IN THE PLACE OF
LAST THINGS

BOOKS BY MICHAEL HELM

The Projectionist (1997)
In the Place of Last Things (2004)

IN THE PLACE OF
LAST THINGS

MICHAEL HELM

National Library of Canada Cataloguing in Publication

Helm, Michael, date
In the place of last things / Michael Helm.

ISBN 0–7710–4125–X

I. Title.

PS8565.E4593I6 2004   C813'.54   C2004-902507-4

We acknowledge the financial support of the Government of Canada through the Book Publishing Industry Development Program and that of the Government of Ontario through the Ontario Media Development Corporation's Ontario Book Initiative. We further acknowledge the support of the Canada Council for the Arts and the Ontario Arts Council for our publishing program.

Typeset in Bembo by M&S, Toronto
Printed and bound in Canada

This book is printed on acid-free paper that is
100% recycled, ancient-forest friendly (100% post-consumer recycled).

McClelland & Stewart Ltd.
The Canadian Publishers
481 University Avenue
Toronto, Ontario
M5G 2E9
www.mcclelland.com

1 2 3 4 5   08 07 06 05 04

Susan, John, Sandra, Richard

It is an expectation, a desire,
A palm that rises up beyond the sea,

A little different from reality.

— Wallace Stevens, "Description without Place"

I

He woke in the new utter dark and swung his feet to the floor, maintaining motion until he was dressed against the chill already gaining the interior. The clock read 2:38. He took the flashlight from the bed table and made his way flight by flight to the basement. In two movements known by touch he turned off all but one breaker and reset the standby power switch, then climbed to the entryway for his parka and boots with his breath breaking there above the beam.

Outside, night sky on the snow. A lone highway sound came miles along crystals of ice hung dimeshining in the quarter moon. When the generator started on the third pull he attached the wire to the ground lug, led the cord out and pressed the head to the 220 outlet. The kitchen light appeared in the empty house. He positioned his father's old anvil against the open door of the garage, then stepped high and deliberate through the knee-deep and crossed to his neighbour's yard. He bent to clean the snow from the runners, gripped both hands on one side of the tool shed's sliding doors and pulled open a space wide enough to move into. A skiff of snow had fingered through the opening where the doors wouldn't meet. The generator was just a few feet inside where he could find it in the dark.

He poured a little gasoline to prime the engine, a line of faintest light bending along the arc. The engine played dead for a time but came to on the seventh pull and the shed was loud and soon there wouldn't be enough air. He turned on the light. A dead cat on its side frozen cuneiform near the wall. He collected it by the tail and thought hatchet.

Back in the garage he removed the torn side bag from the Lawn-Boy. The cat fit exact. He closed up both ends with wire. To repair the holes he removed his gloves and used his fingers to find the end of the duct tape. When the job was done he lay the cat on the concrete and told him he had died a joiner.

His steps along the packed path to the house sounding like nails clawed from old lumber beams, he crossed hare tracks, the delicate passage that lingered there as certain as the ice storm somewhere miles away. Grain elevators soldiered to the north against the dustings of galaxies. The town was in black but for the hospital, its lemon brick pocked in the emergency lamplight of the backup power that still kicked in though the place itself had been shut down since summer, the only services now a clinic three days a week and an ambulance to move the very sick and injured to a town forty miles away. In the fall had been machine accidents, mangled crying along the long highway.

After a minute inside, his breath began to thaw in his eyebrows and nostrils. He towelled his face in the mirror. A 230-pound version of a white man returned from the burning cold,

2

clear eyes, skin flushed the colour of red-figure frescoes he'd studied in books. He'd dreamt the colour that very night, he recalled. In some other season or epoch was a clay wall emanating heat, and some form swept into the pigment ready to awaken and find him there watching.

On the kitchen bench-seat he opened another tin of sweets from the Lions Club, looked, set it aside. They'd given him a turkey plate at Christmas like they did for widowers, and the sweets kept coming. He'd given some to Skidder and to Mrs. Ellis next door but the rest had dried into small, hard consolations on the counter.

The first quality of soul is patience – it was a line from his learning. Patience was his company lately.

After the town lights came up he went out and killed the generators and came back in. He took his place again and sat awake in the kitchen through until dawn.

In the days that followed, the cold broke and the highs reached minus-twenty. In the mornings the ice fog and hoarfrost made the town look like a calendar shot. Russ didn't phone anyone he couldn't visit in person. He took breakfast in the coffee shop of the Flyway Motel, where he sometimes used to, lingered a few minutes in the post office to say his hellos, dropped a thank-you note off at the *Colliston Sentinel* three weeks late. He visited his dad's grave for the first time since the funeral. He bought items at the Co-Op store rather than having them delivered. Eight or ten times a day he received passing condolences and heard an old dog joke he'd resurrected for Skidder the previous week.

At the Credit Union, Russ told loan manager Glen Stockard he'd like to sign something so Glen could look after his bills if anything should happen to him. Glen listened with great circumspection as Russ explained where he was going and why. Behind Glen, in lieu of a window with nearly the same prospect, was an oil painting with a view of the town's grain elevators from the Main Street of twenty years ago. Russ noted to himself that the painting's sad and hopeful quality had less to do with the fact that two of the elevators had since been torn down than that the colours were a little wrong. In '88, after four years of drought and bad markets, Glen and the bank took title to almost half of the family's land and rented it back to Russ's father so someone would be working at the debt. The half that the family kept was under a company name, the Circle L Ranch, whose shareholders were Mike and his brother, Russ's Uncle Reese in Saskatoon. The degree to which Reese hated banks would have been dangerous in most men.

"I can't look after ranch expenses, Russ. You'll need your uncle to sign over power of attorney."

"There's no ranch. All that's left is the lawyer."

"I know that. But I need the signature."

Russ looked out the window at nothing.

"I know how your dad ran things for his brother, but don't you forge this."

Glen pushed himself back from his steel desk and glided until the casters met up with an electrical cord snaked over the carpet, then reclined, laid his hands as if in prayer on his belly. He was a typical homegrown, beefy and thick-limbed, blunted hands and face. He stared a moment at the two cows grazing under-water in the paperweight snow globe on his desk.

God forbid something should happen to Russ while he was taking Jean down to Arizona, Glen explained, then he'd be left holding a lot of questions it wasn't his place to answer.

"If your uncle doesn't know about signing over his authority then things would get muddy."

"You'd send a man out on the road in this cold?"

"There's technology, Canada Post. And the other thing. You're not superstitious, are you?"

"Not even on a bad day."

"I hate to bring up the scenario again but I want to ask about your will. There'd be a helluva mess for your executor with certain estate questions already in probate."

"It's in shape."

"Good. I hear Skidder's going down with you. He's started up again with the stories about his Wild West relative."

"His coming along wasn't my call."

"I bet not. I'll remember you in church."

As he left the office Russ saw the teller counter lined with little white death notices that the paper printed up and distributed. The cards announced the funerals and businesses left them up for a few weeks to collect charity donations. In the last five-week stretch there'd been thirteen funerals, the usual winter kill.

Russ ducked his head back in and asked Glen if there'd been any lost-cat stories in the air. He said no but he'd heard a good dog joke.

"Listen, you've been looking out for me. I can't remember if I thanked you."

"It's my job."

"No, it's not."

"I wasn't gonna ask, Russ, but — it's been a couple months now."

"What is it?"

Glen evidently couldn't find a side door to the matter.

"I don't know. You used to have an entertaining temper. Now you just scare people."

5

"Well spread the news. They can come out of their houses again."

Along the street he walked thinking of the other Russ, whom he knew inside and out like a favourite character in a novel he'd read over and over but never entirely through. The other Russ had been out in the world, schooled to no apparent end. He had a mean corrective streak. He measured all others and himself against his father, and he and they together fell short. He made sense so neatly that Russ had stopped believing in him.

He passed rusting propane tanks stacked upright behind a machine shop, leaning like loaves in a bakery window in an eastern city in October when the bread seeps out into the chill and you go inside to take a number and marvel at the names, all the variations of a simple thing like "bread" worked up from a single crusted syllable. You are at any moment the sum of what you've closed your hand upon or ever hoped to and said the name of. To really forget a thing, you had to forget it in your hands, on your tongue.

This was the place for such a forgetting. White, featureless, cold. His radiant host of the learned dead had followed him to these frozen reaches. They'd been a comfort to him, had even helped him nurse his dying father, though when he died they left town. In his sleepless nights he'd not picked up a book but waited each one out to its end.

And that had left him only duty. He had inherited little else. At the moment it was leading southward and away. Jean was now almost three months late getting to her winter place. He would rather stay, but he had no choice. Duty had released him from choice.

In any season the drive up to Falling Creek was forty-two minutes, rail crossing to rail crossing, though the time on the road was re-cadenced by the disappearance in the last year of two hamlets along the way, their grain elevators torn down and houses moved off or abandoned. In flat winter light the sky endoubted the horizon and the road itself seemed at times to float in a distance without interval until gaining an oil plain and then a sign on the outskirts that told travellers they were entering a town with a future.

The extendacab parked outside the shop identified itself with a magnetic door sign. Meeting Your Brick, Stone, and Marble Needs. Russ parked across the street. Before long a short, thick man left the shop and got into the truck. He was stubble-headed, looked to be in his forties, as he would have looked all his adult life.

Russ followed him for a few blocks and watched him park and head in to the E-lite Cafe. Like everyone else in this cold, he left his vehicle running. Russ pulled in a few spots down the street, got out, and walked past a window of stencil-script signs announcing dances and bantam games, extended New Year's clearance sales. Wayne Bedham's Ford sat high enough that getting into the driver's seat began with the throwback motion of mounting a horse and ended with the sudden apperception of unfamiliar mouldings and instruments that meant you were now in the next model year. Russ adjusted the seat backwards. The cab was well appointed. Digital displays, available four-wheel drive on the run. There was a stacking cd player above the side-positioned gearshift, a remote set into a cradle on the dash, an electronically revolving rack hung below the console.

In time, Bedham approached his truck and stopped short. As the two men stared at one another through the windshield, Russ saw in the other's face a willingness to let the mystery make sense of itself without any effort on his part. Bedham came forward and found the driver's door locked. Russ motioned him to the other side. He walked around the tail and got in, taking in Russ a few seconds before closing the door.

"Should I be hearing bells here?"

"Are you Wayne Bedham?"

"Well, the truck looks familiar."

"Does the name Richard Owen Macdonald mean anything to you?"

Bedham twisted and buttressed himself with an elbow across the seat back and a hand on the dash. "I don't make threats, mister, but then you're sitting here in my truck like it's your habit and not mine."

"I want to know who Richard Macdonald is and why his name is on my dad's gravestone." Russ reached down and rested his hand on the shift.

"You just move your weight right out the door and we'll have our chat outside, but you put this in gear and it's auto theft."

"Just answer me."

"Go on, get out."

Russ shifted into reverse and backed out.

"You stupid sonofabitch."

The street ahead sat down between unbroken banks of exhaust plumes, human shadowfigures ghostly and dumbshow. He eased into motion and then accelerated. For two blocks Bedham spat out stale imprecations until Russ levelled out for the first clear intersection and locked up, spinning the both of them a full panoramic of the town and laying them up against a curb.

"Now you're the dead man," said Bedham.

Russ reached for the gearshift.

"All right, all right. I take it Richard Macdonald isn't your dad."

"That's not the impression I had growing up."

"And you think you know where your dad is buried."

"He's buried under the stone you carved. The name Michael Littlebury is on the top side and Richard Owen Macdonald is upside down on the back side. I didn't notice at the funeral. Now I have."

"I see. Okay, I remember Littlebury – in my business, you know . . . I'm guessing you'd be Russ."

"Unless you have any say."

"The hockey player. The one who punched out the ref. That was a goddam disgrace. They should've pressed charges."

"You're on a dead horse there, Wayne."

Russ revved the engine. The exhaust from the truck enveloped them in a little cloud. Unless a wind got up they would be unseen.

Bedham explained that the current marker was only tempo-rary. "The real stone is all his, of course. What do you expect?"

"I expect what I paid for fifty days ago, not what you dashed off."

"What I remember of the Littlebury account, it's paid by policy so you're not out anything, and as for the stone, I do good work. I don't sucker people, no matter who they are or where they're from or what kind of game they called. Hell, I don't want to get a bad reputation in Colliston – half my tombstones lately come from there."

Russ said nothing. If the comment had come to him two months ago, Bedham would already be pinned against the ceiling, kicking like a child's puppet, but nothing got his blood up so high any more that his strength would be made conscious of itself.

"Don't you go off on me," said Bedham.

Russ used to tell himself his rage was never blind. He liked to think he was strong enough that it never had to be. The truth was that it could take him anywhere.

Bedham had said something that Russ hadn't registered and his silence was somehow deemed threatening. It was simply because Russ was lost in thought, then, that Bedham was able to land a straight right to the side of his head. He cocked his fist immediately again but Russ caught the second punch in his palm like a baseball, and squeezed hard and turned it over like a parent about to force open the hand of a little thief. He held it between them. Bedham shouted a half-word and went silent with pain.

"That's enough," said Russ.

He released the hand. Bedham looked at it a moment as if to see a new shape in it.

"You broke my goddam hand."

"No, I didn't. Why'd you throw at me?"

"A working man needs his hands."

"Listen to me. You and the asshole funeral director up here, we pay you to see something through."

"Aren't you supposed to be some kind of professor? Why don't you go back to your classroom. Christ."

"Here's a classroom. You know any Latin?"

Bedham fluttered his fingers until satisfied that they worked.

"There's not alot of call for it."

Russ took a pen from his coat and wrote on the back of Bedham's injured hand the words "Egregiae Memoriae."

"You'll add this to the stone."

Bedham looked at the words, uncomprehending.

"Gratis," said Russ.

Then he was back in his truck and away to meet his uncle Reese in the coffee shop of a motel where he'd been storm-stayed for three days when he was seventeen. He'd left town for a truck part under a blank slate of sky and rode into Falling Creek in a whiteout with the highway closing behind him. He'd made eyes at the daytime bartender, who was married, and they flirted with each other and it felt pretty good.

For the first time in his life, upon seeing his father's twin, somewhere past the extra pounds and the brush cut, he saw his father.

"I would've drove the full way over."

"That's okay. I had business up here."

Russ laid the documents on the table.

"Sorry about these. It's just if anything happens to me, Glen at the Credit Union needs clearance to take care of things. He knows not to bother you, but I expect if I get killed down there he'll call."

Reese nodded. Russ pointed out where to sign and he did so.

"I don't remember the last time I signed this sort of paper." The waitress set down their coffees. "So you're headin off."

"Yeah." They both stared into their cups. "Let me just ask you one thing about that."

"Shoot."

"Skidder wants to ride down with us and I don't think I should let him."

"So there's your answer." Reese shifted his weight uncertainly. He was almost eighty, the largest old man Russ had ever known.

"Except there's probably another way of seeing it." In the attached lounge area, quarter-scarred sides of keno machines. The space was bright and quiet. "Skidder asked Aunt Jean and she thinks it would be a good education. He's never been off the prairie."

"What do you think Mike would say?"

"He's not here."

"No. He's not."

Two men in a booth watched an old woman pay up and leave. They shook their heads and smiled and one of them said "rare old bird."

"Was he ever wrong about anything in my lifetime, you think?"

"Well, Russ . . . there's a helluva lot worse shadows to grow up in."

"They're all worse." Reese tilted his head and looked down at him like he wanted to say something but wouldn't. "I'm not complaining. I guess you know it the same as I do."

They spoke a while about the government and then Reese said, "One time just after he was saved, I don't know what he'd done, rescued horses from a burning barn or some damn thing, he walked into the house and I told him he took steps like he invented the goddam things, and you know what he said? He said, 'It's not easy to walk when the sun shines out your ass.'" His smile broke fast and hard. "He was my twin brother and, I'm tellin you, after his conversion I would not recognize him as the same man. The man I grew up with was just plain gone, and a part of me didn't want to accept it. I told him I didn't buy his god-fearing act but he never changed back. All's I can say is, you were better off growing up with the second Mike than you would've been the first one. To answer your question, Russ, he made mistakes. He could be wrong about things. But he wasn't usually wrong for the wrong reasons."

Russ wondered what Reese thought the second Mike had ever been wrong about.

"Anyway, it's not a big deal," said Reese. "It's just a car trip."

"Nothing's just a car trip with Skidder."

Reese picked up the check by way of ignoring him but Russ plucked it from his hand. They walked to the till and paid up, then went out into the light-crazed day.

"Word from town is you've gone off the rails. You're scaring people."

"Not since the funeral. I've been keeping to myself lately."

"I can drive her down, you know."

"Where do you get your word from? Is Jean worried about me?"

"No. But then she thinks you're some oversize angel. You don't want to bust up her high opinion of you."

"Don't worry, Reese." They nodded to one another. "I'll call when I get back."

When Reese had gone Russ sat in his truck looking through the window into the motel lounge. Except for the gambling machines the place had been exactly as uninteresting when he was riding out that storm. He'd finally asked the bartender back to his room and thought right away that he'd ruined everything, but she just said no thank you, you're too young and I'm in love with my husband. She said Russ would like her husband, as if that would make a difference to him. He remembered they talked about their ambitions – hers were very specific ones involving children and tropical winterscapes and his were vague, untethered things. Maybe they were lies. He said he wanted to live in many places before he was too old.

He wanted to get lost in huge cities and meet people who'd never heard of Saskatchewan so he could make up all sorts of lives for himself, as if he believed that lives were limited by the places that held them.

By now it didn't matter that in the meantime he'd been to distant cities and lived other lives. When Russ was twenty-five his father told him to quit wasting his winters reading about the world when he could be studying it, and so he enrolled at the University of Saskatchewan. In his last year there, a Cambridge-educated classics professor named Jeanette Leeming had without telling him submitted a term paper he'd written to a competition and thereby nominated him for a travel scholarship. After class one day she asked him to come to her office. She said, "We haven't exchanged twenty words outside of the seminar all term, but we're going to exchange something important right now. You're going to answer a question and then I'm going to give you something you need." Almost everything about her was blunt – her voice, her aimed chin, the cut of her thick and greying and unstyled hair – but she wore a thin, grey cotton cardigan that accentuated the delicate bones of her wrists and naked fingers. She said that a few of the students in class had taken to referring to Russ as "The Deterrent" because they were afraid to launch opinions around him, knowing he'd shoot them down and then unload on them. "You are brilliantly contrary," she said. "I want to know why that is. Is it a simple conditioned reaction, a complex psychological mechanism? Is it a sort of aesthetic response?" Russ asked for her theory. "I think you view academics as a game, and you like to play your games rough." He said only that he guessed it was even more personal than that. She looked away briefly as if she'd had a thought, then told him he was going to Europe.

In Paris he bought a postcard of the Sorbonne and wrote her a note: "London, Oxford, Dublin, Paris: There's no one here to put in their place. They're there and I'm not. Russell Littlebury." He returned home to a letter from the University of Alberta congratulating him on being accepted into the graduate program in Classical Studies, and a letter from Dr. Leeming asking him to forgive her for arranging letters of support and sending an unsigned application. She hoped she'd see him again. He read each letter once more before throwing them both away.

That was six years ago. Since then, the life in which he'd repeated himself and gone back to school after all, the one that saw him in a good job down east, the one where he'd left things forever unfinished. The story was agreeably muddled, enough that he could avoid damaging self-admissions. His particular way of not thinking about himself involved thinking about everything else. Here at home he carried around so much in useless reserve, not just other languages, but other countries, their histories and music and architecture, the banners flown during their revolutions.

Over time he'd evolved the belief that all knowledge touched upon a life if only by lending gravity through its possession, that knowledge put things in layers of context that separated you from sentimentality and the emotions of your past and settled you in the present when, out of nowhere, some small, lapsing moment of the heart came routed through the cortex, delayed, reasoned with. But now the simple mental processes that moved the body or retrieved familiar words weren't to be trusted, and so out on the highway, though it was clear, he made a point of keeping his focus on the road.

The snowy fields ran blank to the horizon and then he was into some unbroken territory of the mind that lay before him, vast, awaiting a lexicon. It was hard to know the names of things in the new dispensation.

At the funeral the minister had told him he'd "joined with death's familiars" and Russ had said he wanted no part of any company and asked not to be thought of that way. He thanked the man for putting his father in the ground and then informed him there was no such thing as common grief.

It was still dark at 8:40 when he walked to Jean's house and picked up her LTD. He took it by the service station, then home to load up his bag. He called her to say he'd be a little late coming around. He made his final checks and locked up the house. From his truck he collected his small emergency kit and his dad's disabled parking permit. He took a brief last look at the house and only then remembered the dead cat in the garage. He retrieved it and laid it in its bag in the truck bed. He briefly considered locking the truck but didn't. Then he climbed into Jean's car and set off.

First light woke before him the shadows of power poles cruciform on the road. North towards the elevators and across the tracks to the neighbourhood of Kilfer, the bastardized version of Killfier, a man long since gone who'd built the first house here in the thirties and opened up the small subdivision that would become prone to the occasional insurance blaze and rat infestation from the nearby nuisance grounds. Skidder's little bungalow had been towed from property to property over the last forty years. It now rented for a hundred dollars a month from the town.

The place contained a mess of such audacity that Russ knew people who had dropped by Skidder's place just to marvel at it.

The kitchen and bathroom sinks both saddle-packed with unwashed dishes featuring odd forms of mould adapted to a deep chill not far above freezing in the cold snaps. All surfaces had been lost to clothes – the floors, tabletops, chairs, lamps, the misshapen owl Skidder collected from a roadside and had stuffed, Skidder himself. He was customarily under here somewhere.

Rather than call his name, Russ simply went to the front room and began kicking the heaps along his path to the bedroom. A heap near the bedroom door cried out.

"We're gone. I'll call from Arizona. Check on the house sometime."

Russ was pulling away when there was Skidder in the rear-view mirror running sockfoot in last night's clothes, carrying, remarkably, a suitcase. He caught up and grabbed the back bumper, held on impressively but lost the bag.

"Don't be so goddam inhuman!"

Five minutes later he emerged from the house again. He wore his dirty white bomber parka. It fit tight to his small body and when the zipper was half open he looked incised.

As they rode, Skidder stared sullenly out at the town he didn't get along with, the houses mixed, styleless, now made conversant by the snow.

"I want so far out of here I forget every pig-ass face in town. Doesn't seem like the place it was back when."

"At forty below nothing seems like anything."

The place where Skidder had grown up was a farm fourteen miles south of town, next to the Littlebury ranch. Nine years ago, when Skidder was eighteen, the uncle who'd raised him was killed in a grain auger and Russ's dad adopted him in all but the legal sense. He'd even lived in the house until Russ came home from his travels in '99. Now he subsisted off death benefits and the land sale.

"Just so you know, when I get down there I'm cashing in my ticket home. Gonna start over somewhere."

"You never started here yet."

"I got this assignment down there. You know Lanny Banks lost his dog in the divorce. Old Mrs. Banks buggered off to Tucson with the dog. You ever meet Lanny's boxer? Name of Mr. Bickles?"

"I saw him once down at the fairgrounds knocking over kids and stealing their hot dogs."

"He was a smart dog, Mr. Bickles. The dog's what really gets up Lanny's ass about this divorce."

"So you're supposed to steal back his dog."

"No, Bickles died. Got bit by something down there, but she cremated him and she keeps him on the tv or somethin."

"You want to steal a dead dog."

"He'll pay five hundred cash, the old bugger."

"So take your truck down and steal it. You've got no encumbrances."

"Money's the cumbrance. And that old pig truck'd never make it that far and back."

Skidder spotted a book on the dash and made one of his slight pecking motions. Everything Russ knew about birds he'd learned from watching Skidder. He picked up the book and tried but failed to say the title out loud – *The Decipherment of Linear B* – and turned it over and read the back-cover description for all of three seconds before he put it down.

"Lanny's new *American Buckhunter* says there's the same number of whitetail deer in North America as Canadians."

"How did you plan to get the dog back up here?"

"I thought we'd keep it somewhere, you'd drive it back when you picked Jean up in the spring."

"So you'd get the money and I'd be the one moving this stolen dead asshole dog over the border."

"Well, like I said, I'd stay down there. But I'd do the stealing. If anyone asks you say it's your dog and it died down there."

"Listen. Skidder. This is Jean's trip. There's people she needs to see who'll want to talk about Mike. It won't always be a galloping good time, but that's the deal. Okay?"

"Yeah, okay."

"If you don't know what to say sometimes, just keep quiet."

"Right."

"You and I have to think about what she wants before it even comes up."

"Right." He tapped the toes of his boots together. "She won't even hear the name."

"What name?"

"Bickles."

They rode into the town proper, Russ trying to imagine details from the houses and yards in other seasons. He recalled reading of a Russian mnemonist who entertained sold-out halls with his unlimited memory. In his mind the man converted lists of letters, words, and numbers into imaginary people and then distributed them on a street familiar to him from his hometown. He'd invent a story that unfolded as he walked along, so that remembering the list simply involved recalling the street and the story. If he'd grown up in the all-effacing snows of Colliston, Russ thought, the Russian wouldn't have retained a thing.

By the time they pulled up to Jean's house Skidder had

already announced he was bored and wanted to drive. Russ went into the house through the glassed-in porch. From the living room he glimpsed Jean through the open bathroom door, applying makeup. A tall woman, especially for her generation, as she liked to point out, in the past year as she neared seventy her hair had gone white and she'd fallen into the habit of never leaving the house without a coat of lipstick or a dusting of powder. He staved off an image of her alone in Tucson, driving her car to some strip mall for a can of coffee. He stepped back to the doorway and knocked.

"Come in, Russell."

"I'll get the bags."

The final business was the call to her daughter in Vancouver. Marlene worked in a car-rental agency and came home to Colliston every second Christmas with her schoolteacher husband, and though this year it had been Jean's turn to fly out west and she stayed with Russ instead, Marlene kept her distance rather than come out and be of any help with Mike. She resented Russ for the persistent unresolved guilt she felt at his being at home looking after her mother while she lived her life.

"You want to say anything?" Jean asked, holding the phone.

Russ took the receiver and said hi.

"Has she got her papers for the border?"

"Yes."

"You've checked?"

"Yeah, we've done this before."

"The car's tuned up?"

"The list is all checked off, Marlene. How're things out there?"

"She tells me Skidder's going."

"Yes."

"Is she standing there?"

"Yes, that's right."

"I don't think you should've invited him, but we can't really discuss it now."

"Well, I'll pass you over and you sign off. Jean'll call when she gets set up. Say hi to Marlon."

"You know damn well it's Marvin."

Outside, Skidder had emerged from the car and was stretching out with his hands on the roof like he was assuming the position for a police frisk. As Russ put Jean's bags in the trunk, Skidder stood straight and howled, his way of expressing any one of several enthusiasms.

"It's a dead dog. What's a dead dog worth? It's like, a misdemeanour."

"The dead part means he won't come on command, which means it's break and enter, which in Arizona probably means a public beating."

"I guess you know all about them." A sly grin. "It's a good thing you won't need me in the spring any more."

Russ didn't know whom or what he'd need in the spring. He didn't even know where he'd be in the world, which likely meant he'd still be here, in town.

"You were always a big help at seeding."

"I get that dog, I'm as good as Californian."

He checked Russ for a reaction.

Russ looked to the southwest sky, so flat it was almost gone. He said, "California. Dead dogs as far as you can see out there. That's the dream, anyway."

A quarter-mile from the Montana border Skidder spotted a tent-eared omen in the ditch staring at him, alert, watching back like maybe Skidder was the omen for the coyote. By the time they reached Port of Climax he was wrapped up in wondering was it a good sign or bad, yes or no. Then patches of snowcrust stained by the drifting earth, his first look at the U.S. looking like it looked here. Still, there it was, he'd never seen it live.

The border crossing was nothing much and then there went Russ into one of his road trances. You sat him on a road, he didn't even have to be moving, and he was off somewhere on the planet Fargon and probably took you with him, you just didn't know it yet because it was like this perfectly parallel universe where they'd made the same mistake of having a Havre, Montana, too. It's all exactly the same except every once in a while something twilight happened, Skidder figured, except it only happened to Russ. The day it happened to Skidder too is the day they get trapped on Fargon. Except you'd never know for sure. It might just be the craziness in this world catching up to you and if you thought about it long enough that's exactly what happened.

Jean was asleep when they stopped for gas. She was a kind old woman, though she always called him David, his given name, or "dear," even after he asked her not to. She was someone on his side, which probably meant she'd be dead soon. She'd told him once he should try to make friends his own age but the ratshits he went to school with wouldn't have him. Lanny was up somewhere in his fifties, and even Russ was thirty-five.

He sat listening to Russ and the man at the pump. Sometimes he liked to put himself so he could hear voices but not really listen to them, it was a funny space you could just barely fit into. The voices outside were all certain and false friendly like so many little endorsements.

When Russ and the pump man had gone inside he got out and looked around at wherever they were. An enormous Star-Spangled Banner sat up high over the station. He wondered what it was about flags down here.

The sky wasn't sure of itself and the bright sun came and went.

When they hadn't said anything for a few miles, Jean nodded off and Russ found Skidder asleep in the rear-view with his head cocked back in a look of slack defiance, fully himself. It was a state Russ could not remember inhabiting. At some time the creature he was had been fractured into consciousness of itself, and yet he couldn't say when it had happened, couldn't name even now its constituent elements.

It was no comfort that he recognized himself best in his intolerance for pomposity or mean ignorance. He'd barely survived his one year of graduate school, with seminar courses he didn't attend and a thesis "On the Myth of the Irreducible" conceived in the spirit of provocation and drafted entirely in the back corner of a diner on Jasper Avenue in Edmonton. The paper put into evidence a daring trust in unreliable translations. In one section he compared Freud's psychobiography of da Vinci with Paul Valéry's essay on Leonardo's genius, a coupling chosen entirely for its unworkability. One crisp morning Russ submitted the bound copy to his adviser, a Dr. Kirkland, who'd been under the impression Russ was writing about Ciceronian influences in Augustine. The next day Kirkland met him in the diner and announced, "This thing's trained on both of us." He said he was going to give Russ a few printed comments to take home and think about. Should Russ agree to the changes he was suggesting, there would be maybe a one-in-ten chance they could call the thesis "interdisciplinary" and sneak it by some other department. "If you don't make them, they'll call your bluff." Russ said he wasn't bluffing. "We're all bluffing, Russ. But they're the only ones who can call."

A single printed page advised name changes. Retitle the thesis (Russ took the suggested title, something so unbeautiful that he'd never been able to recall it). Kirkland outlined a new introduction and additions to the bibliography. The revised version met with enough resistance that an oral defence was arranged, an unusual requirement for the degree, and Russ was made to sit before a panel of faculty members from Philosophy and English and explain himself. Rather than do so, he played the hayseed – he recalled an extended combine-harvester analogy – and at some point the chair of Graduate Studies interrupted him and asked that he leave the room. Instead, he left the campus and walked back to his apartment. That evening Kirkland phoned to say the university would grant the degree on the understanding that he wouldn't apply for another one, a sort of semi-honourable discharge.

Russ thought of his twelve months in graduate school as a surrender to concepts. People like his father understood the very human impulse towards surrender, but what they desired was a state of helplessness wherein all thought and choice and volition are removed. Because they were helpless before a supposed mystery that surpasses understanding, they acquiesced. The only mystery Russ would acknowledge was that the concepts vivified his perceptions. Without claiming too much for his mind, the truth was that he felt powerful.

Back in Colliston living with his father his days were full of quiet thought. The place seemed to have changed on him, though he knew he had changed on it. Mike commented one

25

night that Russ "didn't used to sit around stumped by the weather." He said Russ now had something to ply and he'd better get to work. At the time the advice seemed as close as Russ would ever get to a word from on high, but now he thought of it as a selfless act of deception. It was the earliest sign that Mike was concealing something from him, not just his illness, which soon enough became understood to exist without their ever having spoken of it directly, but his decision to face it alone.

He called Dr. Leeming with a career update and she asked if he wanted to teach.

"It's been leading that way, I guess."

"It should be something you want to do."

"Excepting the creepwork of lawyers and financiers, there aren't many jobs outside the academy where you get paid for being a smartass. The statement of fact is not directed at you, of course."

"Of course not. Give me a few hours."

She called some of her former students, then called back and told him to apply to a college she knew in Toronto. She had a contact name.

"You're always sending me places. I don't want to go east, I wouldn't like Toronto."

"You're a bully, Russ, and I think you should live someplace that's bigger than you. Don't worry, you'll fit perfectly."

The next morning he called Wellington College in Etobicoke and spoke to the chair of Liberal Studies, one of Dr. Leeming's former students, May-Ann Moreau. He was offered a four-month contract based on Leeming's recommendation.

"She says the students will love you."

"Isn't that what it's all about?"

At dinner that night he told Mike he was considering the offer. They'd sold their land and the farmhouse over the winter and bought a place in town so Mike could be closer to his food and money and, as Russ would learn, his medicine. He delivered the job news neutrally, and pretended throughout the conversation to be discussing immediate, short-term matters.

"It sounds like a good deal, son. This woman in the city's looking out for you."

"She's in the habit of giving me options I don't especially want."

"They're about the only ones you got. I'm sure not giving you any."

Mike drank his tea from one of the china cups Russ's mother had collected in the five years of marriage they'd had before she died in a car wreck. The handles were all too fine for him, so he surrounded the cup with his left hand and it disappeared, and the heat never penetrated his calluses. He always seemed to be drinking from his fist.

Russ knew of the strength – he'd seen him lift machinery by hand that other men would put a jack to, seen him pull five-year-old saplings from the ground as if they were garden weeds – but his father's violent past was myth. In story, this most Christian of citizens had once knocked a man unconscious despite having a bastard file stuck in his back, he'd torn a pay telephone from a wall and hurled it thirty feet at an escaping car, he'd subdued an angry buck by gripping its antlers, bulldogging it to the ground and holding it there until the fight was out of it. His scalp held the scars of some said two hundred stitches, most of which he'd sewn himself in a bathroom mirror, and his back had hundreds more. The myth of Mike Littlebury made his conversion all the more remarkable and lent his character a kind of authority that no one born in the faith could ever attain.

Though he may have doubted the stories, Russ didn't doubt his father's faith. The man was fully of a piece, even if the apparent conversion simply involved his having bought into an old lie. After the war he'd raised hell for twelve years. Then he was saved – about the event he'd told Russ only that he'd had another man's blood on him when it happened – and it was seven more years before he married a young woman who sang in the church choir, another four before Russ came along. Even so, after Mike had gathered all that time of straight living, as a boy Russ remembered seeing men cross the street to avoid his father.

"You wanna take your truck down? What kind of shape is she?"

"I don't need a truck. A city that big, you ride cattle cars everywhere."

"It won't be so bad. Even a dumpground rat won't complain much."

"You always see the bright side."

Mike had a way of helping people accept the inevitabilities in their lives. He had come through his hardships with his eyes open, a condition Russ himself would not recommend to everyone, and yet in Mike it seemed to have granted him a kind of broad empathy, a keen awareness of the forces at play in a given life at a given time, owing to his sheer certainty that he knew his own place in the scheme, and knew the particular mysteries he was serving, though mysteries they remained.

In the weeks before Russ left, his father had made at least three unannounced trips to Saskatoon to see specialists, and had returned each time saying that expert opinion was on his side, but offering no details. Russ was prepared to hear the details and take on whatever was ahead of them, but clearly Mike didn't want to discuss them, and Russ thought he'd give his father time to settle himself if that's what he wanted.

The morning of Russ's flight to Toronto, they had breakfast in the dark and were twenty miles along the highway before day broke along narrow ribbons that made Russ think of Homer's "rosy-fingered dawn" and of all the music that is lost in translations. There would be no explaining these moments and this world to anyone he would meet the rest of his life. Through the early morning late summer light, they drove in silence for two hours in colours there were no names for, and then said goodbye with a grasping of hands.

The hotel in Great Falls was an old seven-storey building downtown near the river. Russ let Jean off at the door while he and Skidder parked in the lot and hauled the bags into the lobby, which had the highest ceiling Skidder had ever seen outside of ice rinks or barns. A sign near the desk said Welcome Young Cattlemen of Montana and there was a table set up nearby with a couple of smiling women handing out name tags to a few apparently father-son combinations. The sons were like ten or twelve and had pretty limited variations on the same haircut. One of the women saw Skidder and smiled wider like she was preparing to say something but then she saw Russ and Jean and didn't waste an actual hello welcome. He nodded a hello, wondered if the cattledads would make for a crowded bar.

The room he and Russ shared was about as dim as anything he'd ever stayed in. As Russ showered, Skidder found the hotel stationery and a pen so cheap no one would bother to steal it and wrote some things out he'd almost forgotten so he could remember them. In his high-school years his Uncle Walter would take him and Russ out to teach them about animals. Walter was a hunter crossed over into wildlife groups and he made them memorize certain facts and though Skidder was better than Russ with actual tracking and spotting, he had more trouble remembering the facts than Russ, so Russ taught him about memory shapes. He taught him to write the facts down and draw shapes around the different kinds of animals and then lines between the shapes to show how they connected, and write the numbers and dates out so they sort of hinted at each other.

Over time Russ had helped Skidder devise dozens of memory shapes and on lazy afternoons sometimes he'd cycle through them just to keep them sharp. He had his outlaw relation Levi's life in a shape, his own life too, though there wasn't much in it besides the things he didn't need reminding of. Because the wolf picture was so simple he didn't call it up enough to see it clear any more. It had become a thing he knew but couldn't say.

He began with a circle. Circle means coyote, the c and c. Next, the two fangs of the wolf looking like a tall letter W set below the circle because the wolf descended from the coyote, not the other way around. The numbers Walter had thought were important were from the slaughter years, whether you were talking buffalo or wolf or whatever, and the slaughter years for coyotes and wolves in Saskatchewan were around World War I, the W like the fangs like the World War, when homestead ranchers thought if one animal fell to the wild then there was no telling where it would end. The wolf numbers beside the fangs were 1911 and 270 killed, the 1 and 1 of 11 adding up to the 2 and the sound eleven rhyming with the seven, then remember the zero the same shape as the circle. The coyote numbers were easier because you just had to know 18 times 2 and you had 1918 and 36,000 dead coyotes, the 3 in 36 the same number of zeros after.

And there was his diagram. He could say it if he needed. He folded it and put it in his wallet and felt a bit better that he had learned something in life.

Now that it was gone, he pictured the diagram easy and thought about what it meant. Mike once told him it proved evil in the world.

Skidder checked the tv and found out it was the same as home. He checked the in-house card for a porn channel but no luck. Peeping out the window he tried to imagine the lives out there in the dark but he saw only a few cars, no people on the street, and for some reason it seemed like a sad place.

A wolf is smarter than a dog but you can't train it.

The back wall of the hotel dining room had been given over to a banquet table and half the floor was occupied by ranchers in the middle of a steak dinner and awards ceremony. Jean had decided to put up with the amplified goings-on rather than get in the car again to find a quieter place. Russ noticed her watching Skidder as if he might reveal some plane upon which he might be saved or reformed. Skidder sat angled towards the ranchers, applauding along with them as each young cattlekid went up to collect his award from Nestor's Saddlery in Helena.

"It was me I'd want the bullwhip," he said.

"It's coming to that," said Russ.

"You're the one needs whipping. Have for a long time."

"That's enough, you two."

"We're just having fun, Jean."

She pushed the wine list towards Russ and asked him to choose. He ordered a bottle for the three of them. At some point during dinner Skidder noticed the placemat with its diagrammed history of cattle brands and he fixed upon it like a child with a new toy. Russ thought the letters on the irons looked vaguely Egyptian, the alphabet that moved memory from the mind to the parchment.

"There's people who burn these things on theirself. Black people, mostly. It's just for fashion."

"It has to do with the history, I think, dear."

"No, it's fashion. Or they're all crazy."

"Maybe keep your vast cultural knowledge to yourself."

"You don't need a big education to know what's crazy. You are what you are since the day you were born. Whatever came before's not a part of it."

"So you've got no connection to Levi, then."

"That's different. That's family."

"It's where the history meets the fashion." Russ found he was unwilling to defuse the moment even for Jean's sake. "It's why you're proud to have a cannibal up in the family tree."

"He was no real cannibal. He was white as you and me."

"Listen, you're starting to bother me more than a little."

"Well so you're not dead after all. You should thank me for gettin your hacklers up."

"The word is hackles."

When Skidder reached for the bottle to top off his glass for a third time Russ held it effortlessly on the table and continued eating as Skidder pulled on the neck for a few seconds before relenting.

"You're not my brother." Russ ate one-handed. "Jean, can I have some more wine?"

"You don't need my permission, David. I've never mothered a son and it's too late to start now."

He gave the bottle one last tug, then returned to his plate for a few last forkfuls.

"Well he can't keep his hand on every bottle in town." He pushed his chair back and nodded at Jean. "I'll see you in the mornin, Jean."

"Good night, dear."

When he was gone, Russ observed that he hadn't left any money.

"That's okay. This one's on me," said Jean.

"Just don't think it slipped his mind. All he thinks about is money and women and how he's not set up real well for either one."

"Don't be hard on him, Russ. He's not sorry for himself."

"He's been sniffing around the matter of my inheritance. He can't actually bring himself to ask me if there's anything for him."

"Mike told me once he wished there was more to give you."

"I don't care about that. I don't even think Skidder expects anything, but the way it's laid out for him in increments, he'll maybe take that as a kind of final judgement on his character. He's just smart enough to see it that way."

A woman with highlight streaks in her black hair stepped into the room and stood looking over the scene. She wore loose wool pants and a thin sweater, a metropolitan's clothes that marked her as a passer-through. Russ felt that if she looked his way and smiled he'd bleed all over the table.

"You should say hello," said Jean. She could have said nothing but allowed herself the amusement. The sportive expression was very young on her.

"It's been a long winter."

33

"Mike said you had a girl in Toronto."

For a second he thought he must be dreaming.

"How'd he know that?"

"I don't know. You must've let something slip."

"Well, yes. There was a woman."

"You don't keep in touch?"

"It didn't work out."

"It's none of my business."

Russ had never spoken about her with anyone. He felt as if he'd been hit with a shoe.

"You know, Mike always thought your future was somewhere else."

"I can't very well stick the town with Skidder. Can't just mail in a 'Sorry' notice to the newspaper once a year."

"Well I think you probably *could* do that. I don't think that would be dishonourable."

"I guess you haven't heard, my honour left town a few months ago."

"Of course I heard. But even then you were defending the honour of a woman." Jean had accepted a version of events in which the baited hockey referee lost his good humour, turned to the crowd, and directed a profanity at the first person he saw, an out-of-towner who had come to be called "the offended woman from the north." In this version, Russ had defended the woman from verbal abuse by taking the referee in hand and setting things right.

"I started that story."

"Isn't it true?"

"It's true I prefer it to the actual events."

"There wasn't a woman?"

"Let's say I'm protecting her from further involvement."

"I won't believe you weren't defending anyone."

"The calls he was making were an insult to all human endeavour."

"I'm sure the blame's not all yours, no matter what you say now. You wouldn't just start a fight with a man because he was a bad referee."

"Yeah, well, that's why the offended-woman story got started. I come off better in that one."

Her laugh settled into a smile and for the few seconds it lasted he felt good and let his guard down, and then found himself staring at the one aspect of the whole sorry matter that troubled him. A few weeks before he died, Mike found out about the fight from Skidder. He called Russ into his room and asked him to get out the cigar box from the drawer in his bedside table. Russ set the box under the lamp and opened it. A jade ring, five old watches, a yellowed molar with a gold filling, an Armed Services card, military dog tags, and four war medals. It was the medals Mike wanted to discuss. "I want you to sell them. They won't fetch much but they don't mean anything to me and they shouldn't to you. I never felt right about selling them myself, but they don't mean anything." All right. The king's letters and crown, the blackened silver. "There's things we have to bear forward that we keep to ourselves. If God gives us courage, we carry it in His sight only. We don't make a big deal for others to see." He seemed to want to say more but just turned his head away slightly. "If you need to set something right, do it where no one can see you. Only Him. I don't know what else to tell you. I'm tired." Russ sat with him awhile until he was asleep. He examined one of the medals and wondered how meaning could ever attach to such an object. He fingered the initials. The coin outlasts Tiberius. He squeezed the pointed star in his palm until the pain was general in his hand, then put it away and drew the palm up and inspected the imprint that was fainter than he'd hoped.

"How are you getting on, Jean? I never think to just ask you."

"You know, Russell, if your father hadn't been the man he was, the *person* he was, then people wouldn't feel such a need to talk about him. This whole trip, there are people waiting for us just so they can talk, and some of them will be pretty upset, I guess you should know. But if you find it too hard to hear them out, then that's fine. I don't mind listening to them."

"I just asked how you were."

"I wanted it said, that's all. If it should happen, then it's fine by everyone if you just get up and leave the room."

"All right," he said. "Thank you."

She knew he wouldn't leave a room, it was not an option, not part of the observance. But that she'd pretend for him, pretend not to know. To someone like him, she was a genius of empathy.

An hour after dinner Russ woke into bluejitter screenlight, thinking of the drift. It had presented itself again, not in his dreams, but as a memory in the fugue before waking. The drift of final years, final months and days, a period of time measured for a while in the simple play of dosages and administerings – the MS Contin at fifteen, thirty, sixty milligrams times four, and Ativan, Laxatose, Gravol, the morphine drawn to prescribed lines, the time and effect recorded – but a period marked always by the dissociations of the dying. Oxygen loss and a few more words escape recall. A life shortening from both ends at once, past and future rushing into what is.

He turned over. The dirty white parka on the bed.

Skidder had left town for the end and Mike said not to blame him. And now Russ was thinking about the end, his arm around

36

his father, holding the man up in his final hours, sitting beside him on the bed staring at his own hand clutching the useless notes he'd taken for the doctor.

Russ balled up hard and tried to follow the low-volume voices on the tv. It had something to say about "party machinery" and "press frenzy," familiar words in the predictable tones of barely contained astonishment. Someone wanted a definition of "hard news." Someone said "issues of the moment."

He got up and turned the tv off on his way to the bathroom. Slight separations around the basin signalled a bad refitting but a workable mundanity to bring him back to himself, though re-entry was easier now. For most people recovery was simply another kind of loss, a kind of forgetting, but Russ didn't forget, couldn't forget what he most wanted to. He was a repository of accumulating knowledge and loss. At best the moments were recovered out of sequence, without context or even the illusion of causality. But when they reached a certain frequency he found it hard to pay attention to his life as he was living it.

He left the bathroom door ajar and kept to the half-light in finding his wallet and the number inside. He dialled thinking of distant pre-dawns with his father shirtless in the kitchen. The scars on his shoulders, a German bullet hole counter-navelled in the small of his back.

When someone answered, he turned off the light.

A young man's voice. Russ asked for Joyce Stone.

"Can I say who's calling?"

"The name's Littlebury. She doesn't know me."

". . . Hold on."

He waited a minute, listening for voices or movements set off by the breaking news of his call, but there was nothing until the receiver was taken up.

"Is this Russell?" She'd composed the voice.

"That's right."

"Your father said you'd be calling."

"Did he say he'd be dead?"

She caught herself, he could hear it.

"Yes. He did. He told me alot about you."

"Uh-huh."

"What do you know about me?"

"A couple of weeks before he died he gave me a name and number, and a package to deliver in person. I didn't ask or wonder about you. Speculation hasn't exactly gotten out of hand."

"I see."

"I'll be in your neighbourhood this week if you want it."

"Will you be alone?"

"I can arrange to be."

"Then call a day early. I'm looking forward to meeting you."

"I'll call."

"And Russell?"

"It's Russ."

"Do you know what's in the package, Russ?"

"It's not my concern."

"They're letters I wrote to your father. You're free to look at them. I mean, if you should start wondering who I am."

"Like I said, it's no concern."

"All right, but he asked me to let you know you could read them."

"Now *did* he? It's strange he should have you tell me instead of tell me himself."

"No, it's not. You must know it's not."

"I'll be calling, then."

"I'll see you soon."

After he hung up he briefly considered throwing out the number and mailing her the package. He didn't like people anticipating his emotions, especially people he didn't know. And it was her anticipation, not his father's. Mike would've known Russ wasn't easily shocked, and had no tolerance for moralizing. Each of them knew the other's life must have contained the necessary secrets. Two men with the unspoken agreement that just about everything went without saying. At times Russ regarded this code as so much gender-locked horseshit, but usually he just found it beautiful.

He had come this far believing the need for surety was never misplaced. Pascal argued that the mind was finite and imperfect, and would have to content itself with indefinables, that life was not mathematics. But science had nearly rendered it so. The woman he'd known in Toronto had countered his views with passages from the books he was reading. She'd put forward the "absolute flow of becoming." She'd said that a tree is a new thing at every instant.

Jean had brought her up and now he was thinking of her. And even the dead worthies were straggling back, it seemed.

His thoughts broke off at a sound behind him, the flicking of the old silver lighter his father used for the candles on the Sunday table. He heard it again, at his shoulder, and was seized with the certainty that the man's hand was now in front of him in the dark. He fumbled cold with the lamp switch until the light came on and returned the sensation to memory.

He reasoned that the sound had been in the walls, pipes tapping behind a painting of a trout in mid-air fighting on the line. He tried to assess the artwork. The composition had a sentimental intent that settled him. It hoped to transport the viewer to a summer stream, though in fact it just anchored you in a stale brown Montana hotel room. Now the tapping was just tapping, and the lighter, years distant. It had been only the dark, a young boy's dark, that had closed the time for a moment.

The bartender in the Decoy Room of the Stokes Hotel was a tall, bearded man who liked to flutter his hand over the taps before pulling. The oval bar allowed him to put a short island of glass and refrigeration between him and a customer another bartender could only turn his back to. Skidder had been sitting on a stool for a minute or two addressing the man's bald spot, trying to engage him in conversation. The man was looking up to the ceiling of drinking glasses chandeliered there, tilting his head this way and that. Finally he walked down and adjusted a snifter. The lights beaded in the glasses, repeated themselves, took on a kind of spelling-bee character.

"You got peelers in town?"

No response.

"Peelers meaning strippers. You got a part of town with strippers and hookers and things?"

Like Skidder posed nothing to him, no threat or question, the man spilled out some coins from the tip jar and went over to the jukebox at the back of the room. It was that sort of mixed-up place. Five dozen immaculate goblets staring down on a grimy tip jar and bumper stickers under your drink reading Keep Off Grass. Wilderness – Just Say No. Skidder watched him load the slot and punch in the selections he knew by heart. Though the place was empty, and on his way back he passed right behind him, there was nothing along the lines of acknowledgement.

Skidder was beginning to wonder if maybe he wasn't a little simple. You shouldn't put simple people in this sort of job. A bartender is a key job. He is an important face in the hospitality industry.

Two women came in. The bartender nodded and moved down the bar as they sat. He smiled and slid coasters in front of them and leaned in and said something to make them laugh. The women had maybe ten years on him, Skidder guessed. Their husbands wouldn't know where they were right now.

Sure enough, one of them caught his eye and smiled.

He smiled back and said "Skidder Shute," which caused them to crinkle their brows in sync and laugh some more. One of the women was dark-haired and thinner and kept tucking her chin and talking into her chest. Skidder would glance down and then shift back and look at the bottles of scotch and rum and he couldn't tell what was going on with her. He hoped it wasn't a joke on someone.

Now the bartender was talking to the woman's chest. When he reached out and touched the thing, it just became too much. Skidder leaned over and looked.

There was an animal in there, in her shirt. He thought maybe a toy dog or puppy, but all he saw was living grey fur.

The bigger woman turned to him. "It's wild. Her husband trains wild animals for the movies. They have to get used to people and noise."

It sounded like a cover-up story but he couldn't imagine what the real one could be.

For a time he watched the bar fill up in the mirror and contemplated the devious cruelties of the animal he was. Couples came in, someone called the bartender "Carl." A man's laughter shot out, a hand came down hard on the bar and his beer shivered. Four guys entered and secured the pool table. They hung their parkas over chairs and the hoods tilted forward or back like the heads of men shot dead at a card game.

He was now into his third chaser on some label he didn't recognize. The whisky had the effect of making the room seem unlikely. The woman exposed more of her animal breast, a black-and-white dog trotted by and appeared again on a barstool across the island, facing him, sitting next to a kid in a black cowboy hat. A corner of one of the dog's ears bounced in rhythm with his panting like a little party trick.

At some point Skidder was looking into his wallet for cash and had the idea to pull out the folded-up photocopied newspaper picture of Levi he'd collected from among his father's effects. It seemed a good conversation starter.

"You recognize him?"

He slid the photo towards the woman with the animal. She put an elbow on the bar and turned to him, and kept one hand on her animal. It was sleeping.

"Is he famous?"

"Not like he should be. His name's Levi Shute. He's an outlaw blood relative of mine."

She smiled broadly now. They were getting on fine.

"Let me tell you about him," he said.

He turned the paper over and asked Carl for a pen. There would be no time to run all the details past her so he produced the general picture. The main states, the horse, the nuggets, the pistols and longhorns, the three-legged man, the skull and card, the mountain, the apple and chain, the sling and the noose. She stayed with him as he remembered the dates from the pictures and wrote them down, and then started into the story.

She watched his hand move along the map from Kentucky

down to Texas and over to the coast, but more and more she just looked at him. He found himself not wanting the story to end. The more he said, the more detail he thought to mention. The year 1860 brought a gold strike in Washington Territory and a third nugget to the map that he added on the fly, and Washington west meant Washington east and Lincoln and the Civil War in the form of facing cannons, north and south. Levi killed a card dealer and with the help of fellow secessionists escaped across the border up into the Cariboo Mountains of British Columbia and over to Victoria, where he was jailed for stealing an apple and put to work on a chain gang and she watched his mouth as he spoke and the time was short for Levi. The Canadians released him the day before the extradition papers arrived, so he ducked back down into Washington and then, in 1863, was drawn inevitably as Skidder's hand was drawn towards the final nugget. He saw her watching his mouth and he understood she'd made the connection between Levi and him, and then even as he pointed to the end of his life, he started to wonder what he should do with the impression he'd made. He was hoping she would know. In Virginia City, in Idaho Territory, Levi was arrested by the citizens along with a rogue sheriff and his gang of highwaymen, and all of them hanged until dead.

And then it was over and he was alone with just her and all the wrong things to say.

"Well, that's something," she said. Her voice was full of kindness. It killed him to hear it that way.

Her friend had looked over a few times during the telling and seemed to be waiting for the animal woman to turn back, but a young man with glasses had moved in beside her now and she wasn't in a hurry for her friend any more.

"So what's your, like, mood?" Skidder asked the woman.

"What's my mood?" The kindness had burned off somewhat.

"What d'you wanna do?" He winked at her.

"I beg your huh?"

Her tone came up snake eyes. Like that he slid from his stool and improvised his way across the floor to the Mens, thinking how to explain himself to her. He supposed he'd sort of jumped down the line to the tenth question instead of taking it step by step, but he'd had the sense they were sharing a mood, and he'd just wondered at the name for it.

Above the urinal, weltering graffiti and another bumper sticker. A wolf's head crossed out above the words No Wolves. Skidder took Carl's pen from his shirt pocket and wrote on the sticker, I got it the first time. He became aware that someone had moved in beside him. When he'd made his point, he put away the pen.

He turned. It was the dog's cowboy kid.

"You like it?" asked Skidder.

"No. I don't like it." The kid was involved in a pretty long piss.

"You're right," said Skidder. He fished around in his pocket for something handy and pulled out his room key and went to work on the sticker.

"You deface that thing and I'll break your arm."

Skidder stopped. He contemplated the key.

"Just so you know," said the kid.

"It's that attitude that's killed off the wolf."

"I'm not here to argue. Just leave."

"Same thing you told the Indian, right?"

"What Indian?"

"Same thing you told the Indian and the wolf. Just leave or we'll do some meanness upon you."

"Is it you're insane or just stupid? Where you from anyway?"

Skidder put away the key and put his hand on the door. The kid was about to zip up.

"You're the kind who maltreats his dog."

He flew out and slid undercover along the wall to the jukebox and stared at the revolving cds until they felt like a taunt. Rather than go back to the bar he took a dark hallway leading off the back wall. A sign promised something called Claimstakers, which turned out to be a bleary dance club with a disco ball and a few tables pooled in light like pool tables. From where he stood at the entranceway the place seemed empty but for a lone couple on the dance floor running through the usual mockery of breeding positions and a bouncer who tried to ding him for a three-dollar cover. Skidder declined.

He moved back down through the dark towards the bar, where the jukebox played an early Doobie Brothers tune and everyone else awaited him in low voices. He took his seat beside the girls. The remains of his beer were being poured into a glass ashtray for the dog, who lapped it smartly.

"Welcome back," said the cowboy.

The mistake Russ had made in bringing Skidder coalesced in the image of a restraining device he'd once seen in a magazine in Skidder's shack. A pair of handcuffs was attached to a little wire with a loop in it, so that the detainee could be cuffed behind his back, the wire run down between his legs, and the loop tightened around his scrotum. Then you could just stuff something in the detainee's mouth, carry him back and forth for a few days between hotel rooms and the back seat. If the sight of him bothered your aunt, who really just wanted to enjoy her trip, then you'd dump the little prick in the trunk. Here and there you'd buy a local souvenir and toss it in for him so he'd have memories to cherish later.

He supposed he should go find him but he was tired. He turned off the tv and fell asleep with the lights on.

He woke at the opening of the door. Skidder's face appeared, his hand held to a bloody nose. There was blood on his shirt. When he saw Russ looking at him his eyes went wide and he nodded in acknowledgement.

The neoplatonists believed all things were created out of God's self-contemplation. Around Skidder, Russ often had occasion to hope they were wrong.

Skidder went to the bathroom and cleaned up. Russ turned the lights off and got back into bed.

He didn't want to hear it.

Later, in the dark.

"Hey, Russ."

"Shut up."

"Levi. In those days they wouldn't of talked like we do."

"Russ?"

"We're not talking."

"And you look at it one way, Levi was just mixed up, I guess. The whole country was."

"Yeah, well, ontogeny recapitulates phylogeny."

"Well fuck you and your Latin."

"Shut up then."

She knew superstition left you open to forces, but she noticed that after she heard something like this – CNN said almost four hundred dead in a ferry-boat accident in India – she seemed to read a lot into what happened next. And what happened next was she was staring out her upstairs bedroom window at the mountains south of the city and a dead winter sky, dull white gauze that if you unwrapped it there'd be nothing there, thinking not of four hundred people but of a single soul in all its beauty released, and then four hundred releasings, and then a car pulled into the driveway beside her father's and the three who stepped out were like a consequence of her thought.

She recognized two, Jean and the driver, Russ, who was here last year and looked mean but wasn't, but not the small one taking his hand from his pocket to actually run it along the chrome strip of her dad's old car like a kid leaning over to stroke the dolphin in the Florida ad.

She heard her father greeting them from the doorway, could picture the exaggerated sweep of his long arm, ushering them in.

"The travellers arrive! Come on in."

The little one, the one she didn't know, was stalled in the driveway still petting the car.

"This yours?"

"'63 Ford Galaxie 500. You must be David. I'm Grant Bollins."

Then her dad called up to her.

She came down and stood on the last step.

"You remember Jean and Russ, honey."

"Yes, hello."

There were hellos all around before the one called David introduced himself to her.

"Excuse me?"

"I said Skidder, call me. Double-d as in double."

She felt a little sorry for him not realizing he was being spoken through. She was being told to listen.

She fixed lunch in the kitchen while they sat talking about her dead Uncle Mike, who wasn't really her uncle though she called him that even in prayer on the night they decided not to drive north for the funeral. She didn't have a good sense of him in the hour or two total she'd spent in his presence all her life combined, but she knew he'd offered to take her with his sort of adopted son on some ocean trip in the weeks when her dad had been at the drunk clinic. She saw how she'd have been with this small one all that time and she thanked God her church looked after her instead.

Her father was already practically crying but Jean was talking him down. The other two didn't seem to have much to say.

The motion of her hands on the cutting board trimming cheese singles made her think of work. At the Dairy Hut she spent afternoons serving sundaes and crushing Oreo cookies with a Coke bottle to make the favourite local topping, called black mash, which she supposed was harmless though it was hard to come down on the side of decay or dark references. One thing since she started working there, you had to see the syrups as colours not flavours or you'd feel sick all shift.

It was a place to meet people outside of school or church. It was where she'd met Jack. When she first started, boys came in to see her. They were only boys but she'd been with a couple in their trucks. One of them talked her through when she kissed him down there and then took him in her mouth. Nothing more was expected of her than she was willing to do. The boys were still her friends, though not the girls they had now. So Jack had been prepared for, it seemed like, like he'd been provided to her.

As she set the table, coming and going, she paid more attention to the conversation. They thought she wasn't part of it when really she's the one who saw it forming, rounding into a shape she could pick up and hold like a little world.

Like dirt sifted over the snow scooped into a plastic boat. Driving the streets of Helena, sitting right next to him up high in the truck. He let her pick the radio songs. All of this, and in the morning serving sundaes. As a little girl they were flavours and she loved them and was unjudged.

They said they were going to Virginia City and the small one was digging something out of his wallet.

"They don't wanna see that."

"It's okay, Russ."

"What've you got there?" It was the voice her dad used with kids in his office. He took his bifocals from his shirt pocket and held them out in front of his face without actually putting them on.

"That's him. That's my relative Levi. Only known picture. He's the one we're going to see." He showed the photo to her dad, then handed it up to her. She could feel him studying her face, expecting a big impression. The face in the picture had deep eyes and a long moustache. The creases where the paper'd been

49

folded met dead centre in his forehead. The words below the picture said, "Shute: Ate His Partner."

She asked, "What does it mean, 'ate his partner'?"

"They've sensationalized. They discredit him."

"What it means," said Russ, "is that he literally ate his partner. They were caught in a snowstorm and Levi was hungry so he murdered the man and then ate him."

She felt her dad's alarm that she should hear this.

"Just his leg. And there's no proof he murdered him. He may of just died."

"Anyway, the men of Virginia City were pretty sure he'd murdered a couple dozen people so they hanged him, vigilante style, back in . . . whatever."

"In 1864. Strung him up in a unfinished building. It still stands and we'll see it. Actual building."

"Skidder here thinks Levi oughta be on a trading card or something."

"Actual beam."

She saw it now, what had been given her. She saw the chrome of the car outside reflected in the two brass cylinders covering the lead weights that drew time from the grandfather clock.

"I'd like to see Virginia City."

"Lea, honey, they're just passing through."

"I know, but some day I'd like to. It's only a couple hours from here."

"It'd be best to go in the summer," said Russ. "The tourist stuff won't be open now."

"I think the winter's better," she said. "No tourists, just a town with a story."

And before the clock unnotched another minute, her father

and Jean arranged to catch up with one another while she spent the afternoon in Virginia City with Russ and God's little agent.

On his third trip in from unloading the car Russ finally realized that what was causing the warp in time was the sound of a tv upstairs spewing continuous news though no one was watching. He'd heard it during the visit last year. He only noticed it now because someone had turned it off. A moment of what Leibniz called *petites perceptions*, Russ found himself thinking, then welcomed Leibniz to Montana.

Lea beckoned from the top of the stairs. He carried a load up to her and had to put it down again when she paused and seemed to think about who would sleep where.

"You and Aunt Jean can be across from each other down there." She floated her hand presentationally towards the end of the hallway like a game-show model. "Your brother can take the middle room."

"He's not my brother. Fine."

"I'm sorry I kind of messed things up for you, having to drive me back here tonight. Because of me you have to stay over." Her voice was distracted or insincere. She was looking into the dim light at the end of the hall. Then she turned. She was still too young for him to see how her facial features would assemble into any sort of womanly character, and her hair was in pigtails, but from this distance she wasn't exactly a kid. "I'll make a nice dinner tonight, or we'll probably go out."

"Whatever's fine, Lea."

"I don't know what a hotel room in Idaho looks like but this must be better, right?"

"Yeah, well, we're not hauling ore here. Everything's flexible."

Skidder worked his way to the top of the stairs with the rest of the bags. He tried to pretend he wasn't labouring but when he set them down he didn't have the breath to speak.

"We should probably get going. I'll pack us some snacks."

Skidder nodded and asked for water and she led him down the stairs.

Russ stepped into her room. At the foot of a small bed, the slopes of rooftops and mountains in a window. On one side the gathered lace curtains rested against the tv, which hadn't been turned off after all. On low volume an older, intimidating woman on link-up said that "terrorists tie diplomacy in double binds." Russ bent over and muted the volume. The faint smell of lemon on the screen. Above her dresser, the word "Retropigs" on a poster of a guitarist with his shoulders on an overexposed stage and his legs kicking the air. On the wall beside the door was a small print with elongated figures. An old white-bearded man lay on a road looking up as two demons whipped him with sticks while others flew around wielding serpents. The man had a halo, the demons had horns. A band of calligraphic script below the scene read "ST. ANTHONY TORMENTED BY DEVILS" BIG SKY REPRO, HELENA.

On the dresser itself were a small brass hippo sitting on a cloth and a diary with a brass lock. Under the border of the cloth, a narrow edge of paper. He pulled out a black-and-white photo-booth strip of Lea with a man who looked ten or twelve years older than her. She was mugging differently in each shot but he held one expression. His face and skull were stubbled to about the same depth. His eyes seemed tight, narrowed minutely in fascination or anxiety, as if he saw some portent in the lens. The man didn't want to be there. Russ found nothing written on the back. He looked closely enough to see the pebbled grain. He smelled the lemon again.

The girl had her secrets, of course she had. In her store of the unconfessed was a man her father wouldn't know about. He tucked the strip back under the cloth.

On the screen a woman was smiling and nodding, as if listening to a good song she hadn't heard in years.

Lea rode in the front with him as they left Helena for Virginia City with the sky breaking up all around. Russ saw Skidder in the rear-view staring in wonder at the back of her head. His chin was raised a little, like he intended to inhale all the perfume she'd put on for the outing.

As they approached a Dairy Hut sign on the outskirts Skidder announced he could use a shake.

"We can't go there," said Lea. "I called in sick this morning, which they know doesn't have to mean I'm actually puking, but I can't very well show up and order something."

"We could park and I'll run in."

"It's not happening," said Russ.

"I'd have to duck down," she explained. "It wouldn't feel right."

"That's okay. Your secret's safe with us. Hell, you can tell us anything."

"But I was feeling sick, it's true. Or it was. Though now it's not letter true."

"What's letter true?" asked Skidder.

"I mean like scripture."

"You believe all that?"

"It's not your business, Skidder."

"I had a big argument with my friends about Joshua 10 and could the sun stand still. I figure if it's there at all it could do pretty much whatever."

As if to acknowledge her, the sun broke out fully. Russ fished around under his seat and found his reflecting shades and slid them on. They always made him feel a little silly. He adjusted them in the mirror and saw the road feed into his eyes.

"I'm sorry about your dad."

Russ gave a short nod at the highway. Earlier, Grant had said the same thing, and could barely get the words out before he started to choke up. Since Mike died Russ himself hadn't yet fallen to weeping, or talking as if to expel the pain. He'd been crazy for a few days and scared one or two people who needed scaring, but he hadn't so lost his judgement that he'd tried to talk anything through, and now he was impatient with anyone who did try to, anyone who said any of the usual things, in the usual ways.

"Did you know him?"

"Did I . . . ?"

"Did you know him well enough to be sorry he died?"

"Jesus, Russ, she's just showin manners."

"I know that when your dad died, my dad said he was the best man he ever met. So I'm sorry for my dad that he died on him."

There was a note of childish self-satisfaction in her voice, as if she'd escaped his question through some cleverness. He wondered how the cleverness sat with the letter truths she claimed to hold to. Maybe it all held together through some higher purpose. That was it, he decided. She was a girl full of purposes.

Just past Butte, Skidder started into the long version of the Levi story and Russ let him tell it. She turned every now and then and pretended a great interest in some detail but Russ couldn't help feeling it was less out of kindness towards Skidder than by way of setting him up.

At one point as they were about to pass a truck with bulldogs on the mud flaps and the name Lureen on the door, Russ saw the driver look down at her and do a thing with his tongue. He didn't smile, but she shook her finger in mock sternness and smiled up at him.

A few miles outside Virginia City the snow had formed crests on the gravel tailings standing along the river. For almost an hour Skidder had been moving through Levi's life story, never able to keep moving forward but looping back and making asides about where he'd found a particular detail or how he'd managed to remember it. As a boy Levi rode a horse through the courthouse. His first murder, in Kentucky. His suicide pact with his wife in Texas, his first arrest, his escape from custody and disappearance and the rumours he became an assassin for Brigham Young and stole military livestock at Lodi and massacred immigrants at Mountain Meadows. The stolen horses and pursuit that led him into the mountains to be snowbound, the horses eaten one by one until only the two men were left. The emergence, the shooting of a card dealer, the flight across the border to the Cariboos.

Though he wasn't at the end of the story, as they approached the place where it ended he slowed and soon fell silent.

The main street looked like a movie set. It was completely without signs of life. Patches of snow on the ground. On the low hills above the street sat a few dozen small modern houses. Chimney smoke. A black dog on a chain looking down at them.

He pulled over and they took to the wooden sidewalks that like the buildings had obviously been reconstructed over the years. The structures were flat-fronted and grey.

"It's the saloon!" Skidder shouted. He peered through a window, then tried the door. "Everyfuckinthing's locked up."

Lea had wandered on. Russ caught up to her outside a playhouse studying an old poster advertising the local theatre troupe's production of *A Midsummer Night's Dream*. The top of the poster read, "Ours is the land and age of gold, And ours the laughing time." Below a list of players was the promise that "On the occasion of this entertainment several more Stars of the first magnitude will appear."

The cold came along a gust down the street and Russ felt it on his bare hands.

"I wonder could I come along," she said, still looking into the playhouse. "Could I go with you?"

Russ turned to watch a pickup drive past, as if in its motion he could construe exactly what was afoot here.

"This is where they took him from!" Skidder was standing before the façade of a hotel, pointing at it. "The sons-a-bitches. He had his arm all slung up or they wouldn't of stood a chance." He ran off farther down the street.

"Where do you need to go, Lea?"

"Texas."

"They tell me that's a big place."

He removed his sunglasses and looked up at the sky as it was. He was about to be put into a position.

"What's his name?"

She nodded just slightly.

"Jack. Jack Marks."

"I take it your dad doesn't know about him."

"I know where to find him. I was at his place once when the phone rang. Jack was out to the store and I took the message he should call this guy about the job they'd arranged. I wrote it down." She pulled a piece of paper from her back pants pocket and showed it to him. "That area code is El Paso, Texas."

The message was to call someone named Hec Sullivan.

"I called it, but they pretended they don't know him."

"Maybe he's not who you think he is."

"I know him better than he knows himself."

Lea told him about her Jack. Her first glimpse of him came on a June Sunday. His hair buzzed short like a soldier's, and a wine-red shirt that needed tucking at the side. He was limping up the centre aisle amid old people as the reverend beckoned forward those with pain. When his turn came, the reverend had him sit and he laid hands upon him as a little circle formed and Lea a part of it, though she was the only one not praying, just watching.

"One of the praying men asked Jack if he had troubles besides his leg, troubles with the people in his life, and Jack said there wasn't anyone left in his life, so we all told him he had Jesus, but he said he'd never accepted the Lord, but two minutes later he was up and walking around healed and saved both."

When the service was over, she introduced herself. He said he'd had a vision sitting there looking up at her that she would teach him about the Lord.

"So saved and healed and gifted all at once."

And I bet he got your phone number, Russ thought.

"Maybe he was less than sincere."

"But he was *healed*. Later he told me he'd broken it running from police and it never got set so it healed wrong. It's not the sort of story you just make up to impress someone."

"It could be, Lea."

"Besides, he had the gift of prophecy."

Skidder called out from down the street that he'd found the hanging place. He pressed his face up to a window and cupped his hands around his eyes.

"Just, he'd see two things, a coincidence no one would notice, maybe with numbers or words, and he'd predict they'd show again. And then it would come true. It wouldn't mean anything to him but I helped him understand and he saw what it meant."

"And what's that?"

"It's guidance."

"Uh-huh."

Russ understood that Jack Marks knew how to read religion in a young woman, and that he'd gotten what he'd predicted to himself.

"Did he tell you he was leaving?"

"He said one day he would but there wasn't any warning. Sometimes on his lunch there were places we'd meet. My house, or the church basement, but the last time we were supposed to meet he didn't show up. I went to the church and then his apartment later and he was gone."

"Did he ever use this gift of prophecy? Did he ever even return to church for a service?"

"He wasn't ready yet. The Lord was preparing him."

"Right. But then he skipped out on the Lord."

"That's why I know he'll be back. He'll be back when he's ready."

"Then why go after him?"

"Because the Lord wants me to. Jack's ready, but I've got to lead him back."

Lea showed Russ the silver necklace she was wearing.

"He gave me this."

58

He felt her reading him to see if the necklace was really proof that Marks loved her. No, that wasn't it. She was convinced of the love, it was divinely ordained. She wanted only to know if Russ was a believer.

"Dad'll let me go with you if you ask him. Like he did today. It would only be for a week or two." She touched her hair and looked back at the poster. "I wouldn't have the number if it wasn't meant for me to go find him."

"So God sent you the number and now He's sent me, is that right?"

Skidder was jogging up a path past a sign to Boot Hill.

"Don't you believe in the risen Christ?"

She had never had someone to set her right and now it was likely too late. Now she had convictions and was still young enough to think anything past could be chased down and brought home again.

"What I believe in, Lea, is the skipped-out man and the heartbroken girl. I'm sorry it didn't work out, but if I'm God's messenger then I'm here to tell you to forget about this Jack guy and move on. We're not going to Texas and we aren't taking you partway."

She smiled in her unshakeable faith. It was the first moment in which Russ realized she was, in truth, a little dangerous.

He left her there and walked off towards the hanging place. She waited a moment, then trailed in behind him.

Jack had told her no one could ever know what they'd done because it would be misunderstood because of her age, and then he missed her seventeenth birthday by not even two weeks. She'd been talking about it a lot before he left, so she hoped he'd remember and at least send a card, but there was nothing. Her father gave her a cd player and her friend Tammy bought her a wooden bracelet. Tammy was her best friend but there was basically no telling her anything or it would headline the top of the hour, but she'd really meant the bracelet, and it was one of the things she thought to put in her school bag. She took some bathroom things and a pair of jeans, her favourite red shoes and items from her private drawer – panties and bras and feminine products and a bank card, and then put her diary in with the personal things she left. They'd have to root around through them, and then break the lock if they wanted to look for clues. If she'd had time she'd have written a new one with false clues but she was being looked out for and if a person got in God's way it was "folly" was the youth pastor's word. This way they would have to make the decision to transgress. She hoped her father would be the one.

She stepped into the hallway with her bag and closed the door behind her. All the rooms were dark.

She kept to the wall so the floor wouldn't creak and delivered herself to Skidder's door. She pushed it open and stepped in and closed it all in one motion, and already she felt him awake, like he'd been waiting for her, though he wouldn't know why.

She heard him move.

"Don't turn on the light," she whispered.

"Okay. I just thought maybe you were sleepwalking and –"

"Shhh."

She sat on the bed and turned to him. He sat up just a little. She placed a hand above his knee.

"We need to be quiet," she said.

Russ was the first to wake in the morning. He went downstairs and made coffee. At the kitchen table he listened to the heat blow through the registers. It was forty minutes before Grant appeared in his pyjamas and slippers.

"Good morning, Russ." It was a low, daybreaking voice. Russ supposed he hadn't had a use for it in a long time.

"I don't suppose Lea has any reason to be off to school so early."

"No. She isn't up for an hour yet."

Russ nodded. He took a sip of his coffee.

"Then I think we're looking at an unforeseen circumstance."

Grant stood awkwardly in the middle of the kitchen, one arm hugging the other to his side, the fingers of his free hand looking as if they were squeezing an invisible pencil. He was still in his pyjamas, which somehow looked the more ridiculous for his narrow goatee.

"Skidder's stupid, but his kind of trouble stems from his condition."

"What condition?"

"He's prone to . . . errancy."

"Good Lord. We should call the police."

"By now they're long gone, Grant. This isn't a local matter. If the cops are called this becomes something it isn't. It's not kidnapping or even auto theft and as long as we don't call the cops, no one even has to know about it. I'm not sure how the police would handle this. We don't want their names showing up on tv screens."

"But Lea wouldn't just run off with someone she didn't know."

"Listen, I know where they're going. Did she ever mention a man named Jack?"

Grant raised his head a little higher on his thin neck and shook it slowly.

"She didn't know me but she told me about him. She didn't know Skidder but she convinced him to run off. It's like she was waiting for people she didn't know to show up."

The point was conceded even before he spoke. With thumb and forefinger Grant stroked his little beard and held it for a moment in a pinch.

"Lea and I, we just don't talk about most things."

"Maybe she thinks alot of what she does or would say won't fall on the right side of the ledger."

"What do you mean?"

"I get the impression from her that everything tallies right or wrong around here."

"You don't believe in right and wrong?"

"Forget it. I'm sorry. I'm not trying to tell you —"

"Well do tell me. I want to know if you think we shouldn't teach our children right from wrong."

"All I know is, there's right, there's wrong, there's both of them together, and there's neither one for miles."

Grant sat back in his chair.

"One of the things your father taught me was to pray for wisdom every night. But it isn't always given us, what we pray for, is it?"

"I don't know, Grant."

"It isn't always given." His voice was oddly high and tremulous. "Maybe you better tell me about this Jack."

When Jean heard the news, she turned to Grant and asked him to join her at the table. Crisis management sat on her like a warm coat.

"I'm sorry, Jean. But you know I saw this coming."

"It's just beyond me what David's thinking."

"Your premise is all wrong there."

From Lea's room Russ gathered the photo strip and found in her closet a black-and-gold dealer's cap with the words Bowers Rain Systems stitched on the bill. He looked through her dresser drawers and found the diary he'd seen yesterday and tucked it against the small of his back, inside his belt and his sweater. Downstairs, when he laid the other items on the kitchen table, Grant told him he'd never seen them. He examined the photo strip.

"It's the man from last summer," said Grant. "He came to church and got saved, but he never came back. I didn't know . . ." – he looked away and waved his hand at the pictures – "about this."

Russ tore a yellow page from the directory.

"I'll need the car to go after them, Jean."

"Of course. I'll arrange to fly. Grant will help me."

"Is that okay, Grant?"

"Yes. I guess I'd rather you found them than some state policeman."

"Good. Now tell me, does Lea have much money?"

"She has a few hundred dollars she's saved up in a bank account."

"Do you have any authority over the account?"

"I haven't got around to removing it."

"You need to keep track of the transactions, and don't let it run dry. Skidder doesn't have much money and we don't want them stealing food. Just fifty dollars or so every day or two. We want them poor but not broke."

"All right."

"You should call the school and tell them she'll be missing for a few days."

"I guess I should call her friends. She might have told them where she's going."

"Don't call them. This is between us. And we'll settle it ourselves."

"How are we going to do that?"

"You just leave it to Russ," said Jean. "He'll find them."

The Helena office of Bowers Rain Systems faced the parking lot of an industrial strip mall. In the empty reception area Russ took a seat next to a waterfall fountain featuring simulated rocks and branches. In the back a few men were gathered in the warehouse, and one of them waved to him and came forward. He wore a full beard and another model of the cap in Lea's closet. The name on his shirt was Kerry.

"How are you?"

"I'm hoping you can help me. I'm looking for someone I think used to work here."

With his thumb over Lea, he showed Kerry the photo of Marks. Kerry looked down at it and then failed to look back up.

"Hold on."

After Kerry returned to the back, a short, balding man in tinted glasses appeared. He raised his chin assessingly.

"What's your business with the man in the picture?"

"Well, I don't personally know the guy, but he sort of skipped out on a friend of mine, and the friend's gone after him, and I've got to find the friend, so I want to know all I can about the man in the picture."

He shook his head.

"You know his name?" asked the man.

"My friend thinks his name is Jack Marks. Did he work here?"

"I wouldn't call it work. I employed him for a couple months, but he kind of ruined the morale so I had to let him go."

He extended his hand.

"Richard Vanover."

"Russ Littlebury."

"He didn't say much but he gave the idea he had a big secret. Now and then he'd pretend to let something slip and you could get a little out of him. It was always he claimed to be in the middle of everything. He was in the first Gulf War, he survived some killer hurricane, he was in New York when it all came down."

Kerry came back into the room. He'd been listening.

"It was all bullshit," he said. "After a few of his stories, they were only a minute long but he strung 'em out for an hour or more, you started waiting for the turn. They always took some twisted ghoulshit turn."

"Like what?"

"I don't want to talk about it. I practically get nightmares."

"It's true they're pretty bad," said Richard. "Always people dying in a way you wouldn't want."

"So Richard fires him. And he walks off, and when we get back here to the office, the little fuck, he's slashed our tires and set all these booby traps – one of the platforms back there was all rigged to tip over and the next day we find he's buggered with the hoist which could have killed someone if we weren't

65

lucky. We don't know what else might still be out there. And he stole the picture."

"He stole a picture of my daughter from my office desk."

"But then it turns up in my truck," said Kerry. "He slid it through the window. Like he was planting evidence against me."

"She's thirteen in the picture, you understand."

"Right."

"He was not a model employee."

"If I knew where he was," said Kerry, "I'd find the sonofabitch and drop him like a submersible line shaft."

"My brother-in-law at Fort Harrison offered to get on the case, but you don't call in the army to settle your personal scores. If you're gonna be out there looking, though, I could ask him to check whatever he checks."

"Well, I'd appreciate it. I could call from the road."

Russ took Vanover's card, and both men followed him back out to the car.

"What about his leg. Did he have a limp?"

"Where are you gettin your information?"

"His disability was he's a lazy asshole," said Kerry. "Assholes don't limp. They don't move around much at all, even when they're paid to."

"Right. My friend said he'd had a religious conversion. I take it you didn't see much evidence of that."

Vanover and Kerry exchanged a glance.

"If he did," said Vanover, "then the Lord knew to throw him back."

Russ sat in the car digging loose the brass lock on Lea's diary with a jackknife. He hadn't told Grant he'd found the book for the obvious reason that Grant wouldn't want it opened, and if Russ opened it in front of him he'd feel obligated to learn more about his daughter than she intended he should. Russ expected to find the mostly banal expressions of a young girl getting religion from all directions, but hoped there'd be something to help him get a further read on Jack Marks. He seemed to represent the only real trouble that Skidder and Lea might find. Marks was coming together in the descriptions as an obsessional or pathological type with moderate powers of manipulation. The fact that he had feigned a religious conversion to make time with a sixteen-year-old girl, that he had used her faith against her and set off who knew what miseries and troubles to come, all of it made him a candidate for the kind of retribution that inspired people down here to reach for guns.

He got the job done without gouging the cover, though his knuckle was bleeding. Lea had filled about two thirds of the book with page-long blocks of writing, more than Russ had time to read now. The entries were dated in passing, without breaks or even paragraphs, only slashes between them, as if she wanted to save space. They covered a period between June and November of last year. The first one read, *I know I always quit my diaries but I feel like starting one today June 11. I've got the after school shift all week now. The man Jack from Sunday came by work today. He's older. He looked at me a certain way. He works at some water service. I told him I'd help him understand his gift.* The last, undated entry read simply, *No word.*

He flipped through the blank pages at the back and out fell a small photograph. A shirtless Jack Marks walking away from the camera, looking back over his right shoulder with his brow furrowed, questioning. The location indeterminate. There were trees. For a moment Russ was certain he'd seen the photo before somewhere, and then the moment passed and he tried to account for it. Maybe there'd been a shot like this of Russ himself in a friend's album, or maybe somewhere in the stashed scraps of his inheritance amid the photos of his father on the farm before the war.

Only when he diverted his attention, setting the picture on the dash and checking his watch, did it come to him. Now he held the shot closer. There on the lower back, in the shadow of the spine, a figure. A tattoo? A scar or birthmark? Or just a trick of the light or a flaw on the negative? He couldn't be sure. But a stick figure the length of a thumb, like a primitive drawing on a cave wall, of a man walking.

Russ supposed he'd seen it on first glance in some peripheral part of his mind. That would account for the unlocatedness of his recognition, and what he was recognizing, on the one hand, was the photo itself – Marks was caught roughly in the same position as the figure, if that's what it was. There was an accidental echo of sorts in the shapes. But seeing the parallel opened for Russ the other connection. It was the vision of his father dead. In the early morning, having awoken in his chair in the hallway with the feeling he'd lost a dream of some importance, Russ pushed open the half-closed door. The sheets had fallen off. His father was naked, lying on his side with his arms and legs in mid-stride as if a man so grounded would not fly to his maker when he could walk. Russ didn't go to him, or cover him, no dignity to salvage for unbeing, but left him in the attitude as it had been struck.

Not a trick of the light, then, but one of the mind.

He tucked the picture back between the pages and started away.

II

He moved on alone now, falling into the vast interiors of the continent with nothing and no one to hold the moments in place and almost fearing the course of his thoughts, the oncoming hours as an impossibly long vista changing imperceptibly in its frame.

With road time ahead he kept to the interstate and let it open and his eyes wandered in the slanting light to the cross-movements of distant cars in approach looking insectile and out of season. He drifted without intention along an off-ramp in Butte and saw three deer in a backyard and a sign that read Attorney's at Law, and he thought of people mispurposed in their professions and flashed on an image of a fat man in a blue faux-satin ski jacket lifted off his feet and pushed hard against a panel wall with a fist knotted at his throat as he tried to say something about codes.

On a downtown street he pulled over to ask a teenage boy directions back to the highway, and thanked him and found his way again. He tried not to think of Skidder. The last time he'd been this angry he roughed up the man in the blue jacket, but he simply wasn't ready to replay the events and so instead he reached far back into another part of him and invoked Plotinus and the idea that memory provided the soul an image of itself. Russ wondered if there was any way that the memory of his fist at the fat man's throat could be construed as a contemplation of the divine. Augustine saw religious conversion as an act of memory as the mind remembered God. Maybe what Russ had wanted to share with the fat man was the very memory of God. Maybe he should have told him so.

And then he went back earlier still and saw himself sitting in a cane chair, looking out at the winter city, rooftops peak to peak capped in some indecipherable notation.

"There are no names for those things amongst which one is completely alone." He thought of it as the last line of his formal education. Here was a solitary state he would not call grief, not despair. Such folly to think you knew the names.

In Toronto, May-Ann Moreau had a room ready for him in a downtown house owned by her brother-in-law. He simply took a cab from the airport to the address, where he found a key waiting for him in an envelope with his name on it taped to the door. The house had been subdivided into four apartments, the other three rented to university students. His room was in a converted attic. It was hot and sparsely furnished. He opened the windows at either end of the space and then sat in a cane chair beneath the canted ceiling listening to the wire-humming sound he would learn were cicadas and looked out through the hanging humidity at the rooftops and the birds that seemed like the ghosts of birds until, not having said a word for hours, he fell asleep.

May-Ann called the next day, and the day after that she came by and drove him up to the college. There was a quality of indefatigable good cheer about her that Russ always thought to be either the sort of falseness that was easy to learn and maintain, or a manifestation of some denial and a portent of future emotional disaster. She was older than Russ, approaching forty, he guessed. She was in the habit of dropping her husband's name, Martin, into almost any story or observation, and by the time they reached the college half an hour later, Russ felt he didn't know either of them very well, but knew the version of them that May-Ann liked to put forward. Whether she did so for herself or as a courtesy to others, he couldn't guess.

Wellington College existed in the city's vast and characterless northwestern sprawl. May-Ann explained that their students were in service programs, studying to be chefs, funeral directors, legal assistants, furnace installers, child-care workers. Russ had been hired to teach four sections of a course called The Foundations of Western Thought. When he'd asked her over the phone why such a course would be compulsory, there was a long pause and then a constructed answer about the college's mission of general education.

May-Ann was the only faculty member who knew that Russ had never taught before, and several times over the next few days she stopped by his desk to offer lecture notes and visual aids. He finally told her he didn't plan to use notes.

"What do you mean?"

"I'll just talk."

She pulled up a chair, sat facing him.

"Russ, listen. These students need a *lot* of structure. They lean heavily on the text and on the notes they take, and they absolutely require that the time we spend in class be exceedingly well organized. They don't respond well to formlessness."

"Hey, neither do I. Thanks, May-Ann. I'm sure I'll get to know them."

"I'm not saying you were planning to wing it, but some styles that work in university simply don't work here."

"We'll get by. Thanks."

She started into a question that began with the words "Are you . . . ?" but she thought better of it and instead spoke a pleasantry and left. Russ supposed Dr. Leeming might be getting a call later.

Each class had thirty to forty students, for at least a third of whom English was a second or third language. Some had professional standing or university degrees from other countries that held them in no stead here, and others were a few months out of high school and had never in their lives so much as taken the subway downtown. Some were working people who'd lost their industry or been hurt on the job and forced to retrain. Some had been arrested and tortured in prison, others arrested in an adolescence in which they were still suspended. A few were nearly old men. As Russ guided them along their tour of Western thought, its acute observations, its apparent advances and statements of noble aspiration, they fell quiet together and in what seemed to be reverence, or at least respect for the reverence of others, they met one another. The classroom experience was unparalleled to him, and ludicrous, but seemed worthwhile for reasons that had nothing to do with the learning, and all to do with the common duration, the common mind or even the illusion of it that they created.

He told them at the outset and reminded them now and then that he was telling a story, and that it was pretty much true, except for the story part. He asked them how they conceived of time, and whether or not they distinguished between time and the consciousness of it. Judeo-Christian time began in story, he explained, with the myth of the expulsion. At some point he asked them to imagine the shape of their lives and they drew pictographs – they actually bent over their pages and drew them, hopeless scrawlings or slow geometricals, and he had them reduce their pictures to the essential lines. He transcribed a few onto the board and there emerged human and animal shapes, and the shapes changed to alphabetical characters and then to language, and to gyres and long chalk lines in the dust of lines erased. He invested the lines with the illusions of movement and causality and an awaiting end. He called the lines history and he called them faith. And then he turned the lines back into letters, the letters back to shapes, and then he erased the shapes so they could be reimagined and reclaimed.

At night Russ walked through the city and marvelled at the variety of its artifice. The eighteenth century brought a view of cities as organisms with circulatory and respiratory systems that had to be kept clear of blockage and filth, and he thought just how wrong-headed the analogy was, or had come to be, that the place could have used a little of the quick muck of origins all need to return to from time to time. He listened to enthusiasts talking about their days. He often ended up at the bar of a café where the staff seemed to resent any recognition of him, and he sat drinking and listening to conversations, and one night it all emptied out in the thought that his father was very likely in worse shape than he let on, and now he was sick and alone. They were both alone. And the people Russ was alone with didn't even know what they'd been separated from that made them gather when the night came.

He rode the subway and the bus to work, ninety minutes each way, through the bleak northern reaches of the city, endless single-storey industrial parks and low-rent high-rises, one to the next and receding without horizon. There was nothing for his thoughts to light on but the faces he rode with gone vacant as if having surrendered to the implacable constructions around them. His efforts to read wouldn't take against the passing world, so instead he simply sat, hoping he might see one of his students and they could talk about anything at all.

One late afternoon he was waiting for the bus home with a dozen or so others when someone came to his shoulder and said, "You're Russell Littlebury." His own name sounded strange to him. It had never been said so deliberately.

A woman, about his age: she was of mixed race, he guessed – the skin dusted a half-shade darker than his own, a slight kink in her short hair, her eyes a green he'd never seen before.

"I don't deny it. I'm sorry, I don't remember you."

"We haven't met." He was certain of that. "I asked the secretary, Allison, who you were. We teach in the same division."

She extended her hand and they shook. It was a warm fall day but she wore wool gloves from which the fingers had been cropped.

"I'm Tara Harding."

They rode downtown together and did so again several times in the days that followed. All Russ had to say for himself was imparted in twenty seconds on that first day, but Tara allowed him any question – she actually said teasingly that she'd answer anything he wanted – and so he learned that she was the

74

daughter of a corporate lawyer and his former legal secretary. She had a complicated relationship with her mother, who'd given up her career to a man they both loved though he was an overbearing social conservative whose hackneyed views of the working poor had made Tara more strident than she supposed was healthy. In most areas of her life, she said, she could assert a degree of control through her intelligence, but every so often she'd catch herself narrowing her judgements or reaching a state of unwarranted indignation, and she knew it all ran back to her mother. The woman had made a bad bargain in settling for security and moderate happiness and yet Tara couldn't fault her for giving in to an historical conditioning she wasn't even aware of. She'd had a chance to move her unborn children up the social ladder, and she'd taken it.

Tara had been hired at Wellington as a full-time instructor the previous year. She had a Ph.D. from McGill in labour history. Her thesis was now a forthcoming book, and when it was published she planned to attack the market aggressively and land a university job. She was trilingual, and bisexual.

Recently the race, gender, and class myths evident everywhere in sports media had captured her attention. Her most vocal students didn't seem to share her readings of the politics of colour commentary, though she admitted she had no grasp of the nuances of interior line play or the double switch.

She'd spent a lot of time in Paris and Madrid, both as a girl and a young student. Before she was twenty, she'd read everything there was on the Spanish Civil War, and she could quote Lorca in the original and the translation.

She had a Honda Civic but chose to take public transit to work. Her subway stop was two stations before his, a short walk from a one-bedroom apartment in a house in Little Portugal.

In those first days, when he thought about Tara, as he did often, what Russ thought of was none of these things. It was her body and her voice, and the image of her helping a young blind man off the bus, and the blind man saying nothing, just reaching up and squeezing her wrist in thanks. She'd come back and sat next to him again, and as the bus pulled away she turned to see how the blind man was making out as he moved along the sidewalk, and at that point Russ knew he didn't stand a chance against her.

Three afternoons running, for more than an hour, they sat side by side, touching. On the second Thursday, though his classes ended late, she waited for him. It was near dark. The bus was almost empty, and they seemed to have little to say. He leaned forward and crossed his arms over the back of the seat in front of him and looked out at the oncoming avenue. The lights from strip malls on the verges repeated themselves elongate on the side windows. The engine rolling through the seat. They were just cargo, the two of them, and all of it could fall away and there would remain between them this inclining skin and blood.

"Thanks for waiting," he said. "I really like your company."

She nudged him on the elbow, and he turned. She was smiling. They were looking at one another without ambiguity.

Then he kissed her. He put both hands to her head and he kissed her deeply until she didn't want to stop. And again on the train, and on the walk to his apartment, when they went at it so hard that if there'd been one available to them he would have dragged her down an alley and they would have kept going in reproof of the whole city and the elaborate falsehood that was civility itself.

The recalled events conspire to unsequence themselves, as if in letting them return now he imposes a causality they don't possess, at least not from his vantage, or as if it is in the misremembrance where they remain, the flaw in the memory that gives it purchase on the heart. He feels the temptation to shape his past into a form that holds the line and the mystery at once, that reduces the seeming randomness and reconciles the parts. It was important to think things through, not to fall to dreamy supposition. He knew better than to trust the imagination. It tended towards the dramatic and was full of false consolations and terrors.

She began staying at his place Thursdays through Saturdays. They went to galleries and movies, cheap cafés and bookstores and public lectures. Because they were among strangers they allowed themselves to behave riskily in stairwells and nooks. Sometimes they'd go for walks along streets they didn't know.

The rest of the week they didn't see each other. There was work to do and, anyway, the time apart helped fuel the weekends. When they weren't having sex or talking about it their discussions grew increasingly comfortable, practical, even mundane. Some of Tara's former students from a summer course were in Russ's class and she was keeping tabs on them, and so they talked about work recurrently, though in a glancing way, and a few times they walked down to the Kensington Market and bought fresh fish and a French loaf, and cooked something on the gas stove at Russ's place.

Once, during a dinner he'd made for her, Mike called. Russ put his finger to his lips and she was quiet for the ten minutes or so during which he said everything was fine at his end and asked his father about the weather, the house, how he was feeling. When Russ hung up the phone that night, he understood for the first time the physical actuality that separated them. He felt the geographical distance as if he'd walked it, and the lived one that would always grow greater until one of them was gone and the immediacy of talking together turned over to the metaphors of blood and lineage in the way the moments that bound one generation to the next were lost, set away in the mind, perhaps transcribed to a diagram and tucked into a Bible or photo album to be handed down some day.

"Why don't you want him to know about me?"

She was in the living room, fingering the spine of a book.

"I don't want him thinking I don't want to be home with him."

"Wouldn't he like to hear you're at least happy?" She looked over her shoulder. "Or are you happy?"

The other side of being with her was that responses were required.

"We never really held out for happiness. It's more like devotion through work. Right now his job is to pretend he doesn't need me to look after him, and mine is to see he's looked after without him worrying I'm putting my life on hold."

He'd said more than he intended and now Tara was into some cerebration that was going to extend the matter.

"You didn't say whether or not you're happy," she said.

"I don't think about it. I guess I'm sort of suspicious of the whole phenomenon."

Her smile implied she'd trapped him in something. She came before him, placed her hands on his shoulders and swung her hips into him and held herself there.

"Tell me about the prairies."

"They're flat."

"C'mon. Something must account for your small-town charm."

"You want alot of dust and wind, enduring hearts and all that. I'd rather stick a cattle prod in my eye."

"So tell me what to want. Places have characters."

"Only broadly. What they have are minds, and minds are beyond my powers of description."

"I love how you can be inside and outside your origins at the same time. You say 'minds' like a Belgian film critic but you still have your spurs on."

"You might want to fuck off about now."

"And you're never far away from the hick in your speech."

He lifted her into the air, kicking and laughing, and then allowed her to wrestle him to the floor and pin his arms with her knees.

"I wish you'd let me win sometimes," he said.

"I've got you figured out."

"Then don't tell me."

"I couldn't begin to, I wouldn't know how. And besides, I keep my advantages. There's always an occasion . . ."

She had a way of dropping out of conversations suddenly if stirred to desire. Russ couldn't see it coming but knew instantly when it was upon her. An abrupt silence, and whatever subject was between them – that night it had been the idea that she could make sense of him – was eclipsed for an hour or two, only to return later, often some time after she'd left. The effect, unintended, was so strong, and owing so clearly to her instincts, that Russ couldn't help but feel manipulated. Nothing could punctuate her point like a silence and a provocative parting of her lips.

The sex itself was transporting. It involved no negotiation, only a kind of answering to one another, to themselves. From time to time they fell into patterns of lovemaking, repetition with variation, until something new came upon them. They talked about desire only for desire's sake, and the language they used to express it was understood to be something other than that used in other hours. The point seemed to be to lose everything. They would lose themselves, lose their minds. Utterly bereft. Russ felt close at times to losing consciousness of everything except Tara, her breath and body, the taste of her, as if he were a stranger to himself. Only the returns from these moments were weighted.

"We form a sort of obvious truth," she said.

"Goes without saying."

"Why not say it?"

"Quiet. Please."

"At least admit to your anti-rationalist tendencies."

"Okay, I admit everything. I hope you'll found a cult. We'll wear a meaningless symbol around our necks and gesture to the stars and invent new words for things."

She pulled the pillow from under his head and put it under hers.

"If you arrive anywhere through something other than reason, you can't explain yourself."

"Why explain myself? Apparently I'm obvious to you. Fine."

"Help me with this. Who can I quote at you?"

"I have to help you make a case against my, what, personality."

"As an expression of affection, yes. It's all I'll accept right now."

"You change currencies like this. Well, I don't know. Nietzsche thought that the ascendance of knowledge over the past few centuries has left humans removed from instinct."

"That's clever – you know I don't want to quote Nietzsche. But okay, we've lost our instinct."

"Right," said Russ. "But our teeth line up."

In the mornings and afternoons sex was followed by music or a gallery show. Once on Queen Street they encountered photos of El Salvador. Families living in garbage dumps, men and children who'd lost limbs, starving dogs crowded into the doorway of a church. An older man and woman just ahead of them seemed to find the shots in bad taste. The woman kept peering close to see the sale price.

Something in the photographs, their stark and unlearned lessons maybe, got Tara thinking about a former student of hers in a course called The Contemporary World, who was now in Russ's class. John Overstreet was a flat-faced fifty-some man with thick glasses who sat by himself in the back corner of the classroom. He never missed class and he never said a word. He had failed all three of the short, easy tests Russ had devised to keep the group's spirits up. Tara said that he had worked almost twenty years at the Inglis household-appliance plant before it closed down and the jobs went south to Ohio. He'd been in construction since then, but there wasn't enough work, so he decided to use his retraining money to become an electrician.

"As far as I can tell, the guy can't read or write," said Russ. "How did he ever pass your course?"

She went quiet. She tugged his sleeve and led him into a smaller room, where the photos were of homemade shrines to the war dead. They were alone. She kissed him.

"Sometimes I get carried away," she said.

"It's sex. You're supposed to get carried away. Not arrested but —"

"I don't mean sex. Russ, I did something you'll think is a little stupid."

"When? What are you talking about?"

"John Overstreet. He needed the credit."

81

She squeezed his bicep through his shirt.

"I don't hear confessions."

"I'm not confessing, I'm informing."

The older couple wandered in a few steps and regarded the photos from a distance.

"Well, I hope he doesn't think that all his instructors are just going to pass him."

"I get the idea," said the man. He stood straight and looked down to button his coat.

"He doesn't need them to. Only the ones in his two compulsory, non-program courses."

"The courses where reading and writing matter. The ones you and I teach."

"Yes. Those ones."

The man and woman had stalled. They seemed to be waiting for an excuse to leave.

"It's sad," said the woman. "But they all seem to be managing."

"Yeah, I'm feeling pretty hopeful," Russ said to them. The couple turned, astonished, as if they'd been addressed by a lamppost. The man pointed his chin at Russ to size him up.

"She wasn't talking to you," he said.

Tara took Russ by the arm and led him into the next room, where the photos were of laundry.

"I know you're committed to your students, Russ, but it's easy to forget what's at stake for them. And John's the oldest one in each class. He won't make it without some help."

"He needs a tutor."

"He's too proud to be tutored by a kid not half his age. But he'll listen to you. You can counsel him."

"I don't believe that."

"It doesn't matter what you believe, it matters what he does. You can say what he needs, he'll take it in. He sees you as a man."

"You've spoken to him?"

"I keep in touch."

He knew then what had occasioned Tara's first inquiry about him to the secretary. She'd found out who Overstreet's instructor was, and she introduced herself. Not that her motive diminished what had happened between them, but Russ had liked the illusion that in the beginning, behind everything, they had been just two dumb biting animals.

Later that week, during a mid-period class break, Russ bummed a cigarette from one of his students – he'd quit the habit in his teens but was not above using a prop – and walked up to John Overstreet where he sat smoking on a concrete bench.

"How's it goin in there?" Russ asked.

"You lost me back when you opened your mouth."

Russ remembers smiling.

"Then you come and see me after class and we'll redraw the map."

"That's okay."

"Half the class has already been by my office."

In the act of taking a drag, Overstreet assumed a character. He let the silence sit uneasily between them. His bearing became preclusive, seemed intended to challenge conversation. He looked at Russ when he spoke but not when Russ spoke to him.

"Tell me the truth," he said. "You think your Hobbes and Marx are gonna help me wire a house?"

"They don't know anything about that."

"No. They don't."

"You can guess what I'm supposed to say though."

"You're all wrong there."

"The diploma you're after will prove what an informed citizen you are."

"Yeah, well, I know a thing or two already."

"I believe you. So what d'you say? You come on by."

But he didn't come by after class and a few days later when Russ stopped him in a hallway to ask him again Overstreet just shook his head.

"I'm too old for this shit," he said.

He took his jacket off and held out his arms, bare in a black t-shirt with an acronym and the number of a union local. He used his left hand to pick up the skin at the top of his right forearm and squeezed it hard.

"You see that? I'm getting loose in here. I don't even fit my own skin any more. And nothing you say can change that."

"Quit pissing around, John. Let's sit down right now and sort it all out."

"Listen, I know why you're hounding me – we're both getting something from that girl – but I can't pass your course by the book, so either do like she says, or don't and face the music."

The comment confirmed what Russ had suspected, that he didn't like Overstreet, and made it easier to let him go as a lost cause. The complication was that Tara would not let him go. When she asked for Russ's impression of him, he said the man was "bitter, defeated, and pissed off." She concurred. He didn't tell her what Overstreet had said to him.

"The stakes aren't so high, Tara. He'll get some kind of work."

"Can you imagine what it must be like to lose the only job you've known that late in life? He needs some kind of affirmation."

"So you prove to him you think he can't earn the credit the straight way. That's hardly going to boost his morale."

Russ had put some effort into making dinner and he resented that Overstreet had more of Tara's attention than he did.

"You know something," he said, "sentimental country songs, I sometimes cry to hear them. I mean I fucking abhor sentimentality in all things except country songs. Why is that I wonder?"

She laughed. It was not the response he'd hoped to provoke.

"You think I'm sentimental."

"I didn't —"

"Well, first of all, we could use a little more sentimentality in human affairs. At least of the clear-eyed kind. But what I did for John had nothing to do with that. I just decided early in my teaching career that people deserve credit for their lives, and that I wasn't going to fail any older students who couldn't cut it in my course, despite my efforts and theirs, if they were passing all the others. As long as they learn the skills they signed up for, who cares if they can argue a clear thesis. After a certain point, people deserve marks for just surviving."

Over a Spanish casserole she pretended to move on to new subjects. She talked about the view of the city from the train, the way the light receded unevenly in the fall. He pictured her sitting there in the subway car as it emerged from the tunnel, reflecting, under the hammered metal of late-day sky. The woman caused a mind to wander far, but her own thoughts were always purposive and measured.

The colours had delivered her a discovery, she said, that even the sky had a political aspect. In the cold months, northern countries were enervated by the sheer tonal dreariness, which stilled the radical heart.

"What fun it must be to arrive at theories without having to do the footwork."

"What can I say, they're inspired. Come the revolution, even the sun is ours."

"The bright sun usually makes me want to curl up and take a nap. I guess we're not all cut out for the warrior class."

"You stand and watch, Russ, or you step forward."

"Maybe I don't take the broad forces of history quite so personally."

"Well they take you that way."

They toasted their two views of the broad forces. For the rest of the dinner they seemed to be searching for subjects. They told each other about their friends back home. Russ told a story about a date he'd once had with a young woman who turned out to be the daughter of a reactionary provincial politician, how the next day he'd felt guilty that maybe he'd slept with her for the wrong reason. Tara described an article she was working on examining euphemism in Canadian newspaper accounts of adultery in the 1950s. She hoped it would be included in an edited collection on the social history of Canadian women. They toasted friends, and adultery, the practice of history, and twice they toasted women.

Later, when they were in bed, Skidder called. Russ usually phoned him on Sundays but he'd missed him twice and they had a few weeks to catch up on. It took them less than a minute.

"Have you seen him lately?"

"Yeah."

"Is he getting out?"

"Not much, I guess. I'm getting the mail and the pills."

"Did he mention a date for his next treatment?"

"He says he's not having any more."

"What?"

"He says he's —"

"When did he say this?"

"I don't know, last week."

"Jesus! And you're telling me now?"

"I didn't wanna tell you. I knew you'd make it my fault and then get mad at him and he'd know I told you. I don't know what to say to him, anyways. He's not my dad."

"What's that supposed to mean? He's your dad enough when you need money."

"Fuck off, Russ."

"Christ." He felt a hand on his forearm, a little touch from his alter life. "All right, I'm sorry. What did he say exactly?"

"I don't remember exactly. I guess he just figures he'll take his lumps."

After the call, Russ got out of bed and got dressed. He told Tara he had to go out and that he'd see her at the college the next day. She asked what was wrong and without looking back at her he held up a hand, to quiet her or in farewell, he couldn't have said. What he needed most just then was not a lover, no one he knew, but a stranger he could talk to. He allowed himself to imagine the first exchanges of a heart-to-heart between him and his father, but it wouldn't come together because they had no way of that kind between them.

Past eleven he walked down to Bloor Street, into the usual place. It was half-full. He had a drink at the bar, and the girl bartending smiled at him once, but it was no use.

He sat at a poolside bar watching a young woman play in the shallows with her two kids. Her thin, strong body was most beautiful where her stomach slackened over her bikini bottom as she bent down to them. Every so often she'd look around uncertainly at the strangers angled towards her, six or seven men sitting outside their rooms along the inner courtyard, and this one man at the bar. The woman and her children had their own lighting, and against the far window and the snow falling beyond, they formed a consoling spectacle.

On his drink napkin Russ sketched a version of the narrative map of Levi's life that he'd once helped Skidder devise. Despite its detail it was easy to reproduce. In designing it Russ had employed the classical principles of the art of memory, forming constellations of images whose spatial relation was vivified by distortions, pictographs twisted or violently detailed, pathologized, and so struck hard into the imagination. If it was true, as Russ had read somewhere, that the crucifixion confirmed that the soul is moved most profoundly by images that are disfigured and in pain, then the life of Levi Shute was indeed memorable. Whether it was worthy of the soul's attention was another question.

Of the two routes south from Helena, Skidder would want to take the one to the west of the mountains, the one Levi had travelled so murderously. He drew a rudimentary man carrying a leg on his shoulders in Utah. Then, in San Francisco, a grinning skull on a playing card above the date 1854. A man dealing faro had smiled at Levi's run of bad luck until it became his own. In the popular historical account, Levi drove his hunting knife through the dealer's hand and the jack he was holding, then drew his pistol and held it to the man's forehead and blew the top of his head off. He then removed the knife and let the man fall back, stepped onto and over the table, crouched over the dealer, again with his knife, and carved the smile back into his face.

He wouldn't go to the coast – Lea would bend him her way – but he'd take as commemorative a line as he could get away with. Not owing to Levi, that would take them through Vegas, where Skidder would either call from jail or at least get hung up for longer than he intended. Russ had taken the leeward route. When he'd finished the map, he tried to calculate if there would be time to discharge yet another obligation before cutting the runaways off at the pass in Tucson, but he couldn't precisely locate himself at the moment. There were three fingers of scotch before him that he only vaguely recalled having ordered. They had been there for some time.

He called the bartender over.

"Where am I exactly?"

"Sorry?"

"The snow's pretty heavy out there and I just drove till I couldn't see straight. Then I saw this place."

"Well, some would say you're just outside of south Cheyenne, some would say you're just north of north Denver. I wouldn't say neither myself."

In his fatigue Russ detected countless layers in the man's words. He nodded. He looked back for the woman and her kids only to find they were gone.

"You didn't want that on a tab, I hope."

He slid the man a ten and tucked away the map.

He took the drink back to his room, put in a wake-up call for 4:00 a.m., undressed, and got into bed with the scotch and Lea's diary.

Her father and friends were hardly mentioned. The fragments were unified by the lone subject of Jack Marks. In the early passages she was not apparently working through questions or uncovering parts of her mind she hoped to articulate.

If anything, the record was almost absent of reflection or even conflict. *Today June 28 Jack said scripture is off limits so I'll be Christian in other ways.* For all the mystery he presented her, there was no stated wonder. *Jack said a word denature I'd never heard before and said we would hear it in time and when we stopped for burgers some old guy told the waitress he wanted it well done to cook out the animal nature and Jack said there it was though it wasn't the exact word.* Except when she wrote of imagined divine gifts, the effect of reading the progression of events between her and Marks, laid out as it was in transparent, factual language, was of someone leaving almost everything of importance to herself off the record. She wrote of when he came by to pick her up after work, where they drove, where she was dropped off and when.

In an entry three weeks after their meeting in the church, the diary began to change. *July 8 Jack showed me a video today in his apartment someone took of a burning car with a man inside it he said was his brother dying. The car is across the highway in the ditch and the camera moves closer, then half way around to the driver's side, then it cuts out. You can see the flames licking at him but there's no sound. Jack said he couldn't help but watch it sometimes. I didn't know what to say and he turned it off. Later he said the movie was illegal but anyone could order it if they knew the title which was one-sixty fireball. You could see people die in all sorts of ways he described.*

He put the diary face down on the bed and set aside the drink on the night table. The only way through the moment was to close his eyes and envision a sudden violence. There were not to be several scenarios. Only one. The time or place didn't matter, only the blunt explosion of force. He felt himself lifting Marks off the ground with one hand and then driving his fist repeatedly, breaking the man's nose and orbital bones until he lost consciousness.

In time, he resumed reading.

Apparently the descriptions were just sharp and burnished enough to work as Marks may have wanted them to. Whenever their physical involvement had begun, the first passing mention of it appeared in the next entry. *Kids came by all day (the 12th) in their swimsuits. They smell like chlorine and have dirty feet which I always tease one little girl Melissa about. Myself I'm clean but when I look at my hands working sometimes I can imagine they still smell like Jack. He picked me up after 5 and gave me a swan figurine. I was home by 7:30. Tammy teased me in Christian Youth tonight but she doesn't know who I'm seeing or why the cute guy from that Sunday never came back.*

Two days later, *I've been thinking today July 14 about Jack's brother and the flames and how it's kind of been made up to him the same way. On the day of the Pentecost the Holy Spirit appeared to the apostles upon tongues of fire and filled them with language and prophecy. I can't tell him but the car wreck makes me think of the gift of prophecy and when I think of the Holy Spirit I think of the burning car but I can't tell him.*

And so she was broken, Russ thought, or anyway that was the sense he got from reading the entries successively while knowing them to be the record of a growing obsession.

Russ picked up the scotch and stared down at it, then reached over and turned the light off and took a sip in the dark. He thought of the burning car. He wanted to tell Lea it was just the way the mind works. Tongues of flame, not actual, or even filmed, but remembered, made her think of the Pentecost. They delivered Russ any number of places. Fire-breathing villains in old comic books, deceivers in medieval allegories. Though compelling, such images could never yield real meaning, for the next thought took you to some other connection, on some other plane. Lea had mistaken simple thought association for the language of God.

Except there are times, he admitted, when even the most disparate of thoughts want to cohere. At the moment, Russ understood it was the scotch that brought it together for him. Three fingers, his usual order and the right hand of his father, a man who after his conversion drank nothing but tea and cold water. Mike had lost one finger to a band saw, the other to the cold in carrying his son from a car wreck and the one look taken to know his wife was dead. It was the scotch and the full vulnerability of a tired mind that wanted to give itself up in prayer, if only there were something to pray to. Deliver us from evil, distance us from bad luck, and grant us thine kind iron will. Now the scotch was gone and he began to feel it as he set the glass on the night table, and he saw the ways in which he was his father's right hand, a real dropping off. And deliver us from the one look, the vision defied and endured to the end through quiet righteousness and deeds when possible committed anonymously and offered for the sake of others and the glory of God. He felt it now, dropping off, as if the man himself was there in the room with him, a good man declared all around, the best and the last, and Russ dropping further stared into the dark and knew he was alone, after all, alone with an absence almost infinite, like a guiding constellation lost to some final dawn growing on a cold world.

In one of the classes John Overstreet missed, and he was missing many now, Russ attempted to say something about art. A chapter in the text provided three-sentence definitions of certain terms.

To "classicism" and "romanticism" Russ added "sentimentalism" and "dreck." The text drew broad, inaccurate analogies between musical, visual, and literary arts. It leaned heavily on truisms of the humans-need-stories and art-is-a-secular-faith kind.

Russ brought to class photocopies of a translation of Rilke's poem "Archaic Torso of Apollo" and they listened together to the stone torso "burst out past all its edges / like a star: for in it is no place / that doesn't see you. You must change your life." They read another one about working in an auto plant in Detroit, and then one set "before electricity" in which farm children in Ontario played hide-and-seek only days before they would die of diphtheria. Russ had the students discuss in what ways the poems were about the same thing, and when they'd nailed that down, he told them to identify the things they could touch, that they could actually put their hands to. He said some art was born out of other art and ideas about the world, and some was born of the world itself. He said the best art was most beautiful in those places where necessity broke out of the form. He told them to consider the shapes they'd drawn of their lives and asked if there weren't lines that would be truer if they were broken.

What he didn't tell them, a justified deception, was that he himself didn't believe the seeming truths of art. Even in its most refined forms, imaginative literature indulged in a kind of emotionalism, like religion, and engaged us mostly at the level of, if not superstition, then intuition. It offered only semblances, and the mind's illusion of self-knowledge. As an instrument for wonder, art was increasingly being replaced not only by evolving and emerging sciences but by history itself, the direct report of which offered things to truly believe in, terrors and joys to witness daily. Even the fiction of objective television news at least presented blunt, powerful pictures that had nothing to do with the so-called truths of metaphor. Nothing that existed only in language or its imagery could ever be more than half true.

The students asked questions and sometimes he fashioned answers, and sometimes he chose not to.

After class an Iranian named Hamid told him he didn't agree that broken forms were beautiful.

"I think we're both right," said Russ. They may mean different things by the word "beauty," Russ told him, but it wasn't the sort of noun they could take in hand and pass between them, so it wasn't worth arguing about.

"But you and I are forms," said Hamid. "And it is better when we are not broken."

"Yes, you're right. But we're all imperfect."

"Art can make us believe lies of this sort."

"It can make some people believe the wrong things, but it can make us see clearly, too, or make us experience honest feelings. It isn't the break in the forms that's beautiful, but the fact that they're bursting with necessity."

"Still, I trust my feelings, even without the art."

"I don't always, and I don't see clearly very often at all."

Hamid said he didn't understand.

"I don't want you to think like I think, Hamid."

"I agree with some of what you say. But some of what you say is . . . it is shit – I'm sorry, I don't know the nice word."

Russ assured Hamid he was obviously a perceptive man. So often when he spoke with students, he didn't recognize himself. His need to convey ideas sprang from somewhere honest, but the very act of trying to explain anything came off false, at least to him. It was not a task he was used to. He was still in the habit of hoping that people wouldn't take him at his every word and gesture.

When May-Ann next showed at his office door she explained that though none of Russ's students had complained, a few in other teachers' sections of the course were of the opinion that his tests and assignments were easier than theirs.

"I'm not taking their side, but the only way I can defend you is to make an actual comparison. That way, when they come to see me I can say —"

"You want to see my tests?"

"Yes."

Russ handed her a copy of the last test he'd given.

"The first section there, identify the authors of the quotations, how do think you'd do on that?"

She read a few lines, then her eyes drifted to the margin and up at him.

"'Don't urinate in springs'?"

"No guesses? It's Hesiod. He also wrote, 'That man's a fool who keeps a constant watch over my thoughts, and quite neglects his own.'"

She read on for a few lines, and reread to no effect.

"What am I to make of all this?"

"Just accept it."

"Accept it."

"Yeah. You're not really with us along the way, May-Ann. 'If you should come upon a sacrifice still burning, do not scoff at things unknown.' Hesiod again."

"How can I defend you when you won't even make any sense for me?"

"Maybe you're onto something."

"Listen. I don't really care what you do as long as the core material gets covered and the students don't complain. I mean, some will always complain, but I don't want there to be a consensus growing here."

"Rest assured that in the last days they'll find themselves gathered there on the bright plain of knowledge, where upon the final, I'll slaughter them."

She left with the comment that she couldn't guarantee he'd get a contract for the coming term.

"It depends on enrolment. But there's a chance."

"Well, I'll cling to it, May-Ann."

Early November brought a hard snow. The city in winter was a new place. As he described it for Mike, the cold was nothing except near the lake. Some nights there was sheet lightning, and some nights fog. He'd seen streetcar lines hung with ice extending in long parallel like an inverse landscape in itself or an instrument for sky and wind. He said the light fell faster in its last hour here and looked best against brick and stone of an age that was rare out west. The place he described was unpeopled. Without saying so, they seemed to have agreed not to talk of Mike's health, except through Skidder, and Russ didn't mention the passing moments when he felt like a lost kid, or the nights he was awake in his room.

On many of those nights Tara was beside him. At work, for reasons they couldn't identify, they pretended to be only colleagues and, even when they weren't surrounded by students, expressed no intimacy now even on the bus and subway rides back downtown. But when they emerged from the last streetcar it began, and they often stole caresses into one another's clothing before even reaching his front door.

Once, after making love, he found himself in his bathroom

on the verge of tears, in the revelation that it was possible to be at once happy and full of dread.

"Are you okay in there?"

Her unfailing instinct.

"Yes. Give me a minute."

When he emerged a long time later she was in the far corner of the room, at his desk, working on his laptop. He went to the kitchen and poured them two glasses of wine as she printed off a page. She'd turned everything off by the time he brought her the wine.

"What was that?"

"Porn. I needed porn."

"You're not going to tell me."

"I had a thought I had to get down. My thoughts look better if I don't handwrite them."

"I have to ask you something. Why did you ask if I was okay? Did you get a vibe?"

"'Vibe.' Well, yes, I get vibes. I got this one from the way you walked out of the room. There was a sadness."

"In my walk. That's bullshit."

"It's true."

"Do I often strike you as sad?"

"You do. But you also strike me as being up to it."

"Uh-huh. Simone Weil wrote that —"

"I don't care, Russ. She wasn't the one walking out of the room."

Until he'd met Tara, Russ had quoted the dead only to himself. But with her he could be allusive, and seemed to remember every idea or fragment of one he'd ever read, as if the dead worthies had gathered at his shoulder. She'd tolerated them for a time, but now she wanted only Russ. The thought of being truly alone with her chilled him. He saw himself falling into a silence, unable to get out on his own.

The next day he was grading papers when he came across one whose author identified himself with the initials J.O. The assignment – John Overstreet hadn't been in class to receive it – asked students to use one of the stories reprinted in the text from Ovid's *Metamorphoses* to help define metaphor and myth in classical thought. The essay argued that the story of Ceyx and Alcyon, outwardly about a love that surpasses death, in fact enacted the very sort of deception which was its central, if concealed, theme. When the grieving Ceyx sets sail to meet the sacred oracle who will comfort him, his wife, Alcyon, has a premonition of his death. She waits fearfully for his return until the gods, pitying her, tell Sleep to send a messenger to inform her that Ceyx is dead. One night, in a dream, Morpheus appears to Alcyon as her husband and confirms her intuition. She awakens, mad with sorrow, and goes to the shore, from which she sees her husband's body afloat in the waves. She is transformed into a bird, flies to him, and then, as Ovid tells us, Ceyx himself is reborn as a bird, and the two live happily thereafter.

"Alcyon was deceived to think her husband appeared to her, and we are deceived if we think the tale ends in a happy reuniting. The ending is the only part of the story in which the metaphorical meaning has no dimension. It's simply a happy ending, and just as simply unbelievable. When in her grief Alcyon goes to the sea, she is determined to join her husband in death. Clearly, she is suicidal, intent on sharing with Ceyx not only the state of death, but the manner of it. Ovid's deception is to tell us that she drowns herself by telling us she doesn't. It's a lie he must expect us to see through at some level."

In the last test he'd written, Overstreet had declined to identify a passage from the tale of Orpheus and Eurydice, writing only the words, "Its a car tune, its for kids." Somehow in the ensuing weeks he'd evolved not just a different view, but an implausible sophistication of expression.

The paper was a provocation. It angered him. He found himself going back and forth over it, finding ever more aspects that seemed pointed, particular to the position he'd been put in. Foremost, the essayist read the story as a deception that was intended to be recognized, surely the way he was expected to read the paper itself. Ovid allowed for a happy ending. Was Russ to allow for one, too? The question preoccupied him. He hoped some line of reasoning would reveal the symmetries as accidental, but he settled more readily, if less easily, on the thought that though Tara wouldn't attempt a simple deception, she was capable of a layered one.

From his office, he called her at home.

"Why did you forge a paper for John?"

"Oh. Fine, thanks. A little busy but —"

"Tara."

"Did you see me put this unsigned essay in your folder?"

"You can't write his papers." She sighed dramatically, as if he were ruining the game. "What, are you planning to sit the final exam for him, too?"

"Look, Russ, I'm just pointing out that John doesn't need to know those dumb stories. He just needs a wage for changing light switches. These tests and essays, they're such small things for someone's future to be riding on."

"You know perfectly well that the value of the dumb stories is that they're *worth* dismissing. And they have to know the stories before they can do that. Most of our students have it tough. But you can't sneak them by just because your dad paid your way through school."

He wanted her to see her motivation – motives were never as complicated as people liked to imagine – but, too, he'd ventured a conversational gambit. Of course, she saw it, and batted it away effortlessly.

"Oh, come on. You think class guilt is behind this? It's a narrow imagination that would reduce me to that. This just isn't about me, Russ. It really isn't."

"Some people can't be helped."

"Have you given up on him?"

"I'm still coming to class. He's not."

In this way he found himself taking a strong position on the Overstreet question, and it was a defensible position, but he had no confidence in his reasons for taking it.

Later that day they met at a music store that she especially liked. She would flip through the cds in the jazz and contemporary sections and Russ would busy himself watching her. He loved seeing her excitement at each find. Before long she'd load him up with ten or twelve discs that she knew she couldn't afford and then sadly put them back again. He usually ended up buying one for her.

The moment she arrived she mentioned Overstreet and Russ asked that they not speak of him. She decided then not to speak at all. She was ten minutes into her searches and had apparently found nothing to her liking when she looked up at him.

"What are you thinking?"

"Nothing important."

"Tell me."

"Okay. You know, I wish my mind didn't work this way, but I'm remembering something Sartre wrote. That sincerity could be defined in the same terms as self-deception."

"Did he have anything to say about moral imperatives."

"Don't be dramatic, Tara. We're talking about a credit in a college course."

"No, Russ, we're talking about giving a little help to those who need it because – excuse the jargon – the system doesn't account for them. The systems are either old and inflexible, or new and disregarding of anyone over thirty."

"You know what you are? You're a literalist. You have a monotheistic faith in underclass injustice. That's the god, the single meaning for you behind everything."

She walked out of the store and waited for him in the street. She spoke levelly.

"Why don't you just admit that part of you thinks I'm a schemer – it's the part that probably thinks most women are schemers – and I've attempted to use you to get John a new working life? Another part of you realizes this is ridiculous, you only have to remember what's happened between us. And rather than fight yourself you'd rather just remove John from any consideration whatsoever."

She was right, he realized. But before he could think of what to say she announced she was going home and then walked off down the street.

For the rest of the week he didn't see or hear from her, didn't even run into her at work. She wasn't on the bus. He wondered if she'd begun driving to work. Because of his office location at the end of a far building, he spent his four days a week on campus without having to talk to his colleagues. Announcements of department meetings and guest speakers appeared in his mail-box, but he simply ignored them. He took his lunches in the forested park behind the student residence, with passenger jets in final descent loud but invisible above the treetops.

Each night he had dinner in a café near his apartment. When it was available, he took a seat in the window and marked papers or read. The regulars left one another alone, and the wait staff had at least a friendly inattentiveness that gave the place what passed for character. Out in the street, people from every part of the world underdressed for the season.

Finally one evening she called.

"This essay of unknown provenance, what grade would you assign it?" She had calculated to sound delighted about it all. He felt coerced to play along.

"C. A flat C. The argument lacked gravity. The writing was unpenetrating, all dash and glide. It made a game of a moving story. You're right, it wasn't you. It was insulting of me to think you could have written it."

"Really?"

"Yes. Hugely insulting."

And so they put away the incident in the pretended spirit of fun. They never spoke of the paper again – Russ left it ungraded in his class file – but the thought remained that maybe she hadn't yet been able to let go of Overstreet, even though by now the man had disappeared from both their lives, and from the college altogether.

In the last weeks of the course Russ brought in maps and Breughel prints, paragraphs from diaries and novels, early photos and films. He pointed out errors in the textbook and insisted the students write the corrections in the margins. It wasn't enough to learn a thing generally, he said. All was detail and exactitude.

Otherwise you were just thumbless. The students didn't like defacing their texts, if only because they wouldn't be able to resell them at the end of term, but Russ found supremely compelling the image of them jotting beside the paragraphs, serried edges against the blocks of type.

For the end of class he designed a class on endings. Like every story, he pointed out, the one they'd been following moved forward and backward at the same time, but always towards an end. We live in the expectation that things will make sense in the end, he said, and even if we feel the expectation is false, we have no choice but to look for sequences, patterns, repetitions, understructures that satisfy our fundamental need for meaning. It's important to a good ending that our desires not be fulfilled in a predictable way, that the fulfilment arrives by some unforeseen route, and yet courses such as this did not offer the satisfactions of a good ending, but rather the insipid exercise of examining where things now stood and positing where they may be headed in light of the past. A weak ending not only did nothing to help you remember what had led up to it, but urged you to forget it. What he asked the class to imagine, for the sake of a good ending, was that they were somewhere other than in the middle of an ongoing history of thought. Suppose, he said, that they were at the end of thought. What if we'd exhausted our last idea? What would we most value?

He had lost them, in a sense, but he wanted to strike into them something important. He told them the question would be mandatory on the final exam.

"How would you answer the question?" Tara asked him.

They were walking back to his place from a rep cinema. They'd seen a docudrama about an imposter in Tehran. Russ would have preferred it without the fictional re-creations, and

Tara had said they were the best scenes. The movie had left Russ wishing he'd followed up with his student Hamid on the subject of necessity.

"What do you most value?"

"I don't know," he said. "A good pair of shoes."

She took him by the elbow and pulled him to a stop, swung him around so they were facing their reflection in a store window with ceramic dogs and Virgins.

"You see that?" she asked. "That's us. We've made a monster. We might want to talk about what to do with it."

"We're this . . . Thing."

"Thing, yes. A lurching, stupid creature."

Now she turned him to face her.

"You'll be gone in a couple of weeks. I don't want us at some airport gate in the very hour you find out you're not coming back, trying to work everything out."

"That won't happen."

"You sound pretty certain."

"I'm not coming back, Tara. Even if the college offers me another contract. I need to be with my dad."

In her face he could see that he'd stated the matter too bluntly. He had arrived at the decision more or less as he uttered it to her, but it was reasoned nevertheless. Even though home promised only his attendance at his father's long death – and at some point that attendance would involve nursing, and he could think of no one less suited to it – he was going to get all the time he could with Mike before he died. He was going to see the man through.

She nodded. After a few moments in which they could think of nothing to say, they were walking again.

"So we become lovers torn apart by circumstance."

"You could come west and see me, but you'd hate it. You're not a small-town girl."

"Of course. Then what's the point of seeing you."

"I mean I can't picture you there. It's hard to reconcile that world with this one."

Russ tried to see himself in the same room with Tara and Mike – they were fine with one another, but Russ was absent to both of them, to himself. Absent and mute. If he heard him talking with Tara, Mike would know his own son was a stranger to him. Russ couldn't let him come to know that.

"You're probably right." Her speech was slightly clipped. "You're sensible."

No doubt she wanted declarations and admissions. As if he would know how to say what he felt. As if she didn't know there were some ideas, feelings really, that he wouldn't borrow terms for.

When they got to his street she said she had to go home. The decision wasn't unusual, not on a night before a morning class, but there were other ways to read it now.

He said he'd walk her home but she flagged a cab.

"I like it that you keep things to yourself," she said before getting in. "But sometimes you have to say what needs saying. Or maybe you just said it."

She was gone before he understood from her last comment that she'd heard a note of finality in what he'd said. He hadn't intended to suggest this was the end for them, necessarily. He should have said that he couldn't imagine himself in his small town either.

And that is how the night should have ended. But Russ sees himself a half-hour later fully absorbed in a book. A history of Etruscan art. He was not distracted in any way that he can recall.

Their little troubles were playing out painfully, but he felt only a kind of calm that he may have thought was owing to the knowledge of the greater troubles awaiting him, or maybe just sheer prairie groundedness. He could have called it what he wanted at the time, and called it wrongly, but no amount of self-analysis or greater magnitude of perspective, such as he has now, can prevent him from closing the night away as if it will be of no consequence.

Along I-25 into New Mexico Russ stopped off in Raton for gas and dialled Grant. There'd been no word from Lea. Jean would be landing in Tucson later in the day. One of her neighbours was picking her up at the airport. Grant wanted more reassurances and Russ gave them to him.

Next he checked his phone messages. Glen informed him that no one had claimed the cat so he'd collected it from Russ's truck and sent it out with the garbage. His friend Lyle said he'd visited Lanny Banks and learned that Skidder had called him the previous night. Lyle gave Russ Lanny's number. The third message, received last night from "an outside caller," was a pause, a mumbled profanity, and a hang-up. Skidder caught in a rare second thought.

When Lanny answered, he was anxious to tell Russ that he'd help him out in any way he could. "I always been smart not to get on your bad side," he said. Lanny was a reformed petty thief who'd done jail time and now worked as a janitor's assistant for the school board. Skidder was his only friend. "He didn't say where he was but he's callin again tonight. He wants to know if you been in touch." Russ told him to tell Skidder he'd wire him a thousand dollars in Tucson, once Skidder could confirm he had possession of the dead dog. Lanny understood that Skidder should not be tipped off that Russ had called him.

His last call was to Richard Vanover. He spoke to Kerry, who told him Richard wouldn't be in the office for a couple of days but had left a page to fax Russ if he called. Russ said he'd call back in an hour or two with a fax number.

He set out southward again past rodeo grounds and a desolate RV park looking sad as a zoo bear, into prairie that bounded the road, stubbled and yellow, as it was in the drier winters at home. A lone windmill, a long dugout in the shape of a hockey rink and only a Canuck would sustain thoughts of the national game past a sign for Los Alamos. He remembered the feeling he'd had coming up with Jean last year of having lost the peripheries amid the strange Sonoran plants and land formations, during the slow northward gain. He'd made a point of buying a Peterson's guide just so he'd know the names of things that he'd rather not meet in their full mystery, and now there were the names he'd found and those he hadn't. The apron of land sloping from the mountains to the west was a *bajada*, the huge dormant trees simply stark steel and bone.

He passed a hubcap nailed to a fence post, a hand-painted sign reading only HISTORIC MARKER. The first low cactus, first creosote on the shoulders. Distant high plains to the east and there the gleam of the rail in its bed pacing him. The highway itself in cursive tarpatch and tires shredded in arthropodic contortions. He found himself wanting the names, the illusion of fixedness. He feared his associating mind, but it was warm now, animate, his thoughts to settle like water in the low ground.

There flying along the highway he recovered the orders of memory. From Augustine to neuroscience, memory was thought to have many forms, but in Russ's understanding there was simply the kind of memory people possessed, and the kind that possessed them. The first held what we liked to think were certainties. The second, mysteries. Among the certainties was much of learning, and yet because the learning touched on the inexplicable and was at times intuitive, it sometimes belonged to the second kind. There were mistakes in his life he attributed now to his not having accounted for the second kind of memory.

He had set in motion something ruinous back in Toronto last winter. The mistake was not that he expressed to Tara an apology, but that he'd done so indirectly, with a blind disregard for the others he'd involved. He submitted his grades five days before he was to fly home. May-Ann explained that she'd call him in Saskatchewan later that week to let him know if the college needed him for the coming term. She'd have her brother-in-law hold the room. Then she asked for the students' final exams.

"We keep them on file in case of appeals. It saves us from having to track down former instructors."

He dropped them off with the secretary. Within the hour May-Ann called his office as he was packing and asked that he come by again. He finished loading books and papers into a single green garbage bag, which he carried with him to her office and set outside the door.

She informed him that the grades looked to be within the acceptable range. She said the exam itself seemed fair.

"But there's one missing," she said. "A John Overstreet is on your grade sheet. You've given him a flat 90. The highest mark in the class."

"Yes."

"But his exam isn't here."

He knew he could likely lie his way through this, but hadn't he come around to Tara's position? Wasn't the higher principle on his side, and confrontation over principle his preferred way of engaging with people? The truth was that his heart wasn't in this fight. Tara's was. But if he wasn't returning to the college anyway, why not state her case for her?

"So I lost it."

"I need his paper. I can't put through the grade without it."

"Sure you can."

It was clear to him now, or maybe he'd known it earlier, that she had been tracking his students' results. He had called attention to himself from the first day on campus. She had no doubt suspected the term would not end by the book.

"This guy needs a break," Russ said.

"He's got to make his own breaks."

"He tried."

"Then why didn't he write the final?" Her voice and manner were sharp, but she modulated slightly now towards understanding. "Look, Russ, let me assure you that if you knew what all your students were dealing with, you'd want to help each one."

He knew them enough, he thought. He remembered well the shapes of their lives. Overstreet had drawn a claw hammer inside a box.

"My point is, we all bleed a little for our students. But if you bleed too much, you die."

"So he has trouble with textbooks, okay? The guy just wants to get his electrician's papers."

"Should we give them to him if he can't read them?"

"Of course we should. Historically, I'm talking through the centuries here, May-Ann, the people who do the actual work? They can't fucking read."

"Don't use that language –"

"It's called English. And John Overstreet can use it just fine."

"There's no evidence of that." He'd stupidly provoked her into seeing only two sides to this, and Overstreet was on neither one. "I won't allow you to do this. First of all, you're not helping him. And second, this is a post-secondary institution. We don't graduate illiterates."

"Then you shouldn't admit them."

"The college has a mission –"

"Well not everyone who works here buys the mission."

He knew his mistake instantly and knew she saw it in his face. The administrative offices looked out on a huge horse ring belonging to the equine-studies program. For a few moments Russ simply concentrated his hopes on the chance that a horse might appear.

"You've put people besides yourself in professional danger. Let me tell you what will happen here. I'm going to review this student's performance in the courses he's taken in our department. If there are other irregularities then I'll make a call on each one. I'll have to balance academic standards against the possibility of an appeal or even a lawsuit. Do you want to help me with that calculation?"

"I don't do math."

"Well, you did some kind of math to come up with a 90."

She had him. She'd had him all along. But trouble for others was at large now. And all because he'd behaved true to form.

That night he sat in the cane chair while Tara moved behind him, taking shape in the darkening window. She kept her coat on.

"The insects that hum in the trees," he said, "the cicadas in the summer, I've been reading about them. They live longer than dogs do."

He told her that some nights he dreamed their sound in visions of screeching harpies like those in Dante's seventh circle of hell, where the souls of suicides had been transformed into trees. He didn't mention that the dream had come to him three times since he'd read her forged paper on Ovid. He'd been trying to tell himself something, and the harpies didn't seem open to letting Russ put a good face on whatever it was.

"I haven't had nightmares since I was a kid."

The observation won him nothing.

"You couldn't have hidden him in the mid-range. You had to call attention. You had to make a point."

"The bigger point was that there wasn't a test paper."

"You could have written up an exam and put his name on it," she said.

"Is that what you did last term?"

"I had another student's mid-term exam. He'd dropped the course so I put John's name on it and replaced his final paper with the other guy's mid-term."

"That would hardly pass scrutiny."

"No one looks at the finals unless there's a problem. Or unless they flag you during the year."

"I guess you should have left instructions."

"You'd have ignored them. You wanted this to happen. You wanted to rub my nose in this."

He waited for her reflection to appear again. If he turned and looked at her fully he risked going stupid with anger, apology. With desire.

"There's something about the street from this window. This time of day it all just turns to ink. And the tree nymphs no longer please me."

"What?"

"Virgil."

"Why do you do this?"

"He's lamenting his friend Gallus, a poet who tries to escape his pain in the anaesthesia of travel and war. 'Wilderness is tame. I've seen the blind snowstorms of Macedon, been in absurd swelters of deserts, frozen, baked the hurt, but have it still.'"

"Now you're borrowing your lamentations. Have you ever thought about why you invoke these dead authorities all the time?"

The fact of their being there, inflicting this upon one another, it came to him in eighths and quarters but he didn't know how to bring it all together into anything more.

"And why burn your bridges here? You know something," she said, "you can say what you want about my deceiving myself, but self-destruction is a kind of self-indulgence."

"You don't think I was trying to help him."

"The way it turns out, you get to be the good guy, the victim, and the one who gets to say I told you so."

"That was clever of me."

"And you don't have to come back here. You wrote your ticket home."

"Look. Overstreet couldn't be saved, and I knew I wasn't coming back, so I gave May-Ann a piece of your mind for you. But you want to rip into me for some reason. I'm sure it's for a good reason, I'm just not smart enough to arrive at it myself."

"All you'd have to do is look at me and keep Virgil and Sartre and all the rest of them out of it for now."

He turned the chair into the room and sat back in it. She wouldn't look away. He'd lost confidence in his ability to read her and felt defenceless against her power to read him. The moment dazzled with inevitability.

"May-Ann has called me in for a meeting tomorrow," she said. "Because you messed this up, she read through my exams from last term. She said she caught the paper switch."

Here it was, then. He'd been right. He hadn't wanted to worry her or admit to his error, but here it was.

"I'm still in my probationary period. She already has grounds to fire me."

It was as if he'd known all along that some disaster would roll up on the horizon, but not when or what shape it would take. Now he knew.

"You can say he missed the exam and wrote a supplementary. The bigger danger is that she might provoke you into admitting guilt. Don't let her get to you."

She ran her hands along her hair, pressed it to her skull.

"You know, I've been in school all my life."

"You're not innocent, Tara, but you know you don't deserve to be fired. Just say as little as possible and wait for her tone to register as reasonable. I spoiled for a fight and lost."

"I thought you might have."

She put her hands into the pockets of her long coat and fixed him there below her in the dark, in his memory like an icon on an ancient church wall.

"Go ahead and tell her you're shocked by what I did. I suggest you lie through your teeth."

It seemed for a moment that she wouldn't say anything. She nodded, confirming something to herself.

"You know I can't do that."

She hesitated, then left. He would remember that she paused and he would be hung up in it for a long time that night, knowing they'd been talking about something undeclared and wondering what it might have been.

The hours before he saw her again were heavy. She had been right – he should have known to fold Overstreet's grade into the others, assigned him a C, or should have seen that May-Ann was watching him. His small misjudgement had brought something down on them all. Could he attribute it to inattentiveness, a kind of absence of mind, or even stupidity? Yes, partly. But what was behind the absence of mind? Was it what Tara would call it – wilful destruction? He didn't think so. The simple truth was that he hadn't fabricated the grade for Overstreet, but for her.

By mid-afternoon the next day she hadn't called and wasn't answering her phone. Around five, he decided to drop in on her unannounced. Setting off on the twenty-minute walk he felt the possibility that neither of them would ever really understand what had happened between them. He tried to take his bearings from the neighbourhood. He'd hoped to see before he left a deep snow on these streets and their narrow houses standing shoulder to shoulder but the snow hadn't come. It had been just below freezing for days. The paved school lot he crossed was bare. The young man throwing a Frisbee for his dog at the far end wasn't even wearing gloves. Russ stopped to watch. These were the last minutes before the street lights would come up. The dimming sky, low and flat, transported him to wistful child-hood feelings that didn't belong to him. He did not find it hard to imagine being a boy in this city, in this season. He allowed himself the innocent false memory, until the dog saw him watching and began to bark.

Over the past months he hadn't spent much time at Tara's place. It was more comfortable than his, but going there meant suffering the disapproving scrutiny of the old Polish lady named Stefania who lived below her and seemed to stand guard over the shared entranceway. She was a lonely, crazy woman who had twice detained them with a line of questioning that ended with statements about the sanctity of marriage. Somewhere she'd got the idea that Russ was a cheating husband. On the second of these occasions Russ told her to mind her own business, but Tara waited the woman out both times.

It was Stefania who opened the door when he came up the front steps. He nodded to her and pressed Tara's buzzer.

"The woman not home. Why you come?" There was no sound from upstairs. "You see your wife."

"My wife is in prison. She murdered the gardener."

At this, she fell to her native tongue. He watched her forming the words until he was sure Tara was out, then turned and sat on the front steps.

"You go."

"I stay."

She lingered behind him in the doorway.

"Prison?"

"Yes, prison. Murder. Too much shade for the sage."

There was just enough cold that before long she closed the door on him.

Soon he was rocking to keep warm, and then he saw her down the street, approaching in a slow walk. Not until she was at the yard did she look up to the porch steps and find him.

Rather than say anything, he offered his expectant expression, no doubt lost to the dark.

"Good," she said.

She stepped past him to the door. He followed. They were both on the stairs before he spoke.

"So what happened?"

"I'll tell you."

Stefania appeared and began saying something, but this time Tara ignored her.

When they were inside her apartment she put a kettle on for tea and disappeared into the bathroom. Now he was annoyed.

She came out looking distracted.

"What happened with May-Ann?"

"Nothing."

"Nothing."

"I skipped the meeting."

She glanced at him on her way to the phone and then seemed to set him aside while she picked up her messages. Even her ways of being difficult suggested a talent. She hung up the phone and then looked at him. She was gathering herself.

"You've decided to resign," he said.

She came across and sat down and waited for him to sit opposite. They had never sat together so formally.

She told him that John Overstreet's program coordinator had just confided in her. John was awaiting trial for having violated the terms of a peace bond.

"It turns out he's married. There's a violent history. The wife is estranged and bruised. In fact, by the sounds of it she was badly beaten. This all happened back around the time he stopped coming to class. He'll be put away for a short while, and then he'll get out."

Of course, he thought. All along they'd been hurtling towards chaos. He had mistaken its ambient tones for those of passion, or a clamorous, building need. But they'd both been careless, had exposed themselves to chance. The laws of human event would claim them.

"So I was wrong about him," she said. "And you were right. Did you see this in him?"

"Did he ever threaten you? Was he ever aggressive?"

Her response was inaudible.

"What?"

"I said yes. At first he was just blunt and bitter and defeatist. I was encouraged that he even showed up for our meetings. But a couple of days after he disappeared — just after I wrote the essay for him — he left a message on my machine. He said I'd sold him out . . ."

"What did he say exactly?"

"He said, 'You bargained me away for some cock.'" She sighed heavily. Russ was stunned with rage. "And he said I'd pay for it."

He explored a fantasy of driving his fist into the face of John Overstreet but glossed over the ugly particulars, the bones and torn tissues of it. John would fight back, of course. Very likely he would not be subdued, but would have to be beaten to the ground. He'd be slowed by the sheer surprise in meeting a rage like his own. Men being stupid together. Even sitting there, Russ felt the adrenaline released into his blood.

"Why didn't you tell me?"

"I told the police. You'd just have . . . confronted him and made things worse." She was right, though he had made them worse anyway. "Look, even after the threat I didn't let go of him. But now that he's — Jesus. Her name is Beth. She lives in Burlington. It's all in the public record."

"You spent your day with the public record instead of with May-Ann."

"Yes. The record indicates an escalating violence. If you chart it on a line you can predict the end."

She was looking to him for something. Not solace. Maybe in the hope that he'd say the wrong thing and attach himself as she had to the falling wreckage.

"There's nothing to do," he said.

"The statistics tell us she won't know the statistics."

Here it was, then. Now she had made Overstreet's wife the focus of her concern. She'd found someone caught in another bad system, someone more needy to serve, but only out of desperation or guilt, as if it were anyone but John Overstreet's fault that he'd beaten his wife. She wanted to see the wife, wanted both of them there, helping, and was waiting for the obvious course of action to open before him. They should find the woman named Beth and tell her to disappear. On serious matters, Tara always held to short, declarative thoughts, and Russ got caught up in qualifying phrases and syntax, and got the worst of it.

"You shouldn't have missed the meeting, Tara. You can't escape one crisis by involving yourself in another."

"I'm not the one leaving town." The kettle was whistling in the kitchen. "It doesn't matter. We should stop seeing each other anyway. Lucky us. We timed the end perfectly."

She needed him to free her of this sorry fact, the fact that in some lives, like those of the Overstreets, bad luck and bad judgement were often inseparable, and just a little of either could ruin a person many times over, thinning their will clean through.

"Let me stay tonight."

"Staying's not the problem. It's the leaving. I don't want to wake up to a scene like that."

He could not tolerate the moment. If she could imagine a morning scene, she had probably imagined a future in which both of them were together, something he wouldn't allow himself to conceive of. His foreseeable future was with Mike. He would begin to fail him the moment he allowed himself to think of a world beyond it.

He couldn't tell her. What if she could imagine that world, and could lead him there, make him believe there might be a future for them? What if she could describe that place for him, right here and now?

Her hands and elbows and knees were closed upon one another. She looked small, like someone else. It troubled him, filled him with doubt, when people physically fell out of character.

As if she could read his thoughts, she straightened up, seemed to be drawing back the tears before they could fall. She decided to recover herself, and there she was.

"I'll come to see you off. What time is your flight?"

He told her. They arranged a time to meet at the terminal bar. If only there were a word for it, this thing that was, a thing distant and exact, passed between them like a fossil in a stone.

"The airport, then. Like I predicted."

He spent the night trying to swim out of a dream in which the furniture of his apartment opened its eyes and regarded him. At first he was aware he was dreaming and found the cartoon weirdness of the vision simply ludicrous. But as it progressed it came to seem increasingly real, and the self-consciousness gave way to an eeriness, and then to cold fear. In the dream he was lying in bed with the last light of afternoon coming through

119

the dormer and striking the back of the armchair on which the plush had been worn to a green-grey, and he was looking at a button on the chair, when it blinked at him. Then on the little table he used as a desk, inside the glass drawer knob, a beaded pupil. A standing lamp tilted its shade to expose the wet surface of the bulb as it turned in its socket. From the gathered folds of the throw on the couch, a narrow, reptilian watch. Soon would come an emergence. He was terrified that he would see the creatures whole. The dark came with an impossible slowness. When it had settled, the objects began to grow backs and protrusions, insect wings or limbs, until in his sleep he thrashed and rapped his knuckles against the wall hard enough to wake himself. He turned on the bedside light and found that he was not entirely relieved to be staring at the room he'd just escaped.

From experience he knew that the best way to dispel dread was to read until he found something to take exception to. He chose a book on the grotesque in art, which he examined at some risk, skipping the reproductions from Goya and Francis Bacon, while hoping for a few sentences to tie around the nightmare. Most of the discussions were neither new nor especially comforting. We made monsters as a means of rejecting reason, using the often chance misshapings produced in the unconscious. There was the impulse to revel in abomination, right down to the mixing of artistic genres that was once itself a violation of the norm rather than part of the mainstream aesthetic it had become by the late twentieth century. And so on, and so on. Only stationed critics could bleed dry such a rich subject.

He was rescued, finally, when he formulated an objection to a sentence from a critic named Dorty, who insisted the "value and vitality" of the grotesque "stem from the aberrations of human relationships and acts and therefore from foibles, weakness and irresistible attractions." He had never considered weaknesses or passions as "aberrations," or terror as having anything to do with human relationships. In fact, even on public buildings, in communal settings, or on cathedral archways, grotesques struck him as expressions from deep within the loneliest of souls. And if they were at all instructive, the monstrosities seemed to insist that an open mind is never fully balanced, its parts never reconciled.

He closed the book with a loud clap.

It came to him that there were such things as soulmates. A loneliness seized him. And he knew that in that same hour, maybe in that very instant, Tara had cut him loose.

In the morning, packing, he felt no better. The garish dream had been replaced by self-recriminations for having provoked May-Ann, though at least he understood how it had happened, and a waking dread that out of some cowardice he wasn't allowing himself to fully see what was happening to Tara and him.

He sat down at his small table trying to prepare himself for the goodbye. Anything he might consider saying sounded false, constructed, and yet he knew that in the moment he'd find nothing at all. He wondered if she might try to convince both of them of some plan by which they could see each other in the spring. But whatever happened at the airport, they would not be entering an interlude. They'd be making an observance.

Russ put his course folder of lectures and uncollected assignments into the wastebasket, then took it out again. He opened it and found the blue class lists issued by the registrar, with student ID and phone numbers. There had been thirty-two registered students in Overstreet's class. By the end, about a third had been lost to attrition, and of those remaining, almost a third had failed the course.

He dialled the number. He planned to leave a voice message, but to his surprise Hamid answered.

"Hamid, it's Russell Littlebury, from the college. I won't be back next term. I just wanted to thank you for your work in class."

"You are going away."

"Yes. I'm going home. I wanted to wish you good luck."

"Thank you. Where is home?"

"It's out west. In Saskatchewan."

"With the wheat."

"Yes."

He felt suddenly very dumb.

"I passed the course?"

"Yes. Sorry, the grades aren't posted yet, I forgot. Yes, you did fine."

"Then this is good news?"

"Yes. But I just called to thank you, and to say goodbye."

"Goodbye, sir."

A few hours later he sat in a booth in the Terminal 3 bar amid people nursing their drinks and carry-ons. The glass on the back wall separated the flyers who'd passed security from those who hadn't. At some point a young woman ran past holding her briefcase before her like a shield. A while later Russ overheard a man at the bar elaborately butcher a cannibal joke for the stranger next to him.

There was no one. He had no doubt he was in the right place.

He called Tara's number but there was no answer. He sat back down for a few final minutes, and did her the service of feeling as hurt as she must have hoped he would.

She had forced him to anticipate a resolving scene and then had withheld it. For her, at least, there would be the picture of him in a sterile airport bar failing to conjure some great dead soul and so facing only himself and maybe an examination of his actions, which she held to be certain and discernible. She had been wrong to think he was heartless. He had more heart than his spine could handle.

His window for boarding was about to close. He didn't have to leave, he told himself.

Just before rising to go to his gate, he formed the hope that in the months ahead perhaps a closing of some kind might be conferred upon the open-endedness of his time here. He sat there trying to reduce this closing to its simplest form. At last, he imagined a short note from Tara that read, "I'm now a world traveller. I hope the place never ends." Eleven words. He wondered if in the future there would be occasion to recall them. At least the little fictions he was capable of were useful, he thought, to see him through a tough moment.

In Las Vegas, New Mexico, Russ called Grant at his work number. His receptionist said he was performing surgery but then asked Russ to hold the line. When Grant came on he checked that the secretary wasn't still in the loop, and then, in a voice tinged with either excitement or duress, told Russ that Lea had withdrawn all the money Grant had left for her in the account, about seventy-five dollars.

"She used an ATM in a place called Elsinore, Utah. I looked it up. It's on I-70, which runs east-west. If they're going to Tucson then somehow they got going sideways."

Russ had been right, then. Skidder had taken them down the western route and gotten caught up in Levi country. That meant they'd be angling away from the canyonlands as they came down, and he was a half-day or more ahead of them.

"That's good news, Grant. Now we can steer them. You put, say, fifty bucks into the account and keep track of where she draws it."

"She probably won't check the account. She won't have any reason to think I'd help her."

"We'll see. Just keep track, and don't feed them too much."

When he'd hung up, Russ tried to find the irony in the fact that the day's news had come from a place called Elsinore. It didn't feel like irony, though. It felt like the state of deadfather-dom. He wondered at his increased suggestibility and sharpened eye for coincidence. He had read about the mathematical logic of seeming statistical anomalies, Rorschach tests on swamis, doppelgängers and the compulsion to repeat. Synchronicity apparently all came down to the properties of numbers, the limits of language, and returned childhood anxieties. In Freud, it was hard at times to believe real fathers and sons even existed. And yet how the man could speculate, Russ thought. Did anyone still believe that in totemic religions sons used animal figures to symbolize and worship the fathers they had killed while keeping them from conscious memory? Hadn't it all long ago been debunked by a better determinism? But then no amount of hard science could ever really explain why Freud's response to the long death of his own father was to write *The Interpretation of Dreams*.

The chamber of commerce was housed in the Teddy Roosevelt Rough Riders Memorial Museum, ca. 1940. Russ asked a helpful woman at the Tourism and Investment desk where he could get a fax sent his way. As he'd hoped, she was happy to oblige, so he called Richard Vanover and gave him the number, then signed the guest book and, while waiting for the pages to come through, examined the museum's collection. The entryway was posted with the words of the great man himself: "Far better it is to dare mighty things than to take rank with those poor timid spirits who know neither victory nor defeat." The timid spirits and their descendants were not museum builders, of course, and Russ found no more mention of them, nor of the century of messed-over peoples who had had to endure the aftermath of foreign "liberators." The rifles and war medals were to be expected, but not explained was the relation

125

between the Rough Riders and the piano and the early cameras, or the framed photos of Bill Pickett and Billy the Kid, "cheerful and carefree even in dangerous situations."

With the fax in hand he took lunch across the street from an Italianate bank building, 1880, whose pressed-metal cornice had been fitted with an electronic readout. Sixty degrees at 1:38. The fax included a copy of an e-mail to Vanover's brother-in-law, a man named Rawlings whom Russ had called with specific questions. The e-mail was from some private detective in Denver named Clete Dirks.

> Jackson Paul Marks. Assuming no alias, this is likely him. Born East Lansing, Michigan, '74. No remaining family. No military record, never enlisted. No criminal record. Brother Pete dies in car crash late '97 here in Denver while Jack's roommate. Then nothing for years. Following your lead, last seen Helena, late October. Left Regent Apartments with no forwarding address and insufficient notice. Current whereabouts unknown. Some leads still to hear from but nothing expected.

Below, hand-scrawled, Vanover had added a note for Russ: "You'd think there'd be a damage path. Clete's a family friend but he's not a good detective. You better play your hunches."

A lying heartbreaker, prone to self-reinvention. Described one way, Jack Marks was an American trope, but the unmythologized, actual person was simply a candidate for a thundering comeuppance. He caused trouble, didn't care about damaging emotionally vulnerable women, and he insulted the memory of all the dead, like Mike, who had put faith in divine healing

126

because they thought they'd witnessed it. He'd even used the footage of his brother's death for romantic leverage.

Pondering the satisfaction in redress, in the witnessing of it, even in the anticipation of it, Russ noticed a security camera across the street, sitting high on the corner of the bank. The one constant feeling he had in this country owed to the residual effects of violent U.S. footage and you didn't need to know the right alley to find it. Street assaults, store robberies and murders, aerial shots of gun battles, automatic-weapon shells raining from bridges. Men dying in cars. Because the images were actual they left you dislocated in reality, with the sense you were always about to walk into the frame of a camera that would bring what happened next to a million viewers. And Jack Marks would be there in the frame as someone different to every one of them.

Russ had studied the matter. Violence could grow in any part of a lone soul, from rage or hunger or narcissism. Or from the physical pleasure of using one's strength. Or the beauty of retribution, the elegant simplicity of setting right a wrong through the most direct, least ambiguous of responses. His own indignant anger ended where all angers did. In violence, real or imagined. He belonged to violence, would never be free of it. He hated it for making a lie of reason, the only faith he had ever evolved. The rage would outlive the reason. In someone like Marks, at least as Russ understood him, it had already outlived the rest of him. He would never successfully disappear from himself.

He called the number included in the e-mail. Clete Dirks's machine message evoked the image of a small-voiced man in a small home office with plyboard walls and a small moonscape photo on his desk. Russ explained who he was and asked Dirks to check out the "One-Sixty Fireball" tape. And then he added,

"And while you're at it, you might try to turn up someone else. The name is Tara Harding. Likely in Canada, maybe Montreal or Toronto. I just want a phone number really."

He'd said it on impulse, though he knew an afterthought was no thought at all.

Coming through here last spring, Jean and Russ had stopped in this same café – he remembered the sign on the bank, though not the camera – and then gone into the old town to see a friend of hers who worked at something called the United World College. There had been times when she and Mike had over-nighted here, but the friend's husband was sick and she wasn't up to company. When they headed out on the road again, they talked about Mike and how hard it was to read his condition, which in spite of his having stopped the treatments hadn't seemed to have changed much since Christmas.

When Russ had returned home from Toronto he made a point of getting Mike out of the house. They drove through town in the evenings and one night went to a hockey game together and sat there in the stands as townspeople from every generation came by in procession to say hello. A few were Russ's friends or old schoolmates but even these had come over to see Mike. His health was not spoken of but a couple of the women hugged him and one, whom Russ didn't know, began to cry and had to leave. "She's a good gal," said Mike, "but she bawls at a flat tire." The night didn't go as easily as Russ had hoped, though he should have known how the town would react to his father's illness. It would be easier for everyone, he reasoned, if he and Mike kept mostly to themselves.

Skidder appeared for Christmas morning and again later when Russ roasted a capon. Their gifts missed the mark, as usual. Russ gave his father a book of riddles based on science and philosophy through the ages. It had cartoons. Mike would leave it in the bathroom newsbasket for a week or two and then store it in the basement. Mike gave him a book, another in a series of "contemporary testaments" aimed at born-again Christians and those they hoped to rebirth. Russ barely made it through the awkward title – *The Present Risenness of Christ* – before tucking it away in his closet.

Mike bought Skidder a television that he was to choose himself during the Boxing Week sale period in Saskatoon. Russ drove. There they'd stood before a bank of screens all tuned to some U.S. disaster channel. Programming ads featured floods and tornadoes, knife wounds. When the salesman appeared, Russ asked the questions. Within ten minutes he'd paid and turned with his purchase in his arms to find Skidder transfixed child-like before a few dozen reproductions of high-tech war footage, the baubleshine missiles, their radiant ends. Russ was unprepared for the image and the welling regret overtaking him without known provenance. He maintained himself by remembering Baudelaire's line that the thing he liked about opera was the chandeliers. Made with characteristic indirectness, his father's point was clear to him. Whatever became of Mike, whatever of any of them, Russ was to see to it that Skidder had his chandelier.

One night into the new year as the two of them did the bills at the kitchen table, Russ was surprised when Mike began talking about his health. It was not a subject they had ever ventured into deliberately before, and though Russ had once been willing to talk with him about his health, he found he was not now able to discuss his death.

"When I told them I was done with the treatments, they told me what I could expect. You should probably know it."

"Never mind."

Mike wouldn't wear glasses and he seemed to have to wait a second for the numbers to come into focus on his calculator.

"You should know it."

"Look, it was your call. As long as you're not holding out for miracles then there's no need to start a betting pool."

His father looked up from the calculator. Russ pretended to take an interest in a reminder from the phone company.

"You know everything's connected for me. You don't want to talk health because you don't want to talk religion."

"Fine, you're right."

It astounded him to think the person he was closest to was very probably a creationist. The terms of one or another theology were available to Russ, and though there was no one to admit it to, aspects of Buddhism and Gnosticism offered mythologies in which the engines at least were still running. But myth meant nothing to Mike. He believed in the living word.

"Well, we're gonna talk it."

There was a force in the man. Even then Russ understood it would be the last thing to leave him.

"I don't want to hear how there's no death in the Lord, or how scripture dictates a complete lack of common sense. You're not doing anything to get better."

"Yes, I am. I'm seeing it."

"Seeing what?"

"I'm seeing the tumour. I close my eyes and I see it. It's the size of a grapefruit but I imagine it shrinking. Grapefruit, orange, golf ball, a little pebble, then a speck of dust washed away in the blood. I see it shrinking every day and every night."

At some point Russ had dropped the paper he'd been holding. He now put his hands palm down on the table.

"That oughta take care of it, then."

"I've seen scripture heal people, Russ. It's not a trick and I'm not a fool. Do you think I'm a fool?"

"No."

"I'm a true born-again, son. You won't catch me half naked with some con man slopping chicken blood on my belly and declaring me cured. But I know what it's like to have the Spirit in me, and I know the kind of works it can do."

"Let me tell you what I know. I know that guys in lab coats can induce religious feelings with a little electrical charge to this or that part of the brain."

They could also induce out-of-body experiences, he thought, like the one he was having right then, watching himself watching his father shake his head sadly at this foolishness or betrayal of a son trying to erode his faith. Russ couldn't stop himself.

"You think God is in you when you speak in tongues, but glossolalia is just reproducible nonsense you can teach someone in five minutes for twenty bucks and a pizza coupon."

"Is that as much as you've learned in life?"

"All I'm saying is, the god who made you and me, he made the blood tests and therapies, too."

"It comes down, son, to I don't have your education and you don't have my faith. I'd trade you if I could, but you have to earn your faith. It's pretty clear it can't just be bought or handed over."

"Just don't pretend you're healing yourself when what you've done is give up."

"I'm not pretending one way or the other. I'm exactly as close to God as I've been for forty years."

"Then what was all this about? Why tell me what the doctors said?"

Russ got up from the table but as he passed by his father Mike reached out and held him by the arm.

"They said I'm dying. It might take months. Maybe we'll even be sitting here this time next year. But you can't cut yourself off from the town until it happens. You're not really living a life right now."

"What I'm doing, I don't know any other way to do it."

Mike released him.

"I'm trying to show you the other way. When you're through as a skeptic you'll see it."

In the afternoons when Mike was sleeping or at the kitchen table with his Bible and water, Russ would go to his own room to read from old books he had gathered and new ones he had shipped to him almost daily. He resumed the study of ancient rhetoric, something he'd suspended after grad school. He read again about the lexical lists that Sumerians committed to memory, the Proto-Izi, and Egyptian onomastics. The Greeks regarded memory as the antidote for oblivion, but it seemed to him that the Greeks were wrong, that remembering something like ancient thought was a good way into oblivion, and their being wrong distanced them all the more from the world as he knew it, and so he read on.

Only when Tara's letter arrived was he struck by the enormous remove of his current life from the one he had lived a few months earlier. Seeing his name printed in her hand on the unopened envelope somehow separated him from his experiences in Toronto. She was still present to him, the letter as a physical object sensualized every edge and fold in his room. The whirl of random, senseless involvements back east seemed to have happened to someone else, but Tara herself was immediate. He owed her more than dispassion or at best a casual interest in the characters she'd describe, as if he weren't one of them, so to find the place where the perspective might break down, he tried to let his thoughts go as he opened it, found five pages, handwritten, and began reading.

Russ,

It's morning and I'm miles from anyone, looking out at a winter lake. It's early and the snow is blue. So far from the city, it feels peaceful enough that I can do this in a sitting and be done with it.

In the days after you left I came to understand what you must have known at the end, that anything more you might have said to me really was a risk, that words admit chance, they conjure dramas that can trap us. And we couldn't get trapped together. We had our separate crises, and separate duties, in separate places. I hope you're serving your duty as you would want to.

Let's think of ourselves as just a couple of lovers who parted after three months. Let's put aside for now the outsize consequences of our little deceptions.

A summary of events. I never did meet with May-Ann. I received a letter of intent-to-dismiss two days before Christmas. There were grounds for appeal, no doubt, but I simply went to the college and packed up my desk. It was the first time I'd left my neighbourhood since the day you flew home. When I told you I'd meet you, I think I half believed it. But that afternoon I drove to Burlington and knocked on the door of Beth Overstreet. I hadn't called ahead but she answered without inquiry or hesitation, a short, strong-looking woman, maybe in her early fifties, with her hair pulled back and what I may have imagined were the last signs of a bruise on her cheek. As I introduced myself, I thought of you. I saw myself as you see me, I think, as someone who thinks she always knows what's best. My first moment of doubt flickered then, in the thought of you.

I explained my connection to her. As I spoke she gave me a look that women sometimes recognize in one another when there's a man connecting them. I've learned to distinguish it from the other look I get when someone disapproves of my racial mix. This look – I'm not making too much of it, it was there – this wasn't about racial difference. It was about shared gender.

So there I am, still in the doorway, still working through this look on the face of a woman I've never seen before, and I arrive at the idea that she doesn't think I'm involved with her husband (she would find the thought ridiculous), but that my existence simply explains some-thing to her. I suddenly saw myself as one in a series of women "helpers" who would have come into her life, or her husband's (she hasn't spoken a word yet, hasn't even nodded an acknowledgement). Somehow, that simply, I'm placed as a figure in some long history I'll never know. But whatever it means to her, my being a concerned helper, she knows what it does to John to be around such people. Maybe she thinks it explains why his violence re-emerged after having been under control for so long.

Without so much as a hello, she said there was nothing I could do for her but leave her alone. I got no farther than her doorway. I asked what she expected to happen when John was released? She didn't know, she said, but she wasn't going to run. She said she hadn't even quite given up on him. I pretended to think she was embarrassed or maybe even ashamed to say it, and I couldn't help myself, I persisted. I said I knew what it was to misread a man. She got angry and I said all she should expect was more violence. Then she slapped me. She slapped me across the face and we were both speechless, she was as shocked as I was. My eyes were watering when she literally pushed me out the door.

I understood instantly why she'd hit me. She felt I'd judged her, and her life, and she was right. I felt I knew her story, or rather the rest of it. The climactic, providential part.

Which doesn't change the fact that she's still there, alone with her bad ending. It's just floating in space, awaiting us.

I'm writing you from a place I found on-line, "an off-season rental steal" (a cabin with plumbing) on Manitoulin Island. The lease and the cold up here have me locked in until spring, when I have to give the place up, but it's somewhere I can live for pretty much nothing. I like it that no one I know can imagine me here.

I should have mentioned to Beth that because of her husband I'd thrown away eleven years of expensive schooling. The slap reminded me I'd been blotted, stained. My only hope of restarting my career is to lie. The year and a half at Wellington will have to disappear from my vitae; I'll have to claim illness or kidnapping.

And more immediately, I realized then (in the days afterwards I thought about myself more than about Beth and John), I'd have to find a non-academic job in the short term that would surely kill my slight but precious career momentum. I pictured myself in other lives, as a functionary in a marginal party, an aid worker in French West Africa, as some sort of paid agitator in a social-justice strike force. I didn't tell any of my friends or family – you were the only one I could imagine telling, and you were gone.

There's no tv, just a radio pulling two stations and no CBC. I've brought my work with me, a couple of articles to write on gender myths among early migrant health workers. The only books besides mine are a few Hardy Boys novels, and, astonishingly, the full twenty-six-volume set of the Oxford English Dictionary. For distraction I look up words for stray meanings, strange etymologies. I develop hunches and then confirm or destroy them.

Among the readings I brought with me was your master's thesis. You left it at my place, remember? I thought it might be a useful relief from my own thoughts.

Do you remember writing this?

"In the notebook entry recording the death of his father, Leonardo forgets by the end of the line that he has already written the time of death at the beginning. In a looping conjecture, Freud attributes the forgetting to both a psychosexual root and a rejection of the claims of authority. It matters that the repeated detail is mundane, a number, unattached to the father himself. He argues that Leonardo's scientific achievements were driven by rebellion against his father, the prime authority of his formative years, and quotes Leonardo himself to make the point: 'He who appeals to authority when there is a difference of opinion works with his memory rather than with his reason.' So it was that empirical method advanced as Leonardo rejected the authority of both his father and God the Father."

After reading this it occurred to me that I didn't have to wonder any more why you and I were never alone together, why the authorities, the Spinozas and the Greeks, were always there with us. False authorities, lost gods. Not all your father surrogates were male, but their tradition was.

I'm sure you could argue that I'm being simplistic, but not without naming names and quoting them.

Threshold from a root of thresh meaning crash or rattle, and a second element of unknown origin. You know the meanings, but to me a threshold is for crossing, not demarking.

Beth wore a perfume. It was the middle of the day, and she had a bruise on her cheek, she was alone in the apartment, and she wore a perfume I recognized. The name came to me later it was Obsession. My old housemate in Montreal used to wear it.

Because words prompt us in this way, you'll think I followed an obsession to her door, but you're wrong. It was more like devotion. Obsession, devotion. One is a psychological phenomenon; the other a moral one. The heart needs what it needs. This is the sort of self-evident truth worth saying every so often. For people like me, the expression of devotion is almost impossible to get right.

That last time we were together I lied to you. I didn't get the news of John's arrest from his program coordinator. I got it from the police. They called because when he was arrested John had in his possession a note with my address on it. The police think that if Beth hadn't been home to receive him, I was likely Plan B.

I love men, and I don't mean to be essentialist, but the numbers mean something. Whether or not they express it, men are stupid with violence. So many men, in fact, that it's hard not to hold suspicions about the interior lives of even the meek or civilized male. The testes make you want to hurt things, it's a trend throughout species. It doesn't matter that you agree with me – there's no argument here. All your imperatives are physical, no matter how you disguise or sublimate them. Not to overstate it, you are all about hitting and fucking. For part of every day I wish you'd all go to hell.

I've always thought, or wanted to think, that the presumed difference between men and women could never be reduced to the masculine rational vs. the feminine cyclical-intuitive. I've learned that men aren't mainly rational, you're just ruthlessly linear. In your thought, and in your actions. Not that men aren't devious or their motives concealed. But yours is a world of targets and ends.

I read my research at night with a cup of weak Earl Grey and the beams from snowmobiles passing on the lake. Then I turn off the space heater and go to bed. In the morning I find a half-cup of tea frozen by the window. I warm it in both hands for a minute and then step outside and drop a dark lens into the snow, where little sugar-starved birds I think may be sparrows or something peck it to bits. The same ritual every morning. That first night I simply forgot the tea. Now I remember to leave it.

When I remember it later the snow on the lake is blue in the morning, but as I'm seeing it the blue isn't actually there.

One morning I found a family of four deer in my backyard feeding at the grass where the snow had melted around the water pump. The buck looked up at me in my cold porch. There was nothing between us. We were completely alien to one another. All I could do – and I said it out loud – was to wish him well.

I say lens but that's not exactly it, though without the word I almost wouldn't see the thing at all as a thing. Thing I got from you. Lens from the Latin lentil because of its shape.

Twice a week I drive my Civic seven miles to town for groceries but otherwise I keep to myself. My neighbours here look out for me. An old man named Carruthers comes by almost every afternoon to ask how I'm keeping. A few days ago after he left the thought of his ordinary concern was enough to make me cry. Everyone who grew up in a city should be made to live in the country for a year. But then it would ruin the country, wouldn't it.

I'm not in ruin myself, not even in retreat. I'm simply tending things. The image you must have of me is sad and desperate, I realize, but I hope my voice is steady enough to reassure you that I'm quite together about being here.

Nearer the lake are a few dozen stumps. Obviously, the trees were cleared to afford a better view from the cottage. Humans inscribe their history on a place. It's all parchment to us.

The big picture of human endeavour involves a lot of questing and migration lines that eventually turn back on themselves and knot into cities or turn into lines that aren't human but originate in us, technologies of destruction and defacement with enough heat to melt the poles.

The small picture is the woman along the curve of the shore who every morning goes out and chops kindling with a hatchet, and gathers it into a canvas.

The language closes us off from the world in circles. Canvas means to gather, or solicit, the meaning having taken an unknown route from the noun, from the Latin cannabis, from the Greek kannabis, meaning hemp. I've never had no one to talk to before, the unexpended words collide more and more in my thoughts.

How many times can we be levelled by the same revelation that people are not who they seem? But then who am I addressing here? You fooled me all the time we were together with your allusiveness, your physical presence, your confrontational wit. You fooled me into thinking you were substantial, but you're not. You're made of evasion, and unequipped with the will to remake yourself. You should never have let us go so far, Russ. You must have known your father needed you long before you told me you weren't coming back. But then, having kept me to the very end, and having exposed me to May-Ann, you should have helped me with Beth. You should have stayed even one day longer.

There are small animals out here I don't know the names of.

From mid-afternoon to early evening I miss the city, its beautiful diversions. I miss having conversational angles to play and people to play them for. At night I miss specific people, my parents, a couple of friends back home. I write letters to assure them I'm fine. I live very close to desolation. Which is likely why my work is going well.

Sometimes I want to abandon my past. What more proof is there that I'm clear-headed, and getting on fine?

Tara

On his first day of reading and rereading the letter, unable to ignore the chill in it, he recognized how it had been with them near the end, Tara's growing absorption in everything but him. He now represented to her all that had gone bad. From Overstreet's frustration and the violence it likely contributed to, to her professional disaster, her inability to help Beth, and her own feelings of betrayal. No doubt she'd needed to say what she said, to tell him his mistakes. He'd played everything badly, he agreed.

But there was more to it, he wanted to tell her. A need to respond consumed him. She hadn't provided a return address, but he constructed lines and paragraphs, whole pages that he came to know by heart. He observed that she had read him well, revealed him to himself. That he was certainly evasive, but not in a calculated way. There was no more thought behind it than there was behind his other contrary habits of mind. He confessed that though she'd read him at depths he could never have come to know without her, depths he couldn't sound himself, he wanted to believe there were still greater depths at which, if he could ever reach or draw from them, or see into them for an instant, he would make complete sense. And what seemed like strategies for avoiding emotional truths and moments, whether calling up the dead or simply leaving town, would be revealed as something of his better nature, for which he shouldn't be judged harshly. There was a fuller sense of him at these greater depths. He hoped that in time something might illuminate them.

Then he told her that she'd been right about devotion, and that he'd found a way to express it, or it had found him, and he wouldn't wish the discovery upon anyone.

After another day, he realized that it was only because he knew he could never send the response that he'd imagined it in the first place. It was self-sorry and badly conceived. And though Tara's letter had seemed to be direct with him, she hadn't really earned her judgements so much as meandered into them. The city girl had been stunned by the deep country silence and had understandably fallen into her own attentions. When he understood it more objectively, he let Tara and her letter recede from him. She returned now and then in a sexual musing, he could separate in his memory the physical woman from the whole one, but it wasn't hard to let her go. She didn't belong on the cold prairie, and he had no doubt he was in his rightful place.

In late January Mike suggested that the two of them should get out of the house more. Three times a week they'd take a turn on coffee row at the Salt Lick Cafe, where Mike drank water and insisted on paying two dollars a glass, and they'd head out to the bank or the drugstore and be home in the late afternoon, when Russ would open the wine for himself and cook up a meal for three in case Skidder showed, as he did three or four times a week.

When a call came from the manager of the Colliston Icemen asking Russ to play the last half of the season, he knew that Mike had set up the invitation, and he accepted it. There were daily practices and games twice a week in which Russ took the role of a seldom-used seventh defenceman who sat at the end of the bench. By the end of the first game it became apparent that his value to the team would be as a fighter. Though he had always been good at it, when he was younger he hadn't liked fighting and fought only when challenged. It was part of the game, as fans were fond of saying.

Even as he sat by, his growing reputation hung over the opposition. There were short fights with young enforcers who didn't know any better until they found themselves sitting in the penalty box in their own blood and disillusionment. It didn't matter to the fans that in every other respect Russ was a liability – he didn't skate well, he pinched at the wrong time, his play in the defensive zone seemed drawn from a compendium of bad judgements – he had taken the role of a hockey fighter, and an undefeated fighter at that, one of the last sure things anyone could honour or love.

Every time he looked into the bloodied face of his opponent – the lightest of injuries could look gruesome if the blood ran – Russ reminded himself he was not acting out of some instinct that predated everything he knew about himself. It was true that landing a punch provided an instant of charged connectedness, but he was not senseless with violence. The running joke with his teammates, most of them younger men, was that they disapproved and he was expected to say something funny and obscure after the game to justify the beatings. He always began and ended his line the same way, changing only the middle, where he named the offence. "We were talking before the faceoff and it came up he . . . was a western separatist / didn't practice crop rotation / adhered to the Whig version of history . . . and you don't let shit like that stand."

Spring came, and in the first days of seeding he drove his father into the country from neighbour to neighbour in Mike's pickup, with the sound of his commentary running unbroken beneath that of the tires along the graded roads, and so on for weeks, the early colours changing blue yellow blue in half and quarter miles, through the summer and into September and a new talk in the man. The harvest patter. These are the names of the fields. You see what he's done here, he's opened it up with that old front-end swather but maybe the heads aren't full or do you think it looks a little green yet down there in the distance. That's canola. Winter wheat.

When Mike was no longer up to the drives, Russ would go out into the country alone, usually to visit his friends Lyle and Jackie Cudderly. Lyle was a smart man who didn't say much and Jackie was perhaps the funniest person Russ had ever known. One night the three of them sat on the porch with a cooler of beer watching the stars. Lyle and Jackie were smoking, tipping their ashes into a useless mosquito coil burning between them as Jackie hatched astrological advice.

"Aries, how could you be such a selfish prick? You knew damn well she was saving that money for Hawaii at Christmas."

"You can't live out here without four-wheel drive, I'm sorry."

"Now you've got Pisces on your ass," she said.

"I've had it before."

"I recommend kerosene," said Russ. "Home remedies work best."

"I'm thinking you don't really hear the stars."

"I don't hear them, I read them. I look up there and I see what house you're in and it all just spells jerk."

"The stars don't understand me. You have to weigh in on this, Russ."

"Well, some ancient philosophers believed the heavens were a living creature."

The couple glanced at one another.

"Sorry," said Russ. "It's the view."

"No, tell us," said Jackie. "You mean a creature like in we've been swallowed?"

"No, not like that."

"Who are you talking about?" asked Lyle.

He usually refrained from professing to his friends, but that night he found himself talking about the Stoics and Democritus.

"And later, people like Petrarch thought the universe was providential. Chance springs from the realm of the divine. If we were divine, we wouldn't see it as chance."

"You don't think that's just alot of talk?" Jackie asked.

"It is definitely alot of talk. What the unexplained really makes us reach for is the explaining."

"People like to think there's a reason for everything."

"The worse a thing is, the more people want it to mean something. The Mesopotamians thought disease was delivered by the hand of a deity who just reached out and touched you. The sick didn't have symptoms, they had omens."

Lyle reached into the cooler and found a stone of ice to pop into his mouth.

"Maybe I need a map." He dried his hand on his jeans. "So your dad's not in great shape, eh?"

"That's how it stands."

"I'm sorry."

"Yeah, I know."

Lyle told them about a superstition he'd formed in his last year of high school nights coming home to the farm. He didn't want his father to know how late he was, and he'd cut the headlights as he turned into the laneway so they wouldn't track across the bedroom window. If he forgot, his older brother would wake up and be waiting for him, wanting to know if he'd been drinking and ready to beat him if he had. Lyle came to associate killing the lights with avoiding confrontation so that, after a while, any time of night, even after his brother had left home, he'd turn off the lights before they could hit the house.

"That's not superstition, it's habit," said Jackie.

"I used to think it was style," said Lyle.

"No, it's superstition. Name it and lose it."

The company of friends was keeping him just barely in his right mind, but before much longer even they wouldn't be enough. The certainty touched off a chill that moved up his spine and out into the sky to cover them. For a bleak moment it seemed that everything he thought of was like superstition, everything a lie he couldn't tolerate. The belief in historical progress, the belief in the powers of self-examination. Our trust in just about anything.

"Life's hard enough without losing heart," said Jackie, as if she'd read his mind. Something had upset her. General impending death, he supposed.

"You're right, Jackie."

"Jesus," said Lyle.

146

She was crying now.

"You see that constellation up there, Jackie?" asked Russ.

"He helped us out —"

"Jackie," said Lyle. He was warning her away from this.

"No, I mean, here we are talking about Hawaii and four-by-fours and we never paid him back, he wouldn't let us —"

"It wasn't a loan," Russ said. "He just co-signed something. He knew there'd be returns, and Glen just needed a name to give you a boost."

"Ah, Jesus," said Lyle. "He doesn't want to talk about it."

Lyle was done with the stars. He was looking out across the yard into the dark now.

"He gave us money, too, Russ. I thought you probably knew. He put himself at risk, and you too, and he gave us some money and then wouldn't let us pay it back."

"We wouldn't have all this," she said. "We're paying it back to you, Russ. Don't argue with us."

"He gave it to you, it's yours. I couldn't take it back on him."

"I told you," said Lyle.

It was not the first time someone had felt the need to thank him for who his father was and then required counselling about it.

"That's just him," said Russ. "He wouldn't want you to make a big deal out of it. All he expects is, you know, that we see each other through."

She was nodding for him. She wouldn't say anything more for a while.

"Fuckin stars," said Lyle.

Near Santa Fe there was snow in the ground shadows and a cold had blown in on the mountain gusts. Water from an overpass fell handprint on the windshield and froze there as the traffic picked up in volume and dumb portent with Russ locked for a few minutes behind three U-Hauls and a Covenant Transport truck, and Albuquerque breaking up on the radio.

It was past five when he rode the Cerrillos motel strip. Signs read American Owned and neighbouring signs read Nice Rooms and Nice Nice Coffee. He turned by the vaguest of instincts into a place called the Zuni that advertised cleanliness and a free Playboy Channel. His twenty-six-dollar room featured a view of the snow falling on the neighbouring motel's pool. A window unit rattled heatless. The sheets rode up on one side when he sat on the bed and the tv, anchored to the floor at an angle that obscured the screen in window-light, had the Zuni's name and phone number scratched into the metal top. A sign above the dresser read No Guests, No Exceptions. The room key was attached to a brown plastic frond that would not fit comfortably in any pocket. The familiar charm of cheap motels, bought from the back pages of the catalogues.

He took dinner at a horsemen's café down the road. It was an old place. He ordered green chili at a counter, then squeezed into a small, straight-backed wooden booth. The walls were covered with horse-related items, paintings, cartoons, news clippings, child's crayon drawings. The window ledge was lined with a dozen carved horses. The one other customer was obviously a rancher. When the waitress brought the food she told Russ he looked under the weather, as if she'd seen him before.

When he stepped outside it was colder. In the car he saw the snow in his shoeprints hadn't melted. Where exactly, he wondered, did the off-season around Santa Fe change into the high season around Tucson? He was cold and he needed relief, and supposed he would need it more before he left town.

Back in the room he dialled home and cleared a single phone message. Skidder had worked up his nerve.

> Okay it's me. I hope no one's making a big thing out of this. She's on a hunt and I'm just looking out for her. I expect we'll come back some time. Just so you know, and tell her dad, it was her idea and the car's fine. And something good happened to me . . .

In the pause, Russ heard echoing a bus or train announcement in the recombinant syllables of Kingman Flagstaff Phoenix.

> Russ . . . it's only been two days – I know, I know, but she's worked all that Bible stuff on me so it was in my head even when I wasn't with her, and doing things where you could see how it applied. I mean, I don't praise Jesus to strangers or anything, but you could see how it could end up there. It's hard to explain. I even got Him tattooed on my hand here. I won't twist your arm about it but I'm thinking you might want to try on a more Christian outlook yourself. Okay I'll call again. I'm not saying where we are but some of the places, they're not like they sing about.

Only a fool would parse too closely anything Skidder said, but the last comment and the announcement put odds on Vegas, which seemed a probable place for him to find himself in need of conversion. The Lord apparently hadn't saved Skidder from his own stupidity, or from whatever would happen to him and Lea if Russ missed them in Tucson and they somehow met up with Jack Marks.

He called Jean in Tucson with the news that he was a little ahead of the runaways. He skipped any mention of Skidder's salvation. Then he told her he'd call Grant.

"He'll be glad to hear from you. He doesn't know what to do. He can't start up a prayer circle, so he's feeling sort of useless, I think."

At least there's clarity, Russ thought.

He passed on to Grant an edited version of Skidder's message and assured him that there was a good chance he'd be able to cut the two of them off in Tucson in the next day or so.

"Where in Tucson?"

He was a little loud, a little drunk, Russ thought.

"It's better if you leave it up to me."

"Well then, I'm flying down."

"I don't need any more variables –"

"She's my daughter, for goodness' sake." The anger in his voice mixed with the impression he'd just recently struck upon the thought.

"I'm sorry. But I'll get this done right, I promise you."

He should have come back at Russ but he wouldn't. Whatever was happening to Grant, it had taken the measure of him and he knew it.

"Grant, tell me something. Lea says Jack was healed in church of a leg injury. What do you make of that?"

·"Well, legs are a favourite target among faith healers."

"But you're a medical man. You don't buy into this stuff, do you?"

"Slight disabilities can be healed" – he paused a moment –

150

"can *seem* to be healed when your faith, your conviction overrides the pain of moving an arthritic hand or damaged leg. Some people think faith healing works something like acupuncture or chiropracty."

"You don't see it the way Lea does." You let someone go around believing in miracles and this is what happens.

"The healing I've described only works for believers."

"But Jack Marks wasn't a true believer. He was faking the injury."

"Maybe."

"I don't get it."

"I'm humble enough to know that science can't explain everything." It occurred to Russ that Lea's brand of faith pretty clearly lacked humility. "Listen, I want to thank you for going after those two. I'd hate to think if it was just me."

His last call was to Joyce Stone. He told her he'd arrived and said he was leaving early the next morning.

"Why don't you come up to the house? Tonight if you like."

"Look, Joyce, we'll just say hello tomorrow and I'll hand you the package. There's no point in swapping memories." He gave her the name of the diner across the road from the motel. It opened at six-thirty.

"Okay, I've got it. Strangers at all costs."

"It's no cost at all."

Just before first light on a still, faultless morning, Russ watched from the motel lobby as a young woman already in uniform pulled up across the road and opened the restaurant.

Carrying the packet of letters he went over and took a table in the back, farthest from the front door. The place had windows on three sides and it was just him and the makings of early light. A curtain was half drawn on a small dinner room behind him where the tables were set, cloth napkins mainsailed on the plates. It had warmed again and the snow from the evening before was already melting.

"Coffee'll be a minute," the woman called from the kitchen.

"That's fine."

He studied the laminated menu at his table and tried to occupy himself with the task of arranging the cutlery. Then he reread the menu.

A man wearing a short-sleeved dress shirt and tie came through the door, smiling at Russ as he walked to the counter and collected a Styrofoam cup. The man clipped a bill into the napkin holder and then left without calling so much as a thank-you to the waitress. The transaction may have been a casual, struck-upon arrangement, or something worked up out of histories.

When Russ looked to the front of the restaurant a woman who he knew must be Joyce Stone was already coming through the door. She wore khaki pants and an open sweater over a long, painted t-shirt, with sunglasses perched in thick silver hair pulled back into a long fall. It was a look of the American southwest, something set back in the sixties and left in the sun. She was much younger than Russ had allowed himself to imagine.

He stood as she approached and offered his hand, a gesture she seemed unused to, and they shook and took their seats.

"It's nice to meet you, Russ."

He nodded.

"Right."

The waitress appeared and poured their coffees. They each

152

ordered toast as a boy came in and set down a few copies of the morning news on the counter and left.

"Should we say a little about ourselves?" she asked.

"Let's not. I'm not a subject worth discussing."

"That's not what Mike thought. He told me you —"

"I don't care. Sorry, you can think what you want about my not caring, but I just don't. What he told you was his business."

"All right."

She was looking at him fully now, and she seemed to recognize something and looked down at her coffee. His own cup was nothing, he wanted something more in his hands.

"Why do you think Mike wanted you to meet me?" she asked.

"I'm settling his accounts. You're one of them."

"But he could've had you just send me the letters."

"Maybe he wanted you to meet me, I couldn't say."

He wanted to tell her the moment they were in was pathetic but they didn't have to give in so fast. If only they could sit together without having to say anything.

"I think it's for both of us that we're doing this," she said.

"He had something to tell me but he wasn't much with words. Your sitting here, square in front of me, that's about the best way he could put it."

"It doesn't give you a chance to say anything in response."

"I'm not a priest or a judge. I don't have to respond, I just have to witness you."

"Maybe it's too personal a question, but is there anything you'd want to tell him, if you could?"

"If there was, I wouldn't tell it to a stranger."

She wouldn't look away.

"Maybe a stranger would be best. The right one."

I'm all the stranger I need, he thought.

"There are parts of a life that maybe should stay unspoken of anyway. If I can't improve on people's shabby wisdoms then I'll just let things be until I find my own terms for thinking about them, and it's just too bad if I can't find those terms."

"Well, I hope you find them, Russ."

He recognized that she was stronger than he was. She was here for a reason, and would not relinquish it.

He got up without excusing himself and walked to the counter, where he stood over one of the papers, looking at the headlines without really registering them and having no idea what he was doing here or how he would free himself. He was clearly handling this the wrong way, thoughtlessly, childishly, but the fact was that the actual Joyce Stone wired him straight into a bitter grief that Mike could not have imagined when he thought up this little get-together. And it wasn't the grief but the bitter he felt most, and for all his learning, the only thing he knew any more was to strike at the bitterness before it broke him. He had deceived himself ever to think otherwise.

He sat back down.

He didn't know what he would say until he said it.

"Is this sad for you?"

He'd always thought of "sad" as being a thin word, but it was the right one now. She sat square and held her chin up as if to suggest she knew what was happening and she was prepared for it.

"Yes. But I knew for a long time I wouldn't see him before he died. That's why I wrote the letters."

"I thought it might be something like that. I fetched the mail most mornings. He knew people all over that I'd never heard of, but there were enough letters from Santa Fe that I wasn't going to ask him about them."

She smiled.

"What about you, Russ. Is this sad for you?"

"I don't know. I won't know till later. But it's not . . . important to me especially. Except it's important it doesn't turn all lachrymose."

"Well, whatever that means, you let me know if we're in danger."

"Okay."

Their orders came and they ate together. They were still alone, but soon enough there'd be people around them, going to work, leaving town. Faces familiar or strange to one another, but bound by a shared knowledge of famous names and ad slogans and radio news. One of the headlines had said something about a scandal reaching higher.

"This isn't really the place for saying anything – that's why I picked it."

"Well, I've got a nice house up on Fort Union Road."

"No. Let's stay with it. I guess I can stop being an asshole long enough for you to tell me who you are."

As she laid it out, the children, the husband, the conversion that had broken the marriage a couple of years before she was widowed, Russ looked for anything in her voice or manner that could explain how his father could have built a secret relationship with this woman. And how could she have fallen for him? He'd been an old man.

"Of course he thought I'd lost my mind." She was speaking of her husband. "And of course I had."

Her husband had been a wine rep who spent a lot of time in California, and on one of the trips after he'd moved out of the house, he was side-swiped by a transport truck. There followed four weeks in hospital. A few months later he re-entered for surgery and died on the table for reasons many lawyers were currently trying to determine.

She sat back to signal the end of the story.

"You said all that like you were ordering pizza."

If anything, she took the comment too well, a little astounded, but clearly not put off.

"Well, I didn't tell it for sympathy and I guess I'm not getting any." Her eyes were dark blue and watchful.

"I'm still sitting here. That's about as far as my sympathy extends."

She seemed to wait for a signal to continue, and was satisfied that she detected one.

"What you said about not swapping memories, Russ, I think that's probably a good idea. But there is one thing I'd like to tell you about."

"Do I need to hear it?"

"I don't know, but I'd like to say it. It's nothing dramatic."

"Okay."

"It's how we met. He came through with your aunt on a Saturday, and the next morning he found our church. He'd set your aunt up somewhere. I've never met her and I don't know if she knows about me, and he was alone. I was the one who welcomed him. We talked a while and somehow I found myself opening up to him like I never had to anyone. There was just something about him that got me blabbing and I didn't even feel self-conscious afterwards. When the service ended he told me he'd be back through in a few days. I didn't realize it then but he'd already decided to change his travel plans. The routine was to fly out of Tucson, but he flew home from Santa Fe that year, and every September after that. And in April coming down he'd stay a night in Santa Fe. We saw each other twice a year."

It was her way of saying there was love at first sight. All the time and the letters, and she didn't know Mike any better than to think that. It was as if she hadn't seen that he was a man in his seventies. The mystery of human connection. He found he could not resist it.

"When you talked that first time, what did you talk about?"

"Well, he asked about the church, and how long I'd been involved, and we just talked about churches. I said I was worried the church split me in two, that it had come to be a kind of shelter from the rest of my life, and I didn't know what to do about that."

"And then he said he was coming back."

"Yes. We didn't say much more that first day."

It wasn't love, he thought, it was Christian charity, though she might say they were the same thing. Russ would choose to think they weren't the same, and he'd leave her to her belief. He now had a way of thinking about his father and Joyce Stone. It was more than he had hoped for, not that he'd hoped for anything.

She spoke about her nearing retirement from a teaching job, and about her daughter in San Diego and her son who worked in a local sporting-goods store. He prompted her innocently once or twice and then, it seemed, they were through. They were not.

"He wrote a few times and called me in the summer, so I feel as if I know how he was in the last months, but not right up to the very end. I don't need to know about the end, but Mike asked me to let you tell me about it, if you wanted. He said you wouldn't tell anyone at home, but he knew it'd be hard on you."

Jesus, thought Russ. Every last fucking blaspheming name of Christ.

"That doesn't sound like him, Joyce. You wouldn't misrepresent my own father to me, would you?"

"Maybe we just knew him in different ways."

"He was my father. In the scheme of things, you knew him for about twelve minutes."

"I know he kept things to himself, things he wished he could talk about."

"Then why didn't he?"

"There was no one to tell them to."

Russ nodded. Her certainties came from a script of sorts, he reminded himself.

"Sounds like he told them to you."

"Some, he did. He only told it all to God." Here was something Russ didn't doubt. But you didn't have to know Mike well to know he'd really unload in a prayer. "I'm just saying that you probably have things to say, and I'll be a good listener. If not now, then sometime."

"There won't be any time but this one, and there's no story to tell. I could try to make one up for you but I've never been any good at that."

He sat up higher. If he had to, he'd walk straight to his car without saying another word.

"All right."

The rest of their breakfast was devoted to the subject of Santa Fe. Russ directed the conversation. He called for the bill before she was done eating. When he'd paid the waitress and the meeting was clearly over, she tried him one last time.

"Mike wanted his dying to be an example to you, Russ. An example of the power of faith in a believer."

Well, it didn't come off that way, he wanted to tell her. He had been an example of an old man dying, doped up, in pain. With the wrong one on watch over him.

158

"You were alone with him at the end, weren't you? That boy Mike took in wasn't with you."

"Skidder's no boy. I guess he didn't need the example."

"Mike sent him away for the end. Did you know that?" He thought of getting up, but felt a sudden fatigue. "Russ, did you know that angels appeared to your father?"

Sitting still. He needed out of the moment, needed to disappear from her, but couldn't.

"He had a vision once of an angel in your kitchen, above Skidder, holding his hand over him in protection. He understood it to mean that Skidder is already looked after."

"I see."

"You don't believe it."

"Do you see angels, Joyce?"

"No." She looked down at her hands. "But since he died, I've seen him."

She was a little afraid, he thought. Of the ghost, or of having told him about it.

"Then you need counselling."

"Have you seen him?"

He finally found the strength to get up and leave. She followed, without speaking. Not until they were in the parking lot did he remember to hand over the package of letters.

"It was interesting meeting you, Joyce," he said. "Good luck with the retirement."

He was conscious of keeping a little more distance between them than she could easily cross, and she may have wanted to cross it, for she was stalled in the moment and wasn't saying anything.

He backed off towards the road and lifted his hand.

"I don't know if this was what he hoped for," she said. "It wasn't for the letters, Russ. It was so we'd meet and you could take something from me."

"I don't need it."

She looked at him as if he were a lost child.

"Goodbye, Joyce."

"Just tell me you'll call some time."

"I won't call. Goodbye."

He didn't look back but felt her watching him, even after he'd gone.

For a while the road was pure duration and he sustained a state of non-thought through Albuquerque pooled in its depression and on down where the mountains rose in a silent drama. Billboard proclamations. Old Western Mercantile. Vasectomy Reversals Exit 150. Fireworks, Moccasins, Scorpion Crafts. Community Complex Ahead. The land grew greener and unworked and the earth fell to burlap desert. He slowed for fresh oil laid otterskin past four roadside crosses with flowers and wreaths and saw white-and-green border-patrol trucks repeating themselves in the traffic. He grew hungry contemplating a sign with the lone word Bacon and so he looked for the symbols for gas and food, and took the exit too fast, lifting in a free-floating daze.

An old mongrel dog was sunning itself in the drive-thru so Russ turned off and parked next to a State Corrections truck. He ate his cheeseburger at a plastic table while watching a Greyhound Bus reload outside. A prison officer waited wordlessly on a young man in his charge folding a bandana over and over again until he had it smack and tied it on. The young man rose and went out and the officer saw him onto the bus, went on himself and re-emerged, then sat in his truck watching until the bus was in motion and away.

One by one the cars came to make orders, honked at the dog, and backed off. While the other employees scrambled to recover from the busload, a girl in a headset was catching a break. Russ wondered if it wasn't her dog. Some of the people leaving would pass by the dog and drop food for it. If it landed too far he would get up and scarf it, then move back into his place in the lane. He seemed to know that if they didn't get out of their cars, he wasn't getting any of their food.

An old man near Russ regarded the dog and said, "He's got it all figured out, doesn't he."

"He's found his lucky spot, I guess."

"Making his own luck, is what he's doing. I wouldn't want to have to be the one to move him off there."

On his way out Russ ordered a small dish of ice cream and he held it for the dog while it lapped and specked more white into its grizzled muzzle. It had no collar.

"You hold your ground, mister," Russ told it. "You don't owe the world shit."

When the ice cream was gone he scratched the dog's neck with one hand, then two. When he stood and walked off, the dog twisted its head around to look after him.

A nurse came and they discussed the bidet, and bedsores, the uses of crushed ice and cold water squeezed from a washcloth. One day a woman called long-distance from an agency. Mike had written that he could no longer sponsor the child. "Is Mr. Littlebury not well?" Russ said he was dying. "We thought maybe. I'm sorry. He'll have our prayers." People came at all hours so he put a sign on the door to turn away visitors. At night he moved the recliner into the hallway outside the bedroom and read. He sketched shapes in the margins, and he slept there.

It was all the man could do to sit up on the side of his bed, and then it was more than he could do.

The funeral director wore a blue ski jacket. He and his assistant carried out the draped gurney like they were moving a couch.

When they were gone Russ bundled the sheets and blanket into a ball. He hauled the mattress off the frame and hugged it to him to bend it through the doorways, and put it in the back of the truck with the ball of bedding and tied it all down.

When he'd unloaded he got back in the truck and sat at the dump for a while. There would be people coming by the house all day and in the days ahead. He didn't want to see them. Soon he'd go into town and tell Jean and leave a phone message for Skidder to collect from wherever he'd run to, but now he sat at the lip of the pit. Junk, busted and worn, there was a word for everything below him, and the words would not burn with the trash. Russ thought orphan. He thought patricide.

Someone had thrown away an old toy horse on wheels. It looked homemade. In the field beyond, the shore of a shallow marsh and the frozen passings of snipes and sandpipers, and behind him the truck tracks of the sirekiller.

The horse was the size of a collie, lying on its side, stiff-legged, the paint faded and chipped from its rust saddle. It was beyond him how anyone could let go of something like that.

III

The hours replayed with him and Lea driving through the night so that questions had had time to form and began nipping at him and wanted to be dealt with. There was the question where were they going and where would they stop before getting there, and would they take a room or would it be two they didn't have money for? There was the question of what Russ and Jean would think. A lot of the questions were about Lea and what she wanted from him, and some weren't really questions but mysteries about her he'd wanted to uncover since he first laid eyes on her standing above him on the stairs. While he drove she'd read her dad's road atlas and repeated the sequences of names of the towns that lay ahead. Spencer Dubois Arimo Oxford, Arimo Oxford Woodruff Plymouth, the towns unspooled in order as she called them out of the night. She'd fallen asleep with the atlas on her thighs and he'd looked over at her many times as if to confirm that a car and a girl had fallen into his lap, and maybe even a run from the law. He imagined addressing a judge but the lines weren't all there because he didn't exactly know what they were doing just yet. She said she had a friend in Texas but not the money to get them there. She'd called Skidder a godsend and he had naturally wondered just what kind of sweets an impression like that could buy him.

Your Honour, he began.

Dawn came with him hungry, tired and unsure, the day itself cored and set waiting for use. He reached his hand over and took the atlas from where it had slipped against her hip to read it while he drove. They were following Levi's route. He'd come up the same way they were going down. He entered Idaho Territory in 1863. Before that had been the so-called cannibal episode, which they were then approaching. Skidder assumed Lea wouldn't mind a little detour, so at Spanish Fork, Utah, he left the highway, heading east and then south, bending towards Indianola, and kept on along a narrow road with snow on the shoulders on past Fairview to Ricksford. It was the place Levi had come down to out of the mountains with a human leg strapped across his back, addressing the horrified onlookers, "I am a desperate character. As you will guess, there's a story behind this leg concerning the evils of which I am capable." The lines handed down from eyewitness accounts, though the witnesses missed he was joking.

Past "Ricksford pop 512" was a sign for an historic site so he glided along the main street that had stupidly not been preserved as Levi would have known it, and he found a turnoff leaving town that led to a sign painted yellow on brown and the grainy letters supposed to look wooden.

"The Legend of the Monster in Buckskins"

On this site in 1856 Levi Shute, depraved, degenerate, savage and bestial, emerged from a winter in the Wasatch Mountain Range, carrying on his back the leg of a fellow horse-thief, Elijah Burton, whom he had murdered and eaten. Shute later took up with the remnants of Brigham Young's Danites, but then became a hired killer. Convicted only once, he was among the first Americans to plead insanity, and later escaped from a Missouri asylum. Shute was finally hanged in 1864 in a vigilante uprising in Virginia City, Montana.

The marker was misinformed on the cannibal episode. It had fallen to the same hearsay and exaggeration that in Levi's time would have caused his better side to stop showing.

When he came out of Edwin's General Store and Video, Lea was awake enough to hear how Edwin himself was not interested in the sign's problems. She poked around the bag with the hardware items and ginger ale.

"What's this for?"

He left town a second time and stopped at the sign. With a brush and black paint, he worked at the twenty inches of one-by-eight, then nailed it over the top of the marker.

Levi Shute. Heroiclly Came Down Here With Remanes Of Departed Freind
(Leg All He Could Carry)

And off they went another twenty hours, clear into the next season, drawing the last of Lea's money, napping upright on turnouts where whole families lived and showered just off the interstates. He called Lanny and then Russ's machine but didn't know where to begin and hung up. It was never hard to see himself from Russ's point of view, minus the schooling. They had their troubles together, but Skidder knew Russ held his tongue and his temper around him more often than he didn't. At times Skidder thought he was maybe the only one in town who knew Russ from every side. He didn't know anyone else that way. Not even himself.

Back in the car he put the seat back and stared at Lea sleeping until he nodded off. When he opened his eyes he jolted at the sight of a little girl staring in at him. She was holding the hand of her father, a wrung-out man who'd long let go a beard that had crept up and grew out below his cheekbones. The man tapped on the window and began begging food. ·

"Go away. Jesus, what a country," said Skidder. He straightened his seat upright.

"Sorry, sir," Lea called to the man. "Open the window."

"No."

The kid looked up at him like a puppy. She even had a kind of snout that would be a drawback in future years.

The father was still standing there. He looked around and leaned in a little closer.

"I'll trade you methamphetamines."

"Sorry," said Lea.

"Bugger off."

"All right then. My girl don't need your language."

"Sorry," Skidder said.

"Maybe we should give them something."

"I'll take what you can give, young lady. We sure are in need."

So that Skidder had to forget about his nap and put the car in gear and head out on the highway again now a runner from justice and mercy both.

"Those poor people," she said.

"We don't have money ourselves. Why else am I sleeping in a ditch like that. We're getting a motel. There's no health in this."

She didn't say anything so he didn't press it the way an idiot would. The thought of them with a room together produced enough of a rush that he could make it a little ways farther on a mix of a sex possibility and his worrying about his short sorry stuttering history with women. Skipping over the whole barroom confusion in Great Falls, skipping that, he'd bought a big woman in Calgary a couple of years ago but she'd beaten him up and stole his cash. Before that he had to go clear back to high-school parties, out in his car groping girls in the lower grades who he'd told he was nearly dangerous.

It occurred to him now he'd never been with a girl in a situation he couldn't be arrested for. The Levi in his blood.

They drove another night and fell in hungry along the Vegas strip with the hotel and casino themes throwing a kind of warp into things. It was because the place came at him from all directions that he found himself describing to Lea in detail his uncle's death in a grain auger and how he found him until she asked him not to, saying he who loves the Lord will be loved by God the Father, so he wasn't really a love-starved orphan unless he wasn't worthy of love in the first place.

"You weren't listening," he said. "The man got ate by his own two-hundred-thousand-dollar machine. There's your God for you. Lookit the pirate ship, it says there's free food."

They ate. It was mid-morning when they got the room, and he left again with twenty-one U.S. in his pocket and made out for the strip. Lea wanted to sleep, she said, just stood there waiting for him to leave so she could take her clothes off and get into bed like he didn't have any reason to be tired or rewarded for his work.

"You've been a gentleman. Thank you." Hinting she knew what he was thinking. He noticed she didn't like to say his name.

"A godsend and a gentleman," he said. "And a man under it all."

"I know," she said. "I know you're a man, too. But you haven't given yourself over yet."

"What is that supposed to mean?"

"You'll know what it means when it's your time."

Past greasy lots and rip-off porn shops he puzzled her words until there was carpet for his feet and sunshine above. He heard the ball-peen xylophone music from the slot machines, saw bank upon bank of fools on stools, walking in free to cruise by tables and watch games he didn't know moving a little faster than he could pick up on. At one of the tables a man was crying and the other players asked him to leave and he wouldn't. At another, Skidder hung back watching a woman dealer do her slickwork. The players close to her were all over the cards, but from his position it was her that was the payoff. He compared her to the sequinned lovely assistant on the television hung on the wall behind her advertising some magician mentalist show in some other region of the building, and the dealer came off better. He felt like telling her except she was busy but it wasn't like she hadn't glanced his way a few minutes ago. When she snapped the cards he could practically feel it on his skin.

A man dressed like an organ grinder's monkey stepped in beside him.

"I'm sorry, sir, but you're in violation of the code."

"I wasn't doin nothin."

"It's your shirt, sir. We don't allow that style in the casino."

It was his number 34 muscle shirt.

"At least I don't walk around in a costume."

The man directed Skidder to a shop by the buffet table where there were shirts he could buy. The girl there explained that dress codes were a way of keeping the gangs out.

"They're willing to have their little brains blown all over the sidewalk but they won't wear proper shirts with collars 'cause they think they won't look like they're willing to get their little brains blown away."

On the screen above her the mentalist had turned his assistant into a sailor's knot, with her legs shot out backwards over her shoulders and her head on the floor taking in the reaction. The camera panned over the delighted audience.

He felt he might be sick. The stretch of floor between him and the outside light was so long that in crossing it his breath became shallow and fast like a part of him didn't trust the air itself. The first place he found to sit was a fountain where the water flowed from a mountain down the block and fell just behind where he was sitting and moved on into the casino where people pitched pennies and dimes in it, hoping to change their luck. A sign at the waterfall explained the water was not wasted but cycled back to the mountain to fall again, which because it couldn't run uphill on its own sort of blew the nature effect for anyone who thought about it.

There was a very old person sitting near him, he couldn't tell man or woman, and it had been inching his way for some time.

"I have the papers."

He turned to look. A woman, most likely, clearly outcast and insane. He'd seen a few like her in the cities at home. She wore a long nylon coat, the colour of grain.

"This is my land," she said. "They stole it to build the city here. Don't listen to them. I have the papers."

She reached into her coat and withdrew a page and thrust it at him. He took it just to get her hand away from his face. The paper was thick with grime and heaved by water stains. Under it all, old handwriting he couldn't follow.

He handed it back and turned to look for a casino guard but found he was on his own. His weakness persisted.

"Don't pretend you can't read it," she said.

He didn't pretend anything, he just got up and headed for the street.

"Are you the deceived or the deceiver?" she called out.

He moved faster but she wouldn't fall quiet, and he worried that people would think he'd done her some wrong, though they seemed to ignore him and her both.

When the strip bent away he took an off street down a block of little shops: collectibles, smokes, jewellery. A young guy with rings in his face sitting in the doorway of a tattoo parlour nodded at him.

"Let me fix you up with something," he said. "What d'you need?"

Skidder stopped and looked in the window. There were photos of the actual application and about a hundred options set before him. Eagles, panthers, snakes of different descriptions, cats and dogs, though no wolves he could see. Letters in blocks or a fancyflow. There were pre-set names and sayings, Harley, Goth, Dice N'Slice, Cool Rule. Shapes and symbols, most of them senseless. What did he need? More than anything he felt a need to move things along with Lea. It was time for extreme action, and according to the price list set in the corner of the window, he could just afford one.

Jack took me to a rodeo today. August 3rd. He bought me a Bailey hat and showed me how to wear the brim. We were watching the bullriders and a man behind us was making fun of one of the clowns, he was pretty loud and mean, and when Jack turned around to say something, he just turned back and took me by the arm and made us leave. It took awhile before he'd tell me what happened but he said there was too much past in his life for it not to come back at him, sometimes the same, sometimes with different faces. The people he met were never really new, just old souls returned, even his own old souls. He said it was like seeing ghosts except the old souls weren't dead but he calls them shades. I said maybe they're angels and he said there weren't any angels in the world, there was only shades and God in pieces. I said but he'd felt God in him and he said it was just a piece.

Russ stood by the car at the gas pumps, waiting for the tank to fill. He was less than an hour from Tucson. He took the photo of Marks from the diary and looked again, but the light was too weak, so he held it over the roof of the car. Soon enough he was satisfied that the human figure on Marks's back was attributable simply to a scratch on the negative. It had only seemed otherwise because the echoing human shapes opened the possibility of an intentional pattern, which as an explanation was less plausible even than that chance had inscribed the walking figure on the man walking. The images – of the man, of the flaw in the negative, of his father – connected only in his mind. If you believed Paul Valéry, a mind like da Vinci's could see the

171

correspondences between all things, scientific and humanistic, but Russ saw only himself, or rather evidence of himself, the traces of his thoughts. And they were meaningless.

He looked again at the implicate object that seemed to connect to all things in his small universe. It was doubtful, certainly nothing to navigate by. But there was something else to it.

The shadows, for instance. The picture was taken in daytime, but the shadow Marks cast fell at a more acute angle than those of the trees. Russ didn't know enough about light to account for the effect. He was tempted towards the fanciful idea that the sun had moved in the blink of an aperture so that two times were present at once. He was surprised that the idea appealed to him, but then so did the possibility of a logical explanation. He found he wanted both versions, and to choose between them differently, the one he could believe and the one he could safely make-believe, depending on his need.

Now something had changed in Marks's face. Had he really examined it before now, or had the scar, the flaw, distracted him? The man's eyes looking straight at Russ seemed the most immediate part of the picture, as if of a third, later time, not represented by the shadows. These were the eyes of the man in Lea's diary – the seer of "shades," whatever he meant by the word. If you let it, the esoteric's gaze seemed to promise the whole arcana, right back to the ancient prophets, the great crazies through time, and the neighbourhood percipients of angels and ghosts.

He paid for the gas and got back in the car, drove to the shoulder of the exit ramp, and came to a stop, sure that he'd forgotten something. Trouble takes up in the margins, he thought. He was a little afraid of the margins. That was why he didn't attend to them. And now they were closing in.

To calm himself he tried to recall the name of the place where reason met the imagination. In early Greece the known world met the unknown, unmapped seas at the twin rocks standing at the Straits of Gibraltar that were then called the Pillars of Heracles. The rocks marked the border between the inner world of the Mediterranean and the outer world of the Atlantic, or Hesperios, the boundless Western Ocean. It lay *exo ton stelon*, meaning "beyond the Pillars," and to venture beyond this gate, sailors believed, was to meet death. On his last voyage, Dante's Ulysses went west through the Pillars in a vain quest for knowledge, and instead found his place in hell, perpetually telling his story from within a flame.

More tongues of fire. They seemed to be all around him.

How long had he been sitting there? With a force he'd never experienced before, consciousness hammered.

They sat in the car across the street from the 528 address and Lea would not study the map. He'd committed to the plan a thousand miles ago and he'd stayed with it and followed it here, and now she wouldn't play along. In one way she'd saved him but that wasn't the way he needed now. The way he needed was somewhere in Rand McNally.

"I'm just saying there must be a highway around. I can't drive and read both at once."

"You'll have to plan your own getaway."

He looked at her, then turned and looked at the house. It was hard to imagine Lanny's wife or anyone from Colliston ending up down here with these sunny skies and security systems.

"They'll be at work anyhow. I just get in, get out. Take off."

"It's a crime."

"They're not even full remains. It's just ashes."

She wouldn't look at him. Like she'd never broken a rule.

"I've done worse. I almost stole a body once."

"You what?"

She was looking now.

"Never mind."

"You stole a body?"

She was the kind who wouldn't understand about the body. He wasn't sure he did. He got out of the car.

There was a little boulevard of trees and cactus. The porch was caged in white wrought iron but the gate was open.

He went around the side and back. The doors and windows were all barred, all except the front, and it was hard to see much. It was always hard to do a thing the first time if you hadn't had an example to watch and learn from, but sometimes a man just had to hike up his balls and go to it.

Dear God, You understand all this is not just about the money. Please look out for me. I never hurt anyone physical which cannot be said for them. I just want in and out. And to give Mr. Bickles a proper Christian . . . whatever, Amen.

He pointed to the sky and looked up, then stepped forward.

When he performed the little affirmation she had taught him, Lea wanted to scream and almost got out of the car, but a part of her wanted to watch, wanted to believe she couldn't change his course any more than she could that of a character in a movie. The Lord was guiding this and she must trust in Him. He had put the two of them together. The Lord had chosen for her deliverance and protection this manboy, and though maybe it was hard to see him getting a lot of respect, in scripture it said you who make yourself like a child will be greatest in the kingdom of Heaven.

He was framed in the open side-window. He went up and stood in front of the door a second, then tried it.

What happened next happened all at once – the arm reaching in through the car window and taking the keys from the ignition as the dog flew from the house and lunged at Skidder, who scrambled aside as the dog fell clear off the porch and started back up. Skidder ran for the end of the porch and trapped himself and the man with the keys walked up to the house and she saw who it was as Skidder climbed the bars and started kicking at the dog.

A woman came out and called the dog's name. She took hold of it by the collar and pulled it into the house.

"Jesus, Russ," said Skidder. "Like hell he's dead."

"How's Jackie?"

"I don't know. Her teeth are holding up. The rest is kind of a mystery."

"What're you doing tomorrow night?"

"I'm guessing you're gonna tell me."

"I wouldn't ask if it wasn't Skidder."

"Russ, just say what the gig entails?"

"Well, we're at Jean's place in Tucson now, and I've got him and I'd like to ship him home if I could."

"Right."

"I'll see him onto the plane if you'll see him off it."

"Fine. The highway's clear."

"He's coming in on Air Canada, from Calgary. The other thing, Lyle. Beforehand, could you drop by his place and doctor his truck for me?"

"How bad do you want it?"

175

"Two or three weeks bad."

"Some parts are slow to ship in."

"Yeah."

"Did anybody get hurt down there?"

"Not like they should've. Not like they will."

Skidder woke him in the near dark.

"Jean says it's ready."

When Russ looked up at him Skidder walked to the end of the trailer porch and stared out through the screen. Russ tried to picture an angel floating over him. What would Mike imagine such a creature would look like?

The units angled to the lane in their neat yards, the day waning, corrugated. Nothing moved out there in these arrangements.

"So here we are after all, eh, Russ? I mean, it all worked, I guess."

He'd dreamed of the photo of Marks blowing down the interstate. When he'd collected the diary from the dash, the picture was missing, and though he couldn't remember doing so – he would even say it was unlike him to do so – he must have left it on the roof of the car after examining it. And yet it had been the focus of all his attention. What had distracted him before he got back inside? He had no idea.

"Be like that then."

Outside, the particularized spaces offered this small thing or that for the mind to light upon. In the carport across the lane from Jean's trailer two cow skulls hung by the horns on the supports.

When Jean came onto the porch, Skidder took the opening

to leave. She sat next to Russ. She said she and Lea were fixing a nice dinner and asked if he was hungry.

"Among other things," he said.

"You know, you've done something good for those two, and I think they know that. But they're afraid to say anything. It might be easier on everyone if you could see your way to actually speak to them."

"I will." There'd been a woman in the dream but she was gone now. "Jean, I don't want you to worry about these trips south. I'll get you down here no problem from now on."

"Let's not talk about this now, Russell."

"I like it down here. I mean, maybe the country doesn't work so well, but I like Americans and their weather."

"I wish you weren't always so worked up. What you need is a good dinner. Jim Pryor's coming over. Let's set the table."

Jim Pryor was an old widower Russ had met last year. He spent the early mornings walking his little white terrier around the trailer park and the rest of the day making visits. As Russ recalled from last year's dinner conversation, Jim was slightly untrusting of his younger neighbours but seemed to delight in their children. Jean had described him as having "strong views," which Russ had taken as a warning that her husband's old golf partner was a narrow-minded fool, not to be provoked. In fact, he was simply a man who would not be moved off opinions that were somehow both received and hard won. A proud Republican who valued his property irrationally, he was the first person Russ had ever met who kept a gun for anything but hunting, or at least the first who'd brought it up in conversation.

Yet there was something about the man, something more than the shotgun in the bedroom, that Russ couldn't put together because it seemed to reside wholly in his way of speaking. He examined his statements, tested them against worthwhile possibilities with a kind of folksy thoughtfulness that could be seen to fit with the wariness in his tone or the way his eyes seemed to take in more than was there. Like most things Russ didn't understand down here he just attributed it to the American warp. The warp involved believing yourself to be in a state of perpetual threat, and of course, because the belief had caught on as the guiding constant, the threat was in place. Russ realized there were few regions of the world where something like the American warp didn't hold, but he was from one of them, which made him an outsider, and perhaps a small threat of another kind.

A mild dish of beans and rice was not enough to slake even a quieter day's hunger or to take the courage from the wine. Jim was clearly enjoying the company, though he had sized Skidder up the moment they were introduced. Little Rosco had barked at him until Lea interceded.

"We got the makings of an outing here," said Jim. "We could go off tomorrow to Little Tucson or the Desert Museum."

Russ explained he was spending the day at the airport. Skidder was flying out and Grant was arriving.

"Well, the next day, then. You ever see a javelina or mountain lion, Lea?"

"No, sir."

"They got rattlesnakes, hawks."

"Are they stuffed or is it a zoo?" Skidder had been drinking.

"It's a live museum."

"But the animals are all locked up."

Jim glanced at the tattooed hand with transparent disapproval. "Yes."

"So it's a zoo. I don't support a zoo."

"They take hurt animals and fix them up out there," said Jim.

"If they don't let them go it's a zoo."

Jean stepped in to ask who wanted seconds. Skidder took them.

"You ever get rattlesnakes in the city, Jim?" Russ asked.

"Oh sure. One time a friend of mine found a Mojave curled up with the garden hose. He just said hello and called the police. They killed it for free."

"A mountain lion's got, like, a two-hundred-mile range. It shouldn't be locked up in a box."

"Forget it, Skidder," said Russ. "You're not gonna to be here to go anyway."

"Even if I was I wouldn't. They wouldn't get my money."

"What money would that be?" Russ returned to Jim. "They're deadly, the Mojave?"

"Yeah, without the horse serum."

"That must be what Bickles got," said Skidder.

"Who's that?" asked Jim.

"Yeah, who is it?" asked Russ.

"Oh, I'm just thinking out loud."

"That's not like you, the thinking part."

"Did you phone your dad yet, Lea?" asked Jean.

"After dinner." She'd been quiet since he'd collected the two of them, no doubt stumped by God's failure to point her a way out. Once he'd had them both in Jean's car, he tried to tell her that he'd talk to her dad for her if she wanted, but she hadn't responded. For his part, Skidder had protested being sent home until Russ reminded him that Lea's dad was coming the next day. Then he just wanted to know if he'd be leaving before Grant showed.

"Don't call him until you and I have had a little chat, okay?" said Russ.

She nodded. She was wearing bluejeans and a zip-up sweater. Apparently she hadn't thought to bring warm-weather clothes. Russ supposed that on the trip down with Skidder she'd had many chances to admit to herself that she hadn't quite thought things through.

"What did he say when you spoke to him?" she asked.

"Well, he asked how you were. And he wanted to know if you'd gotten into any trouble, by which he meant crime. I said you brushed hard against it but got lucky."

Skidder looked up as if he'd remembered something.

"It's no luck," he said. "In the Lord there is no crime, Russ."

"What?"

"He means 'sin,'" said Lea. "'In the Lord there is no sin.'"

"Right," said Skidder. "You know what I meant."

"I've never known you to mean anything."

"What's that supposed to mean?"

"All right. That's enough," said Jean. "David, you come help me with the coffee."

When they'd left the table Russ apologized for Skidder.

Jim caught Russ's eye and nodded at Lea. She was sitting still, silently crying. There were rooms she could have gone to, but she chose to stay, and in a few seconds she had recovered herself. She was at least a little strong, Russ thought, and was going to have to continue to be.

"I tell you one thing," said Jim. "The man is right. I guess it is a zoo, isn't it, Lea?"

"I guess so."

"Maybe the animals would be better off without the cages. It should just be a park."

180

"It wouldn't be as educational," said Russ.

"Maybe you save the animals one at a time."

"Or two by two if it's raining," said Lea. She smiled.

Skidder and Jean brought the coffee. The mugs had been fashioned to look like tree stumps with squirrels and birds on them. They reminded Russ of the rhyta from fifth-century Athens, the drinking vessels with animal shapes used in ritual as gifts to the gods and the dead. He chose not to voice the connection.

Jean looked expectantly at Skidder.

"Jim," he said, "I'm sorry I shot down your zoo idea. It's a good idea. I'm just in a mood, I guess. I don't know why."

"We all have moods like that," said Jim. "I always thought that if I could just find the right words to describe those moods I'd be all set."

"There's moods there's no words for," said Skidder. "I've had 'em all."

"Well, suppose someone else felt the same thing, except they were better with words so they could describe the feeling. You know anyone like that?"

Skidder wasn't saying.

"What about you, Lea?"

"I don't know. I guess so."

"All right, so let's say this one just knows he's got eyes for a girl, that one's angry, or this girl knows she's afraid. But there's someone else who can describe what being angry or afraid feels like."

Russ recognized what Jim had entered into. Though it would be lost on Skidder, the exemplum seemed to come out of nothing Russ knew about old men in trailer courts and put him in touch with his vast ignorance.

"Okay," said Russ.

"Okay," said Jim. "Now, the one who can describe it, he can talk to himself, can't he? Maybe he can figure out what's behind the mood and take care of it, or maybe he can't, but at least he can strap the words around it and hold it in place, so he knows where it is and what it is, so it doesn't surprise him the next time he has the feeling. Now that guy is better off than the others, right?"

"But what if the way he describes it to himself only seems right?" asked Russ. "What if he's deceiving himself?"

"Good question. I wonder if he's better off anyway, even if he's wrong."

"But we're talking about how people live their lives," said Jean. "You don't want to make decisions based on the wrong understanding of something important."

"What if he never finds out he's wrong?" asked Lea. "He'd be happier in the end."

"Except some part of him would wonder," said Jim.

"He'd have to be willing to refine the terms if they weren't precise enough," Russ said.

"How did we get here from the zoo?" asked Skidder.

"Just wait," said Jim. "There are people like that. They can find the words for things, but they don't have all the answers and they're willing to change their minds. Now a person like that should tell others what he knows. It might help those other people to have this man's words."

The dialogue hadn't exactly reached Socratic levels but Russ was sure Skidder had never before witnessed the better uses of supposition. An old man who he thought didn't like him had tried to help him work something out. It was more than Russ had done.

After the coffee Russ saw Jim out and walked him back to his trailer.

"Thanks for being so good with those two. I take it you didn't pick all that up from some motivational tape."

"Now that's a sorry industry. I worked alot of jobs, I worked for Burlington Northern, I was a baseball scout, sold lapidary equipment, and I never met anyone whose problems could be cured with a pep talk."

"I can see why Jean values your company. It's easier for me to leave her here knowing she has friends around."

"She has friends everywhere. So did your father. I was sorry to hear about him. I can't say I'm as good a Christian as her and him, but we had some real times, the three of us." They waited for Rosco as he pissed on a prickly pear. "I hate to think this is the last year she'll come down."

"I'll get her down here." Jim looked up at him suddenly, then down again, waiting for the moment to pass. "What did she tell you?"

"She just doesn't have the money, Russ. People our age can't afford to be healthy in this country."

"Well, Christ. Why didn't she tell me?"

"Don't say I said anything. I don't want to catch hell."

"She's harmless."

"You'd be surprised."

They walked on and Russ said he doubted Lea and her father would stay long enough to be part of an outing. "I don't know if I will either."

"That's all right. Jean and me, we'll go for a drive. But you should see that museum sometime. If you get there early enough they let loose the birds and you can watch them hunt."

"Maybe when I'm down in the spring."

"They plant these little telemetry systems on guitar picks in their tail feathers for when the hawks see a rabbit over in Mexico and fly off."

They arrived at the two steps to Jim's porch. He pointed to a plastic owl perched on the edge of his roof.

"That one I can keep track of without much science," he said. Then he gave a short nod and said he'd see Russ in the spring.

Russ walked on through the trailer court at night, past lattice fences and rose bushes, dead sodded grass, pewter wind chimes, a big coach bus converted into someone's home with a ceramic tile set against the wheel with the likeness of the Virgin of Guadeloupe, on by the main office with its mailboxes and fenced-in pool and plastic chairs. Overhead the endless tide of aircraft. There'd been fighter jets all day in twos and fours aloft in their one truth. He thought of the hawks recaptured, the need for intelligence to assert itself meeting the need to recover a wildness.

The prefab names said Homette, Festival, Nashua. His father would walk here alone at night. He'd made the trips every year since Jean's husband died, and Russ himself had planned to make it with her until she died or sold the trailer. As he'd imagined it, before flying out in the fall he would do as Mike had done and rent a car to drive part of the way home. He would come up through the canyonlands, that implausible landscape that dwarfed all histories but its own. He'd find his own places to stop, some he'd return to year to year. He would detour. His route would be covered inefficiently. Now and then he'd simply pull over at a promising spot and take a long walk on the land, ignoring the postings, and maybe get a little lost.

And now she might sell the trailer and he'd have to get lost somewhere else.

Thinking about getting lost, the randomness of life as it was rather than as we liked to imagine it, shaped to a purpose like a tool, he then observed that most things thought to be fixed, the things that orient us, contained within them a hidden variability – geosynchronous orbits, true north, the mathematics of music or verse. The great Homeric epics used a mix of dialects that allowed them to be fitted to an oral poet's needs. To maintain the rigid metrical requirements of a line, the poet could make the sea "wine-dark" or "grey" or a "deep-eddying ocean." The words were chosen from a short set of possibilities, and in this way the poem, pitching one way as the line began, could regain its musical balance as it was told. Sound determined image. Though the main events of the story remained more or less unchanged, and because of the metrics they were more easily recalled, each telling varied, just as in walking a path we have walked before, we pass the same landmarks in the same order, see the same vistas at the same intervals, but don't repeat exactly the same series of footfalls.

Russ couldn't locate exactly when it was that necessity had taken hold in his imagination and begun to erode his reason. The Errant Cause, Plato had called it. A rational mind could bring most of the universe to hand through some language, some algebra, but then there were the mysteries of consciousness itself. Tara would say that you cannot arrive at your gods through reason. If they reside anywhere, it is at the end of thought. And if the gods are there, he wanted to tell her, they may not be the ones we've hoped for.

Each arrival was a small letting-go and brought with it the hope of revelation. He must have been expecting to resolve not just the little adventure with Skidder and Lea, but his very mind. He would arrive in Tucson and set Jean up, and from a distance fit together all that had happened, and then he would plan what to do with the rest of his life. But instead he was experiencing a rare evening instance of the night fear that had kept him awake so often.

Rational understanding was harder to sustain than it was to lose and win back again. He felt he was losing it now, here along the laneway, with that species of yard light upon the orange trees surely not the same as that earlier against the soft mountains to the north of the city. He was losing it to the gods he didn't know.

Jean was reading her Bible by lamplight on the porch. As he passed by, Russ bent down and kissed the top of her head. He hadn't kissed her since he was a boy, he thought, and wondered when was the last time she'd been kissed.

"Thank you," she said. She would want to ask if he was all right but she let it go.

Inside, Skidder and Lea were on the loveseat in the television light, watching U.S. marshals climb into a sewer in pursuit. Lea looked up at Russ a little scared. Skidder saw only the screen.

"I always wanted a job where you clamped a flashlight in your mouth," Skidder said.

She got up and she and Russ went together to the back bedroom and closed the door.

"Is there anything you want to tell me about Jack?"

One shadow moved into another across the window.

"Skidder says you're smart. But a little crazy, too."

"He's right."

"He says you're the real criminal."

"Well, I just came through a crazy time. I guess you know what that's like."

"I'm not through it yet," she said. Her tone disclosed no resignation.

"You mean there's something else, something we haven't put an end to today."

She nodded so slightly he could almost have been imagining it.

"You know what it is, don't you?" she asked.

"I think I can guess. Have you been to a doctor?"

"No."

"But you're in the condition."

"I don't know, I just know."

"But Lea, there are some pretty good indicators."

"I don't need those."

"Well, actually, you do. For one, you can't get pregnant by yourself."

"Mary did."

It was a prepared answer. For weeks she'd been looking for someone to hear it. He pretended to misunderstand.

"If you mean Mary, Queen of Scots, she had what's called an hysterical pregnancy —"

"I don't mean her."

Something on the television brought Skidder to laughter and a lone clap. Russ pictured a gun death. A man slapping an ambulance on the rear door to send it away.

"Look, what did you hope to get out of finding Jack?"

"I just think he should know."

"And you're hoping he'll come back to you."

"He'll do whatever's meant."

The little fist in her lap.

"When were you planning to tell your dad?"

"Pretty soon."

"I'll tell him if you want."

"No."

What she had made passed into him, an inevitability. It was almost enough to make him believe there was something other than chance buffeting them around.

"Then I'll have to ask you to keep it to yourself until at least Idaho. He might want to go after Jack. He'll complicate things."

"He's never any help, really."

"He wants to be. He just doesn't know how." He handed her the diary. "I read this, your dad didn't." She took it and looked away. "I lost the picture. I'm sorry, I don't know what happened to it."

"What picture?"

"The picture of Jack."

"In the diary?"

"The picture of Jack with his shirt off."

"There wasn't any picture in here."

She was embarrassed enough to deny it. That's who she is at this age, he thought. She could admit she was pregnant but not that she'd locked away a picture of her lover.

"All right," he said.

"You really are crazy, aren't you?"

That night he saw a highway blackened against the verges of snow in a flat winter light, passing nameless spaces marked only by the road correcting itself in meter, bend on bend, along the plain. A hand reached for the radio and he slapped it away and it came back holding a felling wedge and they were still, both thinking, This one will get around. They moved like practised thieves past the broken lock and he turned once to look back at the pale beyond. Alone now down the hallway to the room, the door admitting a light on the instruments and the body of his father laid in the open casket he had chosen for him. He said, I've come for you. *Well, I'm not here.* So who am I talking to? *You've found what matters to you, there is something holy after all.*

He awoke, staring up at the furrowed light from the louvred shade dimly hesitant on the trailer's ceiling, seeing parade grounds, canalscapes, microchips and barrel staves and the heart's cage. The tines of a pitchfork his father would straighten by hand into perfect lines so justified to the purpose. It stood in the earth one summer day behind the barn when he was naked with a girl he pressed his fingers to her mouth when she cried out and the horses' legs shifting through the slats.

The undertaker had worn the same blue jacket he always wore. He dealt out the service cards like clubs and spades, and asked Russ to choose one. He read them over. There were better lines in Virgil or Prudentius, but Mike would've wanted it done straight, so he chose an option from Mark. He gave Birkmier the pallbearers' names and then watched him work the calculator. Beneath the antiseptic smell was a sweetness he knew from rats thawing in the empty grain bins on the first warm days of spring.

When Birkmier went back over the list, Russ uttered pronunciations while watching the first fly he'd seen since August enter the room and buzz near a wall calendar featuring a scene of draught horses standing in snow. The fly landed on a Wednesday past and stilled itself into a cryptic reminder.

Birkmier led him back behind the office to a hallway with two rooms. One was closed. In the other were nine burial caskets he was to choose from. There were steel, oak, and cherrywood. Russ pretended to himself that there was some way of comparing them but he couldn't imagine a criterion. He simply pointed to one and walked back out to the office. When Birkmier reappeared he started into his calculator again.

"There's one thing." said Russ. "I want him in the church overnight."

Birkmier hesitated, then finished his column and looked up. "Sorry?"

Russ repeated himself. The fly was now on a horse's back and Russ felt the need of a tail switch.

"That's against code. We can't do that."

"I'll arrange it. You just bring him down the night before. I won't have him spend his last night on earth in this little shithole."

Birkmier nodded and looked down at his desktop for a piece of paper. He wrote something out and passed it to Russ.

"Here's the total." Russ looked at the numbers. The columns were cleanly formed and incomprehensible. "I'm sorry, but we can't fulfil every wish. We can't give up possession of the deceased like that. We'll do it the way it's done. I'm sure everything will be fine."

Birkmier stood as if to signal that the business was concluded. Russ sat looking up at him.

"The burial ceremony, the whole sending-off? It's not really about you and your codes."

"I understand. But we follow the local practice."

Russ got up and stepped around. He took him by the jacket and raised him off the floor to put him up beside the calendar. The fly had lifted off to land elsewhere.

"I can't speak for your family," said Russ. "But when my father dies, it's not fucking local."

190

He walked on out to Skidder waiting in the truck, turned off the radio. Leaving town they passed ice strung on power lines pole to pole.

"He's one of the faithful dead."

"What?"

"Tomorrow night we're breaking him out of there."

"And do what?"

"We're taking him to the church."

"I don't know. It's kinda cold to just put him in the back of the truck. What church?"

"His church."

"Well, I don't know, Russ."

"You don't have to help if you don't want. You haven't so far."

"He's not my dad. What happened back there?"

"Most people don't get to go out very well. If anyone deserved a great exit it was him, but he didn't die a way anyone would want. And there was fuck-all I could do about that."

Skidder nodded at the floor.

"But tomorrow's another last night, and tomorrow I get a say."

At some point on the highway Skidder had a thought.

"What if the church is locked up?"

"It's a church."

"But after the break-ins. I hear they lock it up for the night."

"What break-ins?"

"They kept quiet about it."

"Then how do you know about them?"

Skidder stared ahead noncommittally.

Russ shook his head.

"We'll break in then."

"There's this alarm."

"Christ!"

191

"Hold on now. There's gotta be a way around it, Russ."

Skidder reached for the radio and Russ chopped him hard in the elbow. It was nearly a mile before they spoke again.

"Does Reverend Keeling know you were the one?"

"The way he looked at me the other morning, I'm thinking he sort of accuses me on no evidence."

"Well, what did you steal? We'll give it back and you'll apologize."

"Not much. Candlesticks, the big ones. They look gold but they're not."

He'd had it all before him but it was faltering now.

"He's known it was you all along, and he probably didn't report it because Mike was sick. Did it occur to you you were taking advantage of his dying?"

"I don't . . . No, I guess not."

"You don't even have them, do you?"

"Like I said, no evidence." He sighed dramatically. "Only gold in colour."

An RCMP car was waiting when they pulled up. Russ invited Corporal Rob Gahan into the house. He'd been up before, just after Russ had hit the referee, and Russ had had to ask Jean to stay an extra hour while he went down to the station. That night Gahan had told him the referee wasn't pressing charges but the police still might if the story left town. He said he understood Russ was under stress and the league officials were going to suspend him anyway, and the man he'd hit wasn't badly hurt. He'd asked for Russ's version of what happened, and Russ told him that the referee had joined in with a player from the other team who'd been baiting Russ's defence partner about an incident after a game in their town a few weeks earlier. Russ had taken care of the mouthy player at the end of the first period but then the ref had begun to mumble slurs. "He called him a faggot. I don't know whether he is or isn't and I've known him all my life, and I don't care. But all the homophobes and racists should be rounded up some spring and set on an ice floe. And between you and me, Rob, if I see him again, I'll hit him harder." As it turned out, the story of Russ's short right cross made it around the province but because the assault had taken place on the ice the league was allowed to administer the justice of a lifetime banishment. The story behind the story stayed where it was.

Now the corporal stood again in the doorway.

"I got a call tonight from the Falling Creek detachment, Russ. I guess you know what it's about."

"What's he saying?"

"He says you threatened him and pushed him into a wall."

"I was making a point. Are there charges?'

"Not till the funeral's over. Can you two smooth this over?"

"Mr. Birkmier and I don't really have the good times to call upon."

"You give me something to use and I'll drive up there right now."

"Tell him to take me to court. All his codes will make the paper and even if he has legal grounds for being an insensitive prick he'll lose alot of business. We'll haul our dead off in the other direction, tell him. Ask could he set himself a little more exactly on my wrong side."

"That sounds like a threat. If I do this, Russ, you have to promise me there won't be more trouble."

Skidder had locked himself in the bathroom to listen.

"I can't seem to get arrested in this town."

"Your father built up alot of favours he never called in. But you can't just push people around because you're bigger than they are. There's no good in that."

It was near midnight when the corporal called Russ to say the matter was squared away. He told him to stay out of Falling Creek for a few days and not to call Birkmier or even talk to him at the funeral.

"He says he's willing to forget what happened."

"He never knew it to begin with."

The haze had not lifted by late morning when they left for the airport. Skidder rode in front staring at the back of his hand. When he wriggled his fingers the crucifix rolled like a thing falling away under water. She felt sorry for him not knowing what had happened that he should be here. His whole world was a distraction. He would lose his faith without her.

All this time she had been anticipating one thing and now it was gone and her dad was all she had to look forward to. Her dad and the miles north without the headphones that sometimes helped her along. Before now they'd been as far as Kansas and Canada. After her mom left he'd taken her with him to evangelical revivals in the woods with people speaking in tongues as bats flew through the tent. Organ music and wailing and miracles. The favourite miracle had to do with God making one leg the same length as the other for people who weren't born that way, and most weren't apparently, one leg usually off by a quarter-inch or so. She saw skeptics turned over when the soles of their boots or Hush Puppies evened up right in front of them. It was her first taste of absolute truth and she understood why men might need to preach.

There was a feeling in those tents that wasn't like any other feeling in life and it really was stronger if you lifted your hands in the air to get better reception of the divine signal. She felt like she could float up even before she heard anyone describe the feeling that way. Part of it was fear that she'd be given what her father hadn't had. It was fear she'd receive the gift of tongues. When she felt a voice rising she'd drop her head and stare hard at the ground and think of basketball drills or Saturday-morning cartoon classics — Yosemite Sam could keep the voice down, she didn't want any lost languages in her thank you please — and there was the same floating feeling when she was with Jack.

It bothered her a little when ecstasy was public. It bothered her that people couldn't stop talking about it afterwards. The people who felt no presence would form opinions in its place. When Jack was saved he didn't make a big deal, he just went and sat down like a man.

Russ held opinions about her and had told Jean, and this morning Jean had asked but she'd said what was inside her was her business. Hers and Jack's and God's.

All this that had happened and it ends up here. She didn't know why but the reason would reveal itself in time.

In line Russ asked did he need money.

"Yeah."

"Give me your wallet."

Russ pulled a wad of Canadian twenties from his pocket and began snapping them off one by one, so Skidder handed over the wallet.

"Here's two hundred."

They were up now. Russ put the money in the wallet. He took Skidder's birth certificate and social insurance card from the wallet and handed it to him, then opened the suitcase and tucked the wallet inside. He closed it up and put in on the scale.

"Check it through," he said to the girl. Then he turned to Skidder. "You'll see the cash in Saskatoon. You make sure you make your connections."

"But I need that money, I gotta eat."

From his other pocket Russ pulled a U.S. twenty and slicked it out for him in two fingers while collecting the ticket from the girl. Skidder took the bill. Russ held on to his boarding pass and wouldn't hand it over.

"You'll get it at security."

"Jesus, it's like I'm going to jail or something."

Opposite the security gate Skidder watched old people and business types in loafers. A woman seated nearby was explaining her life to a stranger who kept patting his pockets. She had been a doctor in Mexico but had moved up here to be a research scientist, giving experimental cancer drugs to people who couldn't afford the proven treatments. Her company was private and expanding. When she said it twice it sounded a little dirty and the stranger looked off at the loafers.

Lea was sitting next to him to say goodbye.

"Thank you for trying," she said. "God was working through you."

"Okay."

"Don't forget Him and He won't forget you."

"Yeah."

Then she kissed him on the cheek and it came to him for the first time what it meant that he was leaving.

"Maybe I'll see you again," she said.

He leaned in and whispered in her ear.

"You might work on Russ for me. He's kind of wrote in a day of reckoning."

"All right," she whispered back.

Then they all sat there. Skidder remembered that Lea had said the Lord was working through Russ and that's why he was there to call off Mr. Bickles. He wondered how the Lord was working through him now. Before long he got up and they walked him to the gate. Russ handed him the boarding pass.

"We had some times, huh?" Skidder asked.

Russ was staring him down.

"Goodbye, Skidder," said Lea. "I'll be praying for you."

She walked back to the seats. He found he couldn't just leave.

"I'm sorry, Russ. I never had no adventure before."

Russ looked back at Lea, then turned and tilted the plate of his forehead so that Skidder felt it square upon him. Sometimes he thought it would be better if Russ just did what he wanted and hit him instead of looking down in judgement all the time. What more did he want? Russ got one more day with her, though what kind of story was it when nobody ended up with the girl.

"I thought you two would just sort of do your drive. I didn't think Jean would miss her trip."

"Did Lea ever tell you anything about this friend in Texas she wanted to see?"

He could be of help, then.

"She said he could tell things, predict them. She's hooked up with some con man if you ask me."

"What else?"

"I don't know. You know those paper placemats?"

"Just tell me."

"Well, after she finally said where we were headed we stopped for pie and I turned one over, a paper placemat, and I drew the Texas part of Levi's story."

The Texas picture had two pistols facing one another through the ring in the nose of a longhorn steer. In 1852, Levi married a young girl and for reasons that have not survived in history they made a suicide pact, but backed out when the girl found she was pregnant. Levi left her a few days later and never saw his only known child. Russ had told Skidder once he considered Levi's drawing up the pact the most human detail about him.

"So I told her what it meant and I drew some more things about Levi and said what they meant and she said they reminded her of her friend in Texas."

"Reminded her how? The story or the pictures?"

"I don't know. That's all she said."

Russ nodded. It was time to go. Skidder stepped back. He raised his hand goodbye and then Russ raised his and that was all Skidder needed to turn and set off through the gate.

Now it was just the two of them with their muffins and time to kill before Grant arrived. Every so often she'd look at him directly and then look away. Russ wondered if she hadn't come to realize that she needed someone for guidance and authority from among the world of the living. If she really was ten weeks' pregnant, and she had no one but her father, then Russ himself would seem to her a true guardian.

"You and your dad don't get along."

"We just don't talk very much." Even in this statement he heard a new Lea. He wondered if the girl he'd known a few days ago, so full of confidence in the ways of the Lord, had admitted some ambiguity into her faith. She was not quite such a child. There was something sadder in her now. "He's sort of lost."

"Lost?"

"He used to be an alcoholic. Back before I was born."

"Who told you that?"

"Aunt Jean did. When I asked her. Last year. She said your dad got him into a program and never forgot about him. He'd call all the time and he'd see us twice a year. But since Uncle Mike got sick he's been harder to talk to."

"Did he start drinking again?"

"One night he did. He wanted to drive up and see your dad but he didn't get away in the summer and then there was a storm and later he talked to you or Aunt Jean on the phone and he realized it was too late to visit. I'd never seen him drink before, I didn't even think we had liquor in the house."

"That's all?"

"Yeah. Maybe alcoholic isn't the word. Maybe it isn't what he is."

"Have you talked about this with anyone?"

She shook her head.

"Just Jack."

When they stood at the carousel waiting for the passengers and their bags, what he felt, Russ realized, was Lea's disillusionment. He felt he understood her – this girl he barely knew – better than anyone he could think of.

"Don't tell my dad what I told you. About his drinking," Lea said.

"Right."

"What will you do when we're gone?"

"Lea, would Jack matter to you if you weren't pregnant?"

She turned her face towards him without meeting his eyes. If only she'd made it through a few more years before Marks or someone like him had found her.

"I never met anyone else who sees things like I do," she said. The carousel began to turn. "It's like all the little details in a day are talking at themselves and he can hear them but he thinks other people are better off not knowing what they're saying."

"What do you think they're saying?"

"I don't know. When I see things it's for guidance. You can't explain how you get from what you see to what you think, but you wouldn't have thought it unless you'd seen what you saw."

"Okay."

"It's why you can't always explain why you do what you do," she said.

"People have been doing crazy things since the beginning, Lea. And there are ways of thinking about why."

"But you can't explain everything. Like when Jack predicts things. Sometimes he says things that mean more than he knows."

"So he's an accidental prophet. Were there any of those in scripture?"

"He predicted you."

"I can't even do that."

"He said he'd leave and someone would follow him."

"So he predicted you'd get a new boyfriend."

"I thought it was me, that I was the one who'd follow. But now I see it's not me. It's you."

The passengers began to appear. Lea lifted her shirt-tail and withdrew an envelope from her back pocket. She handed it to Russ. The name Jack was printed in what could only be described as a girlish script.

"It's my message to him. I wrote it this morning." Russ simply tucked it in his pocket. "Whatever happens, I could take it better if I knew he'd read my message."

Russ nodded. He was still a messenger, then. Lea had fixed her attention on the carousel. She paid no attention to the people arriving.

"What if he's got another girl?" she asked. It seemed she was finding ever more truths in her cosmology.

"Do you think he does?"

"He said he knew all about girls' hearts. He said a man's heart just wants a girl, but a girl's heart there's no telling. A girl's heart needs what it needs."

The words were a long white bone turned up in the mind. He wanted to ask if Jack had said it precisely that way, but of course he had. Jack Marks had taken to quoting Tara.

"Lea, can you tell me something? Does Jack have a scar or tattoo or something in the small of his back?"

She pretended to be distracted by the arriving passengers.

"Lea?"

"Why would you want to know something like that?"

"It's hard to explain."

"You still don't believe me."

"It's not that. I don't know the answer, I just have the question."

"I've never met anyone like you, either," she said.

"You're not going to tell me."

"What I know about his person, it's between him and me."

Grant was one of the last to appear through the gate, a tall man with glasses and a dark goatee with a parka folded over his arm. He had the awkward stride of a young deer, a little knock-kneed, swinging his feet before him to land where they might.

He saw them and waved, unsmiling. He looked back and forth between them, as if Russ could instruct him as to how to get through this. He could not, of course, but Lea stepped forward and gave him a hug and Grant instantly let himself go and hugged her back, his glasses jostled down the bridge of his nose, enlarging his closed eyes.

He released her and pushed the glasses back in place. Then he shook Russ's hand with great earnestness.

"Thank you," he said. "I don't know how to say it."

IV

A few miles west of El Paso he pulled into a Texas information rest area. Back in the Edmonton year he'd had a building super whose other job involved exposing insurance fraud.
He told Russ that all it took to be a good detective was a camera,
a phone, and a phone book. Beyond the racks of pamphlets and
audio-visual interactive displays, the rest area offered toll-free
phones and directories.

There was no listing for a Hec Sullivan. Beside the name he
put a question mark in the margin of a free city map. Then he
called directory assistance for a Jack Marks and drew a blank. If
Marks was in El Paso and didn't have a phone then maybe he
was living with his friend. If not, then he likely had a cheap
room somewhere. More than a dozen motels and hotels in the
Yellow Pages bothered to mention weekly rates, so he began
with these. He said he was looking for a Jack Marks who'd said
he'd be staying there. The voices on the other end didn't want

details. Some didn't bother to check the names, and Russ could only hope they'd know anyone who'd been there a while, and that Marks wasn't using an alias. Most of the motel voices were Indian or Pakistani, Russ wasn't sure he'd made himself understood in every case. It came to him how easily he could be defeated. As opposed to genre novels and movies, television's reality crime shows suggested that people's schemes weren't often elaborate, and if they didn't know you were watching or looking for them their every daily motion involved itself in their undoing – unless it turned out your first step was your last because the stranger on the other end was tired or trying to watch his favourite program, or only catching every second word.

He told himself that he would accept not finding Marks and being shut down simply by the distractedness of others, so when he got a hit at a place called the Garrison Hotel he had to acknowledge that because he had been put upon a course and sheer chance had given him his bearings, he felt somewhat elected.

The elect do not examine their motives. He pulled back into the traffic, high-dialling through the Mexican stations where the unbroken unknown tongue kept him from long thoughts. The sky held a certain light he would not try to characterize, though there were lines of poetry in it. "In my room, the world is beyond my understanding; But when I walk I see that it consists of three or four hills and a cloud." And then he thought American poet and the hills and the cloud were no longer themselves. You don't think American and then you do. You think Texas. He knew this place he'd never been only by the shadows it cast, the stories on screen. There were people here who thought they knew the west, but he knew where it began and extended to, where the west and all the wests emptied out.

When the river swung up near I-10 he saw across it the urgent rudiments of shelters growing dense and edgewise. The interstate bent away into the city, the ramps and meridians posted with men in faded fatigue pants and safety vests holding cardboard signs. HUNGRY ANYTHING HELPS PLEASE, THANK YOU. PLEASE HELP ME NOT ASKING MONEY FOR FOOD BUT TICKET HOME. A slight falling-away into the downtown. Immigration/Accidents read the billboard. At some point he got turned around on a series of one-ways and pulled over to orient himself. He rechecked the address. The streets all had state names and he had to ride back through them, California, Nevada, Arizona, Montana, southbound to Franklin and the Garrison.

The lobby of any small hotel ran back to his boyhood. Black marble, red leather, stand-up silver ashtrays with ornate lettering butt-ruined in the sand, numbers lighting in sequence up and down. This one had brown chairs and old wooden cases and picture frames of the place in earlier times, a red telephone booth, and a brass dial above the elevator. Russ briefly studied a display on the Garrison's famous guests and the rooms they had stayed in. The desk clerk nodded as he approached, no doubt the one Russ had just spoken to, the one who'd said, "Marks two-fourteen," as if citing a chapter and verse. He was a tall black man with salted hair. He wore a bolo tie and coarse, dark jeans. Russ smiled at him.

"You got a single?"

"You want a bathroom or is it okay down the hall?"

"I'll take one if you've got it. I stayed here a long time ago. There was a nice room up on the second floor."

"Well, you maybe had the Dillinger. It's five dollars more but it's a corner room and there's a tv and a bath."

"The Dillinger."

"He stayed in it. It tells all about it in the case over there."

"Can I see the room?"

He slid him the key.

"You have to pull hard on the elevator cage or else go up the stairs and just keep turning right through the doors."

He took the stairs. The first-floor door faced the open room of an old man sitting on the side of his bed in his underwear, smoking with his head down. He looked up at Russ without acknowledgement as if he were a passing shadow. The hallways were large and once cream-coloured, and at the turn to take the next flight of stairs the red carpet was worn through to the wood.

The Dillinger was small but clean. It had windows on two sides and the late-afternoon light darkened on the carpet where it was damp near the radiator. There was a television. On opposing walls, the same print of a peacock with other birds crowded around it and a manicured garden in the distance with a fountain and a manor house. The little brass plaque read Ornamental Garden by Marmaduke Craddock 1662-1717.

The room was suitable and, as he'd devised, it was next to the room of Jack Marks.

He went out to the hall and listened at the door to 214. He heard no one.

Back at the desk he paid for one night and filled out the card. The man looked it over.

"The room phone's for local calls. That booth over there's for long-distance. You know your plate?"

"It's a rental. I can go look if you need it."

"Don't bother. We don't have parking but you can leave it in the loading zone. They won't ticket you."

"Okay."

"You're not taking the car into Juarez, I hope. You'll need extra insurance."

"I don't really know."

"If you do, don't stop. Not even the stop signs. If a bunch of 'em set upon you, just get out and walk away. Let 'em take what they want."

"All right."

"You just leave it in the zone there. They haven't been by in a long while."

From the phone booth in the lobby he called Jean. He'd told her last night that he'd decided to take a little vacation now that he was down here. She'd received the news silently, as if she suspected he was up to something and knowing he didn't want her to ask him about it.

She answered on the first ring, and had barely let him say hello before asking where he was.

"I'm in a state of recovery. Just where I want to be."

"You're not up to anything foolish, are you, Russell?"

"Don't worry about me, Jean." He told her to go watch some desert birds with her friends.

Then he picked up the messages from his home number.

"It's Clete Dirks, Mr. Littlebury. I got two things for you. You say the words 'One-Sixty Fireball' to a creep and he starts drooling, but Pete Marks died after the footage was shot, so it's not him in the film. The second thing, I'm sorry as hell, but I tracked down the Harding woman and when I rang her up to confirm she kind of called me on my story and somehow your name came up. I'm sorry as hell. She's smarter than I usually deal with." He left Tara's phone number and e-mail address. She lived in Vancouver.

The second message was from Tara.

"Look, either we keep our distance or we don't. It would've taken you three minutes to get my number yourself. It's just like you to need a go-between to say hello."

He was not prepared for her voice. It wholly returned him to Toronto. She'd struck perfectly the tone they'd had between them, sharp and warm as a knife drawing back. He had in himself the voice he used with her but had no occasion for it now. He couldn't imagine using it – the centred, urbane voice – with anyone else. He hadn't wanted to call her, he told himself, only to have her number. It confirmed the existence of a past life, not one that was over, but one that continued without him. The number was simply to mark the divide between where he was and where he might have been. Her voice, though. He could almost live inside it.

Deep in the night he was brought up from great depths of sleep into wailing and a corpuscular light tracking across the walls. He didn't know where he was, someplace apparently burning. When it came to him he got out of the bed in his shorts and t-shirt and went to the streetside window. Two fire engines and an ambulance had taken positions in front of the stone building next door. He had passed it that evening on his way back from dinner and thought it strange that it had no windows, no name or number. He'd asked the desk man about it and was told it was a detention centre for illegals caught crossing the border. "Every couple nights they pull the fire alarm just to raise hell. They're crazy in there."

He brought the chair nearer the window and sat in the sound of his breathing. His pulse had been accelerated by the sudden waking and the bloodcolour he'd wakened to. It had quickened in him some instinct that survived in the mind through its remakings. The world gave you this, assorted response teams mulling without urgency, radios squawking in the night, a fire truck's lowered side panel, emergency vehicles at chance angles to the street and façades. It gave you this down below you, and you thought of images on screen though a minute ago you were twelve thousand years old.

There was no one else out there. No traffic, no passersby. The famed empty city cores of America.

He was conscious of a slowing now, he was coming back to himself in the way familiar to him. It was Adam Smith, he recalled, who'd used blood circulation as an analogy for the flow of goods and capital in a free-market economy, inspired by a seventeenth-century medical science advanced by experiments on live animals cut open to study their beating hearts. It was a bad night when this was the sort of thought that settled him.

The ambulance attendants emerged from the building with a man on a gurney. His arm was bandaged and there was blood on the sheet that covered him to the ankles, his bare feet registering each new slab of cement as the men rolled him along the side-walk. He kept trying to sit up but one of the attendants held him down with a hand on the shoulder. They came into the brighter light of the street and Russ saw he was just a kid, a teenager. He lay back quietly now. For a moment he looked up at Russ and something crossed his face that Russ could not name.

He pictured Tara asleep near the ocean. On her side, her legs articulated under a blanket whose terrain he knew exactly. He had travelled it many nights before sleep.

They were opening the ambulance doors when the kid made his break. He was on his feet and running before he was free of the sheet and one of the men got a hand on the linen but it fell away without slowing him and he ran on. He was naked. A naked kid escaping into the cold, peopleless streets. A man in uniform came running from the building and took up the chase on foot. The ambulance and fire crews stood watching as the kid cut into a car lot and came up running roof to roof without breaking stride and dropping down again, having made twice the distance on the uniformed man before disappearing in the dark beyond the plastic flags strung along the limits in the sodium light.

From the side window Russ heard a car come hard down the alley between the hotel and the stone building. It rode out into the street and almost hit the ambulance and slowed as the driver looked to the attendants who were pointing like townspeople in an old western. The car sped up and veered into the chase, taking one corner and then another until it was gone.

Bare-assed escape. A little ficelle served up out of nowhere. He found himself wanting the kid to make it somehow, and wondered if any of those in the street wanted it on some level too. The kid had less than nothing so you wanted him to make it, though that wasn't what you expected.

The vehicles departed and left him an empty street, the show over, though unresolved.

He tried to find something in the way the kid's expression had fixed in his mind. What had he seen in Russ's face? Of all his provisional selves, which one looked down tonight and who was it who knew them all?

For the first time in as long as he could remember he wondered about the future. He almost said something aloud in the dark.

Back across the damp carpet to the bed. In time the radiator knocked distantly and he was staring into the open bay of a mechanic shop on Main Street long ago. A truck up high on a column and a man with a torch underneath as another in green overalls came towards him with a grease gun in his hand. He was saying something that Russ couldn't make out amid the knock and hiss. He was late for school and he could smell the grease, a smell he kind of liked. The man was asking him something and when he came forward into the sunlight Russ turned and ran, though even as he ran he couldn't have said why.

He awoke a second time before dawn to the sound of a door closing out in the hallway and he knew he'd missed him and would likely have to wait well into the day now to contrive a meeting. Back towards sleep he fell amid other failed duties, large and small, until one or another unguarded self-admission jolted him upright in bed.

He ran cold water in the shower, thrust his head into the stream, then stood to let the cold run where it would and tracked back into the room.

Eyes open, he told himself. A bright window usually reported a saving idea or two, but there was nothing.

The television doubled as a radio and radios could prove serviceable for slaking the night's disturbances. A woman's voice stressed that the delay would be longer than usual in the northbound lanes where Alameda crossed Paisano. A transport truck had jackknifed into a small car. Russ envisioned the scene, the vehicles but not the victims, the witnesses standing their distance in a little amphitheatre of fascination. He turned off the radio.

For months his mind had been clenched like a fist, now it was wide open and he was not equal to it. I am not equal to myself, he thought. And there it was, words to meet the day with. He'd typed them out on a note card long ago and every so often for years it would turn up in one book or another. It was Paul Valéry on the subject of prayer, something Russ would have said he didn't believe in. The idea was that self-consciousness precludes true prayer, so one had to pray in unknown words. "Render enigma to enigma, enigma for enigma. Lift what is mystery in yourself to what is mystery in itself. There is something in you that is equal to what surpasses you."

Just now he wasn't sure he wanted to know what that thing was, but whatever it was, he could take comfort in the certainty that he would never find the unknown language of true prayer. It was a fool's game even to look for it. The soul's movement was not a progress, but a mere continuance.

The poet's words were enough to get him out of his room, but the moment he was out onto the street, he realized he felt no better. Soon – today, he hoped – he would serve the letter to Marks, in person, so Lea could have no doubt that he had gotten it, and be gone. Something about this place wanted to damage him. He'd felt assailable now and then on the way down, but here the feeling was all around him. Anonymous in a strange place, any emotion might find you.

After a few hours the only words he had spoken were "huevos rancheros" and "thanks" so that the morning disposed itself in scenes he had no part of. Slow-turning racks of godawful shirts in a western-apparel store. Greasy empanadas in a bakery pan. Through the window of an outdoor-equipment shop he peered at a compound bow and a quiver of razor-headed arrows, remembering Skidder once asking him what it meant to say a thing was "stropped better than surgical" and he thought of his non-brother rattling his same toothless key in the lock of every door in his world of doors.

At a service station a man sold chili peppers and jerky from the back of his truck. Russ bought a strip and walked on with the salt taste somehow sharpening his eye for the place. Longhorn Trophy. Electric Tool Rental. He went into a smoke shop expecting magazines and cigars but found a metal-faced kid in a black t-shirt saluting him hello, cases of Zippo lighters, pocket knives, rings and bracelets, and behind it all a shelf of garish hash pipes, then left again with a wave back. It was as if he had been sifting in the random wash of things for an instrument of a certain unreflecting surface. Something to acquire and then drop into his pocket and forget.

He might have waited for Marks in the lobby but somewhat to his surprise, shortly before the checkout time of eleven o'clock, he returned to the hotel and paid for another night. Over the next hour he went up to the second floor three times before the cleaning trolley appeared outside his open door. His room was made up and a Mexican woman about his age who was restocking his towels turned with a short gasp upon seeing him. He invested a smile and she laughed and apologized and went out into the hallway. He closed the door and a minute later stepped back into the hall and walked into Marks's open room with a five-dollar bill. She was at the bed.

"I forgot to leave you something. Here, this is yours."

She smiled and looked down at the bedding as if embarrassed. He took in the room all at once. A wine-red shirt hanging on the chair, a half-full plastic cup of beer on the bedside table. An old Spirit of St. Louis radio with wicker speaker covers and a 360-degree tuning dial.

"Thank you, sir."

The objects on the dresser. A pair of bone dice. A mandrake root strung by the neck with a leather thong. A tattered envelope addressed to someone named Calvin Lu of San Francisco. A brown Gideon Bible.

"I'll just leave it here."

He put the bill on the dresser, next to a bottle of pills. The writing was Spanish. Stamped onto the dosage instructions was the same red caduceus that had appeared on Mike's bottles of morphine.

"Thanks," he said, and walked out.

For the rest of the day he waited for Marks but he didn't return, or maybe returned and left again after Russ fell asleep in his chair. In the evening he finally left for dinner and then came back and listened at the walls but heard nothing. The quiet did not help him sort his thoughts. That night he lay waiting for sounds in the hallway until the idea of Marks no longer involved the photo or the stories of him, but only the objects in the next room that he turned over in his thoughts.

It's Russ.

Sorry about the detective (he gave me this address, though I didn't ask for it). I had other uses for him and you were an add-on. I wouldn't be writing now if you hadn't outsmarted him. I only wanted to know where to imagine you.

You can imagine me in a cybercafe surrounded by students of the University of Texas at El Paso. I'm running an errand down here. I set up an account just to write this.

My father died five weeks ago. I'm currently unemployed with no prospects. Now you're caught up.

It's been a year since your letter arrived and about that long since I last read it, but I remember you accused me of evasion, and acting in bad faith, and a kind of dereliction. It all struck me as true enough. I didn't see everything I might have seen. In my defence I can say only that I wasn't conscious of my failings during the time we were together. Maybe I wanted both lives, the one we were living, and the one I had to return to, so I suspended one and lived the other as if it had its own logic and direction, its own promise.

Or anyway, this is how I see things now. Levi-Strauss (no, I haven't freed myself from the authorities) held that each object, each model of understanding we destroy in favour of a new one is not thereby rendered invalid, but is necessary so that we reach the next object. There is the question of whether or not the cycle of embrace and release leads to a final truth – he thought the inquiry would end in "the one lasting presence" – but even if the final truth is just the necessary fiction we can't get beyond, if we're trying at all we are more or less stuck living our lives letting go of lesser beliefs for better ones. Sometimes we love the ones we let go of, but we let them go even if we fear we may never know that elusive, final embrace.

Which is to say, I can make sense of anything, but can make final sense of very little.

The question that always obtains is, what are the fictions we're living with? The answer should never be obvious, we should have to struggle towards and past it. The answer was never obvious in you. You were always a complicated person. As for me, I don't know – we understand one another, you and I, better than we do ourselves – but you must accept that there are times when a little allusion can deepen an intimate exchange, can fix things with a clarity unavailable in the flutter of everyday moments.

Though we used them with one another, I don't know what we could possibly have meant by words like "heart" and "mind." We might as well ball them up and call them "soul," and say that the soul can't help itself for its availabilities. Like you said, we need what we need. A suspicion of ideas can kill us just as surely as a lack of imagination or wonderment. We need it all to have even the slimmest chance of getting past the last fiction. And even here, as I'm trying to make a rational statement about rational struggle, I see I've lost trust in my line of thought. How far gone am I to ask you to understand me through a model that allows, at best, only a temporary truth?

But there it is. Forgive me.

It was good to hear your voice in the message.

As he was writing the letter, using the language he'd had no use for in a long time, Russ felt especially grounded – as he'd hoped he would. But upon sending it, he was overcome with a kind of objectless desire. It was there in the thought of Tara, in the image of her reading his words on a screen, and in the possibility of her writing back. It was upon him suddenly, touching every motion, every warm surface around him.

Later, looking back, he saw himself leaving the café, walking south, in a state of acute suggestibility brought on by this desire. He had only just begun to calm himself when he was into the mysteries again. There across the plaza, he literally saw red, a man in a wine shirt disappearing down Oregon. Russ hurried to keep sight of him but lost him until, as he drifted south, he picked up the shirt again along a quiet, broken neighbourhood street running east. He followed at a distance.

Russ wasn't close enough to know if it was Marks ahead of him – was it only the shirt that had suggested him? – but the very act of following seemed to weaken the doubt. The man drifted along as Marks would drift. Even the street, the rundown yards, suited him. The buildings he passed were one-storey square, small, many of them adjoining vacant sandy lots. One gutted house exploded in wild barking as he went by. A German shepherd attached to a clothesline put its forepaws on a wire fence and strained against its collar hard enough to choke off its crazed snarling. Marks stopped before it and calmly lit a cigarette. He looked around, though not directly back at Russ, and got on his haunches and spoke softly to the animal until the dog settled down. He extended his hand. The dog consented to sniff it. Its tail swept vaguely. Then Marks stood and leaned over and scratched the animal with one hand, while with the other he took the cigarette from his mouth and cupped it. He brought it in from behind the dog's head and then pressed it fast into the animal's ear. The two of them jumped at once and Marks whipped his hand away from the dog's jaws with a gesture that finished high above him so that for a moment his arm was like that of a dancer, and then he started off down the street as the shepherd yelped in pain and betrayal.

In the time it took to witness this passing cruelty, Russ was reduced to a few stark certainties. That he could neither summon words nor form them. That he was wild with intention. That even as Marks disappeared down another street, Russ was closing ground on him, and that when he'd closed it all, he would beat him in the name of every living thing he'd abused.

By the time Russ saw the shirt again Marks was above him on the footbridge, heading across the border into Mexico. There was nothing to stop Russ from following. His passport was in his back pocket, so the crossing would pose no problem.

It cost twenty-five cents.

He'd lost sight of Marks by the time he arrived into the directed randomness of the Juarez tourist strip. A legless man on a trolley floating amid children with their palms held up,

"Dónde va? Qué quiere?", the merchants beckoning outside the craft shops and the drugstore windows posting prices in the penicillin wars. The awnings, green and yellow, pink and white, all the same age, formerly bright. The place was not Mexico, or even Juarez, but an old lie once easily grasped to be sold to tourists and now overrun by truths that were by-products of what was sold elsewhere.

A taxi driver stepped before him.

"Señor, you want drugs? You want poosy? You want speed? Ampiceelin? Antidote, man?"

"No thanks."

Marks wasn't visible ahead. Russ reasoned he'd gone into a shop. As he walked he was set upon by the merchants and young men whose job was apparently to wrangle him for the others. A broken music was playing up ahead. When he reached the next corner he found a little boy with a busted toy accordion that wheezed a single, failing note. The kid saw him and said "Moneys" and Russ stopped to hand him a dollar.

When he looked back down the street he saw the red shirt disappearing into a taxi parked outside a pharmacy. Seconds later he was in a cab himself, following.

They moved south past a market and a mission, then turned east. At each traffic light they were set upon by the near-dead poor. An old man knocked on the back window, trying to sell him a green balloon. Another whose family stood by on a meridian ran from car to car with a sheet of cellophane candy packets draped over his arm. The little girl with a plastic bag of water.

"You like the city?" asked the cabbie.

The man smiled for him.

"The streets are well maintained."

"The life is strong in these people."

219

He felt his anger easing off. He was slightly amazed at where it had taken him. The traffic picked up and for a short while the city looked like anyplace. A few acres scraped bare opened the prospect of a black plume in the distance. A high-gated mansion passed in white filigree and terra cotta tiles, a man in shades on guard, and then a line of shacks behind a corrugated-iron fence in that familiar way it was in the world where things just wouldn't mix.

"You want the young girl?" The cabbies of Juarez would not relent, not in their particular lifetimes. "I know the young girl. She is very clean."

"No. Just follow the car, please."

The cabbie didn't answer. There was something automated about him but he just wanted his kickback like everyone else. At least the man knew how to follow a car, negotiating the interceding traffic and the stoplights without evident concern. The car ahead turned north for a block, and then south again, a doubling-back that led Russ to worry they'd been made. He settled on the probability that, wherever they were heading, the route would be longer than was strictly necessary.

The taxi ahead stopped at the entrance to a park at the Bridge of the Americas. Marks was out of the car and was well along a path leading into the park by the time Russ had paid and left his cab, stepping into the noise of traffic accelerating hard away from the border. There were no cars parked here, no one to be seen but Marks, up ahead, partly obscured by a thin woods that enclosed a brighter area beyond.

Russ crossed into the sparse cropping of evergreens and what looked like bare birch trees, northern trees. Ahead, the dirt path led to an opening with a low building and an obelisk in a white concrete monument surrounded by a dry moat and a wrought-iron fence. About fifty feet on, where the path left the trees, was a vendor with a cart made up from a kid's wagon. He had liquids in what looked like white plastic gasoline jugs. Though he was only a short distance away, and there was no one else around, the man didn't look over at Marks as he passed.

Now beyond the monument, Marks veered right. Just before he disappeared behind the building he looked back over his shoulder, not at Russ but at something or nothing at all in the distance between them. Despite the shirt and the hair, the last glimpse of him was the very picture of the figure in Lea's photo. A man, this man, in mid-stride, looking back.

Russ came to a standstill at the coincidence. His mind was going on without him again, making meaning from random movements and light. As in the photo, here there were even trees in the background.

He was trapped in a fascination. He almost laughed. There were moments in the flux that asked you to make something of them.

He walked on. Though he heard no movement, there emerged from the shadows of the monument three figures, two young men and a girl. They came into the open and on towards him along the walkway across the moat. The low gate was locked by a chain. One of the young men climbed over, then the two men helped the girl over and the second man came over and took the girl and continued on across the park in the direction of the vendor. The other man stayed and approached Russ.

"You meet somebody, mister?"

Russ could see that he was very young, in his late teens, maybe. He was thin but muscular in a sleeveless t-shirt. His eyebrows were fine and sharp.

"No. I'm just passing through."

The young man drew a pack of cigarettes from the back pocket of his jeans and somewhat theatrically lit a smoke. He looked Russ over and seemed to consider whether or not to offer him one. It was unclear if the moves were stolen from movies or had been stolen by them.

"You want some dope?"

"No thanks."

"Why have you come here?"

There was some commotion behind them. Russ turned to see the kid's male friend arguing with the vendor. The young girl stood slightly apart from them holding one of the jugs.

The kid called to his friend and the friend sullenly handed money to the vendor. Apparently the customers paid by the swig.

"No reason."

"You see the hero?" The kid pointed to the dark head embossed on the monument. Some letters had been lost from the quotation:

"LA LEY HA SIDO SIEMPRE MI E P D Y MI ESCUDO"
Benito Juarez

"What he says, it's a lie. In the city named for Juarez there is no law, only the *espada*." His fist arced backhanded through the air in a cutting motion. Apparently he intended it as a warning.

"Right."

Russ continued walking. When he looked back, the kid was watching his friends return to him. Russ hurried his step to catch another view of Marks. As he rounded the far side of the monument, he saw that the park opened into an empty distance, so he continued a circumnavigation. At each turn he discovered only quiet, open ground. Unless Marks was walking his own circles at the same pace, 180 degrees from Russ, he had disappeared. There was no point at which he could have continued into the park without Russ coming around and seeing him. Yet he was nowhere. In fact, there was no one in any direction, and no human sound.

Russ had the sense he was being toyed with, that the inexplicable was mocking him. When he'd come back around to the east side where he'd first come into the clearing, he stopped and started back, counter-clockwise, and found there was no one behind him. Marks, the kids, the man with the cart, they were all gone.

It will end this way, he thought. With no explanation I'll lose this stranger to whom I've attached an importance I don't even fathom. I'll return to the hotel and find him gone, and that will be it. I won't even know for sure if I saw him.

He was trotting now, looking for any fleeting glimpse of a human form, however far across the park. His thoughts were rampant with calculation. Upon one angle, he supposed, the vendor could have made his way into the trees without Russ seeing him, but he couldn't explain the other disappearances. He ran a little harder. When he was halfway around again, there came into view a man, sitting on a bench, facing the monument. Russ slowed and walked towards him.

He wore a blue suit and sunglasses. His face was freshly minted copper. He looked directly at Russ in approach. They exchanged nods.

"You wish to rest?"

"Yes. Thank you."

The man shifted over and allowed Russ room to sit. He looked as if he'd just come from a barber, the newly exposed skin a little lighter along the neck, where the hair had been shorn.

223

"If I may ask. You were running. Was there some trouble?"

"No. I was . . . there was someone ahead of me. I thought. I was trying to catch up."

"I see."

"But he's disappeared. Did you see anyone?"

"Where could he have gone, your friend?"

"I don't know. There were kids here, too."

The man nodded as if maybe he knew the kids, or that people disappeared around here.

"You are new to Juarez."

"I'm visiting."

"Do you find the light is different in Mexico?"

"The light?"

"Yes."

"I don't know. This is about all the Mexico I've seen."

The man smiled. He looked off to the monument, seemed to watch it as if it were a pond.

"If you don't know the light, it may trick you. You may think you see something you don't see."

"Well, I spoke to one of the kids. He spoke back."

"Then maybe it's the light that hides them from you now." Of course he speaks in riddles, thought Russ. Were there any other kinds of dark-skinned men on foreign benches? "The earth itself is a being of the light."

It was a performance, then. He said this stuff for the tourists. Soon, he'll ask if I'm saved or else offer to guide me for a fee.

"They are still there, these people you followed and spoke to. You just don't see them."

"Do you see them?"

"There is nothing to fear."

In his recollection, Russ couldn't decide if he felt the fear upon hearing the word, or a second later, when he turned and saw the figure. On the thin metal arm of the man's sunglasses were two sets of curving slopes reaching to peaks, one over the other, and a vertical line connecting them so that they seemed like splayed limbs joined by a torso. Behind the arm, in the faintest of crow's feet, leaned the same configuration.

"You are not losing your sense."

There was a tremor in the light. The man was calling into being the very things he said were not. Russ understood that he had to right himself or he'd be in trouble. His focus turned to the sound of his breathing. It was heavy, and hadn't slowed since he'd stopped running and sat down. In fact he was breathing a little harder now, and harder still as he became conscious of it.

"Do you not want to lie down."

He felt a loss upon his tongue. A tingling in his hands. He looked down to find them closing. He tried to say something – what was it? that he felt ill? – but the words wouldn't form and came out slurred and senseless.

He lay on the bench with his arm covering his eyes for what seemed like a long time, though at no point did he lose consciousness. He understood there were words for what he was experiencing, but they weren't present to him and he had no desire to remember them. For a minute or two he had been listening to the distant call of a bird, it sounded like a Canada goose in flight and then separated into two distinct squawks or honkings as the birds came nearer.

In time, Russ sat up. The man was gone. Leaving the path and coming his way was the water vendor. Two wheels of the wagon he pulled were talking their wheeltalk.

He arrived, offered the jug. Russ stood and poured water over his face and down his back, and let the jug run to empty.

Then he gave the man some dollars and began his long walk back to the hotel.

Once, as a boy of ten, working in the farmyard with his father, he'd wondered aloud about the mother he'd never known. It had been a prepared question, made to sound offhand, his earliest memory of calculation. A small question about nothing important that might open space for larger ones. Had his mother liked crabapple jelly? he asked. Mike had been cleaning the inside of a tractor cab and Russ stood by, ready to hand up another cloth. Mike got out of the cab and lifted Russ high up onto the back wheel. "Are you hungry?" Russ said he wasn't. Mike nodded. "Your mother was a good woman. That's all you need to know. Don't ever live in the past, son. You sure won't catch me there."

That night in his room it seemed important that he recall the word that had escaped him in the park, but when it finally came – "hyperventilation" had caused the oxygen debt that had closed down parts of his body – the syllables did nothing for him. A little mystery – as it was happening, Marks's disappearance was inexplicable – and a lot of breath and you had yourself the beginnings of what he supposed could only be called a mystical experience. A dash of the numinous, a pinch of pure consciousness. But the core of it, to Russ, was the loss of language. He thought of the word beyond recall, and of his tongue made useless. He had tried to speak, but uttered nonsense.

He felt he'd been granted an unbeliever's glimpse of the great, transfiguring forces. He didn't pretend to understand their nature, but found it possible to accept that they existed some-where beyond the powers of biology, delusion, or denial. Under the right circumstances, in a certain sort of person in need, even such a small revelation as he had had, a bafflement and a dizzy spell, might open the possibility of full-out religious conversion.

Russ had always accepted the reality of faith, which in his father was as real as his living form, in some ways *was* his living form. Though Russ had no belief in God, he did have faith in faith. What he had never accepted, he now understood, was radical conversion. It occurred to him that he hadn't believed the stories about his father as the feared hellraiser, that once a mind and character had been set, some new mind and charac-ter could take hold permanently. He'd thought that the very idea granted absolute power to false agents, the imagined sav-iours and angels, the sort of creature that Marks and he himself had been mistaken for by Lea, ignoring the obvious fact that memory, habit, biology, all the factors of personal history endure. A person could not be emptied of these things and still have their wits about them.

But he had been wrong. He thought of the Mike he hadn't known, the mean, violent man who'd seen the light. It was nec-essary to believe in that meanness in order not to dismiss or judge harshly what came to be held against it. The stories hadn't been exaggerated after all. That's what he thought, but what he felt, and what would always stay in him, was the memory of Mike, at the end, when the words wouldn't come to him, the names of the angels he couldn't call down, so that he was left with only Russ.

The next morning on almost no sleep he set out in a cool breeze off the mountains and walked to the cybercafé and ordered coffee from a girl with a bronco on her t-shirt. There was no mail from Tara. He put money on the table and left before the coffee arrived.

He found a place that sold scotch and took three bottles up to his room and in the days that followed spent long hours there, driven out by hunger in the evenings.

He made no calls.

He felt closed off in his room and found it possible to believe he would never leave it, that with no one else there he'd remain simply for having no chance to talk his way out.

In bars he let strangers tell him stories so that before long they regarded him as one of their company. One night he inquired about the Juarez park and the monument. From three or four at times competing sources he learned that the monument was a popular place to buy drugs. That you were just as likely to get Faros, cheap cigarettes with the ends cut off. That soldiers from Fort Bliss were always getting caught at the border with baby aspirin called Mejoralitos. He learned that the man in the blue suit fit the description of a narcotics cop named, in two accounts, Camillo, and the rumour was that he worked for someone big in contraband but that this was the rumour on every cop. There were descriptions of trucks leaving maquiladoras loaded with auto parts, and the parts packed with cocaine, Darvon, Percodan, steroids, Ritalin. The theory was put forward that the sight of Camillo had scared off the kids and buyers, who had receded back into the shadows of the monument to hide.

Russ was warned repeatedly by one new friend or another to stay away from drugs in a border town. The point was stressed that this wasn't a movie with these people.

Marks seemed to be spending nights elsewhere, though once Russ overheard a desk man complaining to a maid that he hadn't paid up or checked out. At some point the same man told Russ that liquor wasn't allowed in the rooms.

One night Marks returned to the hotel. Through the wall, Russ heard him moving around, running the water. The very resumption of sounds seemed to hold the promise of some kind of completion. Russ looked at Lea's letter where he had set it out on his night table. It seemed to have nothing to do with his being there.

For parts of the next days Russ followed him on his transits about the city. He trailed him on foot, by car. Twice he boarded the same bus. Never did Russ find Marks looking his way or giving any indication that he knew he was there. When Marks moved out of a space, Russ inhabited it. He followed him like a character in a foreign story, learning his mind through his habits, making sense of his half-familiar world.

He learned who his friends were, that some business had gathered them, and he allowed a sort of plot to emerge. Hec Sullivan and a young blond man seemed to have Marks on call. Together they met him daily, they spoke, then parted. With nothing particular to help him make sense of it, Russ's speculations on their business slid inevitably into crime fantasies, heist movies, takedowns.

The satellite characters included the fat man in San Jacinto Plaza whom Marks sat beside each morning eating his fast-food hotcakes. One morning, after Marks had left, Russ took his seat. The fat man carried a plastic bag containing seven paperback biographies of Michael Jackson at various ages. He and Michael had both been born the same year in Gary, Indiana, but, he pointed out, their lives had taken different courses. If you let him he'd explain forty years of world history in terms of Elvis and Michael Jackson. Russ thought vaguely of palatial bunkers and American men so wealthy and famous they disappear from themselves. He felt no sympathy for these men, but spared a sort of thought for those who did.

Around them were native Indians and blacks and what seemed like whole families of Mexicans climbing in and out of the backs of pickup trucks. A ceramic alligator fountain was surrounded by some pretty nasty looking youths who seemed to have scared off the hairy veggie-hippie kids with their dread-locks and aggressive good cheer who walked in small packs on the streets bordering the square. Marks had watched a well-dressed white woman hurry past and a kid follow her for a few steps until she stopped in her tracks and wheeled on him. Russ thought she would slap him but instead she reached into her purse and gave him money. He imagined Marks picturing her slapping him.

There was the building Marks seemed to stare at as he ate. The building said Anson Mills. Rows of windows chorded into nicotine light like damp brown images hung in strips, a chemical pong in the dark held in mind and now mixed with the cheap smell from the stall of a vendor selling bags of cotton candy to the poor and their many children.

Later, Russ saw him passing Stanton where it rose sharply at the border like a seeming wave of pavement about to crest and break upon him. He moved on west, then south of Paisano along the blocks of dollar stores and places selling jeans, toys, t-shirts, caps, maps, shoes, unspecified Dry Goods that were recessed from the bright street in dim unlit stalls. A moderate sidewalk traffic building with people not his kind. The trade in old gold was everywhere like a form of local worship. Yellow signs read Loans No Checks and Compro Oro Viejo.

230

Farther down, the streets ran empty. Russ found him staring at a composite sketch of a wanted man of indeterminate race taped to a wire fence, a railyard beyond. He walked along the fence and was stopped short by something in the railyard. Russ could see only a Uniglory boxcar, but when Marks had moved on he came up to the fence to find neatly lettered upon the car the words "2 inch comp shoes" and "jack here" and understood that Marks had seen his own name addressed to him like a sign of his personal holy ground.

On past the Ropa Usada shops, Marks watched people of Juarez bathing in the river in their clothes and drying in the cold along the concrete banks and against the graffiti scrawled there, *Viva La Migra*, and blocks along he passed a lurid mural of cowboys and nurses, waiters and cacti bending below the assertion that *God is Mexican*. A white border-patrol truck appeared and slowed and a guard in dark green eyed him as the truck drew even and continued on.

At intervals they passed five Mexican-American men indifferently dressed, huddled around a car that foiled them at ignition. A wide boulevard ran mid-street. Some effort had been made to improve the character of the place. The patchy grass had been cut, the benches and tables wore many coats of deep blue. But on the wires overhead kids had slung a dozen pairs of shoes and they hung by their laces as if cast from the heavens or like remnants of a great flood.

The cirrus haze performed its pearl-handled sky. Russ had spent his life looking at skies, he'd never seen one like it before.

When he looked back down he saw that Marks had stopped and turned, and was looking back at him, or rather through him, past him — their eyes didn't meet — and Russ himself turned and saw then that Marks was looking beyond, at the men now pushing the car through an intersection and disappearing in complete silence.

By the time Russ turned around again, Marks was gone.

He saw him by chance one late afternoon at the fruit stand across from the Walgreens, sitting on the sidewalk with his back against cold stone and seeming to watch people's shadows incline towards them as they rounded the corner. In someone else, the image might make for an insight, Russ thought, but in Marks the very word was false. Insight. The untrue heart of what a thing was called. There was nothing that Marks could see in people, or in himself. He was just some opaque substance borne forward by eddying time. In the quiet minutes, the only thing a man like that felt was the weight of time against him, the physical him that hurled the shadow and the tuck he'd made in his mind that couldn't stop the time the shadow marked.

Buses lined up on the north side of the plaza. Route 31, Fort Bliss via Radford, the light stammered along Main.

Marks took the northbound route. He sat at the front and didn't look up when Russ walked right past him. The bus driver told Marks the story of his Vietnam war buddy dying in hospital last year clutching a laminated postcard of the Virgin of Guadeloupe. She now rode there in the gauges. When the driver stepped off for his coffee, Marks slipped the card into his back pocket and disappeared down a side street, emerging a few minutes later, when the bus had gone on, and making his way into the Crystal Palace Multiplex Cinemas, where the movies were one dollar.

Russ found him on the left-side wall of a theatre showing a film that the poster outside the door suggested was about a blue-collar girl with singing aspirations. He sat behind him, at an angle, and watched the light play on the audience. In the aisles parents attended their toddlers as if at a picnic and here and there heads were turned looking back over the seats to the family behind. Somehow the candies and drinks were apportioned without much talking.

There was fuzz in the speakers.

The girl worked in a foundry, setting metal into a machine that would bend it to one shape or another, alongside her life-long friend, a girl from her neighbourhood. Russ recognized the lead actress but didn't know her name. She was ludicrously beautiful, a fine sweat on her as she worked. It was a genre reprised from the eighties that Tara had once referred to as a "soma flick." Movies like this had nothing to do with life, she'd said. They reproduced only the experience of watching them.

Marks leaned forward, crossed his arms on the seat back. In his intent expression was the man who bought grisly footage through the mail. It was surprising to Russ that a feature film could reach him.

Before the movie let out Russ took a position in the foyer. He had delivered himself into some strangeness and would see it through. He dialled up the message he'd saved from Tara and listened to it over and again until the doors opened. Families passed, the kids darting ahead. There were couples, teen friends. When Marks didn't appear he went back in. The theatre was empty.

There was the morning he woke to his name, spoken unmistakably in his father's voice, from a place somewhere outside his dreaming. The voice would stay with him for hours, he knew, the way a nightmare casts a shadow long into the waking day.

He wondered vaguely at his condition.

There was the lettered window Marks returned to every day. Step by Step Prosthetic Outlet promised Personal Fittings and

Full Natural Articulations, offering a sample of legs and hands like the fading memories of missing parts or the missing parts of memory.

Some days Marks stood outside a restaurant watching the industry in the attached car wash until Sullivan and the blond man came by in an El Camino to pick him up. Once, Russ followed in his car north to where the enormous south-facing houses rode the mountain like the prows of great ships. He parked a block distant and watched as Marks was made to stand before a security camera at the edge of the property and take his shirt off as the blond man inspected his arms for tracks and Sullivan spoke to someone unseen on a headset near the gate. Apparently Marks was not to know his employer. Sullivan was his contact. When the inspection was done, they got into the car and drove off.

It evolved that the El Camino was easy to spot and to follow. Russ followed it once out across the state line to the Sunland Park Racetrack. He parked very near and watched the three men walk up. The blond man was dressed in bluejeans as always. He seemed younger and more country-looking every time Russ saw him. Sullivan, small and prisonyard, the slicked-back hair and a denim shirt with the sleeves cut off. With all its downscale locales, its beater cars and frayed clothing, its mean adherence to the misfit type, there was something not entirely real about the world of these men. The dramatics were so cheap and badly stylized they belonged now to rerun cop shows on television. You looked at Marks and his friends and thought they were headed for a bad ending by the top of the next hour.

A large, uniformed black man stationed at the door of a small casino off the entrance nodded to Russ as he stepped in. The room was dim and near empty but for a few somnambulant old men looking betrayed by their senses before slot machines, mechanically pulling levers with a complete absence of anticipation at the outcome. The grandstand crowd was quieter than he'd have thought, giving the impression it had lost its illusions or was showing respect for the winners and losers among them. Russ knew nothing about the world of local gamblers. In the voices of track insiders, compulsives, a certain narrow strata of the social residuum, he heard words and phrases he recognized but didn't know the meaning of. Bad cover, someone said. Broke in air and quarter post, the trifecta. In every way, the place was foreign to him.

He spotted Marks stepping sidewise along a bench at the top of the stand and taking his seat alone. Russ positioned himself above him, standing over the top rail, looking down at a slight angle to see what Marks was watching. From the numbers turning up on the board trackside, he focused then on something beyond the far stretch in the distance towards the city, and then on the people below him. Bettors trickled down for the next post time, middle-aged women sitting together and older people by themselves, a group of young Latino men, a black man with a little white girl of ten or so who was his daughter. She waved her hand to clear the smoke when an old guy in front of them lit his cigarette one-handed without looking up from the form he was reading. It came off as a neat trick mastered long ago and repeated ten thousand times past any sense of audience once hoped for. When the smoke seemed to want to drift their way the father and daughter moved well clear and the old guy paid no notice.

Marks was now in some penumbral space. Russ saw his fingertips rise and resettle lightly on his thigh as if a tumbler had fallen in his mind. For a few seconds Marks seemed on the cusp of a small revelation. Something was in the periphery of his perception, just there in his blind spot.

At any moment, thought Russ, he'll turn around and see me watching him.

A young tousleheaded kid seated in the row above Marks began to tell the matronly woman next to him about his Kentucky roots. A distant uncle had been the governor. In the fifties you could buy a burger with his family name on it. When Marks lowered his eyes a notch Russ understood he was listening to the story for anything he might use.

Outside, the horses on the far stretch were making their way around with the yellow-jacketed track riders as ahead of them one truck dragged the surface tilling furrows in the pounded earth and another watered them down. Near the waterfall a man in a sequinned black mariachi outfit held a horn at his hip and watched the approach. The track was listed as fast. A dozen televisions that hung from the concourse ceiling began a simulcast from a place called Beulah Park and Define Sam was away early on the rail with the sound just ahead of the picture.

On screen Long Tan Mister now had a neck on Rainpan as the horses here approached the gate. The mariachi man donned an enormous sombrero and was still adjusting it as he brought the horn up and blew. When the horses began to load, the track announcer came on with an East London accent that threw a new sound into things. Above the crowd the lead horse faded as Rainpan held his form to win and then the screens blanked into the words Results Pending.

Russ looked off towards the casino. By chance, because he'd been looking that way, he saw the mirrored door of Riley's Lounge – Reserved Seating Only – swing open and Hec

Sullivan and the blond kid emerge. They walked right in front of Russ without looking at him.

"You shut up when I'm talking," said Sullivan.

"I'm a part of this, too."

They moved down and sat beside Marks.

Then the horses were off. The people broke into a murmur, talking at the horses though not quite cheering. The names now were Real Time and Echo's Boy, Lost Appeal, Feebus, the horses themselves soundless through the window. Over the far rail the riders' colours massed into a toy flotilla of gaming pieces. As they came out of the far turn white birds lifted off from the infield pond. The smoking man still had not looked up from his page, he could have been sitting alone in a rented room. Down the stretch in small groupings they passed over the finish line, an ambulance trailing the field.

Sullivan had been leaning close, speaking to Marks, who hadn't so much as nodded or glanced his way. He was fixed on the ambulance. Russ wondered if Marks too hadn't seen the ambulance episode from his hotel window those nights ago, and now was wondering about the kid who'd escaped and what it all meant. He sat for a few seconds after Sullivan had gotten up to leave, and then they left together.

Russ followed them out to the lot and lost them on the interstate.

"It's quiet."

"I'm reading."

"Reading what?"

Mike had never before asked Russ about his books.

"It's about a military campaign."

"Tell me."

Russ described a Greek army of mercenaries, trapped in the snows of Asia Minor.

"The battle's over and they're starving and cold, walking home through foreign territories. Ten thousand men."

"A story?"

"It's a history."

"History." He was breathless. Minutes passed. There was less and less to distinguish now between his sleeping and waking. His eyes didn't open when he spoke.

One night a few years before, the last summer on the farm, Mike had presented Russ with a gift after supper. A yellowed, stapled pamphlet. It was from the year of his conversion, a sermon on The Last Things. Death, Judgement, Heaven, and Hell, what Russ thought of as the necessary countries of Christian eschatology. "Study on this," he'd said. "Keep it." Russ said he would read it. "It's all real. The judgement is real and you should fear it." Russ agreed that he probably should. "Fear is a Christian duty." Russ had never known his father to fear anything, and the comment returned now as he sat over him. He understood that Mike didn't fear death, or even hell, having known them. He feared only judgement, and had lived his last decades against that moment to come.

It was good to know the nature of your fears, he'd decided, and wondered then what kind of coward he himself was. Not a physical or intellectual coward, it seemed, but surely all the other kinds. Whatever they were called, they were present to him now. There in his father's room, he had never been closer to his fears.

Russ found himself in the phone booth in the lobby, looking across the desk at the back wall where the keys dangled from their numbered slots. The only keys missing on Russ's side of the second floor were the one in his pocket and the one to the neighbouring room. Seeing the empty slots side by side he experienced a refracted moment, a stutter in time, not the sort of feeling he knew how to think about.

He dialled up his messages. He heard Skidder say, "I come home and my truck's shitcanned," and he skipped ahead and past three more calls from him and then listened to Lea say she was home now, and imploring him to "Deliver the message. The message is true."

The last light reflecting off the building across the street dulled and sharpened again with each passing cloud. Russ watched a primordial shadowplay on the lobby carpet.

The elevator dial began its slow counter-clockwise sweep.

A Harley-Davidson had pulled up behind Russ's rental in front of the hotel with two riders in leather pants and jackets. The riders took their helmets off. A young couple, long-haired, Japanese.

He placed the receiver back in the cradle.

Marks stepped out of the elevator. He wore a dull yellow bowling shirt, tucked in, and black jeans and workboots with black electrical tape spatted on the toes. His greasy hair, six or eight weeks longer than in Lea's photos, was combed back now and made his face seem thinner. He nodded to the desk man and began across the lobby.

Russ turned his back and pretended to be talking on the phone. As Marks passed him, Russ turned and saw that he was carrying a brown book that looked like the Bible from his room. Hanging outside his back pocket, a small loop of a fine gold. If he hadn't just heard Lea's voice would he have seen it and pictured the necklace she'd shown him? And yet the Bible and the little loop were enough for him to know that Marks was lonely tonight, and out to do damage, all of it apparent simply in the way he'd walked out of the lobby, looking down at his boots.

A man walks, he thought. He stands in the elevator with the light through the back of the cage dying in the windows of the shaft, he swings the door open, sees facing him a leather chair studded with tacks like rhinestones that make the whole lobby seem false, and because he owes for the night upcoming, as he nods to the desk man Robey he walks on across the lobby and out, where he can't help but smile at the pretty Japanese girl in leather, though her boyfriend is standing right there ready to go judo on him if he doesn't keep walking. We're not two and one, he wanted to tell the Jap boy, but three alone. The pills help me see it, see the differences and connections. Me in my boots and you all over, like the chair inside, reshaping the very skins of creatures in defiance of God's making again and again until the creatures and their maker disappear from us and the only shine is the one we put there, and the only image we see is ourself.

That afternoon he'd stolen a knife from a pawnshop window with the two blades set at three and nine like something to hang over his bed for clemency and had stood with it naked before the mirror and thought the degree to which he needed a woman was some kind of personal record.

He'd shaken three pills out onto the dresser. The kid had said they were for pain, but there was no name he could recognize in the Spanish on the bottle. With his knife he quartered them, then pounded them down with the handle to destroy the time-release mechanisms. He snorted the powder off the thick side of the blade and the burn was as he'd hoped. Then he taped the knife to his hip to wear under his clothes, where he could feel it now.

For blocks and blocks he simply watched his step until he had remembered the exact moment when he'd made himself invisible. It had happened by chance a few weeks ago when he had come to see the steel toes of his boots rubbed bare as two dead eyes staring up at him from the ground wherever he went. He'd bought a marker pen and outlined the matter by drawing lids and lashes but it came off hippie so he spatted them over with black electrical tape, which looked like its own kind of statement though he didn't know what.

Now he knew it had somehow closed the eyes of the world upon him. It had kept him off the maps and under the radars. The knife was a new thing and he would have to see how it went. In his experience steel all of itself could attract trouble but he would not any more be in Sullivan's company without it.

Sullivan. Who did not account for him knowing things cold, like that he was being played for a fool.

The pills conferred a clarity, with the line of things cut harder than what humans could normally perceive, each thing so distinct it made for a greater separation of one thing from the next so you saw that not only were they not connected but the illusion that they were simply could not be maintained.

He passed a funeral parlour that shared a parking lot with an outfit that preserved wedding gowns.

Young girls in church, there was nothing like them.

In his mind he had gone over and over the operation but it wouldn't come together the way Sullivan wanted him to believe. Why would this Pedro want guns? Because he can't move the smack or he'll expose himself, so he trades it for guns, that he can move. If he asks where'd I get them, say Fort Bliss. Bad inventory control. A few automatic weapons, they don't even know they're gone. Just keep talking until he's across. And then it's just a rip-off. Or that's what we want him to think.

"Then he calls in his whole posse and the man whose name shall not pass between us takes numbers and does whatever he does. That's not our concern."

The unnamed man, the one Pedro's sister had stolen from, he had a whole operation moving drugs across the border from the maquiladoras. So why did he need Marks to mule it?

"Because they can't know he's involved. He doesn't need the contraband, he needs the con. So you have to mule it. It's what sells the little badass bandito, man. Just go across, show him the spec sheets, and lead him or whoever he's got lined up back to our side. When they see you're across then they'll come easy for the guns. What do you care anyway? It's fifty thousand dollars. That's more than you get killin princes."

This story repeated with troubling variations every day in person or whenever he called Sullivan's cell.

"This all came together pretty fast."

"It's been in the works the whole time you've been off screwing the border trash. It's all figured, man."

"Sure."

"It's all laid out on the paper. Just don't lose the paper. Everything's figured."

Back in his room he'd removed his boots. As was his custom, he'd laid them left foot forward and pointing towards the door.

The paper was folded into a tent on the night table. Now and then he'd looked at it in preparation for making a decision. It was a photocopied hand-drawn map of downtown Juarez available at the hotel desk. Sullivan had added a few symbols and notes. There was no way of getting from this crude plan to the supposed paymaster with his shipping operation. Sullivan's story was way too elaborate to account for the scribbled map, and because the map was here in hand, then it was the paymaster who wasn't true. Sullivan wanted to rip off the kid, have Marks mule the package, and then rip off Marks himself or worse.

Leaving was an option but then being on to Sullivan's angle might open advantages he would see if he was patient. Times past, when the days made no sense even as they followed one upon the next and now when things came to him a certain way, he understood the base craziness inside each second and believed his seeing it owed to nothing but a belief that the little moments spun the same way as he himself in the endless tumble of his life. The mistake people made was in putting their hand to the craziness instead of letting it run to see what it would say.

He had been granted an understanding and now waited to know what to do with it.

With the church in his sights he felt himself levelling off. From his pocket he took two more of the Mexican pills and swallowed them dry.

He came in just after the start of the service and sat in the back. He could tell right off by the singing that it wasn't a wild enough place. There was no feel at all. What you wanted was girls in groups, a little group of friends with their whispers and giggles, but all the girls were with parents or boyfriends, and nobody anywhere whispered a thing.

Before long he gave it up and left. When he saw a car parked with its wheel on the curb he was inspired to put the hotel Bible under the windshield wiper. He walked uphill with the night sky running now to the horizon. Behind him on the electric plain the border was marked only by the line where the lights burned a little greener in the distance. He caught a bus and stayed to the end, found himself walking along the shoulder of a service road past five or six indistinguishable roadhouses with college kids and cowboys gone loud with the misperception they had the world by the balls.

The bar he turned towards was set off from these by a dark lot and a hand-painted sign saying Nine Acres Prime. It was called Busters. There were tables along the bare walls and a huge open area with square pillars running to risers at the far end. It looked like one of those whore joints for the Mexican workers. The particular dimness was yellowed in the forward reach of light from the bar, where a few staff in aprons leaned on their elbows.

Two girls at one pool table, the other tables empty. From outside came a looping murmur of voices hollowed out that wouldn't form clean. The music was recent enough that he recognized it only from passing doorways and car stereos, but the jukebox speed was off so that for a moment the slow sounds and fast pool-ball colours made you feel submerged over reefs off some island.

He took a seat at the bar and plucked the menu from the clip. The bartender was an older guy, completely bald. He took the order without a word back, then returned with the Wild Turkey.

"You want a pool table?"

"No."

"Clifford over there's looking for someone to split a table with him." He tossed his head at a lightly sweating fat man down the bar. "Sometimes I let him play free but I'm not a charity."

"Me neither."

Marks downed half his drink and swivelled to look at the girls. They looked just legal, a black one and a big-haired brunette. They couldn't really play and he was in love with them. The brunette bent over her shot and from the cleavage of her blouse a leather necklace swung free. Little longhorns made of jade. Some rancher father or boyfriend would have given it to her back in the town she was from, two hundred miles from here. The other girl was her hometown friend and they were both feeling a bit crazy to be on their own and each a little afraid though they wouldn't let on.

The black girl saw him watching and smiled at him before looking away and he felt their whole night with him together hitting him in waves.

"You want on the list to send them a drink?" The bartender apparently had nothing to do but presume to know his thoughts. "Girls like that can practically live free if they want."

"We only want them to drink free," said a man who had just seated himself between Marks and Clifford. "Our intentions aren't really honourable."

"Hey, mister," said Clifford to the man between them, "you wanna split a table?"

"No thanks."

Marks decided he wanted the girls, both or either one. Nothing located you in time like a shooting pain or pussy.

"I don't know pool," said the new arrival. "I know horses. I'm a Kentucky man."

"Bluegrass and all that," said the bartender.

"That's right. Former famous family. We have our own governor's house. A local joint even named a hamburger after us."

So there would be echoes yet to come. Marks turned and glanced at the man. He wore a jean jacket. He was big and square and a little familiar maybe, but just the way anyone was.

When his sandwich came he ordered a second drink. The table numbers hung from filament wire on the light fixtures and swung a little in the air forced from the open ducts along the ceiling. The number above the girls' table had flipped around. It was the only number turned away from him, the number ten. He thought of the way the second hand on that girl Lea's watch would back up on the ten. In all things, a slippage in the works. He would take her clothes off and then pin her down, he never bothered with the watch.

The man between him and Clifford was eyeing him.

"Sorry," the man said. "I'm just trying to think where I know you from. I've seen you before."

"I don't think so, man."

"No, I'm pretty sure. You ever been to Montana?"

And Lea had just crossed his mind.

"That's not me."

"What about Denver then?"

Marks turned. He thought the man would reach out his hand for a shake but he did not.

"The name's Russ Littlebury," he said.

"Jack Marks."

"Do the names mean anything to us?"

"Not to me," said Marks.

"Me neither. But I can't place your face, but I've seen you. Maybe you're a friend of a friend."

"Yeah, maybe."

So now he was not invisible, though he still had the knife on his hip. He had a bright and shining thing that others would never guess at.

"Well, whoever we are, it's good to see you again." The man took to looking at him in the mirror behind the bar. "You're not famous, are you?"

"Look, I never been to Montana or Denver. I don't know you."

He saw him nodding into his drink, smiling at it.

"The day I'm famous," said Littlebury, "I'll be dead."

As if the words promised a bad night, Clifford got up and started away. The brunette waved bye at him and said his name and Clifford winked and smiled at her. The connection was hard to put together.

It was the two of them at the bar now. They were drinking, neither apart nor together, an empty stool between them, glancing at one another in the mirror sometimes eye to eye without turning face to face. Marks knew he should leave, just walk over to the girls and say the things he knew to say. He knew he should but he didn't.

"Jack Marks," said Littlebury, aloud to himself. "What the hell. It's not like I especially want to rake through my past."

"It's not that kind of bar anyway," said the bartender. "You check your baggage at the door."

"Left luggage," said Littlebury. "Just the sinister stuff."

"Well, if it's sinister I could probably hear you out," said the bartender. Marks was liking him less and less.

"It's old, old stuff. A girl gets pregnant, a man runs off. This one comes down to meet a friend who's just an asshole in an El Camino."

Jesus H. Christ. Whatever it was down here, it just would not let him be. He would not be turned away from knowing what he knew, however much he was set upon by connections.

"Troubles ensue," said Littlebury.

"They always do. Did he run off because of the girl or the friend?"

Marks stood with his drink. He intended to move out on the floor to one of the small tables near the girls but he was feeling light-headed. He steadied himself on the bar and tried to focus on them. They looked up and smiled at him and exchanged a little glance.

"You just like to watch?" the brunette asked.

He felt Littlebury still following him in the bar mirror.

The black girl said something to him he didn't exactly hear. For all their beauty, they weren't going to be enough to free him from whatever was happening now.

"I'm not saying the story hangs together. The coherence of lived life is largely illusional. If it exists at all, it's in a lineage that I'm not worthy of and will not extend."

"You got a girl pregnant and left her?" the brunette asked Littlebury. So they had been listening, they were a part of this too.

"I left her and *then* she said she was pregnant. I don't know if I believe her."

"So what do you do if she is?"

"I don't know. She's pretty young to be on her own. What would you do if you were the father, Jack?"

"I don't know the girl," said Marks.

"She's up in Helena. A wild Christian girl."

The room wheeled on him as if to make trouble. He finished his drink but the glass didn't feel right in his fingers. It was the pills playing tricks. The man was probably speaking Spanish and the pills were translating it all wrong.

"They end up with alot of kids, those kind," said the bartender.

"I confess I sort of played her. You figure out the one thing a girl believes and then make yourself into that thing."

Pills or not, he was into something here. He crossed the floor and only then saw the lights and the ring itself framed below the exit sign. In the open air out back was a small floor-show audience of ranchers at dozens of tables running halfway around an empty bullring and he knew at once the sort of place he'd found. A waitress in tight jeans winked at him and pointed to a table, where he took a seat and scanned the faces in fear of any he might recognize.

Littlebury would appear again, he knew. Marks seemed to know a lot of things but he had trouble hanging on to them.

He knew that if he left the bar now he'd just keep going clear out of the city. But to leave would make him a loose end and he didn't want to be made like that if he was wrong about Sullivan. He needed space to think. Never in his life had he had space to think.

There was a cheer as two blue heelers were led through the patio to the ring.

If Littlebury was an old soul come back to haunt him from some distant part of his past, an old soul in the person of a complete fucking stranger, then he should pretty much run for his life. But if he was just spooking himself as he sometimes did, if he didn't respect the actual world that existed outside his head, then he would either make the right move for the wrong reason, or the wrong move that would have very bad consequences for him down the line. If he did the wrong thing, then the next time someone from the past showed up, it would be like in the movies except he wouldn't be around for the credits.

From somewhere unseen a rodeo announcer commenced the spectacle. When the gate opened a young cowboy immediately lost his rhythm and was tossed violently to the ground. People yelled encouragement and applauded as the kid got up and the clowns and dogs led the bull through the exit gate.

The next rider was to be a woman named Darlene. The announcer took pains to insist that she was no novelty act. Marks could see her on the bull's back nodding to go but the men wouldn't open the chute until the introduction was finished, and it ran on another thirty seconds, with the bull slamming her against the bars the whole time. When they finally opened the gate the bull threw her with the first move and then stepped on her hard. Then the bull didn't want to clear the ring. It was some time before the men could drag Darlene off.

At the table next to him an economy-size plastic bottle of Listermint filled with some clear liquid had taken up a route among five young men with ball caps on backwards. One of them saw Marks spot the bottle. He offered it, and Marks took a long pull of some hair-trigger substance and then handed it back. The one who took it now smiled and nodded at Marks as if maybe they knew each other, though if he thought that he was a little stupid. Otherwise he was just making an investment and was maybe a little smart.

The one Hispanic among them was into a story and included Marks in the address. He turned out to be from some town in the mountains. He said at one time his family were the only Mexicans above six thousand feet in all of Colorado. His mom taught high school and his dad was a litigator.

"He gets alot of business from people suing stupid bar owners." He gestured at the ring and smiled. "They're everywhere. Bull riding, live badgers loose on a dance floor. He represents the victims' families."

"He's lying," a kid in a Texas Rangers cap chimed in. "But I knew a guy who wrestled gators for tourists."

"Hell, everyone knows someone like that."

The announcer assured the crowd that Darlene was fine. No one bought it.

"Ape wrestling. *Bear* wrestling. Shit, I *saw* a guy get his spine snapped because *someone forgot to muzzle the bear.* Can you fucking believe? It had all its claws and teeth plucked out but it had these *lethal* gums. Old bear just clamped onto his head and shook him like a scarecrow with his legs all slack and flying around already useless. It was embarrassing."

They mumbled in understanding.

"You ever been to a snake-handling establishment?"

It was Littlebury. He'd taken a seat at Marks's table and had made an audience of the others.

"You mean one of those hillbilly churches?" asked the Hispanic. He seemed by his tone to take Littlebury for a Bible thumper.

"I've seen miracles in church. What about you, Jack?"

"I don't know."

"When I'm fourteen my aunt takes me and my cousins to her church and I see a young guy get his leg healed right in front of me."

"Bullshit," said one of them.

"It's true," said Littlebury. "And then I see how my cousin and all her girlfriends are in love with this kid. And I take note."

He smiled for them and they understood now and began laughing. One of them was reminded of a church story of his own but Littlebury pressed on to the end.

"Nowadays if I'm feeling lonely, I just limp into the right kind of church on Sunday morning and get myself healed."

This was the funniest thing in the world to them. They laughed like demons. Marks understood there were forces assembling here, marshalling against him.

The way to pull the knife involved crossing his arms low down with each hand on a hip, which is how it looked, sort of hip hop, like someone was pointing a camera at you.

When the laughter let off Littlebury said some last words on the subject.

"Then I tell the prettiest girl I'm a prophet."

Marks spun around and faced him.

"Who the fuck are you?"

"Hey," said one of the men.

"Who are you? What d'you want from me?"

"Where do I know you from, Jack? You gotta help me remember. Was it Helena or Denver? Was it back in Michigan as kids?"

He had his hand on the handle but before he could commit, an elbow was brought up hard under his jaw and it sent him to the floor. His senses abandoned him, it was as if he were still falling. The blood in his mouth made him think to scramble away but his legs wouldn't listen.

The pain came on delay. For a second he believed he would die. He looked up to see Littlebury standing back looking at something on the floor. The men in caps had formed themselves into a ragged line and the girls had come out, the black one holding the white one, who was covering her face with her hands like in prayer. He saw what Littlebury saw. In the distance, his knife and the splayed tape like a badly tended wound in the floor.

Marks got to his feet. The way parted. He felt he might pitch forward again as he started walking to the door but kept upright, without thinking, just moving back into the bar and out into the street without looking back and his name in birdsong amid the voices flocking behind in derangement as if cast from a lone tortured soul to the room in general.

He was not followed. A long time later he came to himself in an alley, weeping. Either he was going off the slope or the pills flying him there, or tonight he had met an angel of some kind and then made to cut him. Maybe he'd been right all along, and there was a reason for him being here. Maybe it was as it seemed a place where all parts of his life came together, and in his stupidity he had found confirmation where the worst in him would want it, in the promise of a payoff, when all he had had to do was wait for the signs to collect and arrange themselves before him.

He had slept in alleys but they had never before seemed like the bottom. From each end shadows cast long from street lights laying into one another head to head, water marks on back walls where the rain liked to run. Transformers overhead in their stations on squared frames like gallows. Put it together however you would. He had been given his one-to-one and he had come up no better than the scared shithound he had always been.

Not until he was in a cab going back to the hotel did Russ experience a faint nausea. The man had pulled a knife. That's what it was called, "pulling a knife." Where Russ came from people did not carry concealed weapons that could get you killed in a bar fight. But when the thing was lying there on the floor, what he realized wasn't that he should have expected it, but that he had. A hard fact skidding across the floor as if all along it had been his only intention to bring it out into the open.

Hitting Marks was an admission, a statement about himself he could not otherwise articulate.

He was breathing too hard again. This would keep happening to him until some minor history did him in or until the jagged shard in his memory was finally turned up. He thought of Tara on the coast. She was still there vividly, though he knew she would never imagine him anywhere like this.

Back at the hotel he went straight into the bathroom. He kneeled on the cold tile floor and dry-heaved until at last he sat and leaned back against the tub and felt in the cool porcelain across his back a slow dawning of recognition.

The weather had been warm and grey. For a week Russ had been outside only to start up the trucks but now the temperature had climbed almost to freezing and he went out that afternoon and unplugged the block heaters just as the delivery of groceries arrived. He helped the kid carry the bags into the house, some local son he didn't know, and Russ could think of nothing to say and the kid said nothing, and seemed a little nervous. They nodded at one another.

Jean had been up to cook for him twice a day and spell him with Mike in the early evenings, when Russ would have a drink and call his uncle with an update, and then call Lyle and Jackie just to talk. Skidder had stopped coming around three days earlier. He wasn't answering his phone. Lyle reported that he'd gone by Skidder's shack twice but hadn't found him home, and his truck hadn't been spotted around town. Russ supposed Skidder had seen the end approaching and run off somewhere.

That evening Russ was too tired and Jean had made the calls. She said something about having arranged for a nurse to visit for a few minutes the next day but Russ hadn't been listening and she explained again and he told her there was no point, really. The nurses made no difference now. She gave him a hug and said she'd be by around noon to wait for the nurse herself.

After she had left he filled the tub and went into Mike's room and stood there for a time. The man hadn't been fully awake since before Skidder left. One minute he would open his eyes and seem nearly lucid, and the next he was murmuring in his sleep. Russ went to him and pulled the sheets down and got on one knee and rolled him into his arms. He stood and Mike opened his eyes and looked at him and Russ carried him to the bathroom.

He bathed him. He carried him back to bed. Then he returned to the bathroom and cleaned up and filled the tub again. He took his clothes off to bathe himself but instead sat on the floor against the tub and heaved softly as if to cry. He looked down at his body in wonder that Mike could be weightless in his arms and yet he himself for all his strength was nothing at all. He had almost disappeared from present time, existed only to do what needed doing. By the time he was dressed again he had achieved a near-perfect absence that he felt must be what some called courage. It opened a possibility that he had been blind to.

He didn't begin to return to the present until the next morning, when he called the doctor. The South African intern was thirty-five minutes coming four blocks. They agreed it was the expected thing, and the doctor went in to examine the body, and emerged and nodded to him and said he could call the undertaker. He seemed in a hurry to leave but stopped in the entrance-way looking back at the prints he'd tracked across the carpet. "Sorry about the snow." Russ nodded. He assumed a wooden bearing and waited for the question. "So, in the end, was he having a lot of the morphine?" He was too weak to say what he needed, Russ said. The last day or two, he was too weak. "But you gave him the morphine." He had as much as I thought he needed. I'm no medical expert. "No. Of course not." What happened was the expected thing, wasn't it, Russ said. He would make the intern say it again. He was just a kid, really. Out of harm's way here in Canada. But he'd never imagined a place like this. Wasn't it, Russ repeated. "Yes, it was. Yes."

They were only hours, maybe a day or two of dying that he had taken from his father. He had merely brought the end on a little sooner, a liquid compression of time. He told himself that the act was not uncommon. He'd given him the dose and kissed him on the head and gone to the bathroom and washed up. In the mirror he'd seen he was something of a wreck. It was oddly comforting that he did not look like a man who was equal to what he had been going through. Then he got into the chair and gathered a blanket around himself and sat reading Xenophon.

Marks had the key in the door to his room before he knew there was someone there. The door to the next room was open and at the end of the hall, in front of the fire-escape door, the man Littlebury was asleep in a chair.

Marks stood motionless, silent. Then, for no reason that he could see, Littlebury awoke and recognized him.

"I owe you an explanation."

"I don't need one," said Marks.

He turned the key in the lock.

"It's not such a mystery. I can explain it."

"I'm telling you not to."

Littlebury stood.

"All right."

Russ came to the open door. Marks had turned on the bedside lamp and was at the dresser, and then the hall light closed behind Russ and they were in low shadows and half-shadows. As Marks turned and stepped away he reached back and as if for luck brushed his hand along the curved, narrow shoulder of the radio. He sat at the little table by the window.

Russ came across the small room. He pulled the chair opposite Marks well back from the table and sat. Marks looked out at the city. There was no flight in him now. Some focus had resolved around the moment.

Russ had played stupidly on Marks's paranoia. They were both lucky it hadn't ended worse. The sensible thing was to calm him down with an explanation.

"Maybe you should hear me out."

Marks looked at him briefly, then back out the window.

"They say your past catches up to you. Whichever way you want to explain it, that's what this is here."

Russ felt the questions reassembling. This man really was opaque.

"What were you planning to do with that knife?" Russ asked.

"Little thing like that wouldn't hurt you bad. You just mixed me up, is all. It would of just settled me to know you could bleed."

Marks had had his intuitions turned against him. In that way, at least, he had been brought closer to Lea. Russ didn't know the contents of Lea's message but he had already told Marks of her pregnancy back in the bar. What else did he need to know? Why let Lea expose her heart to him? But not giving Marks the letter would be disrespectful of her faith, in Marks, in the god who she believed looked over her. She thought of Russ as just her earthly guardian, but he knew he was her only one.

"I'm here on behalf of Lea Bollins."

Marks smiled.

"What, are you her consolation man? Maybe you can't stand she says my name when you're on her."

Apparently he meant it as a joke. He wanted to share a little laughter. Earlier Russ had followed him from the hotel to the church and watched him assess the crowd in its devotions, looking for girls. What would I have done, Russ thought, if he'd found one?

He produced the envelope and tossed it onto the table. Marks beheld his name for a moment.

"I'm just here to give you a letter. I'm not anything to her, and I'm not an omen of anything."

"Sure you are. Everyone is."

"I forgot. You're a prophet."

"I see what I see."

"Then you already knew she was pregnant."

Marks laughed meanly.

"Is that the message? Man, she really played you."

"Here's where you tell me you never laid a hand on her."

"You don't get it. That's why I left. She said I knocked her up."

Russ had expected him to lie in his defence, but there was no lie in his voice.

"She was setting the two of us up for this right here."

"Why would she do that?"

"Maybe she thought you wouldn't bother finding me if I was just a guy who ran off. You'd think if I found out she was pregnant I'd come back."

"But if there's no message, why find you at all?"

"She thinks you're God's instrument, man. A big sonofabitch like you could probably wrestle me back up to Montana the way God wants you to. But you don't want me up there anyway. The girl is fucking mixed-up, man."

Marks took hold of the envelope, opened it, and read the letter. It made no impression on his features. He folded it and put it back in the envelope and set it aside. He got up and turned on the radio. There was a moment's pause between the click and the incoming sound of an early blues recording, the single guitar and the voice beginning in the distance and then arriving at once fully present. The voice was there no more than a few seconds before he turned it off. Russ thought he was witnessing some behavioural tic, but Marks had heard something. It would

258

have been the elevator cage opening in the hall. Then there came a knock on the door.

Marks went to the door and spoke through it. The desk man had come to collect for the night and Marks told him he'd pay in the morning, that he'd have money before noon, that he'd missed nights before and had always made them up, that he knew the desk man wasn't the kind to turn him out in the middle of the night. He spoke for a time and then asked the man when his shift ended so he could be sure to give him a gratuity for his understanding, but there was no response. The desk man had left the scene some time ago.

"You showed Lea someone burning in a car."

"So what if I did? We've all seen footage. Every day's a horror show."

Russ said nothing. Marks watched him a moment – nervously, Russ thought – then went to the little sink and ran water into a face cloth.

"I'm out of weapons. And you're not the kind to hurt me just for being what I am."

"And what's that?"

"I don't know the name. I doubt there is one that'd cover it all."

Russ could leave now. There was nothing more for him here. He sat there. Here it was, then. He tried to muster a little feeling for the man. He was aware of wanting to feel goodness, but the truth was that he'd never felt so cold.

Marks took his shirt off and squeezed the cloth at the back of his neck and rubbed under his arms. He took two plastic cups and carried them to the dresser, and as he went about pouring the drinks, Russ saw the scar at the base of his back. It was small and fine, barely raised above the skin. There was no human shape, but a slightly curved vertical line. A crooked stroke like some West Semitic vowel, the earliest of I's.

Marks found a clean shirt in the dresser and put it on. He brought the drinks to the table and sat.

"I knew this educated girl once. She told me a woman is seven times more emotional than a man. A scientific fact."

"That sounds about right."

"How can they stand it? A heart seven times the size of ours. I'd just curl up and let go." He raised his cup. "Here's to our girl Lea."

Russ didn't raise his cup. He watched Marks drink.

"She aint pregnant, you know. I can tell when a story's got a hole in it. I know there's a hole before I even see it."

"You see what you see."

"I see it but I don't always read it right. Earlier tonight I was all mixed-up again, but I see it clear now. The problem is, I don't like what I know is the truth, is that there's just what's here. There's nothin else, nothin beyond. There's just what's here and alot of stories with holes."

He looked at Russ's cup.

"You won't drink in my company, is that it?"

All Russ wanted was to feel something other than he felt, and Marks made it seem less likely with every word. Still, he would wait him out a few more minutes. He took a drink. It was bad tequila.

Marks was looking out the window again.

"You been to Ciudad Juarez, Littlebury?"

"Once."

"It's the shitpipe of the hemisphere. Nobody over there wants to learn anything that'll get them in trouble. And the young girls all get murdered."

"I've read about it."

"They're even running out of water." Russ looked out at the view he knew from his window. "I'm supposed to believe a kid over there named Pedro's getting killed tomorrow."

The words separated Russ from any hope he had that the night would end cleanly.

"Don't waste the story on me."

"It's true. He doesn't know what's coming. I know the feeling."

Russ couldn't see why Marks would lie to him now. And whether the story was true or not, he knew he'd wait to hear it. He drank his drink and listened.

It was a version of one of the stories Russ had heard in the bars, a popular one apparently. The young man Pedro had a sister working in a maquiladora that shipped north, among other things, engine cylinders packed with cocaine. One day her foreman called her into his office and tried to impress her by showing her a brick of coke in his desk. He then told her to take her clothes off. She refused. Before the repercussions, only days later some men marched into the plant and hauled the foreman away, and when the office was empty, the girl went in and took the coke.

Marks shook his head. "She thought she was making some great play when she was just setting herself up to get fucked over. And now her brother's trying to get rid of it under the radar."

"And you're the one who's gonna fuck him over."

"No. Me and Pedro get fucked over together. But I won't have any part of it. Not any more."

"And what happens to him?"

"He was screwed the minute his sister had her big idea." He blinked a couple of times as if remembering something. "She thinks I'm her brother's friend. She's a pretty thing, too. Got a little puppy on a string."

Russ looked away. The Virgin that Marks had stolen from the bus driver had been tacked to the wall above the bed. The story had not been told in the spirit of relinquishment or redress. Marks didn't even seem to care if Russ believed him. Of course he didn't care. He placed no value on anyone else's faith, not of any kind.

Marks looked at him, and nodded at Russ's drink and smiled. Russ saw that his hand was holding the near-empty cup as it rested on the table, but he couldn't feel it in his hand. He lifted his hand away and it drifted slightly outward. Then it seemed he hadn't lifted it away at all. Whatever was happening was happening fast. He knew he was in some trouble. Marks had him now, and would do what he wanted.

Across the room, a folded piece of paper steepled on the table by the lamp cast a shadow that loomed enormously behind Marks. It seemed to billow as if the lamp were a flame or the wind blew there and out through the wall and over the city lights that moved now like stars on a dark sea.

Russ ventured to speak.

"You're under a black sail, Marks."

"What's that mean?"

"Anyone can see you're bad news from a long ways off. You can't fool people any more. There's a black sail. Plain as day."

"Don't you sonofabitchin curse me."

"I just see what I see."

He meant to smile for him but Marks was no longer there and Russ was left to nod at the sail upon the wall that moved with the looseness in the structure of human event. A life could move in any direction, lose its line, grow to twisted shapes. His own life with its many worlds and the many people he was in them. They all swam above him now and he understood the persistence of the unknown and its place in all things. On the wall floated the strange continents and shifting topographies of a perfect hell where his soul guided or only seeming so and completely unsponsored would meet others, one after the next, offering up their spontaneous testaments and confessions.

He saw his boyhood dog on a river island tugging at the skeleton of an enormous sand crane until it reared up as if to lift off. The heel of his uncle's hand punched the throttle on an old truck in procession on the unimproved cemetery road with the stones scattering against the undercarriage as he remembered hiding in the machine shed with his hands over his ears as the hail spent its full worth against the steel roof. Dimeless before bakery sweets and inside the case the hand of a woman who let him look but only teased she'd sneak him a taste. The upright tombstone that was his mother. Two little sisters in plastic shoes fallen and crying that they couldn't walk home up the icy street and a quiet sheet of the river in spring riding into the trees and shearing them along the bank. The haltscript autograph of an old boxing champion kept safe in the wallet of a downtown drunk. The mortar on a mason's trowel dried hard up on the scaffold in the hours after he fell to quadriplegia like the mud football field baked to stone that tore scabs and left the two-bit scars on the backs of his wrists. At the front of an early schoolroom the queen's photoportrait sitting high above the alphabet with Canada in pink on a map of the world until the forty-ninth became a sickle ooze of blood where the fallen drainpipe sliced the lifeline in his palm. A girl crying in his car over some unspeakable family thing he'd never know.

He felt himself borne up as if he were the one to be harrowed from this hell and above him indeed the light strengthened so that he closed his eyes upon it. He awaited the voice but there was none and then understood it was all around him, it would not abandon him, but he had failed to hear it, and to keep it from going he spoke to it and at once it came down as if to smother him, saying *The choice wasn't yours to make.* But ours is the species that intervenes. That's the way we were made. *You would excuse everything.* Don't speak now when you wouldn't then. We both knew I was the wrong Littlebury for the job. *You were my son.* I still am. *My son the usurper.* I don't pretend to fill your shoes. I never wanted to. *It's not me you've usurped.*

When next he was aware of anything, he saw himself as he was. Sprawled and alone. Before him ran a hallway with darkness clotted in doorways and transoms. He saw the animal, regarded it, finally, with just one question in mind.

Was it a hopeful creature?

I was not equal to my duty. For a moment he emptied himself and the whole broken dream was back floating around him in pieces, just out of reach, but then he returned to the thought like a dog to a cemetery stone. There it was. He had said the unsayable thing, and now his one hope was that something, a consolation, a judgement, almost anything, would follow.

He crossed into Juarez and took the first side street one block west into the red-light district, such as it was, dead in the new morning. A few cars were parked along the curbs, the bar doors facing one another chaindraped, heavy-lidded. It was early enough on the strip that none of the tourists had spilled this way. Feeding from a box on the sidewalk a pariah looked up at him, then returned to the box. A lone man asleep in a car. Russ passed by unremarked.

He'd been awake almost an hour and his head had not surmounted the effects of the spiked tequila. He'd awoken in the chair that he'd dragged out into the hallway to await Marks the night before. The door to Marks's room was wide open. He had cleared out. Russ recalled an iron sound in the night and pictured now Marks with his duffel bag passing by Russ and out the door Dillinger once may have used, unfolding the last flight of the fire escape, climbing down, dropping into the alley, running off, a fugitive from his debts and their solicitor.

On the table, Lea's letter.

> My Dear Jack. I know you didn't want a baby. I see that now. If you come back I will take care of it and not have the baby if that is what God decides. He is looking out

for you and loves you. I love you too. If you can't come back now then maybe some day. I think I will always be in Helena. Love Lea.

He looked out at the morning. It was early.

By the lamp was the paper that had cast the shadow of the sail the night before. It was a map of Juarez from the hotel's front desk that listed landmarks and businesses that had some arrangement with the Garrison. Added in the margins were words and phrases in two hands. One was illegible. In the other, someone had jotted "Tuesday morning" on top and had circled the words "Not to Scale." Along the bottom was written, "See P at shoestand." Notations had been added that made a sort of narrative. A dollar sign, a sombrero near the cathedral, a circled X, arrows along the route that eventually curved back onto Avenida Juarez and continued north to the border.

Had Marks not told his story of Pedro, or had Russ not remembered it, the map would have meant nothing. Maybe it meant nothing anyway. But the P, the X, the arrows, they seemed to admit him into a secret, or if not the secret itself, then the knowledge that it existed. The knowledge was enough that the choice to ignore Marks's story and leave for home now was removed. It didn't matter that being in possession of half the facts was no state in which to live dangerously. That he didn't know Pedro or the nature of the trouble, or whether there was trouble, rendered him a carrier of little more than doubt itself. Whatever had brought him into this day hadn't quite prepared him for it.

Onwards, Mariscal angled a little off parallel with the strip and the street grew yet quieter into an empty townscape until he'd made Ugarte and approached a busier intersection where the morning finally broke from its shadowpace with men gathered at the corners watching the early traffic. Some wore jackets or down vests. The younger ones had their hands in their pockets.

The map grew more precise. Up ahead were the cathedral and the square. On his left he saw the sign over the back entrance of an alley. Mercado Tipico, Curios. He saw the Compraventa Dolares a few doors farther south. Seated outside on a small box as if waiting for him was the man represented on the map by the sombrero. His head was bare. Small white scars venulated his cheekbones like thumbprints. He looked up at Russ and spoke without inflection.

"You want the cathedral, sir. I can show you. I know the history."

The man spoke to him as he would to every passing tourist, but because he was there on the map, the offer seemed part of some drama already inscribed, as if both Russ and he were players but only the old man knew their parts.

"I just need some information," said Russ. He handed over a ten before asking the question. "There's someone named Pedro. He has one of the shoe stands. I need to know where he's set up today."

There was no movement. Russ began to repeat himself when the man nodded and held up his palm to silence him. Without speaking, he got to his feet and began walking towards Avenida 16 de Septiembre, and it was a moment before Russ realized he was being led. They came out beside a Wendy's across from the square. The man looked east down the street briefly before turning to face the cathedral. He pointed at it as they spoke.

"Look at the cathedral," he said. Russ did so. "When you look at me, see beyond, on the sidewalk. You see the next block."

Russ looked over the man's shoulder. On the next block was a magazine vendor and two shoeshine stands.

"Do you see?"

"Yes."

"The last one. The farthest one. You understand?"

"Is that him there now? Is that who I'm looking for?"

The man nodded. He let his hand fall.

"Thank you."

The man simply left him there and walked off, not back to where Russ had found him but across the street to the square. Russ waited a few seconds, then went across himself and feigned an interest in a table of knives and rings. The old man was nowhere to be seen.

At the shoe stand a large black tourist in shorts was enjoying the sight of having his sandals shined. His smaller friend stood by laughing as the big man spoke through a cigar at the kid working over his feet. From the square Russ could not get a clear view of Pedro. His lowered head exposed the green and black lines of a tattoo serpent reaching along his shoulder and up his neck. He seemed to be working alone.

"Good morning."

The vendor was Russ's age. He spoke from his stool.

"Good morning."

He said something in Spanish and gestured at the trays of silver and gold.

"Estoy mirando," said Russ. The desk man had prepared him with phrases days ago, and tested him whenever he paid up. "Solamente."

He moved on to the next stall, where a young man on a cell-phone smiled and nodded at him and pointed to his wares. Blankets and belts, ponchos.

Pedro was still bent over his work but the tourist was losing interest in the shine, looking up and down the street as if for the next entertainment. His friend was shaking his head at a poster on a wooden light pole.

Russ checked his watch.

"A blanket for your truck."

"I don't have a truck, thanks."

"For your horse, then." The young man smiled. He was being ironic, for his own amusement, perhaps. Good for you, thought Russ.

He moved on to the curb and stood waiting to cross as soon as the black man paid up and left. The moment was without token. Russ had no feeling for what would happen next, sensed no fleeting memories transforming into an inevitability. He would have thought that by his very movement and the sheer fact of his having come so far he was owed a little surety, that ahead was a consequence nearly fated or at least seeming so. But it turned out that his mind was not in any shape this morning.

A car slowed to let him cross but he waved it on.

The shine was done now. Pedro looked up. It was a boy's face.

The tourist handed over a couple of bills. He caught his friend's eye and went about making a production of digging out another bill and beginning to hand it over, then snatching it back to hold it aloft in his fingers. Pedro stood and waited. The tourist loosened his sandals and removed them together. He straightened his legs and examined his feet in the cool light and saw them cloven by the black polish.

He waited for Pedro to clean them, but the kid simply handed him a cloth, and the black man rubbed the polish free, smiling to himself and his friend. Then he put on the sandals, pocketed the tip, and tossed the cloth to the kid. As the men walked off,

269

Pedro looked after them for a short time and seemed to say something to himself as he climbed into the vacated seat to await another customer.

So there were at least portents, however cheap. It was not an act Russ especially wanted to follow.

Approaching from behind, Russ could see the mechanics of Pedro's little operation, which came down to two car seats mounted on what looked like a sawed-off church pew. Frayed duct tape t-patched the torn vinyl. The whole set-up involved imperfect retrofittings and just making do.

Pedro was already looking at him by the time Russ came around and nodded a greeting. He was very thin, with green eyes. He couldn't have been even twenty years old. Russ expected to be hustled but Pedro said nothing.

"Can I get a shine?"

He looked into the street, then hopped down and offered what was apparently the preferred seat and sat himself on a little footstool.

Russ had barely settled when Pedro set to work on the walking boots. His hands were small and not especially quick but he kept them moving. Right away it was clear he would not make a good job of it, and he didn't care enough even to put on a show. Not once for the first half-minute did he look up at Russ, but now and then he gauged the street. Russ found himself looking at the poster. Below the word "Desaparecida" were three photos of a beautiful young girl, a description, a number to contact.

Russ realized some volition was required of him. He tried to make something of the particulars below. Two shallow, open jars of polish, a dummy stash coffee can of coins and bills, a cheese-cloth in plastic, a stack of clean rags, a box of loose laces, a brush.

On the low partition between the chairs hung a small photo of a man in a suit and a couple of dirty rags on nails. A marker pen. A folded canvas bag into which all of this fit.

"What do you want?"

Pedro looked up only after having asked the question.

"Just a shine."

The kid shook his head.

"You ask for me," he said. "Who are you? What do you want?"

Of course it would take a turn like this. Maybe he'd been set up. Maybe it ran clear back to Marks, he'd never know for sure. He was simply adrift in the midst of pure occurrence.

"Somebody I met last night said you were the guy to see for a shine. He said over in Juarez the kid you want is Pedro."

His hands slowed for a moment as he looked up. He seemed to want to believe him.

"You're him, right?"

"I'm Pedro, yes."

"You've got a good spot here. You been here a long time?"

He went back to work on the boots.

"You're not from Texas."

"I'm from Saskatchewan. Canada."

"Canada." He seemed to like the sound of it. "Then I'm right. Do you take Mexicans in Canada?"

Russ assured him that Canada was the place to be.

"It's not for me to go. It's my sister." He interrupted his work to reach into his back pants pocket. He handed up to Russ a photo of a smiling, round-faced young woman, cheek to cheek with a puppy she held awkwardly on her shoulder. The picture seemed intended to manipulate strangers for their help, or even just for a better tip. He handed it back.

In an instant Russ saw that they might all be safe, he and Pedro and his sister. He imagined Pedro handing Marks the photo, and Marks, as he liked to do, using it to inspire a story just to have at hand if he needed it. He'd used it last night to evoke for Russ a world where great forces were at play that no one could be expected to stand against.

Pedro looked up at Russ and then pointed his chin at the stack of rags. He reached down and turned back the top half to reveal a cellphone.

"You see now?" He smiled. "A friend calls and tells me you asked for me. I have friends everywhere."

"Yeah."

"There is no mystery."

The map was from the hotel desk. Russ hoped it had been the desk man who'd written on it.

"I'm staying at the Garrison Hotel. Someone there told me about you."

Pedro nodded.

"Listen." He spoke lower, though there was no one to over-hear him. "You go to the new *mercado*. For gold, if they say two hundred, you say one hundred."

"All right. Thanks."

"See Mr. Mancilla. Booth thirty-one. Say my name."

Up came his hand again, now with the portrait photo. It was an old shot. The man was thin, unsmiling, quarter-turned from the lens.

"I see a resemblance."

"You see what?"

"He looks a little like you. Is he your father?"

"No." Russ handed back the picture. "He is gone, my father."

"Mine too."

Russ saw that the shine had been worked up after all. It was there in place but Pedro kept at it. There was a lesson here about determined attention.

"Is he dead?" Russ asked. "Your father."

Pedro looked up at him now, then down again.

"I think he is dead. Yes."

Russ nodded, though Pedro was not looking at him.

"Mine too."

He had buffed the shoes and now he got out the cheesecloth. A fat young man with small glasses walked by the booth and set down a can of Coke for him, then moved on without a word.

"My sister is in trouble." That simply, it all fell apart again. Pedro said nothing for a moment, though now he did not pretend to concentrate on his work. "She made a big mistake."

"I see."

Russ tried to recover the possibility that the kid was playing him, but it was gone. Pedro seemed to want to say more but fell silent. Then his hands stopped. He was done with the cloth now. The shine was apparently over.

He stood and gave Russ room to step down. When Russ offered a ten he hesitated a second and then took it.

Pedro produced a cigarette and lit it. He offered one to Russ. It was a courtesy only, and Russ declined, sensing that the kid felt he'd said too much already, and wanted him to leave before he said more.

"Pedro, I met a man named Jack Marks in El Paso last night. Do you know him?"

He looked at Russ quickly and then bent down to the rags and folded them back over the phone, then unfolded them again and put the phone in his pocket.

"No."

"If you know him, if you have any arrangement with him, then you should know that he's gone. It's not happening."

For a moment it seemed Pedro would try on a smile but it never came up.

"I don't know this man."

"He's a coward. So is his friend Sullivan. They're nothing but trouble. You can't trust them. Marks told me you'd get hurt today."

Pedro looked at him one last time and then turned away and looked at the cigarette where he cupped it in his hand.

"I need my seat back."

He stubbed the cigarette on the step that served as his table and put it back into the pack. When he took out his cellphone and walked off down the block, Russ felt himself forgotten.

About forty minutes past the time when Russ could have been back in El Paso to check out of his room, he spotted the El Camino moving south down Avenida Juarez. Sullivan drove and the other man Russ had seen the day before rode shotgun. Russ stepped from the doorway of the Yankee Bar and crossed over as the car turned left on Mejia and stopped at the curb. Sullivan jabbed the heel of his hand against the steering wheel and swore and the fair-haired one got out and looked around. For a second he paused over Russ, watching them from his position, then climbed back in even as the car started away.

Russ moved south along the strip with men calling him from stalls and then calling the others he walked past. The light seemed to fail on the buildings, became sallow, convalescent. He would remember this morning, whatever happened next, as belonging to a certain value of light. He turned onto the avenue and looked along the run of streetside shops with the buildings jury-rigged and jammed shoulder to shoulder all facing the square in their chance assemblage.

Almost two blocks from the scene, he heard the intervening pedestrian and street traffic, a nearby conversation between two well-dressed women who liked to laugh together, a hawker across the street, so that the sounds from what he witnessed came too weak and broken to make out. Cars and trucks turning a block distant interrupted the line of sight, leaving him a view of the men in changing tableau and the figures that seemed to insist a meaning be found in their interjacence.

The car pulling up with the blond man in the back now, sitting on a canvas sheet. Pedro stepping forward with his arms crossed, Sullivan out and almost even with the back of the car, Pedro obscured by the stall. Pedro now with his back turned to Sullivan, his arms still crossed, and the blond man intent on his face.

Pedro looking down the street to see Russ watching.

The image of what happened then, or so it seemed a minute later as Russ lost himself in the stream towards the border, will remain laid over all that comes after. Pedro looking into a shop window. Then all at once turning and releasing his hand, long with the knife, and Sullivan having caught the arm safely, though Pedro keeps turning his body and his other hand. He has delivered a punch to no effect. The blond man swinging out of the car, stepping forward as Sullivan now holds both of Pedro's arms, and coming around in front, and with a motion beginning below his hip, his fist closed around something that can't exactly be seen, lifting a hand into Pedro's side.

The face stopped, wordlessly annunciatory. The picture, as Russ thinks of it, is static and composed and utterly knowable, the mind resolved in its most sudden apprehensions.

Pedro is down, Sullivan and his partner in flight across the street to the square as other young men from the streets and doorways take up the chase. A small crowd closes the scene.

"The work is done."

It was the man from the park bench, Camillo. He wore the same blue suit. He stepped past Russ without looking at him and moved on towards the gathered crowd, speaking into a walkie-talkie. Russ wasn't certain that he himself had been addressed.

He watched as six or eight young men, maybe Pedro's friends, maybe not, ran after Sullivan. Soon they were surrounded by others, only slightly older, and tackled, handcuffed. Through the crowd Russ had the impression that no one was attending to Pedro. By the time the traffic cleared and the crowd began moving again he saw that Pedro was gone. There was no commotion, no sign that he'd ever fallen. Camillo and the police, or whoever they were, were all across the street in the square. The young men with their hands cuffed behind them were being made to sit in a row. Pedro was not among them. He hadn't been stabbed, Russ decided. He'd had the wind punched out of him and fallen, then gathered himself and run off.

As if the weak pedestrian tide were enough to sweep him along, Russ found himself moving north. Even now he understood that the events were changing on him as he worked them over. He didn't know what had happened or why, or what his part was, if he had one. What was Camillo's involvement in this? And whom did he take Russ to be? Had Pedro's seeing him there, watching, confirmed some misconception in the kid's mind?

Whatever had gone down, he knew only what it had looked like in jump-cut actuality. Like a movie, as people were in the habit of saying. Except a little less dramatic, a little confusing, too sudden. It was like a form of local street theatre, badly blocked and paced. So which is the world as it is, and which the world pretended? In most places, such scenes were the givens, Russ told himself, and even for those who lived in them, the safer, domesticized territories had always been a little make-believe, perched on imaginary footings.

It was no surprise to him, then, that as he approached the bridge he became aware he was being followed. It was Pedro's friend, the fat boy with the glasses. He was about twenty feet behind him. Russ looked back twice — there was no attempt to close the gap — and looked again as he fell in line with the others at the bridge. The boy had stopped and was watching him and reporting it all by cellphone.

Along the bridge he walked past the low murals spanked on the concrete barriers and the fire-breathers moving amid the cars and the sniffer dogs held tight by their short-hair partners.

When he was clear, he saw a young woman walking ahead of him. She carried a white paper bag and her jacket was the colour of green that Arizonans call Aztec. She walked at his pace, and if she had turned off and hadn't passed the man standing on the sidewalk looking south, watching Russ, he would have missed seeing him and walked into his ambit.

He was about Russ's age, a large Mexican with a pockmarked face. As Russ slowed the man looked off to his right and Russ saw a younger man start towards him from the opposite side of the street. The way to the east was clear but even as he took it Russ realized his mistake. The streets were empty. There were no cars. The two men were following now and he was in a dead neighbourhood.

The younger man took off running, then reappeared a block north, pacing him. Russ was hemmed in by the border to the south and the older man behind him. At some point he would have to get into it with them unless there were some way of explaining. They had made a mistake to think he was part of whatever was supposed to go down in Juarez. Maybe they thought he was with Sullivan or Marks. Maybe they didn't care who he was.

He turned north. The young man wasn't in sight but he'd be waiting somewhere. The narrowing shadows, the half-sunlit street. He saw where it would happen, an empty, junk-strewn lot up ahead, and when he came to it, he turned to the man behind him and found that the younger one and another, a shirt-less teen, had joined him.

"I don't want trouble. You and I have no problem."

"You got a big problem, mister," said the kid.

"Manny," said the man. Russ couldn't tell if the name was spoken in caution or command. Then the man smiled at him and he felt his stomach tighten.

He thought he could show them his passport if only to prove he wasn't Marks, but it wouldn't matter. They had the fat boy's word that he had been at the scene and had said the names and had some connection to them.

"What's that there?" asked the man. He was looking at the map tucked into Russ's shirt pocket.

Russ handed it over, knowing it only made things worse for him, though he didn't know exactly how.

He started again and walked into the lot as if cutting across it but kept his eyes sharp for something to take hold of. It was only human to fashion a thing from materials at hand.

They'd gone quiet and he felt them ready to close now, but it was already too late. The blow came above his ear. He was on the ground and bleeding. He scrambled forward to all fours and took a kick in the face and another to his stomach but managed to navigate a roll over the broken frame of a child's bed, so that he came up holding an angle iron. He stood.

"You think we're not armed?" asked the man. "A neighbourhood like this?" He smiled and patted his front pants pocket. "If you don't drop that thing I'll have to bring out El Campeón."

Russ shook his head. It was no gamble from where he was standing. They all knew what was next though who could say why.

The kid was holding a hollow pipe and now picked up a handful of dirt and circled slowly. He wanted to make Russ turn his back to the others, but Russ stepped to the side and cut him off so that all but one of the possibilities before them closed.

The kid threw the dirt into his face and ran hard at him to get inside the blow but Russ fought for his sight and shortened the swing and caught him hard in the ribs. Manny cried out and his eyes closed and he fell ungoverned. When his eyes opened, there was surprise in them, and Russ saw that he'd never been hit like that before. The pain had made for a senseless arrangement of features.

Russ dropped the iron and ran.

The man and the other teen started after him.

"Get the truck!" called the man, and then it was just the two of them and Russ was opening ground.

There was no one ahead to cut him off so he took to the street and kept running as he looked and found he was not pursued. The man was back with Manny, hauling the boy to his feet. Manny looked up and saw Russ. He seemed to try to say something but he didn't have his breath yet and his ribs were broken and the words wouldn't form. The man helped him walk towards the street. When the teen arrived with the truck, Russ knew, they would come after him.

He ran west to the market streets and ducked into a shop and watched the traffic. He bought a bandana and wrapped it around his wounded head, and a cheap pair of shades and a Corona t-shirt. Before he left the shop he took his shirt off and put on the t-shirt and tied the other at his waist.

He angled west and north into the downtown, keeping his distance from the square. His wits told him to wait before returning to the hotel.

Into a library. There were five or six people, a young man at the desk who looked up at him only briefly when he entered. In the Mens he washed the blood from his hair and the bandana, and then reapplied it. He saw that the doors had been removed from the stalls and understood there was no place to hide. In the mirror he saw a beaten stranger. He was a thousand miles from last night's dream, the lazy drift of a narcotized mind going out.

When he stepped out he took a book randomly from the nearest shelf and found a seat at a window table, where he sat wondering about the kid Manny and how badly he was hurt. Through the iron he'd felt the ribs give way. People hurt each other with the simplest motions they were capable of. They hadn't even touched but through the iron. He looked at his hand where it rested on the book. He felt the kid there still.

When he had packed his bag, he stopped in the hallway. The door to the next room was still open. He stepped inside. It was as it had been earlier that morning. There were towels in the sink. The plastic cups were still at the table with Lea's letter. On the dresser, traces of white powder.

The top drawer was slightly ajar. He pulled it open. It was empty but for three little pills that must have fallen from the edge. He collected them one by one and tucked them into the small side pocket at his hip. Then he went to the phone and rang the desk.

"This is Mr. Marks. Any messages for me?"

"You owe for two nights."

"I'll square up with you in a minute. Did anyone call?"

"No."

When he set the receiver down he felt suddenly weak.

He was about to sit when he heard the elevator cage open in the hallway and went cold. He couldn't make the fire escape without being seen. He moved to the door and closed it.

Before he could answer the knock, a voice told him not to open the door.

"Who is this?"

"You alone?"

"What do you want?"

"I'm leaving this out here. Wait till I'm gone but don't let it sit around."

He couldn't hear the steps but heard the cage again. When he opened the door he found on the floor a large camera case. He took it into his own room and closed the door and sat on the bed. When he opened the case and saw the money, he knew that the news was bad for everyone. For Pedro, whether or not he'd escaped this morning, and for his sister and his crew, the endings were in place. It was all contained in the case he held, with its certain volume and heft. He could think of nothing to do for them.

It was still morning when he checked out.

V

In the southern middle of nowhere he stood at the edge of a parking lot looking at the long outlet store set back from the I-10. Painted words along the roof promised Moccasins, Black Hills Gold, Southwest Rugs, Dreamcatchers, Ponchos, Fireworks. A man and his wife were arguing over a purchase as they walked to their car. The man carried a stuffed rattlesnake under glass and held up the creature, slung over a few twigs and rocks, while impressing upon his wife the words "natural habitat." On the billboard near the highway was a representation of an early rock drawing of a human with its arms raised to the sky. It was what anthropologists called a hallelujah man, Russ remembered, the earliest picture behind written characters in many languages. Every smart, profane, fallen word had within it the image of the soul longing. Over in the shop it was available on t-shirts and key chains.

He started to dial and stopped, started over and misdialled, and stopped again and hung up the receiver. Years of manual work and yet his hands could lose their precision like their calluses in just two weeks of driving.

Somehow a teenager working under his car in the parking lot made Russ think of the name Chekov.

At a gas station a few miles back he'd washed up again in a bathroom sink and satisfied himself that the head wound had stopped bleeding. Then he tied a bag of ice into a towel he'd stolen from the Garrison and pressed it to the side of his swollen face as he drove.

He had seen a young man maybe get stabbed and here he was that same day looking at nothing. A scene with nothing going down. If he chose to, he might even imagine that he had witnessed a murder, and if not, had at least seen the beginnings of some nasty injustice. And he had some unknown relation to it. Sheer chance might just as easily have hurt him worse or released him unharmed. Either the pieces do not fit together or they do only in an unknowable way. Or the way can be known briefly but not retained. A teenager on a canvas groundsheet gathered at one edge like the stage curtain imperfectly closed in a university theatre in cold Alberta where the shows were all Russian or prairie, sitting there in the dark before the first act with lines memorized from a Latin primer. It is possible to believe there is a defile in the mind where all our past fleeting attentions lie dormant. He hoped he'd registered something in Juarez that would return to him someday with all the answers.

This time he dialled another number.

"Hello?"

"Jean, it's me."

"Well praise be."

He apologized for not having called.

"I was a little worried."

"I know. I'm sorry."

"I thought you probably just needed the time for yourself. You haven't had time for yourself since the funeral."

"I guess not."

A little girl getting out of her father's truck looked back and caught sight of him and hurried ahead to her dad. Only then did he realize he couldn't let Jean see him. In truth, he was unprepared to see her. Even speaking to her now, she was completely unreal to him.

"You just missed Jim Pryor. We were talking about Lea. Jim thinks Grant maybe isn't up to the job of raising her. He said she's her own woman more than he's his own man."

"That's about it. You know what, Jean, I'm not even two hours from you but my flight's this afternoon so I won't have time to come by. Sorry."

"Well, that's too bad. I thought I'd see you."

Russ said he'd call her next week.

"That's fine, dear. You just go home and unwind. It's time you looked after yourself for a while."

He hung up and stepped towards the parking lot and, for just a moment, he had no idea where he was.

At the Tucson airport he dropped off the car and cashed his ticket to Saskatoon. To fly to Helena and then Calgary on short notice would cost over twelve hundred dollars, so he bought a standby to Denver, and planned to put it together from there. He was in no hurry to find company anyway. When the man at the security gate opened the case and saw the money, he checked and rechecked Russ's other carry-on until he was at a loss for further procedures.

In Denver he took a cab to the bus terminal and bought a ticket north. It was a long ride, by night and day. He sat near the front and half slept through until morning and found that a new driver had come in somewhere along the route. The overcast sky was backlit and it lay like sheet metal over the hours. At some point he'd passed into true winter again.

There was a fine dust in his clothes and on his shoes. However many miles it was, he was only a few steps from the desert. He observed that he could use a shine.

In that moment when she hears the man moving downstairs who is not her father she knows how prayer can leave her at times in a burst without words like a puff of smoke from the chimney there in her window and then like smoke be gone and forgotten because the prayer was selfish and full of childish need. Not her father, who'd have called out before he was even inside, who didn't weigh upon the floor so much that you could hear it upstairs like you could Jack. He came in the way Jack would but the moment and the prayer were past and she knew who it would be. She turned off the television.

"Lea?"

When she came down, his suitcase and boots were in the entryway. He was standing in the kitchen in his socks.

She went to put the coffee on and he said no thanks so she put the kettle on for tea and he waited.

"When does your dad get home?"

"After six."

His face was swollen around one eye.

"I didn't call ahead because I didn't know what he knew."

Maybe because she didn't respond he sat at the kitchen table to make himself smaller for her. He was the kind who thought of things like that.

She made up a plate of assorteds and put it on the table. He nodded and took one and she felt him looking at her as she moved to see was there anything to give away. She scalded the little pot and poured it out, made the tea and made up a tray for two though she hadn't asked him. She set it down and sat across from him with the plate and the tray between them making his being here seem formally arranged. They sat in silence just long enough for her to understand that she was out of things to do.

"So I found him, Lea."

"All right. I want to thank you first."

"Okay."

"I guess he's not waiting out in the front yard."

"No."

"And you gave him the letter."

"Yeah." He took two more biscuits in hand. "I saw him read it."

"Whatever you think about him," she said, "whatever he said, it's not for us to question."

There were crumbs on the tablecloth. She got up and swept them into her palm and brushed them into the sink. She was always cleaning up this place she hated. There was nothing of her anywhere but in her room, and not much of her father. It was still after all this time her grandmother's house, with its cut-glass lilacs and sheer lacy curtains in the dining room, and dark, smoky paintings of child angels and impossible fields, and her father hadn't thought to make it his as if to do so were to dishonour his mother or maybe the woman who would have made it hers if she'd had the time. Jack had hated it too, even her room until she put the plush dog in her closet. She'd known not to tell him it had a name.

"So he maybe thinks he won't come back."

"Yes. That's what he thinks. I don't know if he ever intended to, Lea, but he kind of trails trouble around. I guess that's why he's disappeared again."

"Not from God he hasn't."

"But from the rest of us, he has." She sort of knew it. "Did you tell your dad?"

"No."

Sometimes she left things to see if he'd notice. Flies raisined along the windowsill, a lone spot of mildew on the bathroom tile. A little grease on the stove dial that made it hers somehow. When she finally scrubbed it off she worked it over and over until some of the numbers disappeared and it looked like a clock with half a face that she knew the lost positions by heart. She could keep it all running with her eyes closed if she wanted.

"Why not?"

"It doesn't matter any more."

"Jack's coming back or not doesn't change what matters."

She nodded at a space between them.

"What is it, Lea?" He was leaning towards her.

"I really thought I was pregnant. But like you say, there's definite signs, I guess."

"You were never pregnant. You know that now."

"I thought it would make sense that I would be."

It was true in a way. Believing and half believing were almost the same thing.

"Jack was pretty sure you weren't. But not so sure that you didn't scare him off by saying you were."

Of course Jack would tell him.

He looked up at the little painting of the show dog. She should ask about his face but she didn't want to know.

"The other thing. He left some money for you."

"He left money?"

"Yeah. Some. I guess it was all he had."

"I don't need it."

"I'll give it to your dad."

"He's got too much already. It isn't money we need."

"Well, I can't take it across the border."

"Then bury it somewhere." There being money made her feel dirty somehow. "Do you believe he's disappeared from God?"

He didn't answer. For just a second she imagined what it would be like to be in love with this man, but there was something in the way of it so she tried to imagine the kind of woman who would love him. She didn't even know what clothes she'd wear. But she knew she'd like to meet the woman someday.

"You back at school?"

"Everything's like I never left. I knew it would be."

"I'm going to stop in and see your dad."

"Okay."

"He'll invite me back here but I've got a bus to catch."

He asked her for directions to the office. When he was in the doorway she went to the kitchen and came back with a half-dozen biscuits wrapped in plastic.

He thanked her.

"I'll stop in with Jean when we come up in the spring."

"Okay."

He picked up his bag.

"He wasn't what you expected, was he?"

"It was a mistake to expect anything. It's better not to have expectations."

"Do you have him figured out now?"

"All I know is you can't help someone like him, Lea. I'm sorry how it turned out."

She wondered if he thought there was something wrong with her and would it always be wrong, and by spring would she be able to ask him. Until then she would stay clear of vanity.

She was not so smart she couldn't take guidance now and then.

Little by little he disappeared into the falling snow until she couldn't see him through the window and the baby was gone and Jack wasn't coming back. She saw how she could pretend she was back before it all started, like none of it had happened, but it would only be pretending, like a kid would, and she was old enough now that pretending wasn't in her any more. Where does it go? she wondered. It was not the sort of question that she ever committed to prayer but it seemed important now to know the answer before she got any older and forgot the question. Tonight before sleep she would remember to pray for the answer, though she couldn't imagine how it could ever be made clear to her.

When he left the house a wind was blowing off the mountains and wet snow thickened branches and overhead lines, the riggings of fences and schoolyard backstops. By the time he reached Grant's office the lights downtown had come up and he saw in the reception area bright through the window an old man waiting his turn with two young mothers and their children. He went inside and left Grant a note at the desk, saying he'd stopped in but had to make a connection and he'd see him soon enough and he hoped he and Lea were well. He tried to think of one smart thing to say, something that could help Grant with his daughter, but it wouldn't come to him. He was out of smarts, didn't trust them above any other faculty, or any resource he might draw upon to meet the general run of things. For a minute or more he stood still at the desk with the receptionist on the phone and the patients waiting together, ignoring a game show on a television mounted up high near the ceiling. Then he printed his name on the note and nodded a thanks to the girl and he felt her and the mothers and the old man all watching him as he picked up his bag and walked out again into the weather.

Back in the bus station he dozed for more than two hours amid the sounds of coin-operated games and a young couple bickering about years of sly intentions. When the bus finally came and he boarded, the streets had slowed to nothing and it rode the tracks of semi-trailers out onto the interstate with the headlights caught up in the falling swirls until it was up to speed and the snow seemed suspended in the air and the whole world in ashes.

The last stop was in Sweetgrass and the Port of Coutts. A few blocks south was a café that opened an hour before the border did. He waited outside in the snow with his bag until a man drove up and nodded to him and opened it up to let him in. He had the biggest breakfast on the menu, alone in the room with the man in the kitchen making dire predictions about eventual accumulations and clashing systems. It was earlier than it had been in Santa Fe that morning, waiting for Joyce. Of the debts he was coming home with, the one to her at least could be cleared. He owed an apology. He promised himself to write her soon if he could just make it home.

It was still dark.

He fished from the bottom of his bag the book he'd stolen from the library the previous day. He'd simply walked out with it, not absently but with the firm intent to make this randomly chosen object his belonging, if only to serve as a charm, a detail of his appearance that would ward off the dangers out there looking for him.

He could make no sense of the book beyond its appearance. A small, old hardcover with faded lettering almost rubbed out of the canvas. He scraped off the call number taped to the spine. Now he could say it was something he'd bought for a dollar in a second-hand store. He couldn't ask for a better prop.

Seeing it before him now, he knew what he'd decided. He was going to try to cross the border with an undeclared sum of fifty thousand American dollars. He didn't know what he was risking. If he was caught he'd likely have to pay a fine and the duty, or maybe it would be worse than that – the borders weren't what they used to be. It was stupid of him, but the moment he'd seen the money, he knew he'd take it, and when Lea had turned it down Russ realized he'd already imagined uses for it. Everything of any consequence he'd ever done was worked through below the wakeline so that when it surfaced it seemed a revelation, and right in all its parts even when. Even when he knew there were errors of the heart worked into it.

Twenty minutes later the book sat in his lap in a waiting room at the border. If the bus schedules were on time, he had reason to wait another half-hour. Looking down from the wall were the faces of hundreds of missing children and women, most of them smiling, and the men suspected of being involved in their disappearance. Faces on every partition, from knee level to ceiling. Clearly the room was not big enough for all the lost faces, Russ imagined a thousand others that went unposted.

His own face was still pulling away from him. He had been saving the pills in his pocket to get high if one or another kind of pain set in, and though it seemed to be now, he thought he might try to stay lucid the rest of the way.

Only minutes before he was to walk across the border, his wait paid off when another bus pulled in and emptied a half-load of people who looked as tired, if not as bad, as he did. He took the pills from his pocket and considered them, then dropped them into a garbage can. He allowed a line to form and stepped in about halfway.

One man was handling the interviews. Russ gauged him to be in his forties, at mid-career. His eyes, not unfriendly, were crowfooted like those of someone who'd spent years out on the snow. Russ reminded himself to answer only what was asked.

When his turn came, holding his passport and the book in one hand and his bag in the other, he stated his citizenship and said he had nothing more than a Corona t-shirt to declare.

"Where you coming from?"

"Tucson."

"What happened to your face?"

Russ had forgotten to prepare an answer.

"I was playing with some kids. Took a ground ball in the eye."

"What were you doing in Tucson?"

"My aunt winters down there. I drive her down and then bus back home."

"Where's home?"

"Colliston, Saskatchewan."

The man nodded slightly.

"Never been."

He asked for Russ's passport and opened it and stared a moment at the photo, and then a moment longer as if to wait for a passing thought.

"Did you get the runner?"

"Sorry?"

"Your face."

"Oh. No. I didn't even get a throw off."

The man smiled and handed back the passport, and tossed his head to indicate the business was concluded.

All this time he'd felt he was being led by some form or force of his imagining, but now as he rode up through Lethbridge, sleep-deprived, at times memory-shocked or dreaming, he felt unguided, abandoned even, so that when he reached Calgary, because it was open to him to do so, he went east and he went west.

Going east towards home he sat on the right side of a bus with the lamp of winter sun lying low to the south. His dreams kept close to him. They emerged from his thoughts before sleep, the scenes he played out, his way of putting things, not only the words he spoke but the chronology of events he tried to hold in sequence.

Going west, things are distilled, often without transition. He descends by jet to a coastal city lit up under low clouds so that he seems impossibly to be dropping upwards into the sky and the constellations beyond. In the terminal he studies a street map that won't stay still for him and then in the dark he's looking at a house that he can't quite make sense of – the stairs along the outside disappear around a corner and then seem to turn back on themselves like an Escher drawing. Where they finally come to ground he finds no mailbox or light switch. He takes the grated steps without seeing them, in trust, like a thief, and finds a mail slot in the door below the painted-on 2A. Then, as he pushes the note in, he wonders if Tara is alone and what troubles he might cause by reaching her this way, so he withdraws it again and catches the slot so it won't sound and makes his way back down in the dark.

But even as he leaves her door, he opens it and steps inside. It's full night, the windowlight is nothing. A digital clock on the stove reads 11:20. He walks through the apartment to the bedroom where he knows it will be. The door is open. He sees her there, alone, asleep with her back to him. He says her name and she turns. He says his name and then they are naked together and he remembers her.

But going west he has retreated from her door and is in a room somewhere dreaming this, falling hard and headfirst. He's walking through an outdoor arcade with the sound of someone weeping behind him, and when he turns, the figure is lost to the neon lights slurred drunkenly through tears and he knows it's he himself who follows. When he awakes in the dark he discovers his eyes are dry and he's completely at a loss to name his condition, and then it's morning and he's walking through a heavy shore fog that seems born of his spirit with the mere suggestions of cars and people weakly conceived in the light.

He was wide awake now on the eastbound schedule, thinking it all through. For months he had tried and failed to keep Tara from his thoughts but now there was no reason not to admit her. He would never know what it was to be his father – fully human, with regrets and secrets, having suffered great sunderings, yet utterly good. But Tara's goodness was flawed and self-deceiving in ways he understood. It could be an example to him.

There was something building in him again. He hadn't slept well. He returned to the moment of the possible stabbing, the image of Pedro's face looking back at him. The idea was to keep the face before him, and let its after-effects register. Otherwise it would fall through him and return even worse on delay. The longer in coming was the discharge, the harder it was to localize.

The day was failing now, as it would be in an hour or so on the coast.

All he could do was wait it out until he found new consolations conferred upon him from a source he hadn't yet learned the workings of, and so could accept.

It all lay before him. In Falling Creek he asks the driver to let him off by the side of the highway. A young woman gets off with him and they stand together in the four-thirty dark watching the bus roll away, and say hello and then goodbye, and she recedes down the service road with a cardboard suitcase twice her age, the family name markered on both sides and binder twine braided into a strap gripped bare-handed in the cold. Russ waits until she has turned into a motel parking lot and climbed into the back of a rusted old Mustang, and then he starts in the other direction.

Along the pebbled snowcrust in the ditch the wind scuttles seeds of ice that form a grain and then a new grain. Yes, it was more or less like that. Something has freed him from his habits of perception. He feels like a dreamer wondering at the particulars of a dream – a glove button, a strand of hair curled over an ear, or simply the spaces, a dance hall or an airport terminal, some vast architecture. Things that don't command his waking attention but must always be there. It's as if the verges have opened up and everything is available now.

Jackie and Lyle are waiting in the window of the all-night restaurant where Russ met his uncle three weeks ago. They smile as he approaches. In the truck he sits with his bag on his lap and fends off questions about Skidder and his stories about women and God. He learns of a fire drill gone bad, a broken hydrant and a road torn up, every emergency vehicle in town now frozen tight until spring.

Russ speaks at length only once, to enlist his friends in a deceit. In the spring they'll turn up at Jean's door and ask her to relieve them of the unpaid debt to his father that Russ won't accept. Jackie will do the talking. She'll make Jean promise to spend it on herself. Then she'll hand her the money in cash.

The cash will have come from Russ. He'll have told them Mike had wanted to leave it to Jean but knew she wouldn't take it, would give it to Russ or to charity, so he left Russ the money and the task of getting it to her sideways.

In truth the cash will have been changed from American currency in a dozen transactions over three months conducted in Glen Stockard's office. On the first of these occasions Glen will ask Russ for the name of the bird from that old poem they did back in school, and Russ will say albatross. Glen will accuse him of train robbery and Russ will swear that the money is orphaned. Together they'll lament the state of the local economy. Thereafter the business will be unspoken-of even as it is conducted, hand to hand, the sums converted without ever passing through an account.

Grey smoke from a farmhouse past a windbreak off the road. The yard lights bent through ice on the trees as if through leaden windows with thin distorting panes that let the cold into old churches or schoolhouses long lost to spilled stove fires or the wind that erased everything in time. Wind, ice and fire, and an ambulance stuck until thaw. The smoke is beautiful. He can see the dance in it.

He senses that Jackie is worried. She knows something has changed in him. When they drop him off she says the town doesn't have facilities for him, he needs therapies and shrinks. He gets out and nods a thank-you. Tomorrow, says Lyle. Jackie says advanced drugs and constant monitoring, says it in jest but that's not the way she looks at him.

He comes in to the red flashing message light. Versions of the news from Clete Dirks run through his mind, that the kid he'd hit was hurt worse than he'd seemed, that the kid he'd tried to warn and his friends are missing, or have turned up dead, but the imagination of disaster feels forced and hollow. Rather than wait to take the message by day, then, he listens to it. Clete says hello and explains that it's hard to get much on a medical matter, and El Paso isn't his town or these his people, but there's nothing on a Manny with ribs, which means the Manny in question wasn't treated, or is likely not insured and so maybe got taken care of under another name. As for Juarez, the events described did not make the papers, though people do die off the record down there.

The record does not hold up, so the damage is not redressable. He concedes it's a fact he will have trouble living with.

In the thinning dark he falls asleep in his bed. If there are dreams, they don't remain. He wakes to the colours of his room seeming strangely intense. Lying there, he understands a new snow has fallen and now the sky has cleared. He goes to the window. The yard is a blank sheet of raw, punishing light. I have been a rebel to the light, he thinks. They have not known his ways. Neither have they returned by his paths.

Downtown he collects the mail. Awaiting him are seven books that he ordered in the days before leaving. He pays the return postage and sends them back unopened.

Some time that afternoon he steps through the front door of Skidder's shack and finds him sitting in his parka watching a cartoon on television and squeezing the contents of a brown plastic bottle of maple-flavoured syrup onto a last toasted pancake on a plate in his lap. His mouth is too full to speak so he turns and waves, starts to get up and almost spills his plate, and sits back down and waves again.

Before swallowing, he asks, When the fuck did you hit town?

Don't you have a furnace in this place?

It costs like hell to run it.

Russ walks in and takes a reading from the thermostat. The room temperature is eight degrees Celsius.

Don't touch that – it's a personal setting. And I don't have the mouse problem most people do.

He gestures at the screen with the bottle.

What d'you make of them there?

What are you asking me?

You can't tell if they're animal or not.

Onscreen are two green figures with round bellies and round ears. They possess no clear snouts or tails.

Is it cats or dogs or made-up things? I been sittin here and I don't think you can tell.

Russ goes to the window and looks out to the yard.

Come here.

I'm just watching my program here.

Come on.

Skidder casts his eyes around as if gauging an escape.

I been praying for your humour, Russ.

He comes warily to the window and looks out.

So what do you think of it?

The black three-quarter-ton Chevy truck in profile.

What, it's a test-drive?

Yeah.

I seen that one on the lot. There's a blue bugger, too.

You like the blue better?

No, the black's got more options. Smaller engine if you use it for work, though. What the hell you want with a new truck?

Let's go for a ride.

Both of them already dressed for the cold, they walk out. Skidder goes soft in the face, like a girl looking at a newborn foal.

You drive, says Russ.

He directs him out to the old highway and tells him to open it up. Skidder smiles as he steps into the pedal. The truck is still pushing them heavy in their seats when he levels off.

Find the top end.

Skidder shakes his head at the wonder of it all. He yips like a coyote, wide-eyed upon the road. The blacktop has no centre line, the snow runs to the horizon in all directions. Where the acceleration ends they can't feel the speed but know it precisely by the readout on the dash.

This here's a good idea.

Yes, it is.

They're speaking loud above the engine.

Thanks for letting me drive.

Russ nods.

Thank Mike, he says.

The engine cuts away and they coast for a time. It's a quarter-mile before they're stopped on the shoulder. Skidder is still looking straight ahead.

Did you hear me?

I don't know.

Mike's the one who put you behind the wheel.

His mouth forms into a silent oh. He fingers the logo embossed on the wheel.

The will is executed in stages. This part just came through.

He nods solemnly.

I didn't really expect . . . I talked trucks with him sometimes. He must've had it picked out.

Yeah.

Did he say the black one in the will?

It's whatever you want. You can take the money instead.

But he must've thought the truck. He knew the money I'd just piss it away.

He squeezes the plastic beartooth toggles of his hood. They're both a little high to come down from the speed, stunned into black and white, with nothing moving for miles.

Shit, Russ. There was a reason. About my leaving.

Never mind. I know.

You know?

Yeah. The last time you saw him. What did he say?

I don't know. Nothin much. It wasn't a big scene or anything. He said it was gonna be hard on you but you were the type to handle it better alone. He said you'd just want the quiet.

The quiet.

Yeah. He wasn't up to saying alot. It took him a while to get that much out.

Uh-huh.

And he asked if I'd look out for you, keep you out of trouble.

You're kidding.

No.

302

This strikes them both as funny.

Then, you know, I just thanked him and said goodbye.

Russ nods.

Then you did the right thing.

I don't deserve no credit. To tell the truth, I think I would've took off on my own anyway.

After a moment Skidder pretends to take an interest in the defrost setting. He says, It sure fucked you up.

Yeah.

I mean for a while. The whole lead-up and the thing itself.

It did.

They say he used to really raise hell himself.

That's what they say.

You ever ask him about all that?

No.

I believe it, though. You're a little like him maybe.

Russ laughs.

What?

I'm just picturing us here, working it all out.

You don't have to picture it, we're sittin right here.

Yeah.

We better get back maybe.

All right. I'll see you when I get home.

What are you talking about?

We'll set everything right and be happy. We'll all be converted. The skies will all be promising.

What the hell? You're worse now than when you left.

I've come all the way back and then some, Skidder. I feel fine.

Once, passing by an open classroom door at Wellington, he'd heard her voice. Her lecturer's tone accentuated something that was there, he realized, in her every utterance. This is how it is, she seemed to be saying. I'm telling you what matters, and it matters whether or not you listen and in ways quite outside those prescribed by our being here. For the class, whatever the subject, the distinctive timbre and rhythms must have summoned grave certainties, that the world is made of broken things, history reconstructs the very place you stand, the most distant remnants prevail, the smallest elements adhere everywhere, they have unguessed-at meanings. To Russ, the voice said, I'm ahead of you, I know how to put this together, now trust me.

What he'd forgotten about her voice until he'd heard the message she'd left and now her recorded phone greeting were the small fragments of speech audible within it. She instructed the caller to try another number, which he committed to memory, but at the end of the message she seemed to pause, as if trying to remember which key was pound and which star, and softly vocalized to herself something he knew. It wasn't a word, but a sound she often made when listening, or just prior to speaking, the sound that broke before a syllable could form. Something both early and young, a first gathering from the human need to say.

The number was for something called the Bread Exchange. He dialled, and there she was.

"Hello."

"Tara. It's me."

"Me who?" And before he could answer, "Oh."

"Yeah." He couldn't hear her so much as breathing. "I'm on my way back up from Texas and I was in the neighbourhood."

She waited out a rumble behind her that sounded like steel filing cabinets on trolleys. It subsided and died.

"Really. What neighbourhood is that?"

In miles, he'd come an impressive distance to see her, but in reality it was only so many dollars that he hadn't earned and a few minutes of light turbulence over the mountains.

"Calgary."

"Calgary. But you're in Vancouver now."

"Yes. I'd like to get together."

"Hold on."

She put the phone down and began giving directions to someone, maybe the person with the trolley. Her heard her take up the receiver again.

"Here it is, a busy morning, another dopey sky, and you're calling to tell me you're here."

"Yes. And I want to see you."

"Why just show up and spring this? It feels kind of desperate and creepy."

Because it is desperate, he thought.

"Let's call it crazy."

"Right. I hope you've thought this through, Russ."

They established that he was in town for the day, that she had a night class and would be too tired to see him afterwards, so they would meet that afternoon. She gave him a time, an address, the name of the man who lived there. He wanted to ask if they'd have a chance to talk alone, but managed not to, trusting she would know what was best.

He contrived to be twenty minutes late so the entrance would be his and not hers. The manner of his arrival had come to seem important when he'd spied his face in a mirrored pillar in the hotel lobby. The swelling was less pronounced, the bruising shaded to lighter pastels except for the shiner. He wished he looked better and then was glad he didn't. Better to create a slight shock. Whatever might happen between them, whatever his having come to her out of the blue would be thought to mean, she would always remember the moment of his reappearance. If he got it right, she would never be free of it.

He'd told the driver from the airport to take him to the best hotel, where he stored his bag without checking in. It was a trick he'd learned travelling in Europe. You could get a locker at the bus station or else lie to a concierge about your late-arriving wife and her company card and have your luggage stowed for free to kill a few hours in relative comfort. The luxury places were crass and removed but the bathrooms were better and as long as you were out before the nightly jazz trio started up the drinks cost the same whether you were staring at an old licence plate or an ocean.

Outside, the sky was weak blue. He got into a taxi at the hotel stand and gave the address to a nodding white man with long hair and a bald spot who looked in recovery from a wasting addiction. Though he'd been in Vancouver a few times, Russ never knew precisely where in the city he was. Downtown somewhere, on the water. He'd never gotten the hang of the layout. With its rivers and bays, creeks and straits, the place always turned him around. All that was familiar was the ride itself, the cabbie consulting a ring-bound street directory while driving, and snickering at the halved dialogue on his radio as the dispatcher ridiculed another driver, mimicking his accent, a mispronounced name, calling the lot of them morons and chimps.

The address turned out to be on a street off of East Hastings. He knew the neighbourhood from CBC documentaries on the heroin skid row and prostitute killings. A girl he'd gone to school with until grade eight had ended up here. No one back home had recalled her until she OD'd.

The number he wanted was stencilled on a door beside a used-appliance store with stoves on the sidewalk. There was no buzzer. He entered a narrow stairwell that smelled like something three days dead. The carpet felt wet beneath his shoes as he climbed up to the landing. Wherever he was headed was no place for sweet reunions. The number from the street repeated itself on the apartment door. There were no sounds inside. He knocked.

After a long, silent interval the door was opened wide and incautiously by a thin, elderly man who stood squinting at him.

"Hello. I might have the wrong address. I'm here to meet Tara Harding. Are you William?"

The man stood squinting, in torn slippers, shirt untucked, his hands at his sides, clutching the plaid polyester.

"My name's Russ Littlebury."

The man nodded.

"I had a cat name of Russ. He caught the brain cancer and died."

"I'm sorry. Is Tara here?"

"No. You come on in, 'less you're a homo-setshool killer."

"I try not to be."

"You look beat-up. There's nothin to rob in here."

"Okay."

William led the way, his shoulder bones pronounced in the shirt as if it had been hung on a picket fence.

The little space was clean and orderly, with features to be expected in a room in this neighbourhood — a hot plate, a mini-fridge, a single-size mattress on a low steel frame, a greasy window with its clouded impression of the street – though Russ doubted there was anyone to form the expectation. A table covered with papers. Old photographs lined the walls, some in frames, most simply taped at the corners. Many were unpeopled. A sad bungalow somewhere, a river bend, farmscapes. It seemed Tara was still involving herself in hard cases and lost causes.

"She put them pitchers up."

"Tara?"

"She thinks there's memories for me but most I don't know where they're took or who took 'em."

A dog on a couch. A young man long ago, in uniform.

"Are you a veteran, William?"

"Not no more. I gave it up."

"You gave up being a veteran?"

"I did. Nothin counts for nothin. The world's all changed. She puts up the pitchers and reads me them papers."

He pointed to the small table by the kitchenette covered with loose pages and open books.

"That's her project there she's workin on. A box of papers my old mom give me. My dad didn't have her education so he didn't leave papers. I sort of took after him."

"What's she doing with the papers?"

"She's puttin them in shape for my daughter when I'm gone. The daughter's not partial to me."

Russ saw that the old man had not managed two of the snaps on his shirt, but even as it gaped there wasn't visible within so much as a rib.

"Hey, let's drink a hello. I used to hide a bottle from my nurse up in that cupboard up there." He pointed. "I can't get up there no more. I ast Tara she wouldn't check it."

Though he'd just spoken to her, and of her, it was oddly thrilling to hear her name on the tongue of this unlikely host. Russ moved a chair over and stepped up to the counter.

"Back in there. I don't know if there is one."

"There's nothing in here."

"Prob'ly in the back there."

"There's nothing."

"All right."

He climbed back down.

"Don't say I sent you up there."

"I won't."

From somewhere, William had produced two tiny pills in the palm of his hand. In a gesture of mock horror he brought his hand up suddenly to his open mouth and then swallowed them dry.

"Don't you want water with those?"

"You help yourself. The food, you'll have to wait for the Meals on Wheels. They'll be by if you just wait. The thing is, I don't have alotta entertainment."

"That's all right."

William stooped down to the mini-fridge now and brought out a jar of what appeared to be lentils.

"Lentils," he said. "You can boil 'em up."

"That's all right."

"I worked for the Wheat Pool. I could sell a lentil like no one you ever met."

"I'm not hungry, William."

As he put the jar back, William paused to take an interest in the other contents of the fridge. Russ was left to wonder whether Tara had planned to be late and what end she supposed would be served by this encounter. Maybe she thought a few minutes with William would shake free any hopeful illusions he may have held. He couldn't suppress the memory of a noisy airport lounge, and strangers beyond a glass wall silently parading to their flights.

William had some trouble straightening up again but he waved Russ off when he tried to help him. Eventually he moved somewhat stooped to his bed.

"I use'ly lie down after my pills."

"You go ahead."

"I thought we could drink together but my plan went to shit."

"Can I read your papers?"

"Just don't mess 'em up. I did one time and she damn near spanked me."

William lay down and soon there began a shallow wheezing that accompanied Russ as he sat at the table and read. Tara was cataloguing the papers in a spiral-bound notebook. She'd put question marks beside undated documents, but most of her work seemed to involve matching the dates of letters against those in an old sewn hardcover book that she described as The Diary of a Logger's Wife. The woman, William's mother presumably, was named Rebecca Pryce. Tara had had to invent short-form titles for each undated entry. The Journey. Gospel Meeting 3. Husband's Shoes. A Bear Sighting. Beside the descriptors she'd noted details or words she thought important. Some had cross-references, others had prompted questions or short interpretations. This was how she practised history, Russ knew. From the bottom up. And here on this table, in this room, was about as hard against the bottom as she could hope to be.

Russ turned to an entry called The Premonition.

In the catalogue she'd determined the year to be 1914. The place unknown, somewhere in the Canadian Rockies. Rebecca had been out walking with her husband when they came to a narrow pass marked by tall rock walls that the sun didn't penetrate. The facets looked green in the reflected sunlight and something about the colour overwhelmed her with foreboding. Her husband didn't understand her fear, and laughed at her reluctance to enter the passage. If she didn't walk on, she knew, the ridicule would increase and she'd have to endure it again later in front of his friends. As she stepped ahead he gestured for her to lead the way, and she kept going.

The day had been still. The sky above was peaceful. But as we walked a strong wind blew and disturbed the path before us without grass or flowers to root the soil. I turned my face to shield my eyes and saw my husband in a countenance of fixed terror. He was looking beyond me. When I turned back I saw what had distressed him. Perhaps our eyes had grown used to the dim light, or perhaps the wind had exposed the floor, but there before us, as far as could be seen and gaining under our very feet, was an aisle of bones. They must have numbered in the hundreds. Seeing them, I knew at once the source of my bodement which yet had left me and seemed twice stronger now in my husband, whose fear was not of the remains, but of me. It was my intimation that had struck him cold. He beheld me as if I were a ghost, and backed away. When he turned in retreat I implored him, commanded him, to stop. 'We must walk through,' I told him. I couldn't have said why, and cannot now, but I

311

knew it as certainly as I had known something awaited us there. I said no more, and now it was he who reluctantly continued.

As we covered the ground I saw that the bones were of humans and beasts both. The wind blew strong again and we walked on, unspeaking, until we were through the pass. We spoke no more of the incident, and came back along a path of our own making that led us above the pass. Tonight I have no one to tell of this event. For fear of my husband's regard I will never describe to him the nature of my second presentiment. It was that if we retreated the wind that had revealed the bones would blow ever stronger, and lift them up not to their former shapes, but in new arrangements, not only fitting one man to another, but animal to animal, horse to woman, and these new shapes would change everything, so that we, the living, would seem senseless, and we become the bones under their passage.

In looking up from the page Russ felt suddenly light-headed, as if he'd risen through submarine depths at a great speed. William lay on his side, small as a child. It would be ten or more years before he was conceived. In this moment, the mother was a greater presence than her son there on the bed.

He consulted Tara's commentary on the entry.

"If a woman has a vision in the woods and there's no one to call her hysterical . . . ? The formal language again as elsewhere attaches to gender position – how did she end up in such isolation, with this man? What prospects for an educated woman? The imagery: she'd regard bones made into new creatures as an abomination of God's work. She's angry at God but afraid of a

312

godless world. She can't bring herself to declare the anger so she envisions the abomination and then records it (is she reliable? does she change the vision while recording?). Compare the unimpassioned tone used to record the gospel meetings."

For some reason, though he recognized her thinking, her words filled him with despair. It wasn't that she was conducting a professional reading on the side – at least it was like her to have a shadow motive – but that he would have thought she understood that the diary passage called not for a response, but for contemplation. He himself felt the impulse to say something back, something about, but it had nothing to do with the need to understand. The entry unsettled him in ways he didn't want to be alone with, that made him want to escape upon a stream of interpretation. But it wouldn't be enough for him, not any more. The passage recorded an infinite loneliness, and left no possibility of speaking back, at least not in a way that fashioned an immediate sense. The best thing, really, was silence. The Tara he remembered had known when to call upon her narrow, academic language, and when not to. But her notes seemed a retreat from mystery. He knew the path of retreat very well.

He studied Tara's script, the elided vowels, imagined the sure passage of her hand across the page. She would have her reasons for entering this woman into the record, and she would believe in them. Russ didn't have to accept her reasons to love her belief. He told himself he was making too much of this feeling that she was now the one sheltering herself in ideas, but the feeling remained.

Under her commentary he drew a small star, then turned to a blank page near the end of the catalogue. There, inside the slim possibility the words might never be discovered, he drew the star again and wrote her what he thought of as a love letter.

What is revelation?

To begin, as are all real mysteries, it is extremely rare. The only fitting response to it is a silence full of knowing. The knowing resides beyond all rational understanding, but it's necessary to move through that understanding, to expend all the terms, all the common language, in order to arrive there. It may not be possible, then, to communicate the mystery, but if it is, the language of that communication will have been made strange to us.

In the face of revelation, fear is immeasurable. Not because it is unfounded or without substance, but because it is everywhere and various, and because, again, language falls short.

Through fear, revelation casts us not outside of time, but into a simultaneous past and future. Revelatory fear looks forward with dread. The dread is of loss, which is to say, of some future longing.

Dread, then, is a premonition of longing yet to come. And longing is fear reflected.

The very lonely are more prone to visionary revelation. The vision itself may not comfort them as much as the possibility it has come to them by something other than chance, that it has been directed to them by an Intender.

They fear they are alone, and they fear they are not.

It can happen that revelation finds us not upon winds or through weeping icons or even ordinary things, but through someone else.

Certain others can be the unknowing keepers of our visions.

You're the only one who ever got me half right.

There's another way of saying this, but then the words wouldn't be mine.

He turned the book back to the page she'd been working on. In the star he saw his hand under hers, saw it in an instant and then let it be. Her words made a physical thing, drawn physically. He pictured her skin slightly mottled under her ear, the muscles softening there in the moments after she spoke like wet sand pursed around a fading print.

For a long time he stood at the window and stared through its imperfections and grime, waiting for her to appear. The buildings had a shambling quality of no architectural type. They hadn't been made to be looked at or spoken of.

A red old-style V-bug passed by. It seemed to recede along a runnel in the glass.

At first he didn't recognize her. Her hair was no longer cropped, but pulled back. She wore a collar that looked Japanese or clerical. By some instinct he stepped back from the window in case she looked up.

William was still lying on his side.

He listened for her up the stairs. When she made the landing he opened the door.

He would have said he remembered her face but he was only now recovering it and the way it worked upon him. As if he couldn't hold them both in his mind at once, he forgot himself, and for a second or two he watched her speaking that voice without the sense he was being addressed, and had to loop back to gather her meaning.

She had asked what had happened to his face.

"I was mistaken for someone else."

She decided to accept this and nodded once.

"Lucky him."

She stepped up and kissed him on the cheek.

"Hello," she said.

They were catching up to the moment.

"Yes," he said. He almost reached out and touched her shoulder, but then she was past him and into the room.

He took an interest in the objects she'd brought in with her for William. A written reminder of an upcoming lawyer's appointment. A sealed letter on hospital stationery, care of the Bread Exchange. Clipped together, a social insurance card with William's name and a laminated card from a mission house with his photo and address. She unclipped them and handed them to him one at a time so they would register.

"These will do for now. Don't lose them again."

She and William were sitting side by side on the bed. For some reason, Russ had ended up with them, sitting at the foot end. He should have taken the chair at the table and now he was part of the group.

"I always tell 'em," William told him, "you want somethin done, Tara's your man."

"I can't stay today, William, but I'll call tomorrow and I'll come by on Friday. I'll have the table cleared off by the weekend."

"That's okay. I clear it off to eat and then dump it all back on there."

She stood and focused her concern on the table. William winked at Russ and grinned in delight.

"Yeah, I just went through and shuffled them for you," said Russ. "Now it's a deck you can deal with."

She looked at him and he thought she would make a face. She'd made it once in Toronto, the mouth pulled to one side, the eyes crossed, head trembling with cartoon rage, and they'd agreed making faces was nearly a lost art.

"So you read it?"

"Some of it. Yes."

This was not the place to discuss what he'd read – for Russ, there was no such place – and she swept her hands towards the door to signal an exit. She bent down and kissed William on the forehead, and was out and descending the stairs before Russ got to his feet. He lingered at the door to shake the old man's hand.

"It was nice meeting you," said Russ.

"You come by, we'll have a soup."

"Next time I'm in town."

William lowered his voice.

"Don't step wrong with her."

Russ expected another wink but William turned away.

"It might be too late," said Russ.

The old man made for the bed. Russ waited for him to sit and turn back towards him, and then he raised his hand but the wave was not returned, and William didn't even look up as Russ closed the door.

"He's dying."

"Yes. He's old. His liver's older."

They were in her Civic. Tara seemed to know her way to the hotel. Along the route she told Russ how she'd ended up here. Last February, while she was living in the cabin she'd written him from, a diverted letter arrived from a woman she'd gone to grad school with. The woman now taught at Simon Fraser and her department was advertising a limited-term appointment in Tara's field. A colleague of hers had favourably reviewed Tara's book in galleys, she said, and both he and her friend were on the hiring committee.

"By the time I called, I assumed the job had been filled, but they hadn't found anyone to their liking. I explained that I'd moved to the cabin to write and the mail had gone to the wrong address and so on. Through my teeth."

"Like I once advised you."

She briefly narrowed her gaze at the street.

"Did you?" He was surprised that she'd forgotten. Surprised and disconcerted. "And so anyway, here I am. I watch the ocean every day for three minutes. It calms me stupid."

She didn't seem especially calm. Her strategy seemed designed to keep Russ from saying much of anything. Otherwise they'd have met in a restaurant. Looking as he did, she now may have thought he intended to ruin himself against her.

"I'm sorry about your father, Russ."

"Okay. Then you got my e-mail."

"I hope you weren't expecting a response. I started one but it turns out I'm no good at virtual condolences. Maybe I'm out of step with the times."

"We're never off the hook for the times."

She seemed to lose her train of thought. Maybe he'd disarmed her to suggest the old debates weren't in play. The suggestion was accidental. Their old debates, the harmless ones anyway, had a specific friction that warmed him.

She looked at him briefly.

"Jesus."

"What?"

"You look terrible. You just show up here from the world of detectives and beatings." The beatings are of the times, too, he thought. But then, she knew that. "So what should I ask? How's life?"

"Turns out it's bigger than me," he said.

"That's better than the alternative. William is eighty years old and his life is the size of that room."

Now she told him about the Bread Exchange, a volunteer-run haven for the dispossessed. It put people in touch with services and lobbied the private sector for funding. On the recent day that a provincial government minister mentioned them by name in announcing in the legislature that she was not in the business of funding "special-interest groups," Tara had gone out and bought William a radio. The first voice they heard upon plugging it in was the minister's. When Tara left, he pawned it and got a neighbour to buy him some gin.

"That would count as a stark lesson."

"So we lobby privately and fail to get by that way instead."

He stole a glance at her hands upon the wheel. He was completely unprepared for them.

"And what did you think of Rebecca's diary?"

"It seems like a real find," he said. "Will it end up in a publication?"

She shook her head and smiled slightly.

"There you are."

"What?"

"Never mind."

"I insist."

"I'm not trespassing on William's life. I've read him the pages aloud. Yes. I might use them, but I have his permission."

"To publish them?"

"To quote from them."

"Right. What did you mean, 'There you are'?"

"Nothing, I'm just touchy. Some days I think everyone looks for some human failing behind any good thing to make it count for less."

If only she hadn't generalized the comment it would have pierced him, not unpleasantly, and he might have said that he knew what untainted goodness looked like. He'd seen the real thing, it wasn't compromised. Or self-conscious. A true selflessness, he would never understand.

How strange that he should crave her old contentiousness. He weighed telling her that he'd never known her to be serving only one principle at a time. There were the principles, but then there was their promotion. And capital-H History, and her side of every argument, old and new. All the best things going. But he could think of nothing he himself believed in enough to make her come back at him as hard as he needed her to, not even a provocative quote from the dead. Name my failing, he thought. Light into me.

Now he was the sentimental one, it seemed.

"Why are you at the posh Pan Pacific?"

"I'm not, my luggage is."

"And you're leaving for home tonight."

"Yes."

"Is that where you belong, you think? Home?"

"I don't seem to belong anywhere. Home's just where they tolerate me."

She had been pulling cds up from under her seat, made her selection and opened it one-handed, and inserted it into the player. They rode the rest of the way listening to Chet Baker singing. Now he was between them. She had apparently forgotten that they'd played it once after a late dinner at her place. To the voice of Chet Baker they'd fallen asleep on a cheap, plush throw rug.

"I saw your interpretation of Rebecca's vision. Do you think she'd want just anyone to read her thoughts and then weigh in with an opinion?"

For a moment she evinced no response, as if she hadn't heard him.

"What do you want me to say, Russ? Do you care? Or are you just poking a stick in a hole to see what might come out?"

Hadn't he come here with something else in mind? So why was he now looking to invoke her judgement? Tara had set him up to meet William, to remind him of their past differences, but hadn't allowed them to share a half-minute of silence. She had made up her mind about Russ long ago, he realized, and now he couldn't save himself. He couldn't give her up when he loved even her calculations, all her layered deceptions.

He was struck by the truth of his conclusion. A moment from the past presented itself. He'd woken from a dream of grotesques, and read to calm himself, closed the book, and understood that he had lost her. It had happened then. There was no cause for hope now. To be so physically close to her and yet free of hope left him speechless.

She asked him to haul up her briefcase from the back seat.

"Open the back zipper pocket."

He did so and withdrew a ten-by-twelve sheet with a colour image of a young smiling couple seated on a plaid couch. The man's plastic frames, tinted lenses, and the woman's blue bell-bottoms dated them in the seventies. Her brown hair, parted in the middle, fell to either side of her bright face. The man's hair was combed back, not especially long. Because he was smiling Russ almost didn't recognize him.

"I take it you wouldn't have this if there wasn't a bad ending to their story."

"Not yet there isn't. He'll have been released by now. Beth still lives where she used to. She's not dead or in hospital. That's all I know."

Through some delicate recognition, he understood that he and Tara, at least, were going to get their ending. It was close upon them now.

"Then how did you come by this?"

"I made that copy from a Polaroid. It was mixed in with William's other pictures."

He knew at once that he'd been wrong to think she may be in retreat. It was just that her devotion had found a new way of expressing itself. He remembered from her letter the lines on devotion, that it was not to be confused with obsession. She'd written that one was a psychological phenomenon, the other a moral one, but he couldn't make the distinction now.

"All that time I spent with the public record, one thing I tracked down was Beth's family. I thought someone might take her in for a while. I ended up on the phone with an aunt on her mother's side. She hadn't seen Beth in years or had anything to do with the family since her sister died. The last she'd heard, Beth was estranged from her father, and her father was a skid-row drunk in Vancouver." She ducked her head to read a street sign. "I forgot about him until a few weeks after I moved here. One night – I'd been drinking a little myself – he occurred to me. I looked him up. He's in the book. A message directed all enquiries to the Bread Exchange. I dropped in the next day."

"And joined up on the spot."

"More or less."

"And took over William's case."

"We don't have cases. We all just do whatever."

"But why? What were you hoping to accomplish?"

"There's no grand scheme, Russ. I don't hold out for tearful reunions. I just wanted to do something for her, and then it became for William. And then I discovered Rebecca and kind of fell in love with her. I know how it sounds to say I was drawn there for a reason, but it feels that way."

He did know how it sounded, and he knew the feeling, too.

"So Beth will get a box in the mail after he dies."

Tara had called her a few weeks ago. She'd said her name – it didn't seem to ring any bells with Beth, and if it had, she fully expected to be stung again for meddling – and began to tell her about William. At first Beth didn't want to hear it, she said she didn't care, but then Tara asked if she'd ever known her grand-mother, Rebecca. She knew nothing except that she was named after her. By the end of the conversation, Beth said she'd accept the papers and photos.

"I'll send them off to her when I get them in order."

"And William doesn't know the whole story."

"Nobody knows. I wasn't going to tell you but now I have."

She turned off the cd and they rode in silence finally for what seemed a long time.

"So you got your career back, and Beth gets a little connec-tion out of the blue. William gets your help. And maybe every-body survives. Sounds like you got lucky, Tara."

"You might think I'm just transferring my own needs from one person to the next, but it's all I can do. So be it. I'm not hurting anyone, am I?"

"No."

"So I focus on William."

"You're loading alot onto a frail old man."

"And a long-dead woman. Yes, I guess I am."

He decided that she knew she would always be in trouble about one sad thing or another.

Since leaving William's room it had felt as if he existed for her only at some great distance, a distance opened without effort, within her sense of passing time. But now he knew that she'd had to try to forget him, or half forget him, as she had the Overstreets. He wondered where she focused her attention when she didn't want to think of him directly.

They stopped in some residential neighbourhood, a block uphill from the water.

"Where are we?"

"I live here."

They got out of the car and she led him into her condominium. There were hardwood floors and a view of the water. He recognized none of the artwork or rugs. Her new life looked nothing like her old one.

She seemed to understand there was nothing to say. She left him in her living room and disappeared.

The lights were coming up around the bay. He found himself predicting where they'd appear next based on where the land lay dark on the water, and he got it mostly wrong. The sequence wouldn't hold to its projected shape, but broke into something new, something other. It would all be over in a minute.

She returned and held a hand out to him, and he took it and she led him into her bedroom. It was a powerfully strange moment, but she'd seen beyond it already, already knew it was the only way to resolution. It was a way of sharing their mutual past, of acknowledging it, though it had never been this palpably sad. That she would end it this way was in keeping with her sense of charity, and he felt at least a little like one of her projects, another lost cause to attach herself to, but the truth was that he needed the charity.

The lovemaking was without urgency or language. In this sense it was new, but mostly it moved with the motions of memory. He found himself remembering her, the surfaces and textures, her ribs articulated when she raised her arms in slow hunger, the thin discoloured line like a salt stain on her breastbone that an old lover had made her self-conscious of, the speckling of scars on her shin, the vein coming up there on her forehead when she lay back. Remembering too his own need, a mimetic desire to return energy in kind to the form he drew it from. They were suspended in their past unions, but now there was something else. Russ was conscious of registering her body, the way her face changed when he was inside her, knowing he was in a future memory that he would return to again and again for years.

When it was over she left the room without lingering. When she hadn't returned after a few minutes he got dressed and went out. She was standing in the kitchen with her jacket on, her back to him. He wondered if she'd been crying, but when she turned and nodded to him, he saw that she hadn't. She looked different somehow, almost unfamiliar.

He waited while she turned all the lights off but one. Then they went down to the car.

He tried to know what she was thinking. It wasn't that she had a lover here or anything so straightforward. It wasn't common disappointment at life, or a lesson in managing losses. It was that the important things in your past needed a form, they had to be closed into something whole that they might be placed safely away. He couldn't decide if they had closed their past or not. Maybe they'd made a lie of it.

They parked in a lot near the hotel and walked. At one point he reached out and held her arm and she smiled and leaned into him for only a second and then separated and he let her go.

They walked into the lobby amid a moderate traffic of guests and crossed past a sushi restaurant and a coffee shop to the bar and stepped down to a sunken floor with tables shaped to suggest protozoic islands in the Sound.

When they were seated with their drinks Russ became acutely aware of the time left to them. Tara wouldn't allow this last scene to run too long. Soon the need to talk things through would assert itself and they'd lose this shared understanding that the work of finding the real mysteries amid all the false ones was to be best done out of sight, without long lines of shared intelligible speech.

A cruise ship loomed in the harbour. It was admitted to them to try to recall the name of the bar they used to drink in with the old photos of ships along the walls. Russ said it was the Fox in the Forest on King Street, and Tara said he was wrong, that she couldn't remember the name, but that wasn't it. Russ could have said he knew the place down to its layout, and the little hallway leading nowhere off the back booth where they'd kissed and reached into one another's clothing like teenagers, and he could have said which ship was there with them, but he let it go. The *Endurance* trapped in the south polar ice.

Quite suddenly the lounge began to fill up with small clusters of conventioneers as the dinner hour approached, no doubt those very Pacific Rim Traders being welcomed on the electronic sign at the entrance. A ruddy-faced fat man spotted Tara, the only woman in the room, and nudged his friend. Before long pretty much all the groups had made their appraisals. Russ wanted a second scotch but their waiter was attending to the drinkers on expense accounts.

"There's a word for this," she said.

"A word for what?"

"That's just it, there's an exact word and I can't think of it."

A few men at the bar looked their way and broke into laughter. Holding forth was a square-headed, buzz-cut type, some small-time lewd wit. He wasn't as mean as he looked, Russ decided. He would cut the blockhead some slack.

"You're creating a stir. I'm hoping they'll send drinks."

"You look too scary." She put her head down for a second. "I do this in class. I stop and wait for the word. The ones that don't come kind of haunt me."

"Maybe they don't exist."

"Some of them do. They come to me later."

Until you knew them all, there was no letting go of words. Only days ago, in a hotel corridor, he had found himself hoping for clarity or something like it. Against his stated principles, he'd been a sly believer in something like grace, in hope without illusion, but the old words had not summoned a thing except violence. Having sought the consolations he'd once forsworn, like everyone he'd come to see that his hope lay beyond him. Today it had nearly been bestowed. Tomorrow he would try not to wait for it.

To Russ's surprise, the waiter appeared with more scotch and white wine.

"It's from a man at the bar." The waiter set down a business card. Orrin Carr of Tacoma. Eastern Motifs. The card had a sea-blue border.

Russ raised his glass to the men at the bar. He counted five hands raised in return.

"I could vanquish the suitors."

"I'd rather you took their money. We'll give it to the poor."

"Sure. The poor get the money."

"And the rich learn humility."

"And the gods love us for the benefaction. They pay us off in beauty. Everyone wins."

He imagined using the old words to ask for her heart, like in the songs. If he could win it, if only he knew how, he would give his own to her.

Something was making him maudlin. The booze, the species. He felt like the very sap in *H. sap*, and didn't care.

From her jacket she produced a little plastic wallet. She placed three blue fives on the table. They filled him with regret. She turned her chair and looked back to the bar. The men were exchanging their plastic name tags. One of them smiled at her.

She turned back.

"I have to go, Russ."

He nodded.

"What's happened to us," she said, "it's really pretty common. It will help to remember that."

He pretended his best response wasn't a day's ride away.

"You're wrong," he said. Nothing else came to him.

"You used to be harder on me, Russ. I liked that about you."

He got to his feet and accompanied her out of the lounge. The lobby was busy now, the human sound crowded in on them. They were making for the door when she stopped and turned to him and held him in place. Her brave expression was not quite holding together.

"I got to start over here," she said. "You're right. I got lucky. It's hard to get over being so lucky."

She waited a moment for him to say something, and then without touching him again, she left. She was through the door and gone before he could bring himself to move.

He drifted back into the lounge and sat at the bar for a last drink. The new bartender was a dark-haired young woman with a small birthmark on the side of her neck. He ordered a scotch. The suitors kept their distance.

He was going to drink his drink and then he'd be a little drunk. He would concentrate on hitting a note of light drunkenness and holding it through the flight and to the bus station and onward through the hours until Lyle met him in Falling Creek. He would need to find a bottle somewhere.

The bartender set up his scotch.

"Can I buy that vessel from you? Our little secret?"

"Only in singles and doubles. And I don't keep little secrets. Sorry."

She smiled.

He turned to look out at the water but there was only the dark drapery upon which the lounge recalled itself in the glass. He found a figment with his shape and watched the drink come to his lips. Down on the floor their uncleared table held its artifacts in place. It killed him a little to see it and a little to look away. He picked up its reflection, sitting light upon the mind, and met a figure ghosted there, just a movement really, a faint uncoiling sleeve falling over the table and then rising and gone before rounding into a meaningful gesture, then reappearing as a hand full of light, and the light passed on. Outside the window, a ritual sharing in the night.

A man had separated himself from the group and was walking down the bar to the till. He smiled at Russ and Russ nodded. He was Chinese, or Chinese Canadian. The name tag he'd ended up with read Orrin Carr.

"You're not from the ship, are you?" he asked, glancing at Russ's unidentifying lapel.

"No."

They looked out at the ship together.

"When it's just sitting there, without the shuffleboard and the cruise director, it kind of has a pull, doesn't it?"

Russ agreed that it did.

The bartender came down and the man paid his tab.

When the man left, Russ went down to the table. He pocketed the business card and finished both of their drinks.

At the front desk he collected his bag and was assured by one of the clerks that a courier could pick up his delivery in the morning. He asked for a phone book, and printed the name and address of the Bread Exchange on an envelope with the hotel's name and logo. In plain view, though no one seemed to be watching him, he counted out a thousand dollars in American fifties and put them inside. There were uses ahead for the rest of the money. He'd already thought of them. On the back of Orrin Carr's business card he wrote, "For your good works." He sent forth the hope that he would be repaid in beauty. He dropped the card inside, sealed the envelope, and waited until the clerk returned and relieved him of it. Then he picked up his bag and stepped out into the throng of other travellers to begin the last leg home.

ACKNOWLEDGEMENTS

Thank you – James Adams, Joanna Birenbaum, *Brick*, the Canada Council for the Arts, Gary Hopkinson, Ellen Levine, the Ontario Arts Council, and Anne Simard. And Ellen Seligman, for her talents and devotion; Michael Redhill, a great friend of the cause; and Juanita DeBarros, for every minute of the long haul there and back.

•

The Wallace Stevens quotations from "Description without Place" and, on page 204, from "Of the Surface of Things" are taken from *The Collected Poems of Wallace Stevens* by Wallace Stevens, copyright © 1954 by Wallace Stevens and renewed 1982 by Holly Stevens. Used by permission of Alfred A. Knopf, a division of Random House, Inc.

The poems alluded to on page 93 are Philip Levine's "Detroit Grease Shop Poem" and Margaret Atwood's "Game After Supper."

The lines from Rainer Maria Rilke's "Archaic Torso of Apollo" on page 93 are taken from *The Essential Rilke* by Rainer Maria